THE SWINGING DETECTIVE

by

Henry McDonald

GIBSON SQUARE

This edition published by Gibson Square for the first time

UK Tel: +44 (0)20 7096 1100
US Tel: +1 646 216 9813

info@gibsonsquare.com
www.gibsonsquare.com

ISBN 9781783341177
eISBN 9781783341160

Papers used by Gibson Square are natural, recyclable products made from wood grown in sustainable forests; inks used are vegetable based. Manufacturing conforms to ISO 14001, and is accredited to FSC and PEFC chain of custody schemes. Colour-printing is through a certified CarbonNeutral® company that offsets its CO2 emissions.

Prologue

Belfast

Inside the white workman's van with the blacked out back windows, sweating due to the summer heat and the lack of ventilation, Martin Peters deliberately shoved the gun into the right trouser leg pocket of his workman's overalls.

His palms were sweaty. He hoped he wouldn't have to slip his hand down to pull the pistol out, especially given that his companion sitting across him in the back was nursing a Heckler and Koch machine gun, stroking it as if he was holding a baby in them soothing the infant to sleep. Even after many operations as an undercover agent Peters still loathed the idea of a 'wet job'.

Peters' companion hadn't spoken a word since they had left the briefing room in a downtown police station close to the banks of the River Lagan earlier that morning. He was a surly looking Scot with thinning red hair on top and reddish stubble dressed like a grizzled painter and decorator in the same white working gear that Peters was wearing for the 'job'. Bullish shaped with a tight scowl around the thick lips and hazel eyes that were focused on something far far in the distance, way beyond the reinforced armour of their undercover surveillance van. Down at his feet was a battered green holdall into which the Scot eventually carefully laid his Heckler Koch into before zipping it up.

There was a crackle of static from the driver's cabin and then a knuckled rattle on the glass to tell Peters and his silent colleague to get ready. Peters picked up a paint tin with one hand and a brush in the other, and followed his fellow soldier out the back door.

As they walked along the side of the Crumlin Road up past the Victorian Jail that was a temporary home to hundreds of prisoners who would have dearly loved to kill them both, Peters first heard and then saw the motorbike approaching.

The undercover soldiers crossed the junction with Tenant Street and increased their pace until they reached the garage close to another cop shop just as the bike came roaring south, in the direction of the city centre, before turning sharply into a route back towards the Protestant Shankill.

There were two of them, rider and pillion passenger, as they swerved at top speed around into Cambria Street when the ginger Scot dropped his bag, opened it and lifted out the machine gun pointing at the pair to stop. The one on the back raised a right arm and opened fire with an Uzi, the rounds whizzing over Peters' head, some of the bullets striking the tarmac on the road and clipping the side of a taxi accelerating along the southbound lane towards central Belfast.

Seconds later the motorbike buckled and suddenly collapsed onto its right side flinging the driver and the shooter at the back up into the air. The Scot ran over towards the rider when he hit the road, firing one shot into the ground beside him and speaking for the first time that day, screaming out in the guttural accent of Glasgow, 'If you move you die.' The man on the road wasn't moving at all.

Peters crept towards the pillion rider who was sitting up on their honkers, apparently dazed from the crash, one hand on leather biker trousers, the other fumbling for something lying close by. It was the Uzi which the shooter was drawing slowly, spasmodically towards them, the gloved hand shaking all the time as the Israeli machine pistol was raised up feebly and pointed directly now at Peters.

He reached into the side trouser pocket of his overalls as a reflex, drawing out the Walter PPK and seconds before the injured passenger was about to squeeze the Uzi's trigger, Peters opened fire instead, directing two shots straight through the visor of the motorbike helmet. The helmet then jerked back twice, its glass cracked almost in half from the bullets' impact and the body slumped to one side, blood starting to seep out from under the visor and onto the padded black motorbike jacket, red spray sprinkling over an array of pointy studs that crowned each side of the shoulders.

He had always hated 'wet jobs' even when those on the receiving end of his army unit that dared-not-speak-its-name were ruthless killers whose idea of being at 'war' was to ambush off duty soldiers driving kids on school buses or mow down part-time local coppers coming out of Sunday services with their families. Peters took no part in the barrack's mess post-ritual pass-the-picture crime scenes snaps of the 'flip-top terrorists' whose skulls were blown off when they happened to be surprised by 'real' soldiers. He always made himself scarce when the champagne corks popped as undercover troops clinked their glasses in celebration of a successful operation.

Yet this one, here on the squalid oil slicked forecourt of a Belfast filling station, felt wholly different. He observed the hour-glass shaped body of the dead terrorist coiled up on the ground beneath him. He shuddered at the attire the killer was wearing because it reminded him of his younger self.

As an old Punk Peters instantly recognised the way the leather had been decorated with pointy studs. He walked around the body to see if there was anything on the back side of the jacket. There was the faintest of outlines of a familiar stenciled image from the early 80s. He recognised it immediately. It was the trace of a circle with a giant 'A' inside it. Anarchy in the UK. It was only a decade and a half that he had stencilled one on his own jacket.

As sirens started to scream for attention in the fresh Saturday morning air Peters was transfixed by the sudden disjunction between the studded, stencilled leather motorcycle jacket, his rebellion and the teenage rampage, and the lifeless figure who had committed sectarian murder less than 500 yards up the same road.

One

Lothar Blucher belched and the already-dense air inside the sauna of 'Der Zug' swingers club was filled with the sour stench of barely digested garlic sausage and onion.

Blucher was a bloated Buddha of a man with folds of fat tumbling over the white towel that was wrapped tightly around his waist like a giant nappy. The absence of hair anywhere on his huge frame made him look even more like a pumped up baby.

Balanced on his lap, cross-kneed, sat one of Blucher's purchases from a recent trip to the Far East. An unusually tall woman, or what appeared to be one, with crimped hair, pert exposed breasts, one of which was pierced, thickly veined hands that resembled swollen river deltas, and a bulging thong shifted on Blucher's knee.

Blucher took off his thick steamed up bi-focals and appealed for help.

'Someone is trying to kill me, Herr Peters. I am sure of it.'

He was addressing Martin Peters, a detective inspector with the Berlin Police who spent every Saturday evening relaxing, drinking and, if he was lucky, fucking inside 'Der Zug'.

'I'm not talking to you until we are alone, Blucher,' the detective replied coldly.

Immediately, Blucher slapped the thigh of his Thai boy-girl who got up, minced over to Peters and hissed an incomprehensible insult into the policeman's ear, before wrenching back the door to the sauna, letting in a blast of welcome, fresh cool air.

Blucher had been an informant for nearly twenty years, mostly for Peters, who had a long history of helping him out when he was in trouble with Berlin Vice.

'OK, go on then, Blucher,' Peters said reassuringly, once the lady-boy had gone. 'So who's trying to kill you now?'

'Enough of your bloody English understatement. Someone is really trying to kill me and you have to help.'

Peters realised he would have to get to the point before the couples started filing in after their conga-dance around the club: that was where 'Der Zug' got its name from; the train, a human locomotion of limbs and protruding pieces of flesh locked together, slowly pacing its way through the premises, stopping to grope and slide into each other in rhythm to Lil Louis' House-Porn Groove anthem 'French Kiss.'

'Who is it, Lothar?' he asked sharply.

The owner of the 'Boyz R Us' gay sex shop leaned forward and the folds of fat wobbled; escarpments of blubber shaking off beads of sweat. He held out his right hand and produced a key.

'Locker 71 in Friedrichstrasse Station, to section to the left of the information centre. It's all in there, Herr Peters.'

'Stop being so cryptic. Some of my friends will be joining us soon and they are way too normal for you Lothar. Anyway why did you choose this place? It's perfectly straight!'

There was a grunt from Blucher and then a smile: 'Perfect place to meet you then. No one is going to follow Lothar Blucher to a straight swingers club, are they? Who'd believe I'd be seen anywhere near a place like this?'

'Here's another one.... why are you going for a half-way liner this time? I thought you lived strictly by the motto of your shop. Boys only.'

'I thought a change would be good for me but I am starting to regret that.'

'So, what about the Russian? I thought that's why you summoned me here, Lothar.'

'Never mind the Russian. I'm in danger this time and you have to help.'

The Russian: those two headless corpses washed up from the Havel. They had been found separately within weeks of each other just after Christmas in the exact same spot out at Wansee, both naked, young men in their twenties or perhaps early thirties, no signs of bruising or wounding on their bodies, no DNA trace, nothing to identify them at all except for a single word on each of their left arms, tattooed in Cyrillic script: 'Kursk' and 'Kharkov.' It was now mid-March and Peters, the Senior Investigating Officer in the case, had no breakthroughs on who they were, let alone who might have killed them.

'You'll be ok with me, Lothar. Just don't forget the Russian. I take it he has nothing to do with your current troubles...whatever they are.'

'I hope not Herr Peters. I sincerely hope not,' Blucher added, as if in hope that nothing more could get worse for him.

There was the muffled sound of a fracas just outside the sauna door, close to the changing rooms. Squeals and squawks that Blucher instantly recognised as belonging to him, to his Oriental companion, to his latest indulgence.

'Anika!' Blucher bellowed, more in anger than alarm.

Peters opened the sauna door and marched straight over to the melee. 'Der Zug's' diminutive owner Marion was trying in vain to separate an inflamed young couple lashing out at Blucher's lady boy.

'Right, shut up. I'm a police officer, which some of you already know. Don't make me embarrass us all by making the call,' Peters shouted above them.

Blucher pulled away Anika in a reverse rugby tackle, dragging her into the changing rooms and a quick exit. Marion meanwhile calmed the couple down with promises of free champagne. When the fuss finally died down, Peters touched Marion on the forearm and nodded towards the sauna. This place was turning into his second office, he thought. Marion and he had a few encounters in 'Der Zug', normally in the presence of her husband who liked to watch down in the basement room where it was 'strictly watching-room only'.

There was a new row now, Anika screeching and yelling at Blucher who cried out in Peters' direction as he left the building.

'Don't forget. 71 in Friedrichstrasse Station, next to the

Information. I chose the Palace of Tears because it will fuck your head up.'

When Blucher and his companion left Peters apologised to his hostess.

'I didn't invite them here. What happened?'

Peters felt re-invigorated on seeing Marion tearing off her black top which already exposed one shoulder. He felt a new surging urge inside to take her to the basement.

Marion, now topless, her compact body exposed, reddening rapidly in the searing heat, explained the commotion.

'The tranny went down below to watch them in the basement and he got a little carried away.' She giggled. 'The two of them got a full spray, which as you know is against the rules down there.' Peters smiled and put his arm around Marion but she slipped politely out from his grasp.

'Not tonight, Martin. I've got to keep that couple sweet. They're regulars. I'm just hot from the sauna not that kind of hot. Sorry.'

The detective tried not to look too disappointed. Even before Blucher had appeared in the sauna it had been an evening of knock-backs, jealous first-timer husbands and endless spectating. Peters' last resort was the train which he had always vowed to avoid. A sapping lassitude, brought on by several trips to the steam room and the stress of Blucher's astonishing apparition in the club, was engulfing him. It was almost time to go home. There was just one good deed to do before dawn after a night of observing but not actually participating in so much sin.

Peters eventually found the boy in an underground passageway running underneath the concourses of Berlin Zoo station. He was lying on a spread out piece of cardboard, hunched into a puffed up sleeping bag, the sleeves of the green Parka Peters had donated to him pulled up to reveal colonies of track marks on the rake thin lower arms and the claret and blue bobble hat with the West Ham crest in the middle where it covered his forehead; the hat that the boy had asked Peters to bring back for him from one of the English detective's pilgrimages back to Upton Park. This was before the boy fell into the vortex of bad company and addiction; before the boy was lost to his father preferring to sleep in the innards of a station where for years now adults and children who had succumbed to the needle and later the crack pipe begged, stole or sold themselves.

It was the sight of the Hammers' colours on the boy's head that almost moved Peters to tears. The claret and blue hat reminded him of when the boy was still a bundle of pre teen energy and innocent effervescence who because of Peters closeness to his father had adopted West Ham as his favourite team rather than Herta or worse still, Bayern. What had happened to this boy whose face was now covered in scratchy stubble and whose eyes were underlined with dark rings? What changed in a few years from a boy who improved his English by reading old copies of Peters' 'Shoot' magazine collection to this wretch paralysed by the opiate coursing through his blood stream and central nervous system? Peters could not find find an answer because the boy's father was a good man, a colleague, a friend. All the Englishman could do was seek out the boy and ensure he could secrete enough money into his clothing each night to keep him out of the hands of men who would abuse him. The detective admitted to himself that he was still funding the boy's habit but this was the least worst option in Peters' mind, at least until he started a campaign to lead his secret charge towards rehab.

He told nobody least of all the boy's father about his nightly quests to seek the lad out and help where he could. Peters ruffled the top of the bobble hat to rouse the boy.

'Paul, there's fifty euros in your left breast pocket. Tell nobody it's there son. I'll try and find you tomorrow again. Don't forget the money!' he whispered in case any of Paul's so-called friends made an appearance.

The boy shrinking into Peter's old Parka emitted the faintest of sounds in reply which lifted the heart of the Englishman watching over him, 'Up the Hammers.'

Two

The wind howled all the way from the east up all the Allee's and Damms and Strasses right to the western edge of the city, it whipped through the forests and the pathways of the Grunewald and raced along one of the main approaches west into the centre, it came unchallenged, barking mad, down Heer Strasse where Martin Peters' two bedroom fifth floor apartment overlooked the local S-Bahn station on the other side of the road.

It was approaching eleven o'clock on Sunday morning– Peters' favourite time of the weekend – and most of his three and a half million fellow citizens were seemingly still asleep. Normally woken by the roar of traffic and the clatter of the S-Bahn trains coursing eastwards towards the Mitte, Peters noticed that Heer Strasse today was completely deserted, barring the odd jogger heading for Berlin's most expansive green space.

He poured his third cup of Earl Grey from the Regimental tea pot he had liberated from his old home base back in England and stepped outside the living room and onto the narrow balcony above the road. Shivering in the cold, Peters wondered when winter would finally give up. The trees remained bare, puddles were cracked and frozen, sleet blessed the pavements below. He remembered a particularly un-seasonal Easter in Berlin when it snowed for almost the entire duration of Holy Week. The memory of it depressed him.

Peters was determined to put off the journey to Friedrichstrasse and Blucher's mystery package for as long as he could. He wanted to enjoy those few hours in the week when he was totally alone, surrounded only by all the mementoes of service and the memories of half a life spent in uniform, under orders. The high-ceilinged room inside contained trophies from campaigns in the Gulf: the captured, deactivated AK47 above the main wall incongruous amid the framed contemporary art miniatures he bought in the bohemian market near the Landwehr canal every Saturday morning; the photographs of his class at Sandhurst; a picture of himself atop of a captured Iraqi T-54; the shields of various units he had liaised with in Berlin before the Wall fell; and the East German General's hat on top of the only wardrobe in the living area, a present from one of the Intelligence Corps' most valuable sources, who had crossed over in '88, just a year before the sudden collapse of '89. The hat had come later, a present to Peters from the General after German reunification; a token, perhaps, of his atonement for getting it all wrong: he'd insisted all along there would be a bloodbath before the regime packed its bags and retired.

The sleet was transmuting into snow and Peters shivered, sliding back the balcony window and returning to the living room. On this way into the kitchen to deposit the tea and root out the leaves for the compost bin, Peters looked up at the poster. His father had cherished it from the day he bought it in June 1966, the England team including the old man's favourite player Martin Peters. His son had come into world the following July on the very day of England's most famous sporting triumph. Watching Moore lift the trophy in a bar not far from St. Barts where his son had just been born, Kurt Peters, a leftwing refugee from Hitler, was determined his only child would be called after one of the heroes from the team he had long adopted as his own. Peters Junior would take on the same name as the West Ham midfielder. In later life his mother would tell her son that this was Kurt's last revenge on the Fatherland.

The razor-thin mobile trilled and vibrated along Peters' kitchen worktop. The flashing number on the LCD showed that Blucher was clearly getting impatient.

'It's Sunday morning, Lothar. Am I not allowed a day off for good behaviour?'

'When have you ever been guilty of good behaviour, Herr Peters?' Blucher asked breathlessly.

'Have you fished out my present to you, yet?'

Peters dreaded the thought of Blucher's 'surprise' secreted in a locker in the old border station where he first saw that other apparition for the first time, when he was transferred from Belfast to Berlin after the shooting, when he was detailed to pose as the western tourist attending the 40th birthday party of the DDR, when he had to descend into the U-bahn below the earth and first stirred up the spectre of the woman he had killed.

Peters pretended to be indifferent towards Blucher's latest offering.

'No. I went for a run in the Grunewald, then I'm having lunch, maybe a little drink and then a siesta. I'll come and collect it in the morning.'

'Make sure you do as you bloody…...' Blucher then disconnected.

Was he out of coverage or simply throwing a strop? Wondered Peters. Blucher wasn't like the majority of his informers and sources. Usually they were nervous, haunted, weak men with secrets desperate to bury, dead men on leave who clung onto Peters like he was some flotsam after a wreck, their only means of not going under. Blucher normally played up the Prussian bearing, exuding confidence in deference to his alleged aristocratic roots.

He immediately felt guilty for stringing Blucher out: after all, the day was yet to be filled by Peter's mental filing system. At work they had a nickname for the former soldier-turned-cop – Filofaxhead. Because he ordered his work, no, his entire life, into neat, methodical segments. Like in his old undercover life Peters still religiously kept to schedules and time constraints. He organised others around him in much the same way. The former spy constructed patterns that suited his planning. Unknown to the gossips at Kotbusser Strasse, he even timetabled his sex life.

On Sunday nights he would take the U-Bahn west to Halensee and make the short journey to the little bar on Westfalische Strasse. The tiny liquor store was run by a widow in her mid 60s who loved to flirt with the virtually all-male clientele of Hertha supporters and Formula 1 fans. She was a glamorous grandmother in leather trousers pouring Kindl and snap shots amid a forest of Mullets, puffed up jackets and swollen stomachs. Peters, unable to sleep, had stumbled into her bar one wet autumn evening 18 months earlier, took her flirtation as a direct invitation to bed and promptly proposition the patron.

The widow Schuster was flattered at the attention she was receiving from the fit, neatly turned out younger Englishman still with his own hair and teeth; so much so that on their first night together she revealed that she and her late husband had been doyens of Berlin's dungeon scene.

Where most widows and widowers were inclined to keep a suit or a dress belonging to their late loved one neatly pressed, in pristine condition, mothballed in a cupboard of a bedroom, Frau Schuster told Peters that she couldn't bear disposing of hers and her husband's S&M garments and toys. So they remained locked in a stout seventies-style dark blue suit case beneath her bed. On their second Sunday night together back at her Charlottenberg home, Peters persuaded her to unlock the case and model for him. Thus began his dalliance with sub-dom games played out with an experienced mistress who started her routine back in the pub by turning Peters into her evening busboy who wiped down the tables, emptied the ashtrays, swept the floor and on command lit the widow Schuster's cigarette or poured her favourite tipple, bone dry white wine from the Saar-Mosel, into her glass. All tasks completed without pay.

The only reward was the widow's genuine flattery and her modest bewilderment over the attention he was giving her. Privately he took comfort from her re-assuring him that he was handsomely furtive with Slavic features, sharp cheekbones and china blue eyes despite being small for a policeman (five foot five) and at least one of flab now around the midriff Peters toiled in vain to shed. He was grateful to her for restoring his confidence in between the episodes of the spectre's appearances. The widow was non-judgemental shelter. She could sense the haunting around Peters but soothed him with her only verbal order in their evenings together ,'Keep it shallow Martin my dear, keep it shallow.'

A night of tasks and rewards at the Pub and later Haus Schuster lay ahead of him but there were still hours and hours to eat up before he set off by S and U-Bahn to his older lover. He thought about the two other women he was involved with and the strictly allocated quantity of time he allotted to each of them. 'Ms Thursday' was Miriam, a married Turkish born woman from Kreuzberg who was shunned by her increasingly devout husband because she believed she could never bare him a son. She was in her late 30s and in contrast to the dumpy, busty widow Schuster was long legged, slim and carried herself with benighted elegance.

Between Monday to Wednesday Peters punched in 12, sometimes 14 hours at the station daily in Kreuzberg where he worked. He built up enough hours by midweek to knock off earlier on Thursdays, giving him time to visit the Turkish food stores in search of spices and fresh food, for the meal he always cooked for Miriam. Peters would steal menus from restaurants, invade kitchens to catch a word with an Indian or Iranian chef, download recipes online, anything to impress his married lover with his culinary skills.

Whatever he and Miriam did not finish, Peters would put in the fridge to be wolfed down the next Friday evening before his night out with Karen, the youngest of the women of his week.. She was a 22 year-old architecture student at the Free University whom he met a year before while investigating the deaths of three young men on campus who had been mired in a gothic triple suicide pact. Karen had dated one of the students for a short while and broke down while being questioned by Peters in the university bar. He bought her a drink and then passed on his business card. Peters was astonished when this dark haired girl with Italianate looks and olive skin nearly half his age from Stuttgart rang his mobile a month after the suicide's funerals and asked HIM for a date. It was not so much a lack of self belief but a conviction that he didn't really deserve the interest any of the three of them showed in him. They certainly wouldn't have if they had known what he had done back in Belfast.

Karen was also his key to unlock the doors to alternative Berlin: the hyper all night parties in Friedrichshain thrown by one of her boho-class mates; the clubs in Prenzlauer Berg that blared out chest thumping techno from midnight to dawn and the seedy eastern basement bars where students, artists and wannabee rock stars mixed with spaced out hookers and their paranoid pimps.

Siberia was rattling again at all the windows of Heer Strasse, sleet and rain streaked across the panes making Peters blink momentarily as he stared out over the desolate cityscape. Back in Kreuzberg they wondered and whispered about why Peters had never married. If only they knew, he thought slyly. No, he often panicked inwardly, far better that they never knew. It was already too much for some of them that Peters, a foreigner, had risen through the ranks relatively quickly to become second-in-command of the station's murder squad, one of the most revered of all the homicide units in Berlin.

Peters took out the key Blucher had handed over in the 'Der Zug' the previous night and yawned.

Three

The screaming stopped for a few seconds when the hood was pulled off and his face was revealed. He sucked in the air before the pleading started but no one could hear him.

The ordeal had left him unable to express any horror through his facial muscles or eyes. All he could do was stare directly into the camera, a blank, doomed expression of someone who had given up the fight.

For about ten to fifteen minutes his naked body had sustained blow after blow from a baseball bat. He had been tied to a chair, unable to escape the relentless battering. All he could do was sway back and forth trying in vain to dodge the assault. A helpless bruised body being knocked to and fro, a ticking metronome of terror whose flesh was growing increasingly dark with every new swing.

The volume had been turned down to zero. Even when his visage was exposed there was no sound, or even an expression, no tic nor twitch, of any kind of fear or pain. Just that blank stare down the lens, hopeless, pathetic, resigned but an image held long enough to make sure that he would be identified. Then came the final blow, the figure in black standing behind the subject of his torture game, swinging the bat and then bringing it crashing onto the back of his victim's head and the object of that ordeal falling to the ground.

At first Peters had thought he was watching some ghoulish kidnap and murder DVD from Iraq. Perhaps even a recording from Abu Grahib. It was only when Peters saw the face that he realised that Lothar Blucher might have known this man.

The detective continued to rewind and freeze frame the penultimate scene, the hapless picture of a man who has been battered to the point of absolute surrender.

Why Blucher? Why was the film sent to him? Peters wondered. The woman beside him seemed to sense his thoughts exactly.

'He must have known him. Your contact must have known the victim.'

Angelika Domath put one of her perfectly manicured, purple painted finger nails onto the screen, the noise of its impact made Peter's teeth chatter.

Angelika was diplomatic enough never to ask her boss as to who the identities of his sources were because everyone in the station knew that Martin Peters kept all their secrets closely guarded. She was eleven years younger than Peters but an inch or two taller, swarthy skin and china blue eyes, a synthesis of the Steppes and the North German plain. Her blonde hair, accentuated by so much dyeing that it appeared as brittle as glass, when at work was always combed back and held in place by a series of multi coloured hair-clips. Peters' favourite thing about her however was her lower lip which was fatter than the upper one, ripe red and plumped up only by nature.

The men underneath her in the unit's pecking order ran a guerrilla war against Angelika. Hostilities were opened on her first day in the office, with graffiti scraped onto the wall of the female toilets. 'Angi-Stasi'. Quite a welcome.

Her father had been a colonel in the East German National People's Army, which once afforded Angelika the privileged perks of a family loyal to the old regime. Her mother had been Russian. Angi had just joined the Communist youth movement, the FDJ, when 'The Turn' began and the dictatorship crumbled amid mass protests, Gorbachev's removal of the Red Army crutch and the panic of the party leaders offering far too little, far too late. Although she was only 12 in that pivotal year Angelika eventually moved West first to the Free University's Science department, then to police college and finally her posting in the homicide division of Kotbusser Strasse, where open season was declared on the uppity 'Ossi' who had vaulted over the older, more experienced men in the unit.

Her promotion had won her several enemies inside the station, the chief of whom was Gunther Riedel, the division's very own

Iago who had first spread the rumour of Stasi-connections. Riedel came over with the legions of those other ambitious westerners seeking to cultivate blooming landscapes in the east after the fall. A native of Stuttgart, he constantly dreamt of promotion, a Porsche in the driveway, a second home in Majorca, a season ticket for Bayern, a clatter of kids and a submissive stay-at-home wife.

Peters looked at Angelika and admired the way she was fixated at the image freeze-framed on the television; she exuded dedication and seriousness; unlike Riedel and his mid-week five-a-side companions in the unit, she would never have made light or cracked a joke about such a vision of horror. To Peters Angi appeared to have a calling more than just a career; she cared about catching the killers, the rapists, the abusers, the traffickers. In Angelika Domath, Peters knew, the victims had a true ally.

'So tell me, Angie: if my contact knows him, then why not tell me straight away'? Peters asked.

She tapped another nail against the glass.

'Whatever the reason I'm sure of it. Your contact knows this man or at least has come across him.'

'Right then, I'll call the contact and arrange another meeting. If you're right then there's a game going on here'

Peters hesitated and drew breath.

'You don't suppose the whole thing is a set-up, a joke maybe?'

'Absolutely not. I can tell from the injuries that this is, sorry was, for real. I recognise the colouring and wounds from my post-mortem studies, Angelika added.

10 A.M Monday morning and the unsolved murder count had just clicked up to 3.

'Shit. I'd better go and tell Stannheim we have another stiff on our hands.'

Every Monday morning Mannfred Stannheim posed the exact same question to Martin Peters: 'When are you going to take over and let me retire?' And every Monday morning Peters would refuse to answer.

Stannheim was old enough to remember the privations of the Berlin Air Luft when Stalin sought to starve West Berliners into submission. He had stood on a mound of earth close to the flats in working class Wedding as the RAF planes swooped low towards Templehof carrying the food and fuel that kept the free western sector out of Soviet hands. For Stannheim that bravery and ingenuity in keeping his city fed and warm erased the memory of the blitz Berlin received during the War. For the rest of his life he remained an Anglophile and so was delighted to learn than an ambitious young German-speaking British soldier had applied to join his division.

Martin Peters was also the son Stannheim wished he and his late wife had had. His real son had drifted from secondary school into the arms of a gaggle of junkies. Graduating from hash to heroin and ending up on the crack pipe, Paul Stannheim spent his days begging, cadging cigarettes, committing the odd petty theft around the Zoo Station and (according at least to Riedel and his cabal) renting his ass to friendless or abandoned old queens who often frequented places like 'Boyz R Us.' Just as he had done on Sunday morning Peters regularly stopped off more often in the late afternoons on the way back to Heer Strasse at the Zoo, his pockets bulging with Euro coins intended to keep Paul Stannheim from the more humiliating means of funding his habit.

'Come in, Martin. If you are not going to take over you might as well tell me how your headless horsemen are coming on.'

Stannheim was wreathed in cigarette smoke which had stained his hair, lined his face, cracked his skin, discoloured his teeth and blunted his appetite.

'I'm afraid it's got nothing to do with the corpses from the Havel, sir. think.'

Peters handed over the DVD Blucher had left for him.

'It was given to me by one of my best sources, sir. Another murder. And this time captured on film.

Four

To: heike.numann@wams.de
From: st.christopher@hotmail.com
Subject: A wake up call
Fraulein,
Please take a moment to read the link below. By the way - I have always admired your work.
www.thewrath.com

She had been bitten too many times before. Cranks confessing to crimes never committed. Perverts sending in pictures of their penises captured on Polaroid. Conspiracy theorists warning of Jewish-Bolshevik plans to unleash World War 3 from German soil. Heike Numann had her fill of the time-wasters and the weirdoes. It was Monday morning and all she wanted was to roll back into bed and sleep through the morning.

It was just as she was about to leave for lunch near Checkpoint Charlie when the computer beeped again. It was from the same address as her earlier 'wake-up call'.

To: heike.numann@wams.de
From: st.christopher@hotmail.com
Subject: the wrath
Fraulein, this is just a reminder that you should click on the link below. Do it before someone else gets the scoop.
www.thewrath.com

Instantly Heike Numann was sniffing an exclusive - what were the bodies of the two headless corpses found in the Havel all about? And she could never resist the allure of the magic word scoop. It was her solemn duty. As one of the first wave of female crime reporters on a national paper Heike drove herself beyond the point where others around her would never cross. She sacrificed weekends away with friends, disappointed and eventually ditched lovers, rarely took holidays, paid few visits to her parents at their home near Bonn, hardly had the time to read a novel anymore and had even abandoned her weekly trip to the cinema.

She clicked on the web link, it opened, and what played out on her screen turned her stomach.

The volume turned down to zero. A'nother hooded man, otherwise fully naked, handcuffed to a chair directly facing the camera. There was a figure in black, the face unexposed, carving his captive to pieces with a sword. Blood was splattering the camera until the tableau of terror was obscured. Yet there was still no sound. The lens was wiped down and the man in the chair passed out. The hood was ripped off to reveal an unconscious specimen. His attacker was standing still, reversing the blade behind his body and then the weapon then frozen behind the swordsman's shoulder. Finally the killer swung it around in an arc severing the head in one clean, savage swipe. The film dissolved and a symbol appeared on screen. A badge. A stout man in a toga, a staff in a river and a child on his shoulders.

She wretched and didn't make it in time to her bathroom. There was a green, viscous pool on her carpet. It had travelled down her nostrils as well as her throat. The membranes inside her nose were stinging. She could not speak or barely breathe. Shortly after came the freeze, her blood chilling, she was overcome with cold, shaking and shivering as if she had been doused in ice.

She couldn't look, at let alone touch the computer. She sat in the corner of her living room on her honkers staring into space.

It took her half an hour to make the call. No, it would be easier if he came around to see her. Yes, she didn't want to talk about it. Not now. Later. Much later. He could look for himself.

Across Berlin another recipient of Christopher's wrath had just closed the link. He too had just shared Heike Numann's experience.

From Kottbuser Strasse by U-Bahn it took Martin Peters fifteen minutes to reach Heike's apartment. They had known each other for about three years after meeting at a Christmas drinks party organised for the press by the Berlin Polizei Media department. Peters had asked her to lunch in Sale E Tabacci, a favourite Italian haunt for journalists, politicos, architects and lawyers just a few yards from Koch Strasse U-Bahn and around the corner from the Checkpoint Charlie Museum. It became a monthly regular rendezvous, Heike extracting snippets of information on cases and crimes from the English detective with the impeccable manners and a comical German accent. He had provided her with the barest details about the headless horsemen first and the mystery surrounding their identities. She had been good to her word and kept it out of the paper, at least until he gave her the nod.

He was met at the apartment door in Schiller Strasse by a tear stained, pale, still shaking Heike. On entering the flat she pointed back to her workstation and the computer, which was constantly bleeping. Peters went over, sat down in the seat in front of the screen and used the mouse to click on a new mail.

To: heike.numann@wams.de
From: st.christopher@hotmail.com
Subject: wrath revealed
Well, Fraulein, I hope that wasn't too distressing. But it's time the People out there got to know me a bit better.

'What does this mean, Heike?' Peters called out across the room.

She was trying to light a cigarette, her hands trembling unable to torch up. Her voice was quivering.

'Read the previous one...I'm sorry, watch it.'

Even before Peters opened the mail he had a sinking feeling.

But this one was different. The face wasn't to be revealed until after the fatal blow had been administered. This time life was to be extinguished before exposure. His stomach lurched too at the sight of the severed head held up for a second to the lens and tossed away and then the dissolve to the symbol that Heike had recognised immediately.

'It's Saint Christopher,' she murmured, 'He is crossing the river holding the baby Jesus.'

She was getting her voice back slowly, composing herself as she slid upwards along the wall.

'My father gave me a Saint Christopher medal the morning I left for Berlin five years ago. He told me the saint would protect me in "that place". He spoke as if I was just about to walk into the Valley of Death.'

'You're in it now,' as Peters replayed those final macabre moments of the second condemned man's life.

'St. Christopher's wrath,' Heike whispered.

Peters knew she was slowly recovering because she was already thinking in headlines. Already at work. Planning her next big story. And he knew he had to stop her.

'Heike, I have to ask something of you,' Peters spoke in a faked softer tone. He moved over to where she still leaned against the living room wall. Peters noticed that her entire flat was covered in papers, ring binders, files, reference books, discarded printer cartridges, Dictaphone tapes.

'Heike, I have to ask a favour.' She just stared into space.

'I want you to keep this to yourself. At least until we find out who we're dealing with here. Whoever he is he wants to be talked about and a bit more famous than just for 15 minutes.'

She was back in the room again, on earth, re-engaged, Peters' plea snapping her out of her semi-catatonic state.

'You have to be joking Martin. That mail was for me alone. You have no right to stop me. No right.'

The detective was filled with panic. He had to put her off, at least for now. He had an image of Stannheim in his mind now, barking at him, throwing down a copy of WAMS onto his desk in the Kotbusser Strasse, the lurid headlines, the wrath of St. Christopher. Peters knew only too well how dogged she could be in pursuit of a story even when the story was him! When they first dating he had told her early on about the apparition that now haunted him on the U-bahns.It was after a panic attack when Heike enticed him onto underground the line going east towards Pankow one evening. Peters saw her, the destroyed side of the face leaning on Heike's shoulder, the good eye winking at him, that knowing sinister smile that forced the detective off out of his seat and towards the door at only the first station from when they had boarded at Alexanderplatz. He marvelled at Heike's chicanery especially the way she tried to convince him that by telling his story of what about what happened that summer morning in Belfast in the same year that The Wall fell it would be his personal therapy; it would help him cope with the trauma. He had stopped her then writing about what he had done for Queen and Country , and now he needed stop her again.

'Heike, maybe we can do a trade?'

'A trade? What have you got that's a better story than that?' she gestured towards the computer.

The two headless cadavers thrown up by the Havel flashed across his brain.

'The two cadavers in the lake. There's something we haven't released yet.'

Her hands had steadied now, she was lighting up her cigarette at last, listening intently for the offer that was coming.

'There was something odd written on their bodies. Their right arms to be precise,' Peters said.

Heike's eyes widened, What exactly?'

'Kursk and Kharkov. Two battles from the Second World War.'

'Big deal Martin. How could that be a new lead?'

'Because they were written in Russian.'

The expression instantly changed on Heike's face. Peters realised he now had a trade.

'Russian? So that means a Mafia killing. It's a gangland double murder, isn't it?'

Peters interrupted: 'No Heike. Let's not get carried away here. Just because it's Cyrillic writing doesn't necessarily mean it's Russian gangsters. Be careful.'

'I'll be careful, Martin. Don't patronise me. I've just watched a man hacked to death on my computer and you're telling me not to write about it. I'll do it for you Martin but don't tell me how to write my stories in my paper.'

He walked back to the workstation and sat down. 'I'm going to forward this to my own mail back in the station. Radio silence won't be forever Heike. You can have the story once I consult with the brass back in HQ.'

Pressing the send button to his own address, Peters then shut down the computer and swivelled in the chair towards her.

'Heike, I have to go and report this. Will you be alright? Is there anyone I can call to be with you?' Peters realised instantly he had delivered an insult.

'What kind of wimp do you think I am?' she snapped. 'I'm perfectly fine on my own.'

'Good. I'll call you later. Maybe you can take to me to lunch at Sale and put it on expenses. I'll probably have more information on the headless horsemen by then.'

'Martin?'

'What?' Peters replied softly.

'That's the second time in five minutes you have patronised me.'

Five

In the summer the lake would have been packed with bathers, in the grim hiatus between winter and spring it had always been the perfect spot for espionage. Teufelsberg. The devil's hill. The location of Peters' first intelligence triumph.

It was where Blucher had placed the photographs in a dead drop in the year of 'Die Wende'. They were grainy stills of a customer poring over that section of 'Boyz R Us' with the collection of portraits of young boys' faces including the iconic one of the pubescent kid on the front of the U2 album. The subject captured on Blucher's hidden CCTV cameras was a member of the SED-West Berlin, the DDR's Trojan horse inside the free western citadel.

Shortly after receiving the pictures Peters hauled the communist agent in to the British Army's HQ near the Olympic Stadium. He was offered a choice: Work for him or see his name in print and disgrace on the pages of 'Bild' or 'BZ'. He would then be arrested by Berlin vice, arraigned before a court charged with possessing paedophile material. A journalist by his Stasi legend for 'Neues Deutschland', their West Berlin correspondent, the agent chose instead to be in the pay of two masters rather than none and ultimately jail. Military intelligence had dug through into another passageway of the decaying regime beyond the Wall and another agent compromised within its allies on his side of the divide. The spook started working for Peters and became an invaluable if somewhat short-lived source.

Lothar Blucher's sacred duty was to believe in nothing. 'Anti' was his only ideology. He was never for but always against. Thus, anti-communism before the 'Turn' came easy to him. It also came with lost territory: the Bluchers claimed lineage back to the rescue of the British at Waterloo, the Prussian general whose cavalry had made that final decisive charge slicing through the lines of Napoleonic troops. The imagined blood-line could be traced to those lost territories to the east. Peters always remembered that Blucher never referred to Gdansk by its Polish name; for his original source in Berlin it would always be Danzig. This was what they shared in common: Two sons from the evacuated eastern lands, one with his roots in East Prussia, the other the child of a reluctant Sudeten.

There was a bench by the lake and beside it the waste-basket where Blucher had left those first incriminating photos. Sixteen years later Peters' informer had chosen a reunion at the very same spot in line of sight of the earth mound where the American listening post used to be. There were rumours of a new hotel and conference centre from where the Yanks used to eavesdrop into the east.

Blucher was already seated, wrapped up against the elements in a black crombie coat, wine-dark scarf and an incongruous Russian winter hat complete with the flaps pulled down to protect his flabby, cauliflower ears. Sharp jets of freezing breath were emitting from Blucher's mouth as he gulped down air, wheezing and coughing.

'A sentimental journey, Herr Peters. Please sit down.'

Peters observed his oldest source in Berlin. He wondered if Blucher was about to have a heart attack.

'Don't tell me you walked all the way through the Grunewald to get here, Lothar?'

'Certainly not. Anika is parked over there. I try to avoid public transport.'

'What's the problem? Panic attacks on the S-Bahn?

The informer shuffled his huge frame along the wooden bench.

'Not so much the panic attacks. It is that word "public" I don't like. I fear the general public and tend to avoid them if possible.'

For a man who made his money out of other people's perversions this sounded like a strange thing to say. Because he revelled in being in the know over the private tastes of his customers, which he would from time to time share with Peters.

'Why here Lothar? Get to the point.'

'Well it's better than that place you frequent every Saturday. By the way, do your bosses know you are a swinger?'

Get to the point.' Peters was wearying of Blucher's games.

'Someone sent me an email….' before Blucher could finish Peters butted in.

'Of someone having their head chopped off.'

Blucher looked stunned.

'It's alright, Lothar. It was sent to a friend of mine as well, a journalist. I've seen it too.'

The informer took out a handkerchief from the crombie and wiped off the sweat gathering along his forehead.

'Why was it sent to me? I'll tell you why. Because I'm next.'

Peters said nothing. This time around he wanted to encourage Blucher's fear.

'You've got to give me protection. This is where I made you. This is where I got you your man. This is where you pay me back.'

The detective waited pausing for Blucher to reach the edge.

'You aren't saying anything? ? You've seen the video. He cuts off his head. He slashes him to bits and to pieces. And you say nothing!'

Peters stood up, bent over and touched his toes. Then he reversed back upwards and cracked his fingers, the sound of gristle and bone grinding together made Blucher wince in the seat. Blucher was made all the more uncomfortable by the metallic pecking of a lone magpie at the foot of the tree behind the bench.

'Damn, violent birds,' Blucher complained. 'Are they bad luck in England too?'

'Only unless you don't say 'Good Morning' and ask them how their wife is doing?' Peters replied.

'The English truly are mad, Herr Peters. You talk to magpies in the trees. And you are the maddest of all. You have said nothing and you have seen those images. My life is probably under threat here and all you can do is say "good morning" to a bloody bird. I could be next in the firing line.'

A smile flashed across Peters' face as he watched Lothar squirm under the pressure.

'And you saw them too. An old acquaintance perhaps, or maybe a loyal customer, being hacked to death in front of the camera. He wasn't a hostage in some Baghdad stink-hole, was he Lothar? You knew him.'

His informer was holding his head in his hands now, on the verge of sobbing, not for the man whose death he had witnessed in cyberspace but only for himself. For Lothar Blucher, the director of 'Man Everyday', his one and only porn movie, a gay take on the Robinson Crusoe story, a castaway character with an exotic partner for each day of the week, cared for no one but himself and the fulfilment of his pleasures, which extended to him taking a bit part in the film as the English sea captain who rescued the hero and his new friends from the desert island. Martin Peters could never fully warm to his old source and felt no guilt for applying further pressure to the exposed nerve.

'You knew him Lothar. You fucking knew him,' Peters said. 'That's why you are shitting yourself. Who is he?'

Blucher raised his head up. The Russian hat had collapsed over his eyes.

'All I know is that he came into the shop. Quite a few times. He and the other one.'

To ward off the cold Peters was jogging on the spot, trying to keep warm.

'The first one. That's what you mean, isn't it Lothar? You knew the first one as well. I would call that obstructing a police inquiry.'

He could see the panic taking hold on Blucher's face, the sweat re-appearing on his forehead. Peters put his hand on his informer's right shoulder.

'Don't worry Lothar; I'm not going to charge you with anything. All you have to do is tell me about them.'

'What is there to tell? They both came into the shop. They liked the section with the younger boys. The first one I had to ask to leave eventually. He was pestering one of my staff.'

'Pestering? Who?'

'That doesn't matter. He was pestering him for videos, of younger guys, the younger the better. I thought it was best we bar him from the shop. I didn't want a reputation.'

Peters burst out laughing.

'*A reputation? That preceded you a long time ago Lothar.*'

He kept jogging on the same spot watching the magpie get closer to them, its pecking growing louder.

'I have a request Herr Peters. I want to call in a favour too. I don't feel safe anymore.'

'No you are right. We'll have to close down the shop, move you out of your house,' Peters glanced towards the car park. A column of smoke wafted from a rolled down window of Blucher's VW Beetle.

'And your Thai friend too of course.'

'Absolutely not. The shop can't close. No way. I'll barricade myself in if necessary. "Boyz R Us" will never close.' The thought of lower profit margins seemed to be dispelling Blucher's fear.

'Ok, Lothar, ok,' Peters said reassuringly. 'We will book you into a guest house for a few days. Get you out of Charlottenberg, you and your young friend.'

For the first time since they sat down at Teufelsberg, Blucher was smiling.

'A guest house for Detective Inspector Martin Peters' greatest source! Absolutely not. I want the executive suite at the Marriott on Potsdamer Platz if it's available. Apparently the architect modelled the interior on Notre Dame in Paris. A cathedral for good taste and modern art. Anika and I will be very happy there.'

Good taste! Blucher's tastes were anything but.

Yet he had to keep his source sweet not only because of the link to the two men on film but also what he knew about the headless horsemen and a possible Russian connection.

'And what of the Russian, Lothar? '

'Ah, the Russian. For that alone you will put me in front of a Russkie firing squad. I'll tell you more about him over a Marguerite in the Marriott bar.'

'But you have heard something haven't you?'

'I have my sources and my contacts in that particular community that go back to when the Wall was still up but you will have to see me in the hotel before I talk about that ," Blucher replied.

Peters wanted to go back to Kottbusser Strasse; he was desperate to share what he learned about the men on camera from Blucher with Angelika.

'You go off now and play with your Thai friend. I'll make the arrangements and call you. '

Blucher got up, took Peters hand and shook it vigorously. Then he clicked his heels, the clocking noise of two shoes together an echo of his Junker roots and then bowed before waddling off towards the car park. When he had driven off Peters noticed that the magpie had flown off in the same direction as Blucher, eastwards towards the sun.

Six

Mannfred Stannheim always preferred to sit right at the back of the morning conference, pulling on his first cigarette of the morning, playing the disruptive schoolboy at the rear end of the bus. And he waited until near the conclusion, when his English protégé was wrapping up, to toss the awkward question into the middle, to launch the verbal grenade with the pin pulled out.

They had gathered in the incident room to discuss the two killings captured on film and posted on the Internet. Two gay men with a taste for younger men killed brutally, their deaths shown for a reason. A gay basher taking things to the extreme terminus of homophobia? A religious fanatic obsessed with Sodom and in search of smiting Gomorrah? The grim visages of the two men were blown up and pinned to a white board. In front of it Peters held court, Angelika by his side and Riedel looking on enviously from a knot of plain clothes officers seated in front.

'The only thing we know about these two men were that they both frequented a gay sex shop not far from Sauvigny Platz. That they liked very young men and that they were deliberately exposed for the benefit of the camera. Whoever killed them wanted us to see them.

'I want all reports of missing persons, of missing middle aged men from 45 to 60 specifically. I want details of any psychos, any with a history of attacking gay men, who have recently been released from jail. And I want a complete black-out on this until we have established who these men were and who we are now dealing with. So if there are no further questions I suggest we get on with it.'

Stannheim shot his hand up.

'Just one question Detective Inspector,' the head of the

Kotbusser Strasse murder squad was evidently enjoying himself.

Stannheim went on. 'If the last one is posted on the Internet won't the press get their hands on this sooner or later?'

Peters smouldered. Stannheim was paying him back for his latest refusal to take over the murder squad.

'We can't be certain that he has already sent this to someone in the media.'

He walked across the room to Stannheim and whispered impatiently into his ear.

'Sir. Please, if we can have a word in your office in private.'

Stannheim nodded and they walked towards the nerve centre of Kotbusser Strasse. Once inside his boss' office, Peters shut the door.

'Well, Martin what is it you couldn't say to me in front of your fellow officers?'

'An email was sent to a journalist. The fortunate thing is that I know her.'

'Another one of your conquests, Martin?' Stannheim asked acidly. He knew. He must have known about Peters' private life. Mannfred Stannheim was nothing if not thorough even in the monitoring of his subalterns' existence far beyond the walls of Kottbusser Strasse.

Peters wondered if Stannheim had been keeping tabs on him even paying one of his old contacts from the Cold War to spy on his English detective. The thought of him being stalked on the orders of his own boss provoked Peters to wound the old man.

'No sir. But I do trust her. And as you well know I am good at keeping secrets and I certainly don't gossip.'

Stannheim never dropped his guard even though the vaguest mention of Paul his sons Peters knew would hurt.

'You mean you traded with her? What did you have to give her?'

'The headless horsemen sir. I told her about the tattoos. The references to the battles. It was the only thing I had to trade. It bought us a bit of time.'

He sized Peters up and down for a moment and then reached over to his desk fishing out a document buried underneath an untidy mound of papers. Stannheim shoved one under the English detective's nose.

'By the way, this is a bit steep Martin, isn't it? Are you sure he's worth it?'

Peters felt as though he had spent half his career in the Berlin Polizei defending the fiduciary demands of Lothar Blucher.

'He's come up with the goods in the past sir and I'm confident he will again. Not just about the Russian, maybe the recent killings too.'

His boss gave him a world-weary look.

'What does he know about our friends taken from the Havel?'

'He knows about a Russian connection even though we've kept the tattoos under wraps. I'm certain he has more to tell. It's just his way of working; he likes it teased out of him.'

'You mean he enjoys the largesse of the Berlin Polizei.' Stannheim said rifling through one of his drawers and taking out a stamper. As he rolled the department's seal of approval along the account chit, Stannheim whispered.

'Make bloody sure you're right because we have no real leads either on the headless horsemen or our stars on film. Four murders in one month and not a single fucking in-road. If your lady friend at WAMS falls out with us and prints we are all screwed.'

Peters was in a vengeful mood when he left Stannheim's office, so much so that he made his way directly to where Riedel and his clique were sitting, gossiping by their workstations, sniggering into their plastic cups filled with filtered water and organic juices.

He first addressed Riedel's number one ally in Kottbusser Strasse, Hermann Bauer, a former Vopo from eastern Berlin whom his former colleagues in Prenzlauer Berg swore rose through the ranks of the old force by beating up dissidents and informing on his colleagues.

'Herr Bauer,' said Peters delivering a mate-like slap onto his back. 'I have a special operation for you. Get yourself a pool car and then take a walk on the wild side.'

Bauer looked bewildered. He could never fathom the Englishman's oblique sarcasm.

'I want you to check out every gay bar in a radius starting from

Sauvingy Platz. Try the pubs first; the ones were the older men frequent. Our two friends were probably less likely to attend the more extreme clubs. Too much sweat and effort for them I imagine. Angelika will provide you with photographs of the victims.'

He then turned to Riedel himself, the source of so much back biting and barrack room rebellion in Kottbusser Strasse.

'And I have a special task for you Herr Riedel. Grab your coat we are off to Potsdamer Platz to get you a job.'

Riedel looked back to Bauer who was fuming in his seat. Peters nodded to both of them and then gestured with his head towards the door.

'Come on gentlemen we have a lunatic to catch.'

As they left the incident room Peters deliberately bumped into Angelika and winked at her.

Seven

The cackling echoed around the foyer of the Marriot Hotel on Potsdamer Platz. Peters heard Anika before he could see him/her.

Blucher's lover was standing at the bar, one hand on hip, the other balancing a cocktail glass through the fingers, flirting with one of the Filipino waiters. The man who brought Anika to Berlin was sitting in a chair near the entrance, prodding on the key board of his lap-top, one mobile glued to his left ear, the other ringing on the table beside his computer. The two of them were already fitting in.

'The Executive Suite was already booked. They've given us a room on the ninth floor instead. It's small and the sauna isn't working today either. The Berlin Polizei has let me down, Herr Peters.'Blucher snorted in protest.

The detective had come to take the keys to 'Boyz R Us' off its owner. He calculated that his informer might be in danger; instead he would put Riedel behind the counter, once Peters found him something appropriate to wear.

'The keys Lothar please. I've a detective out there who is just dying to get into those leather shorts you have hanging up in the shop.'

'I must come over and see him modelling them. Here take the keys and let me work out how much I've lost today,' Blucher continued complaining.

Peters thumbed over his shoulder towards the bar from where the cackling was coming.

'At least your friend is enjoying it.'

'It keeps her happy Herr Peters. As long as there's something left to entertain me I don't mind the flirting.'

'Something left in the tank for Lothar', Peters said with a trace of sarcasm.

The lobby was full of slickly dressed business types carrying wafer thin lap tops under their arms, sitting down to talks with partners under the layered balconies leading up to the roof of the hotel. There was a hum overlaying the hotel atmosphere, the murmur of polite 21st century commerce. Peters admired the women in their dark suits and designer glasses, all poised and elegant and immaculately made-up. Peters felt at home in places like this, inside these post-modern cathedrals of good taste and impeccable manners. It was all a far cry from the odorous back-biting, the bitchiness and the claustrophobia of Kottbusser Strasse.

'How long have I got here?' Blucher asked.

'As long as it takes, Lothar just don't take the piss and order champagne every night.'

'I'll just stick to the Sekt then. Here's to the Berlin Polizei.' Blucher lifted up a glass and swigged back the fizzy, golden liquid. It had just turned eleven o'clock in the morning.

Before leaving, Peters grabbed the glass out of Blucher's hand and slammed it down onto the table, some droplets falling on his keyboard. Peters wanted to remind his informer that there was another reason why they were meeting - the Russians and the headless horsemen from the Havel.

'Damn you this is my office on the go for as long you keep me out of the shop.'

'You haven't mentioned the Russian Lothar. You said you had information about the men in the Havel. I think it's time you stopped being so obscure. I've got a nervous wreck of a commander breaking my balls to get a lead, any lead, into the Havel corpses and you sit there guzzling back the Sekt at our expense telling me nothing.'

Blucher shook his head feigning sadnesss and the look of someone who had just been deeply insulted.

'If there is anything dodgy going on with a Russian link in Berlin then it all flows back to one Avi Yanaev.'

Peters didn't recognise the name. His attention was diverted by the cackling from the bar. Anika had snatched the Filipino waiter's hand and shoved it up her skirt. Blucher ignored the scene and continued texting.

'Yanaev? Never heard of him. Who is he?' Peters inquired.

'What is he - that is the real question here,' Blucher said while sending a text message on one of his mobiles before continuing.

'He's a Jewish émigré from the depths of Siberia. Made his money in property down in the Russian quarter in Kopenick. Lives in a big house there with electronic gates and drives about in a blacked out Mercedes. Rumour has it the houses and flats he owns are just fronts for his other businesses. There's a knocking shop down in Schoenberg full of Russian and Ukrainian girls. Seven stories high. A different kink on every floor. One of Yanaev's partners owns the place but he's just the front man.'

'Who's the partner?'

Blucher winked at Peters and sent another text he was clicking out on his dial pad.

'He's a friend of mine who's fond of talking when I've plied him too with much vodka.'

'Then bring him over here and put the Stolychnya on us.'

'Me and the Russians have form, Herr Peters. I still owe them.'

Peters sensed that Blucher, despite the protests, was also enjoying himself.

'You and your lost lands in East Prussia. You really ought to get over it.'

'Never Herr Peters! And you should know.'

Peters left the hotel shuddering at the notion that he and Blucher were alike. They could both trace their roots to lost Germanic lands beyond the Rivers Rhine and Oder. The thought of such a connection, however tentative, repulsed him.

Riedel was fuming in the driver's seat, already irritated for having to drive around Potsdamer Platz several times while Peters held talks with his prized source. Peters had insisted he did not come inside with him. He was not going to let Riedel find out about Blucher.

'Head over to the Ku'damm Herr Riedel and I'll direct you from there.' he said coldly.

Still a building site! Peters wondered if Berlin was a city that would ever be finished. For the place he had adopted as home was in constant flux, new pieces of architecture being constantly bolted incongruously onto old ones. This was a hodge-podge of a capital, with rival urban themes either clashing or coalescing. A bastard child of history and post-modernity; a home where everything and everyone was temporary and transient in a departure lounge for plots and dreams.

After the Ku'damm they turned left mid-way down the west end shopping thoroughfare and onto a Wilhemine side street. 'Boyz R Us' was situated on a corner, its shiny black sign above the door the only hint of what was on offer inside.

Once he unlocked the door, Peters had to shut down the alarm on the inside wall and illuminate the shop. When the lights came on they revealed a cornucopia of fetish clothing, racks of porn DVDs, gay sex magazines wrapped up in plastic and a terrifying range of sex toys, some of which posed unimaginable anatomical challenges to their future owners. Riedel looked as if he was about to throw up.

'Come on, Riedel. Don't be so squeamish. There's not much difference between what they do and what you get up to at the weekend. Just the portals are not the same.'

When Riedel failed to rise to the bait Peters plucked an enormous double-ended vibrator from one of the shelves and waved it in his face.

'Lighten up Herr Riedel. You'll have to get used to all this stuff while working here.'

'What exactly do you want me to do here?' Riedel asked as his eyes wandered over the shop.

'There is a link between this shop and the two men killed on film. They both used this place for their kicks. Whoever did them in probably knew that. Maybe he has been here too. I just want you to look out for anyone suspicious.'

Riedel looked at Peters as if he had lost his mind. Suspicous? Everyone, Riedel and Peters both knew, who came into the shop, would probably look suspicious. Furtiveness was an unspoken code in sex shops across the world, gay or straight and especially in any establishment belonging to Lothar Blucher.

'Just keep me posted on this place.' Peters added as he twirled his car keys around his fingers relieved to be leaving the shop to Riedel and his paranoid imagination.

Eight

There was something there. She was sure of it. Something engraved on the blade. Slowed down on the screen in normal size it was just a dark grey blur.

She fiddled with the touch pad, the mouse icon whirring around the sword until she clicked on that part of the cold steel where the word was to become enlarged.

She recognised the style of writing instantly. Cyrillic. One word. A message carved out in the second language of her childhood.

Angelika had spent the morning in Kotbusser Strasse rewinding the brief horror shows depicting the death of two of Lothar Blucher's clients on her computer. The first thing she noticed was that both men had indents on the bridges of their noses. Whoever had captured them, bound them up and prepared them for their final ordeal had removed their spectacles. She wondered if either of them could see properly when the camera lens was pointed directly at them.

She pushed the enlargement from the sword to its limit and then copied and pasted the word onto a blank file. She knew she had recognised it almost right away. But Angelika was nothing but meticulous. She had to be certain before she took it to Peters.

'Tavarich'.

'Comrade.'

After printing it out she crossed the murder room floor, making her way to Peters' desk just outside Stannheim's office. She waited until she was sure the superintendent was out of earshot and laid the picture she printed off in front of the Englishman.

'What's this?' he said looking up from his laptop.

'Something I spotted on the blade that killed number 2, sir.'

Peters lifted it up and read the enlarged letters marking the word of solidarity on the sword.

'Comrade! Mmmm. Not another Russian angle, Angi.'

'I can't say sir. But I'm sure it's a Russian blade. I think I've seen one before.'

'Where?'

'In my father's house.'

Peters knew that Angi's father had been a colonel in the old communist National People's Army. This had been the reason for all the jibes and the cheap shots levelled at her in Kotbusser Strasse. A loyal and faithful servant of the regime who had remained trapped inside his Pankow apartment since the Turn, the old man raging against the changes all around him, while surrounded and kept warm by the souvenirs from where the past was literally another country.

'I'd like to see that sword.'

'I'll call him, sir. Ask him to see us.'

'Us? You want me to come with you.'

'I think he might enjoy the experience besides he's not likely to hand over such a prized possession even to me.'

They took the U-Bahn from Alexanderplatz to Viner Strasse and then by two S-bahn stops to Pankow, alighting at Borkhum Strasse and taking a right past the abandoned prison down Bornholmer Strasse. The roads were still pitted with cobble stones, the walls of the grey apartment blocks still peeling and pockmarked with wartime bullet holes. Mid way down was the Domath family's block; a flat accessed via an inner courtyard with reeking bins and rusting chained up bikes. Impenetrable graffiti, Arabic-like, curled and swirled around the exterior walls and also inside around the stairwells leading to the apartments; Lt Colonel Hans Domath (retired) lived on the fourth floor.

Angelika used an old rusting key to unlock the door into a small, narrow hallway surrounded on either side by bookcases, each end of the four shelves shored up by iron busts of Marx, Engels, Lenin and Thalmann. Underneath his feet Peters felt the squeak, squeak of cheap oil cloth. Angelika gestured to him to shake off his shoes and take a right.

The main living room, even during daytime, was illuminated by a low level orange light. Peters surveyed the shelves and the tops of the wooden cabinets on which sat toy T54's, plastic tiny troop carriers, a model of a Soyuz rocket, a perfectly clipped together MiG 16 fighter. The sight of the miniature tank reminded him of those lines of rotting and rusting Iraqi fighting vehicles strewn across the Kuwaiti desert. He remembered at the time thinking as if he was in the junk yard of Soviet communism surrounded by the system that had so ingloriously failed. The system that his 'betters' in military int once told him in Berlin only a few years before the '91 Gulf War was likely to survive the upheavals elsewhere in Central Europe. Remembering how wrong they had been as he recalled the wreckage of Saddam's Soviet armour, sitting now in Angi's father's living room, he felt that exact same emotion.

On the walls there were pennants of F.C. Berlin and the Felix Derzinshky Regiment; a poster demonstrating support for the MPLA in Angola; a black and white picture of Sigmund Jahn, the first German in space. There were bottles too, empty ones all sitting atop white doilies strategically positioned across shelves, record player lids and tables. All of them beers that were no longer brewed in the city. And above them hanging on the wall nearest the window, a sword in its sheath. Peters thought how remarkably similar it all this was to his own apartment several miles away in the far, far west.

Angi's father sat up bolt upright in a battered, moth eaten chair. He was breathing heavily through a thick, angular nose. The colonel's sonorous inhaling and exhaling created the impression in Peter's mind that he was inside the belly of some rumbling, latent beast.

He was a tall man, about six foot three, thin, free from any excess weight. He had blue, watery eyes and a colony of wiry red hair on his head.

'You will have a beer, then?' he asked without even looking at Peters.

'Yes please, a Kindl would be great.'

The colonel instantly rose to Peters' bait.

'We don't drink that shit here. We drink our own beer.'

He stormed off to the kitchen and then returned with three

bottles under his arm and a tin opener clamped between his teeth; the top of it revealing the colours of the German flag and the familiar DDR icons of the hammer of the workers and the dividers representing the 'progressive intelligentsia.'

As he popped off the beer tops the colonel launched into a tirade.

'We only drink Vernesgruner. We keep to our own. It's all we have left, Herr Peters.'

After handing the bottles out and ignoring the protests of his daughter who reminded him that she was on duty, the colonel fixed his glare on Peters.

'My daughter tells me that you used to be a British soldier.'

'Yes, sir here in Berlin just before the Wall fell.'

'Then you were in that nest of spies over near the Olympic stadium?'

'If that's what you want to call it. Yes. I was there right up until it all fell apart across here.'

The colonel laughed and slapped Peters on the back.

'You speak German like a Swabian. I take it your teacher was from Stuttgart.'

Peters remembered that summer of 1980 in the capital of Baden Wurtemberg, camping in the Black Forest, drinking apple beer and his first awkward sexual experience as a 14 year old virgin lying about his age to an older girl in purple dungarees and a Nuclear Power-No Thanks badge clipped near one of her breasts; the two of them fondling and pulling each other furtively in the university residence halls.

'You are very perceptive Colonel Domath,' Peters said also remembering the exact same comment from another member of the NVA when there was still such a thing as the Warsaw Pact and a wall that defined all of their lives.

'Know thine enemy. Now how can I help you Herr Peters? My daughter said you need my help.'

Angelika interrupted and explained to her father about the two murders on film, the second one with the sword and the strange Cyrillic message engraved on the steel. The colonel marched over to the wall and with both hands took down the sword. He unsheathed it and moved back across the floor, his right hand gripped on the handle, the sword pointing straight into the direction towards Peters' stomach.

He could run this right through me now and he wouldn't flinch. No, not now,. But back then, when the Wall was up and the Cold War was running. If Domath had captured Peters he would have not hesitated for a second in dispatching the English spy and all the 'traitors' he once controlled. Peters swigged back the beer and then handed the colonel's bottle back to him. The ex-NVA colonel took a sip and sat down, balancing the sword on his knees.

'Sir, there was a word engraved into the blade used to kill our second man.'

'The word was Tavarich. Or 'Comrade' as any linguist-spy in the British Army would have known,' Colonel Domath said impatiently.

'Yes, Comrade. What is the significance of that, sir?'

The colonel held up the sword to the light and pointed to an engraving on the side. Peters leaned forward and read.

'Tavarich.'

The old man collapsed back into the decaying seat and again sipped at his beer. Then he bent forward, clasping his bony hands together as if in prayer.

'I was not like the rest of the jackals. You must understand that Herr Peters. Unlike the others I didn't cross the line once the anti-fascist protection barrier came down to offer my services. Oh I know. That was your job. You must have interviewed all those ex NVA and Stasi officers willing to offer up our most closely guarded secrets. Well I wasn't one of them.'

'I don't quite follow how this is connected to our investigation.'

Angelika again interrupted: 'What we want to know, what Herr Peters needs to know, is who would have access to such a sword?'

'Oh come my Angi. I think you already know the answer to that question.'

His daughter blushed; Peters looked up and spotted a framed coloured photo, fading now, blurred slightly, almost ghost-like, of a young Angelika, bedecked in the royal blue shirt of the Free German Youth, a bunch of flowers in her arms, beside the humongous tonsured outline of Ernst Thalmann, the adopted home grown communist hero of the DDR who had died in Buchenwald concentration camp.

The colonel was staring longingly at the sword, gently shaking and twirling the blade around by his hand.

'What Angi knows is that such a sword is quite a collector's item, Herr Peters. That there are, that there were, only a limited number in existence.'

'How come?' Peters was bewildered.

'They were only given out to specialist units. Units in the NVA that worked alongside our Soviet comrades. Hence Tavarich.'

'So they were only given to Germans.'

'Of course. Only to special forces. Men who had fought in Afghanistan against the medievalist fascists. You know those people that your British Army is still fighting today. Or men who had trained the freedom fighters in Angola and Mozambique.'

Peters realised this was potentially worse than he could ever have imagined. He was reading his thoughts out loud.

'So, our man is, was, a soldier?'

'No, not just an ordinary soldier. Someone with experience in Special Forces. Someone who is very good at killing people.' The Colonel seemed delighted to be relaying this.

They sat there in the indeterminate orange glow in silence for about thirty seconds before Peters interrupted with a banal hope.

'But surely this could just be someone who bought such a sword in an antique shop. Or of one of the stalls at Checkpoint Charlie.'

The colonel dismissed Peters' desperate theory with supreme confidence.

'Not a chance. No soldier from that unit would hand over such an honour. They were not mercenaries.'

'So we should be worried then, colonel?'

The old man suppressed a smile.

'I would say that that is a fair assumption my British comrade.'

Again silence. They sat draining the dregs of their beer. Peters and Angelika taking in what her father had just told them. A sword for a special forces' soldier. Now a trained, efficient assassin loose on the streets of Berlin. Still on a roll.

'Colonel, your advice has been invaluable.'

'I would say it's been a double-edged sword,' the old boy said barely able to silence his sniggering. Even now, 16 years after all that was dear to him had collapsed in ignominy, Angi's father was still at war.

Nine

Armed Germans prowled outside the synagogue on Oranienburger Strasse and around the corner up Tucholvsky Strasse in front of the Beth Café. Their presence was a small, daily act of atonement.

The middle age cops bulging out of their olive green overcoats, their Heckler and Koch machine guns pointed away from pavements and passers-by, were there to ward off old threats and new. They were there not only to protect the small Jewish quarter wedged between Friedrichstrasse and the Hackesher Markt from the emulators of Nazism, but also from other smouldering avengers from the dust, the dirt, the heat of thousands of miles away.

Peters nodded to the two officers patrolling outside the café with a curt 'Tag' before going inside. In their sitting smoking, reading a Hebrew language newspaper, legs crossed, fiddling with her straight shiny black hair was Irit Weissman, cultural officer at the Israeli embassy in Berlin with a husband allegedly still back at home in Tel Aviv. She was here at the table only because she owed Peters.

'You look as if you haven't slept in weeks, Martin. You're having too much of a good time.'

'That's Berlin for you. You ought to get out more, Irit. You're looking far too healthy.'

They embraced, Peters landing kisses on either of her cheeks, he caught a whiff of her scent, a new perfume, the aroma of chocolate and spices.

Irit clasped her hands together, the cigarette clamped between her lips and stared into Peters' eyes who half expected this woman to shoot up from her seat, place her hand on her hips and bark out orders. He instantly recalled flying to Israel via El Al from Heathrow and those sharp minded, bright eyed young women, the security officers who gazed into your pupils to detect minute signs of fear or evasion when they asked: 'Are you bringing a bomb onto this plane?'

She took the cigarette from her mouth and crushed it into the ashtray, blowing a jet of smoke into the air above their table.

'So why does the Berlin Polizei's finest want to see me?'

'I have a favour to ask you. Or rather to call in.'

'Go on,' Irit prompted.

He took a sip from the coffee cup just laid down on their table.

'Do you know a man called Avi Yanaev?'

Peters studied her for a reaction but the force-field Irit Weissman was always able to erect 'was as impenetrable as ever.

'What? No response?' he asked.

Irit lit another cigarette, again blowing a jet of smoke in a straight column towards the ceiling before returning to her coffee.

'Avi Yanaev? Of course we do. Why would the Berlin Polizei be interested in such a fine pillar of the city's Jewish community?'

'A pillar of salt or a pillar of fire?' Peters asked. She jolted backwards in her seat, smiled and then laughed.

'Herr Yanaev finances a number of projects in the city including the Berlin Jewish film festival. It starts this weekend,' Irit was now surveying Peters coldly.

'You haven't told me yet why you are interested in him. Why? What's he done?'

He didn't need to remind Irit about the Palestinian taxi drivers operating along the Ku-damm just a couple of years ago, especially the one Peters' station had picked up drunk late one evening near the Schifferbauerdamm, boasting about the Zionists they had fooled from the Embassy, one of whom had left his ID card in the Arab's car. Peters later unravelled a plot to kidnap the diplomat, which Stannheim's Cold War comrades in the BND prevented with a deportation order and a one-way ticket for the loose talking taxi-man all the way back permanently to Amman.

'At long last I can ask you out on a date,' Peters said before hesitating and adding.

'As long as your husband is back working in Tel Aviv.'

Peters remembered a tall, blonde man with flawless German, speaking refined nord-deutsch. In reality, Irit's spouse was probably acting out a part somewhere east of The Jordan, marooned in some stinkhole, playing the role of the affable businessman from Hamburg or Bremen for his Arab hosts.

'The launch party for the film festival is at the Maritim hotel this Saturday, Martin. Formal wear. You have to dress like that so I can buy a new frock.' Irit was flirting, strategically, ignoring his remark about her husband's possible true whereabouts.

Saturday, thought Peters. He had no one on Saturday. This was going to be a perfectly fulfilled weekend and there was always 'Der Zug' later if Irit Weissman was still preoccupied with her man on a mission far beyond the borders of their homeland.

'I assume Yanaev is going to be there?'

'Of course. He's at the top table with the ambassador.'

'So we can be introduced then?' he asked.

'Naturally, I hope you aren't going to cause a scene. The Mayor of Berlin will be there with his gay partner too.'

'And good luck to the both of them but my interest in is Yanaev.'

Peters studied the Israeli diplomat for her reaction. The force-field was still in place. It suddenly occurred to him that Yanaev might have been working for her bosses for all he knew. If this was so there could be no further way into the mystery that Lothar Blucher had partially opened for him.

'One more thing before I go Irit. Is Herr Yanaev on your side? Is he on the books?'

She seemed disappointed by the question: 'Come on, Martin, that is out of order. I don't go around asking who's working for you.'

'But he isn't, is he?' Peters insisted.

'I need to know.'

Irit Wiseman stared into Peters' eyes; there was just a flicker from hers, a non-verbal signal that the detective was safe to pry into the affairs of Avi Yanaev, that he needn't worry about Mossad covering the Russian's back.

After embracing Irit once more he left the Beth Café tickled at the thought of what the glamorous Israeli spy would have made of one Lothar Blucher.

Outside, the police guards were getting drenched by a deluge, salty ice water needles from the Baltic stinging their faces and those of everyone else passing by on the pavements. Peters moved back down Tulchovsky Strasse then right up the Oranienberger towards Friedrichstrasse and the U-Bahn station. Amid the gathering gloom, filed up in parallel to the outdoor heaters of the Indian restaurants and bars stood a line of East European hookers all clad in their winter-street uniform of hip length white puffed up fake fur lined jackets, skin tight jeans and knee boots. One of them smiled at Peters before disappearing inside a jeep with blacked out windows, which then shot off in the opposite direction from where the detective was walking, eastwards towards the ever-dimming twilight.

Ten

The S-Bahn to Spandau pulled out of Friedrichstrasse and the eastern Berlin skyline started to slowly disappear in the decaying light. The winking beacon at the summit of the TV tower at Alexanderplatz was the only landmark still visible as the train coursed slowly westward through the lush green affluence of the Tiergarten, then on past the seedy drabness of the west end towards the Grunewald and the ultimate destination - the old British military headquarters near the notorious prison. Peters suddenly realised tomorrow was Thursday, Miriam's day of arrival.

His mobile rang and he fished it out of his jacket. It was Heike Numann.

'Martin?'

'Heike, what's up?'

'He's been in touch again. Another email. A different address.'

'What's he been saying?'

'Can we meet up? I printed out the mail. Let's have a drink somewhere.'

Peters noticed that the next stop was Sauvingy Platz, the square close to Blucher's shop. If he jumped off and grabbed a cab he could be at Checkpoint Charlie in ten or fifteen minutes. Peters assumed Heike was back at work, inside WAMS headquarters in the gleaming, hyper modern skyscraper on Zimmer Strasse that Axel Springer built to show off his empire to the citizens once trapped just behind the Wall facing onto his offices.

'How about Café Adler? I take it you are still at work in the Springer Building.'

'Sure. Adler is perfect. Twenty minutes?'

Café Adler was situated to the left of Checkpoint Charlie, the bar that was once the pub at the edge of the world, a spit's distance from the old Cold War barrier, now a stop-off hostelry for tourists milling around the former frontier zone.

After entering the bar, elbowing past a group of Japanese tourists fresh in from a tour of the museum across the street, Peters ordered a wheat beer and sat down by a table overlooking Zimmer Strasse.

Heike Numman was half an hour late; Peters guessed she was held back by the paper's fact checkers assiduously editing her copy. She apologised for her tardiness and asked the waiter for a bottle of Schultheiss beer. Peters was already on to his second wheat beer. Heike then neatly rolled out a photocopy of the email in front of the detective.

To: heike.numann@wams.de
From: st-christopher@clara.net
Subject: 'the next phase.'
Well. Well. I hope you are busy with your story. You will have plenty to write about. This is only the beginning.

Peters wondered if he had been wasting his time cancelling his journey home to be with the WAMS journalist.

'He doesn't give much away does he?'

The reporter shrugged her shoulders and sipped at the beer bottle placed in front of her.

'If he commits one more murder Martin I can't not write about Christopher. He'll go elsewhere if I ignore him. I've just written the report on the Russian murders. But if he strikes again then our deal is off.'

She was obviously serious, Peters realised his agreement with her hung on what she and him now called Christopher did next.

'Grant it, he's probably preparing for another one. But if he holds fire until the weekend then our deal stands, Heike.' She was the only link to the killer barring Lothar Blucher. There was only one move he could make.

'I want someone from the station to shadow you, Heike'

When she bridled at the thought, Peters added determinedly:

'I'll go to the top if you don't agree with it. You could be in danger, Heike. Besides you are only real connection to the murderer. Let's not forget that - he is a murderer.'

Heike detected something in the Englishman's tone, something beyond the call of professional duty. They had been lovers once, albeit for a short time. She refused to commit herself to anyone in her life while building her career although that was not why she had 'ended it. But she still felt a common bond with the detective, her reticence about over-involvement overlapping with his refusal even as he hit his forties to be tied down either to one person. And yet there was still something in his voice, something that told her that she remained somehow special to the ever elusive Martin Peters. He was stirred once more surveying those intense hazel-green eyes that were focussed on his reaction, the porcelain skin devoid of any make up and the way she kept her dyed black hair with purple tinge cut in that new romantic wedge.

'Okay, Martin. We'll give it to the weekend to see what Christopher does next. If he sees nothing in the paper on Sunday he might cut me off. But seeing as it's you Herr Peters I don't think I have a choice.'

Peters liked it when Heike flirted with him; it was more like a cat toying with a mouse, he succumbing as always to her game.

'Oh, I don't think even I could ever control WAMS' finest,' he said staring into Heike's eyes. 'I don't think even your editor could keep you in check.'

She drew back in her seat and shot him a lascivious smile:

'Oh, I remember a time when you used to regularly keep me in check,' she said licking froth from her upper lip.

'You used to say it was "my therapy". Remember?'

He blushed, remembering a short passionate six months a couple of years ago before Frau Schuster, Miriam or Karen, when Heike would stay over on weekend nights in Heer Strasse, when they played games with each other until one of them 'lost' and paid the price over the knee. Embarrassed at the memory, Peters darkened the mood once more.

'Still, I insist that we get someone in to shadow you at work. We need someone who can be there if he rings, emails or who knows, even makes a courtesy call.'

Even when she jolted at the thought of it, Peters stood his ground.

'I'm deadly serious Heike. If I have to I'll get Stannheim to call your boss. He has pull all over this city. We have no inroads into Christopher barring you,' he added lying, thinking again about Blucher.

She knocked back her Schultheiss and immediately ordered another from the waiter. Peters resisted another wheat beer and instead asked for coffee. He wanted a clear head in the morning for his face-to-face with Stannheim.

'Since you've handed me my scoop for the week and it's only Wednesday how about a night on the town?' Heike asked, bristling with confidence. Peters noticed the line of yellow cabs outside Adler's door. He was too tired to go by U-Bahn all the way to Friedrichstrasse and re-trace his S-Bahn journey west back to Heer Strasse; he was far too tired either to fall for Heike's temptation.

'When all this is over Heike you and I are going to go on a real bender, a force 9 one all over this city. We'll pub crawl all the way from Hallensee to Friedrichshain and back again. But not tonight. I'm sorry. Unlike you I've to go to my boss tomorrow morning completely empty-handed.'

'That's a pity,' Heike replied curtly, stood up, marched out and left Peters to his coffee in a café filling up with more Japanese tourists. He was relieved to see that none of the tourists outside were hailing taxis. He couldn't face the endless east-to-west-west-to-east pull that drove him back and forth over memories and history. For some reason he could not explain it was only travelling by car could he feel that he was living in a reunited whole.

Later, in those penumbral hours between the darkness and light, with the night sky gently crumbling away towards morning, Peters paced around his apartment, naked, unsettled, unable to sleep. The television plasma screen flickered in the corner of the living room, the volume muted, the ever changing images of scantily clad women speaking into telephones, different numbers from Germany, Austria and Switzerland flashing up and below the smaller digits below constantly reminding the caller of the cost in Euro and Swiss Francs per minute.

He sat down on the couch facing the TV and the women who even with the volume turned up would still have been saying nothing. Peters looked up towards the area above the door into the main room where the captured Kalashnikov hung. He thought about Angi's father far way on the other side of the city, the sword hanging on his wall, his obvious delight that the swordsman who sliced and then hacked the second victim to pieces was probably one of Herr Domath's old comrades. Then Peters thought about his own father and his long agonising death during that final six month posting to Northern Ireland just before the ceasefires; his tour of duty constantly interrupted by phone calls from his mother and her daily dispatches from the medical front; all of his R&R spent at the bedside in that very same hospital where he had born on the day of the World Cup triumph. All Peters could recall from their final conversations was Kurt's continual amusement that his son was leaving the army to go back to Berlin and join the German police. His father was so stunned by the news of his son's ambition that he shared it with all the other men in the cancer ward or as Kurt had described it on first entering, 'Terminal One.'

For the next two nights Peters decided he could not be completely alone. So he was grateful for the insomnia and the isolation that sleeplessness brought. As he tried desperately to shift his thoughts towards the sword as well as the enigma of Avi Yanaev, Peters realised that his face was wet. For the last few minutes he had been unaware that tears were streaming down. He hated to admit but it was then that Peters regretted spurning Heike's offer.

Eleven

It wasn't the alarm clock but her mobile that was bleeping.

The phone must have been ringing for at least five minutes, on/off, on/off until Heike Numann was finally roused from her booze sodden slumber. She was still in her clothes, which smelt of smoke and sweat, both hers and others. She had gone on from Adler back to the Springer building and then joined some colleagues in the ground floor wine bar of the high rise media centre. From there it was on to the Russian disco in Prenzlauer Berg. Her increasingly frenetic consumption evolved from the Schultzheiss with Peters onto a bottle of Riesling and finally a toxic rainbow of different coloured shots in the nightclub, downed until she finally keeled over. All she could remember was stumbling out of her taxi into her apartment in Neun Kollen as the birds were starting to twitter. Heike knew she'd gone off at the deep end.

'Hello. Who is it?'

'Fraulein, good morning.' She noticed that his German was formal, clipped, officiously polite.

'Aren't you supposed to be in the WAMS building by now?' he went on.

She was still groggy, her antennae blunted by her overnight/early morning indulgences.

'I'm sorry if this is someone from work but I'm not due in until midday.'

'Fraulein. May I introduce myself? I am Christopher your friend from the email.'

No one at work was aware of what she had seen. It had until now been a secret between herself and Peters and he would never play games with her head like this.

'Christopher? You're the one that's been mailing me?' she was breathless now, her heart thumping until she would hear the blood pounding in her ears and feel her palms weeping.

'I ring to apologise to you. I know the material you saw was unpleasant. I hope you weren't too offended.'

She glanced at the LCD screen on the cell phone; the number was withheld of course. Heike immediately thought of Peters and wished she had persuaded him to stay with her.

'Fraulein. You are very quiet. There is no need to be afraid.'

Heike yearned for a cigarette and rummaged around her bed and through her clothes but found nothing.

'How...how did you get my number?'

'It's very simple. I just looked up the reporters' contact details on the "WAMS" website and there it was. I hope you don't find that too intrusive.'

If she had gone home last night, if she had went in early to the Springer building, she would have bought time to at least have had the call recorded. In her hazy state Heike knew she would lose details and be only vague in her recollections of voice, diction and intonation. For some unknown reason she started to apologise to the killer.

'I'm sorry. I'm in a fragile state this morning. You were the last person I expected to call.'

He laughed gently: 'We are both apologising to each other here. There really is no need.'

Those manners again, she thought, and the old fashioned pronunciation which hinted at an education and upbringing in the east.

She was so thrown by him Heike could only offer the kind on banal question a news editor would despair at .

'No. No need. So why are you calling me?'

'It's very simple Fraulein. I've chosen you to explain what I'm doing. By the way, have you worked it out yet?'

'What's to work out? Two men killed on film and you are seeking publicity for it,' the moment she said it Heike wondered where she had gotten her brashness from.

'Fraulien. Let's just see how you deal with the incidents.'

'Then explain to me why. Why these men? Who are they?'

There was a pause on the line, deep breathing through his nose.

'To tell you who they are is to tell you why they were chosen, Fraulein. The struggle isn't over yet... .' the line went dead.

Heike started swearing in frustration. Like the email he had told her next to nothing. She kept frantically pressing 1471 but continually that anonymous female phone voice told her it was a blocked call. She decided to take a shower and head into work, to get away from the bastard tormenting on her on the end of the line. Heike depressed the power button and switched the phone off.

She couldn't bear the short journey via S-Bahn and then U-Bahn to Koch Strasse and the paper's HQ around the corner. Instead she took a taxi, all the while in the cab thinking about the last word Christopher had uttered: 'struggle.' Struggle for what? Heike asked herself over and over again on the journey across central Berlin through Postdamer Platz, across the former frontier towards 'Charlie' and then Zimmer Strasse. Struggle! What a curious way to describe the slaughter of two old defenceless elderly queens in front of a camera.

Later, at her desk in the open plan office on the 12th floor of the Springer Building, Heike felt the weight of her secret pressing down on her. She wanted to scream out to the reporters and sub-editors hunched over computer screens, whispering in near silence down the telephone line or huddling together in small groups of two and three, mapping out their various sections of Sunday's paper, what she had seen and now heard.

Heike noticed that fat, black clouds pregnant with precipitation were now bulging around the top of the TV tower. She yearned for the downpour and longed to be outside in the sharp, static air, showering herself in the threatening storm about to break over Berlin. Heike also needed Peters.

Across the invisible border inside Kottbusser Strasse the English detective was about to hold court again in front of his murder squad. All were gathered there except Riedel whom Peters had called in to see at 'Boyz R Us' that morning. The only interesting thing Riedel had to report was that the few men flicking through the magazine and DVD racks were only talking about one thing –

rumours that one of the 'regulars' hadn't been seen for weeks. They pondered on whether he had had another heart attack. 'Too much sniffing of the poppers' one of them quipped provoking a round of sniggering from the others that day in 'Boyz R Us.'

Back in the station Peters looked worried. Stannheim sat in his usual recalcitrant pose at the back playing, no threatening, to be the disturber of the peace. Angi was standing beside her boss holding a mounted photograph of the sword, two black arrows pointing at the blown up Cyrillic word on the weapon's side.

'What Angi is holding up is a picture of the murder weapon and one word engraved in the blade,' Peters announced. As he did so the team opened their files and each lifted up A4 photocopies of the sword from their desks.

'The word for those of you who never benefited from a DDR education is Russian. It means 'Comrade'. And you can't buy it from one of the hucksters flogging East German memorabilia outside Checkpoint Charlie or the Brandenburg Gate,' Peters continued.

'Angi and I have discovered that the sword is a collectors' item, not commonly or widely available. They were manufactured by the Soviets and given to their most trusted East German comrades. Members of the old NVA who fought with the Russkies in Afghanistan or Africa. Unless our man has stolen the sword I would guess he was given this before the Wall came down. Which as I'm sure you can guess means that he may have been a soldier.'

Peters wasn't the least bit surprised that it was Bauer, the suspected former Stasi-nark who used accusations against Angi as a shield to deflect attention from his own past, that put his hand up first.

'Sir, I have a few old NVA contacts that might be able to help us there.'

The Englishman was tempted to say 'I suppose it's better than spending all of your day in gay bars' but he resisted. Bauer probably did have contacts in the East German military, possibly even some of those in the more elite units linked into the old party's apparatus of power and terror.

'Go east Bauer and dig them up. Find out exactly which units were awarded these swords. Ask if any of ex-soldiers have gone weird lately. Maybe they've started to frequent gay pubs. And don't forget to wonder out loud if any of them own a quiet lock up somewhere deep in the east, somewhere where no one will hear you scream.'

He detailed the rest of them to check other police districts for reports of missing relatives; to quietly issue photographs of the two victims in stations across the city; to check out if any of the doomed duo had a record and to track anyone with a history of homophobic violence. When the team dispersed to their desks, or in Bauer's case disappeared to the car pool, Peters sat alone in a chair beneath blown up pictures of the dead men. He was aware that Stannheim was staring at him, slyly.

'How is your media management campaign coming on?' the superintendent asked.

'Our deal still stands sir,' Peters said with renewed confidence. 'Heike Numann will be as good as her word.'

Stannheim marched across the incident room floor until he was directly facing Peters. The station's chief reeked of tobacco and his breath betrayed a night at home downing snaps waiting for his son to arrive back, as usual an effort made in vain.

'You have just made a classic error Martin.'

The accusation stung Peters.

'What on earth do you mean, sir?'

'Too much unnecessary detail to too many officers. The thing about the sword should have been kept between you, me and Angi. Instead you blurted it out in front of the entire squad. On the law of averages I would guess that at least one of them has a contact in the lower end of the media food chain.'

'I don't follow, sir,' Peters said with barely concealed sarcasm.

'What I'm saying Martin is that it's going to get out. All the juicy bits are there now. A former soldier slaughtering older gay men with a Russian sword, the tabloids will hyperventilate over all that one.'

'Then I'll make sure there won't be a leak because if there is I'll have their balls off and turned into Easter Eggs.'

'Who says the leak will come from the men?' Stannheim interjected.

'So you do trust your troops after all sir?'

'An awful lot more than I would trust any journalist.'

'Heike Numann will honour our agreement, sir. That at least I can promise.'

On the mention of her name his mobile rang. Peters had had a bizarre feeling that the call was from her. It turned out to be perfect timing. He would be released from Stannheim, a man whom he loved and feared in equal measure.

'Excuse me for a moment, sir.'

'Never mind a moment, Martin, I'm off to Anna's'

'Anna's' was an old fashioned kniepe-Berlin corner pub in a street parallel to their station. Stannheim had gone off in search of his early morning cure.

Peters ran to his desk and snatched up his mobile, pressing the green answer button at the sixth and final ring.

'Hello.'

'Martin, it's Heike.'

'I know. I was expecting you.'

'Then you must be telepathic.'

'Just intuition. Anyway, how can I help you?'

'Martin. I need to see as soon as I can.'

There was a hint of panic again in her voice, just like the first time when her morning and, perhaps, her sanity was partly fractured by the horror show sent to her through cyberspace.

'Heike, are you ok?'

'Not really. He's called this time. On this number. I've managed to hear his voice.'

She sounded captivated and Peters was filled by panic, fearful that Stannheim's prophecy was about to come to pass.

Twelve

'Anna's' was the casualty ward for the over-indulgent, the mournful, the traumatised and the permanently passed-over. Officers from Peters' station around the corner sought solace here amid the gloomy décor and the brothel-red lights. Its proprietor, a widower who named the corner pub after his late wife, hardly ever left the premises. Every time Peters and the Kottbuser Strasse murder squad came here to wash away the dirt from their finger nails along with the sordid details of their days amid the dead and deranged, the owner was always propped up behind the bar, his waxen, taut skin translucent in the crimson glow of the pub lights. And today was no different when Peters walked into 'Anna's' with Heike Numann beside him.

'Good day Herr Peters,' the landlord growled . 'And who is this lovely fraulein I see before me?'

'This is Heike Numann, one of the Berlin press's finest and she will have a Kindl and a Korn. I'll have a double brandy.'

Heads were already turning at the bar. The leering brigade from uniform elbowing each other at the sight of Heike sliding into a snug with Peters behind her clasping beer and spirits to his chest.

When they sat down Heike lit a cigarette and downed the Korn in one go.

'Struggle?' Peters asked.

'Struggle? Why would he use a word like that to describe what he is doing?'

'That is exactly what I thought, Martin. A strange word indeed.'

He almost blurted out that it wasn't unusual for an ex-soldier to employ the language of war. But he resisted, remembering his pact with the journalist and the fact that the days were ticking away towards the weekend and publication.

'This is very interesting, Heike. I promise you can use all this once we get a better picture of our man. No one else is talking to us directly.'

She seemed placated by what Peters had said and that gave him confidence to ask for more from her.

'Angi is coming to WAMS tomorrow to shadow you. She's the best I have and totally trustworthy,' he hesitated.

'Heike, if he rings again try and engage with him, keep him on the line, make him feel important, as if you want to tell his life story. Then the second he puts the phone down, write everything down that you've heard, instantly and then call me.'

They sat for a while enjoying their drinks, watching the hunched over and the hung over throw back shots and drain beer glasses. Peters was as ever on the look-out for Stannheim but there was still no sign of the boss. He remembered Mannfred's warning about the danger of disclosing the details. *To hell with him.* It was worth the risk.

'Oh, Heike ask him this: Does he think he is a soldier?'

'A soldier? Whatever for?'

'He might think he's at war. Angi will join you in the newsroom tomorrow morning. Stay close to her and let her know everything about him. Now I have to go and avoid someone.'

As they left 'Anna's' he spotted Stannheim coming around the corner from Kottbusser Strasse. He had been too late. The chief was already waving wildly over at his favourite officer. 'Time for a beer, my friend,' he bellowed across the street. Peters nodded to Heike to get off sight quickly.

Back once more inside the pub Stannheim simply nodded to the landlord who poured out two large Kindls and left them on the table where the two men had sat down.

'Prosit,' said Stannheim lifting up his glass and clinking it against Peters'.

'Did you have company?' he asked slyly as if not knowing.

'Yes, Heike Numann.'

'Is our journalist friend still co-operating with us?'

'Yes sir. She's on for the Russian story still. Nothing about Christopher.'

'Listen to me Martin. It's going to get out. You must know that. Someone in the investigation is going to blabber to someone else who happens to know someone in the media and there we go. So we don't have much time left. When he sees that Frau Numann hasn't bothered putting him on the front page he is going elsewhere with his manifesto.'

'You are a prophet of doom Mannfred. How is Paul by the way?' Peters tried to shift the focus of his boss' attention onto another more personal source of misery.

The old man suddenly looked crushed, his face sunken, his entire frame deflating. Peters expected the worst about the errant son. It was the reason why Mannfred Stannheim consistently cleared the room in 'Anna's'. No one wanted to hear his rolling tales of filial woe.

'He stayed over last night. Found him rifling through the room where I keep my wife's things. I lock up the money every evening in a safe. Paul only has a key to the house. There's nothing for him to take. So he was searching for something from her room to sell. We had a huge row when I caught him on. Jesus Christ, Martin.'

His boss was on the verge of tears now.

'When he's like that anything is possible. He had one of her necklaces in his hand. One I bought her years ago. All he cares about is his fucking fix.'

Peters gripped Stannheim by the shoulder, steadying the ship, preventing the old man from breaking down in front of the remaining flotsam and jetsam in the bar.

'Get a grip Sir. You have to lead from the front.'

'Spare me your old regimental mottos, Martin.' He was wiping the water from his eyes with a handkerchief flicked out of his ash stained jacket.

'He's a fucking arsehole Martin. You know that. I know that.'

'It's the smack sir, that's all. It's not him. I've seen it hundreds of time before. So have you. He's a nice lad deep down. It's an illness sir.'

Stannheim waved away Peters' excuses.

'Well it's too late to even care about that. He's slipped away from me a long time ago. Anyway, you be careful with that Fraulein Numann. If she loses Christopher to some other hack there'll be hell to pay.'

With that Peters' boss stood up, gripped onto the table to steady himself before marching off towards the door of 'Anna's'.

Miriam arrived as always in her taxi, the light on top switched off to avoid being hailed down, the car then parked quietly up against the space at the side of the building where Peters' car should have been had he ever had bothered to get one. He watched her from his bedroom five storeys up, noticing the crown of her head and that permanent neat parting exposing a line of her skull that separated her long jet black hair, hearing momentarily the muffled wail of Middle Eastern music from her stereo before she switched it off, opened the door, slammed it shut and flicked the alarm on to de-activate.

Inside his apartment he had lit scented candles, the aroma of lemons and limes wafting across the flat more for the benefit of his Turkish born lover than himself.

'You look tense, Martin,' Miriam remarked the second she came through the door, her hazel eyes swimming in sympathetic water.

She put one of her hands to his face and stroked his cheek gently, her touch forcing Peters to close his own eyes.

'Let me massage you, Martin. I think you've had as terrible a day as I have.'

Thoughts, theories, conspiracies were all ricocheting like a pin-ball through his weary brain. Lights and noise rattling across his consciousness, flashing up images of headless cadavers and tortured doomed captives. He was trying to calm down and let Miriam relax him. She began rubbing one of her forefingers up and down the back of his neck, then knead them deep into his muscle tissue. But Peters didn't want to be soothed. There was only one way to turn off the machine. By trip-switching it with a burst of lust laden energy. He grabbed Miriam roughly around the stomach and lifted her off her feet. Within seconds they were in his bedroom and he was working off her tracksuit bottoms and pants until he was over her, effortlessly entering her. By the time he was thrusting deep into Miriam she was digging her ankles into either side of his spine.

Later they lay together, Miriam stroking his head, her hand movements creating shadow play in the candle light.

'I can feel your blood throbbing, Martin.'

'That's down to you, love', he said flattering her.

'No, I would prefer if it was singing instead. It's a sign that you are tense. A hard day?' she whispered.

'You don't want to know. Was yours any better?'

She sat up in bed then reached down to the floor where she had dropped her handbag, fished around inside and produced cigarettes and lighter.

Peters watched her light up in the semi-darkness, caressing her nipples while she smoked.

'Yol is getting worse by the day,' Miriam said, her voice almost croaking. 'For him everything in Germany now is shit, corrupt, filthy. He won't even watch Turkish TV because he says it's infected by the west. Those channels from the Gulf are on constantly except at the weekends of course when he turns back to the football.'

'Why did he come here then?'

Miriam sighed as if Peters had just asked a stupid question.

'Because when he left Turkey the army was in charge and his family were left wing. He used to believe in Marx not the Mosque, just like his father. Twenty years of life in Berlin has turned him inside out. It's funny but it was the Wall that did it for him in the end.'

'As it did for a lot of socialists darling,' Peters interjected.

But Miriam was losing her patience, gently but firmly for not being fully understood.

'No Martin! He was depressed when it came down. While it was up things were simple. The socialists on one side, the imperialists on the other. He loved the idea of all those pro-American Germans trapped inside West Berlin. He used to laugh at them and say one day the East is going to cross over and then they will know the score. He loved the idea of being so close to real power.'

'Why didn't he go over there then?'

'He wasn't that stupid. It was just his perversity, his kink, his kick. He enjoyed being on the edge of something and when that disappeared, well...'

'He sought out another crutch.'

Miriam moved closer to him, until he could smell the dry-rot reek of tobacco on her breath and body.

'Yol has needed a crutch all his life, Martin. First there was his father, then the party back in Turkey and now, after the Turn, the Imams. He is a weak man and they are the ones I fear most of all.'

Peters almost blurted it out, his one secret desire, the wish he kept suppressing, the easy temptation of commitment. But he managed, just in time, to stop himself from saying: 'Leave him. Come and live with me instead.'

She seemed to sense that he was tensing up and stroked his face again.

'Enough of him, Martin. Tell me about what's happened.'

'No, not now. We will eat and then you'll go home pretending you've been driving around the west end all night.' Momentarily he couldn't believe how resentful that had sounded.

He had a phrase for it, her ritual of departure after they had made love: they lay together for a short time and then dined, after that it was her 'nightly ablution' when she would disappear into his bathroom to wash and shower away any scent of him off her body. Peters had even learned to remember never to wear aftershave on Thursday nights. He imagined her husband, his paranoia increasing with every sermon denouncing the decadence of the west, sheet-sniffing around everything external that Miriam came into contact with.

Sometimes he felt the same way towards Miriam as he did with all those informers past and present, the believers and refuseniks behind the Wall who lived in constant fear of exposure and ten years in solitary confinement or the firing squad, or the criminal ones today who, through baser motives, risked a slower, more brutal demise for their betrayals. Spy and later policeman, it was dawning slowly on Peters that he was putting Miriam in the line of her husband's ire.

They had first come across each other at a dinner party organised by an English bookseller in Friedrichshain who specialised in detective and Cold War thrillers as well as novels, plays, poetry and even old football books from the former DDR. Bob Carew, the shop owner, had been a sergeant in the 14th Intelligence with Peters at the time of the Turn and, like his company commander, decided to return to Berlin after reunification in search of a fortune amid Helmut Kohl's promised blooming landscapes.

Before taking up taxi work to escape the evening rantings and railings of her husband at yet another example of western corruption on television, Miriam had worked as an assistant in Carew' 'Ostbooks'. Lucky then for Peters, unlucky maybe for Miriam, that Carew had organised the party on the weekend of her husband's annual trip to see his family back in Anatolia.

As Miriam was slipping her tracksuit bottoms back on, sniffing all over the top that Peters had ripped off when he overpowered her, he lay back on one of his sofas, still completely naked and looked her over.

'If you think this is too risky...'

She quickly crossed the room, leant over his face and put one finger on his lips to shut him up.

'Please Martin. No acting up. Stop playing the self-sacrificing martyr. If you can't bring yourself to end it then don't ask me to do it for you.'

Miriam released her finger and he sank to the floor and clung to her legs burying his head in between her knees. Afterwards when she had left the apartment and Peters could hear the engine of her Mercedes revving up in the still early Spring night he realised he was kneeling naked on the floor frozen in the same state of suspended, miserable submission. He hated to admit it. The idea of being alone through the night and the nagging fear that his spectral companion would arise from the Berlin underground to haunt him in the place he called home sent a chill through his body.

Thirteen

Two headless corpses the Berlin Polizei found in Lake Havel are Russians and may be linked to new post-Soviet mafia feuding in the city.

Welt am Sonntag has discovered that the bodies last weekend were washed ashore near Wansee according to sources close to the investigation.

Officially, the Polizei are refusing to comment on the discovery of the cadavers but sources say they are certain the victims were Russian.

Wams has also established that both males had mysterious tattoos on their bodies.

'They were two words "Kursk" and "Kharkov" - references to battles of the Second World War in the Soviet Union,' said one source in the Polizei.

'This would indicate that a message was being transmitted, a message that whoever did this was serious........'

Numann has run out of road, thought Angi. Good. She was searching around for words to pad out the meagre morsels of information her boss had given the journalist. But Peters would still be furious with that reference to 'one source in the Polizei'. She was sure of it. Stannheim, and worse again his underlings in Kottbusser Strasse, wouldn't take long to work out who the 'one source' happened to be. They had all seen Peters with Numann before. Then the whispering games would begin.

Angi wished she could wipe the copy from the computer screen and persuade Numann's editor to kill the story. But she was only there inside the top floor of the Springer Building to watch and wait for another call to Numann from Christopher.

Her editor Christian Littbarski had reluctantly agreed to allow

Angi to shadow Numann. He was not or ever would be prepared to let a police officer dictate the content of his paper let alone potentially a front page splash.

The journalist returned from the bathroom, resentment still etched over her face about Angi's order that she leave her mobile at all times on her workstation.

'Look I'm unarmed! Satisfied?' Heike Numann asked when she reached her Apple Mac. 'Nothing to call me on. Has the new man in my life rang me yet?'

'I'm sorry but Peters insisted. Mobile and phone stays in one spot where we can track it.'

'But course - you are only obeying orders,' Heike shot back.

'And Herr Litbarski has agreed to our request Heike.'

'Look it's Friday evening and do you know what that means? While you and Martin Peters and everyone else in the murder squad are normally taking your weekly dose of Soma in "Anna's" I'm about to enter the busiest time of MY week. I need to get this piece finished before the evening conference, so I can convince my boss that this is more important than Angi Merkel making some inane remarks about Afghanistan or EU expansion.'

'And so?'

'So please give me some space to get this finished before five,' Heike pleaded.

'Sure thing but I'm taking your handy with me. If it rings I'll just be over by the window overlooking Zimmer Strasse. I promise to be quick; I used to be a sprinter when I was a kid.'

Numann had folded her arms: 'Bully for you. I'm sure the local party hacks in Prenz'l Berg were proud of you.'

The policewoman didn't respond. She was immune now to the toxic back references to her past, to those years she couldn't erase, to that upbringing as one of the chosen pampered few in the republic of near empty.

Angi's phone did eventually ring, it was Peters sounding nervous, like he was in the centre of a tumultuous threesome, diplomatically slinking off the sheets and out of the bedroom.

'Hi. Any sign of our man?'

'No sir. Not a word.'

'And how's Heike? She ok?'

'Look it's hard to talk here. She's written that report about our headless horsemen. Mentioned the tattoos in her piece and you.'

There was a pause down the line.

'What! She named me. No way.'

'No sir, not named. Hinted at maybe. Source in the Polizei.'

She spotted Numann advancing towards her from her desk.

'Sir I have to go. Hard to talk as I say....'

Numann snatched her mobile from the policewoman. *I would slap that bitch if this was elsewhere.*

'Hello. Hello. Is this Martin? Yes I suppose it is hard to talk. It's hard to think or write or breathe either in these conditions.'

Peters tried to be diplomatic, 'Heike, listen. You know why we are doing this. We have to take precautions because this man is extremely dangerous, more dangerous than we first thought.'

'Martin you are such a tease. This story is a guaranteed front page splash.'

'You are getting full chapter and verse on this once we get an inroad into Christopher. First up. And you have the Russians meantime. You're away ahead of everyone else, so don't complain.' The line went dead. Peters had lost his temper.

Heike Numann turned her glare from the tiny screen up to Angi's face.

'How can you work with such a shit?'

'That's easy. He's about the best in a bad barrel of them.'

'Really? And how do you know him then?'

At that moment Angi realised that her boss had once slept with Numann.

She gave the journalist the once over, scanning her small, tight body without an ounce of flab or any physical disproportion. Heike had thick upper and lower lips, a button nose and translucent sky blue eyes that sparkled and twinkled even after 12 hours under the hum and glare of the strip lighted ceiling on the top tier of the Springer builder. Only her skin, the colour of dish water, betrayed any sign that inside she was an exhausted, raging, conflicted mess.

Angi thought better of even hinting that Heike and Peters had been lovers. Instead she dared to offer some journalistic advice.

'You forgot to mention there was an official statement. On the Russians. There were a couple of quotes to use.'

'What are you the press office?' Heike snapped. 'If I'm looking for some insight into forensics I shall call you since Martin tells me you are such an expert. Otherwise leave the writing to me, darling.'

'No. Not the press office. Just someone obeying orders,' Angi bit back shuddering at the thought that they had to spend the whole night together.

Further out east, inside the ear splitting atmosphere of 'Taceles' on Oranienburger Strasse, Peters could barely hear himself think let alone anyone speak or listen to anyone else. A band, the 'Vomitorium,' from out in the sticks, the Saarland, were screaming and screeching about 'Pigs' and 'Nazis' in front of a juddering mass of sweat and steam. Somewhere in the middle of the torn up bike jackets and ripped shirts and bondage trousers was Karen Stock, clutching a bottle of Becks, swaying and bending to the quivering, hypnotic trance of the band's bass guitar. With her bobbed hair, Med looks and short flower patterned dress she looked even more out of place in 'Taceles' than Peters did. He wore his favourite T-shirt, the one given to him from the boys in the regiment at his leaving-do, the one of the Clash standing dazed and puzzled outside the Henry Taggart Army Base in west Belfast. It had been a private joke shared between comrades in the 14th Int. Peters had served inside there on his first tour of duty when he was charged with shadowing some of Ireland's finest. If only Joe Strummer had lived longer and Peters had had the chance to meet the Clash singer, just to tell him that one of his biggest fans had once worked for imperialism inside the 'Taggart.'

Before the Wall had come down Peters had used that same T-shirt as a 'passport' to gain entry into the world of the those disgruntled, alienated, constantly harassed youths who in their tartan trousers and graffitied and spiked biker jackets Peters decided to make contact with in the centre of East Berlin. The Ossie punks had been impressed by Peters' original Clash T-Shirt, a superimposed black and white photograph of Joe Strummer, Mick Jones, Paul Simonen and Topper Headen posting outside an army base back in Belfast around '77, in the the same station where he had probably fired off some rounds in the cramped shooting range, taken tea with the ordinary Squaddies holed up in the base.

In Berlin his first hand reports of building resentment from the bottom up and the regime's complete loss of its youth such as the Punks were mostly ignored in favour of Oxbridge educated Soviet bloc 'experts' in intelligence who could see no end to the party's monopoly of power or any real challenge to it. When he was sent to Belfast in THAT year and THAT operation Peters often wondered if his temporary transfer back to Northern Ireland was some kind of punishment for what he had been filing back then from inside East Berlin in the months before the Wall came down; for what they didn't want to hear. And he had fretted, too, that his masters might never let him return to Germany again. Inside the same base he recalled rifling through a forest of photographs taken from the fortified Sangars of IRA suspects from the estates directly across the Springfield Road.

As the three chord blunders in Taceles came to the climax of yet another three-minute rant, Peters thought about Angi and barely suppressed a guilty laugh. He imagined her settling down for the night on Heike's sofa bed amid the chaos of the journalist's apartment and her hostess' acidic hospitality.

'What's so funny babe?' Karen said stumbling back into her chair at the back of the bar.

'Oh nothing. I was just thinking about a friend of mine. No, just two friends of mine actually whom fate has thrown together.'

Karen swigged on her bottle: 'I hope they fall in love.'

'A cessation of hostilities for the night would be enough.'

'Are you talking about them or us, Martin?'

Before 'Taceles,' inside the Irish pub around the corner in Friedrichstrasse she had been pestering him to move in with her. The author of a PHD on 'Misogyny and Media in the Springer Empire' insisted that he 'show some commitment eventually.' How thoroughly old fashioned of her, Peters mused.

'I don't even know where you live.' Karen cried in protest above the din.

'Somewhere way out west Karen. Over the Wall and far away.'

'You never talk about your work either, Martin.'

'What's there to say. People do bad things; you try to catch them. Sometimes you do, sometimes you don't. The details don't interest me once I go out the door and then breathe again.'

'You are so passive aggressive sometimes,' Karen chided. 'You should seek a shrink. I can recommend a few.'

At the mention of Karen's counselling tips, Peters judged he would rather seem ridiculous than be mentally microwaved. He leapt out of his chair and dived onto the dance floor to join the throbbing mass pogoing on the floor.

Thank God for 'Vomitorium' and a terrible rendition of 'White Riot,' Peters thought.

Fourteen

In the cloudless glassy dawn, there were two jet-trails, scar tissues torn across the sky, far above the Grunewald where Peters was working off his hangover.

His early jog towards his favourite rendezvous point with Blucher, the sound of Japan's 'Suburban Berlin' booming in his ears from his iPod, the curt polite silent nods of fellow runners, the latticed patterns of light filtering through trees and vegetation, the crackling sensation of twigs breaking beneath pounding feet, the best time of the day, that time of retreat back into the comfort blanket of the forest.

He was sweating out his other Berlin, leaving it behind temporarily, at least that was until he came across the bulging, wobbling frame of his closest source, a reminder of that other side of the city and all its toxic temptations.

When he reached 'their' bench Blucher was already sitting down beating his two hands together in an attempt to ward off the cold which Peters had stopped feeling about twenty minutes earlier.

'A clear blue day. It's probably going to freeze over later. Wouldn't it be nicer to be up there in one of them heading somewhere warmer?' Peters said pointing to the fading back-wisps of smoke escaping from the planes arcing north far above.

'I hate flying!' Blucher snorted. 'Always did. It's a necessary evil....'

Peters interrupted: 'Another necessary evil you get to add to your case, Lothar.'

'Don't be facetious, Englishman. We are here to do business.'

'Perish the thought,' Peters said stretching out his body against the tree where the magpies normally foraged.

'You wanted more on our Russian friend for starters. Well there isn't much more I can give you.'

'Go on Lothar, you might surprise me. You normally do.'

'Last night I was with my Russian pal in the Marriot. Anika was out clubbing, not my scene, so my old mate and I played chess in the bar. He is a good player, like many Russians. A shrewd tactician who knows all the moves, the smart ones and the stupid ones.'

Blucher continued to warm his hands and slapped the top of his arms.

'It was when I asked about Yanaev that he started talking about chess. He told me what the smart move was.'

'Which was what?'

'To stay well clear of that particular dark knight. My friend said that anyone crossing Yanaev would be knocked out of the game. Permanently.'

'So your source has dried up Lothar? That isn't very impressive. My boss back in Kottbusser Strasser will be wondering if it's worth picking up your tab anymore.'

'I didn't say he had gone completely silent,' Blucher barked back. 'He just sent a friendly warning. Yanaev is dangerous.'

'Now you don't say. Two headless corpses you think are connected to Yanaev and a chess game metaphor is what makes him dangerous. You're making me regret my morning run. I could have been still in bed down in Friedricshain with a student nearly half my age.'

Blucher's mood lightened: 'So we have more in common than you think. Not just our fathers from the lost lands, eh? A taste for youthful flesh.' Blucher smiled wide at Peters' wince.

'But I have more for you, not about the Russian, rather about our friends on film.'

'Go on then.'

'I remember now that the two of them came into the shop regularly. In fact, they were part of a little group that used to huddle around in front of the snaps of the younger boys. All legal of course, barely but still legal. There were three or four of them.

I remember thinking they were a close little band.'

'Three or four of them? Then the others will be back, is that the usual MO with your pervier clientele?'

'If you put it like that, yes. There's a pattern to their behaviour, all of them. You can set your watch to some of them, to the exact time they sneak through the door for their weekly fix. It's good to know that. It's re-assuring for a businessman like me operating on the smallest of margins.'

Peters' thoughts turned to Riedel, reluctantly serving undercover in 'Boyz R Us'. He recalled what Riedel had told him, the conversation among some of Blucher's clients, their concern over absentees from the shop and he realised Kottbusser Strasse's Iago might have stumbled across an entry point.

'As always my heart bleeds for you Lothar especially when you don't even know you are being useful to the Berlin Polizei.'

Blucher seemed pleased with the back compliment: 'Lothar Blucher has never, ever let you down in all these years we have worked together.'

He always wanted to be thought of as someone important, a player in the big game, Peters remembered.

'Anything else Lothar? Names maybe, addresses, credit card details we could pull down and check on for their purchases in the shop?'

His informer's huge frame was shaking, no longer from cold but rather laughter, the mocking of an innocent beside him.

'How many of my clients would use plastic to buy anything from me? It's cash over the counter mostly. No names neither, just faces. If you showed me some faces I might be able to connect them to our two film stars.'

First thing Monday morning Peters would speak to the techno-boys about putting a hidden camera in the shop but he decided to keep it back from Blucher. And then there was Riedel, forever smouldering in sullen plots, suddenly becoming a vital link in the trail towards 'Christopher.' Peters at once resented the idea that Angi's secret tormentor was potential pathfinder to their quarry. He shook himself down by the tree, slapped Blucher on the back and bade his source farewell for now, this time running off to escape from his thoughts of Riedel's breakthrough. As he beat a path back to Heer Strasse Peters switched his mind towards an evening with Irit Weissman and Avi Yanaev and then cried out back in Blucher's direction: 'I'll get that Russian bastard myself Lothar, believe me!'

Fifteen

Irit Weissman's 'frock' for the occasion turned out to be a rippling blue chiffon dress that seemed to shimmer in sync with the contours of her body as she glided across the floor of the Martin's low ceilinged ballroom. She kissed and mwaw'd her way through a thicket of Berlin senators and their wives or significant others. The Israeli's glass tinkled constantly as her face lit up almost automatically at the sight of each German, foreign diplomat and benefactor in town for the opening of the film festival. Her visage transformed from flirtatious to serious as she moved from the glittering correspondents of society magazines to the chin stroking critics and from the culture sections of the more upmarket Berlin papers. And all the time as she slalomed around the politicians, the journalists, the dignitaries, the entrepreneurs, the photographers, the battalions of hotel staff milling around, Weissman was focussed on coursing her way towards one particular table in the centre of the room, the one where Avi Yanaev would be sitting.

At her side, his hands shoved into the pockets of his dinner jacket, looking and feeling ill at ease, miffed too, that she hadn't allowed him to link one of her perfectly bronzed arms, was Peters smiling nervously at everyone she had greeted, cocking his head above the throngs of guests and waiters in the direction Weissman was heading obviously heading for. On their journey together he kept thinking about chess moves, of what Blucher had said to him, of Yanaev and the way he ruthlessly dispatched any piece of the board that stood in his way.

Yet what greeted him, literally, when the Israeli woman's progress slowed to a halt, shocked Peters. He had expected some bling'd-up bloated oligarch looking more like a bouncer than a businessman flanked on either side by younger trophy women. Instead Peters was towering over a small, slight man with a short wispy moustache and nervous, darting brown eyes. It was difficult to hear what the man he sought was saying above the hubbub of those gathered for the Jewish film festival and the stains of Schubert from the Israeli quartet flown in by the embassy for the occasion. Peters strained to hear the Russian but did feel a weak shake of his right followed by a polite nod that bordered on the edge of a deferential bow. It took Weissman to amplify the greetings with a throaty introduction from a voice rubbed by years of smoking.

'This is Martin Peters, one of the Berlin Polizei's top detectives...well that is what he tells me all the time.'

The other diners around Yanaev, which included at least one journalist and one politico Peters vaguely recognised, issued polite collective laughter from their table.

Peters felt those shifting eyes sizing him up, something about Yanaev suggested that this stooped, wan, translucent image of a man was a mask hiding a deeper, darker interior. It was there in the eyes, Peters noticed, just a hint that another man lay beneath.

'Thank you for coming to our festival Herr Peters. We always appreciate the support of the Berlin Polizei,' he heard Yanaev say when the Russian was only a breath away. He then realised he had been staring at Yanaev for too long.

'It's always a pleasure to take Irit on a date, any excuse will do,' Peters said wrapping his arm around the Israeli's waist, guessing her to be somewhere between a size 8 and 10.

Yanaev made a pointing sign at Peters, a gesture almost like a child making a gun with their fingers and thumb.

'You are not German. You are English.' The Russian wasn't wagging his fingers around; instead he kept his gesture frozen on Peter's body. 'What is an Englishman doing in the Berlin Polizei?'

He noticed that Weissman was looking a little alarmed at where all this was going.

'Like a lot of people after the Cold War, I was facing redundancy and boredom. No more beasty Easties to spy on anymore now that we were friends all of a sudden,' Peters replied ignoring his partner-for-the-evening's visible concern.

'I've never met a spy before. How intriguing,' said Yanaev.

'I wasn't a spy I was a soldier, Herr Yanaev.'

'I see sir. Maybe you should write a book about your time as a soldier of course.'

'Actually I'm more interested in the here and now. Every new case brings a new challenge. Like the one that the Havel threw up. Did you read about it at all Herr Yanaev?'

The Russian didn't flinch, nothing was betrayed in his reaction. He retreated back into his facade and sipped at a glass of fizzy water. Peters noted that there was no sign of any booze around his plates or cutlery.

'I have to apologise to you. Which case was this?'

Peters leaned over, a little too intrusively and in a near whisper said:

'The one Tavarich of the two headless corpses that were washed up on the lake shore. Do you know what someone had printed on their arms? '

Inexplicably Yanaev started sniggering, nervously, Peters unclear if this was an authentic response or yet another stratagem to cloak what lay behind.

'You didn't ask me what was on their arms.'

'Do I really need to know that Herr Peters?'

'It was Kharkov and Kursk. You recognise those names?'

'Of course I do. Battles of the Great Patriotic War. Any soldier would know that especially one who used to serve amongst our once gallant allies like you.' Yanaev replied.

'Why would anyone leave those marks on these men?'

'How on earth would I know? That's your job, you're the detective. I hope to read about the end of this mystery when you solve it. I really love a good detective story.'

He felt Weissman gripping his arm, the pressure that she was applying increasingly painful.

'One more thing sir,' Peters said wincing from his partner-for-the-evening's vice on his forearm,

'I think this was a Russian hit and that these men were from the motherland.'

The last remark seemed to send a jolt through Yanaev who suddenly rose from his chair again.

'What makes you think those men were Russians at all,' Yanaev hissed, 'You jump too quickly to conclusions Herr Peters and now if you don't mind I'd like to sit down to dinner.'

This time it was Peters who was bowing politely, beating a retreat from the table, quietly pleased that he had punched through the defences around this diminutive Russian in an ill-fitting tuxedo.

After appetites had been satisfied and thirsts slaked, the ballroom was plunged into near darkness as a series of film clips for the festival were presented on a giant screen, Weissman squeezed Peters' leg under their table and leaned to whisper into his ear.

'Did you deliberately seek out to piss our Avi off, Martin?'

Peters retaliated with a tighter squeeze on one of the Israeli agent's thighs.

'I'll tell you why if you come back to Heer Strasse with me tonight.'

'Lousy try Martin. And you still have to answer my question – were you here just to raise his heckles all night?'

'No, I came for the nouvelle cuisine and a glimpse of the movies on offer. Fancy coming to the pictures with me next week?'

'You never give up. That's why I like you.'

Peters hoped Yanaev thought something similar of him, that he would dog him to the end. He was certain that Blucher was right about the connection, he knew it in his bones. Now that he had come face to face the name linked to that horrific discovery two weeks to the day Peters could turn his thoughts to obliterating the rest of the night. He checked his watch and realised there was plenty of time left to spend in Der Zug now that the elusive Irit Weissman was thinking about her bed alone.

Sixteen

To: heike.numann@wams.de
From: christophswrath@hotmail.com
Subject: coverage
Fraulein Numann. Naturally I was disappointed when I opened up my copy of WAMS this morning and found nothing inside about this struggle. Instead I read about headless corpses washed up on the Havel's shore. Please try and take what I am doing more seriously. I shall be in touch....soon.

Was it out of spite, duty or fear that Heike had forwarded the mail to Peters' work address overnight on Sunday? It had been the first portent for a week that would test him and the squad in Kottbusser Strasse to their utmost limits. She hadn't resorted to screaming abuse down the line or turning up at Heer Strasse in a strop. Instead she had decided to post Christopher's latest, terse, affronted communiqué, coldly to his office for Monday morning. Peters realised his media management campaign was about to spectacularly backfire.

He had spent Sunday morning in bed recovering after his date with Irit Weissman which had been followed by an energetic evening at Der Zug entertaining a brace of housewives in town from Magdeburg for the weekend. On Sunday night he suffered from a sulking Frau Schuster who had taken exception to his rejection of her offer of a free Med cruise shortly after Easter, and had gone home early instead back to his apartment after the widow announced she wanted to spend the rest of the night alone. The two of them had more in common than Peters cared to admit.

He was about to take a print-out of the email to Stannheim's office when he saw the lanky frame of the unit's commanding officer towering over his desk. There was a dull thud on the table as Stannheim dropped a pile of newspapers onto the table.

'Take a look at these Martin. No doubt your friend at WAMS will be delighted at the coverage too,' Stannheim growled.

Peters stared open mouthed at the headlines screaming up at him from below on the desk. Thick black lines with huge exclamation marks emblazoned across front pages complimented by blurred stills of the doomed men on film that were somehow connected to Lothar Blucher. 'Christopher' had had a busy Sunday.

'CRAZED KILLER FILMS VICTIMS'
'SLASHED, BEATEN AND BROADCAST'
'GHOULS ON FILM'

The last one from the stable of BZ almost amused Peters with its cheeky, tasteless, back reference to Duran Duran. But he was glad he didn't visibly see the funny side of the final headline: Stannheim's manner was graveyard grim.

'Fuck me Martin we have well and truly screwed up,' he muttered and gestured, nodding back towards his office. Both men walked over to Stannheim's lair and the boss of the Kottbusser murder squad gingerly closed the door behind them.

Stannheim checked to see if anyone was watching them and then went around the glass box that was his HQ, closing each of the three sets of blinds until they were fully obscured from view. He sat down in his chair, pointed to Peters to sit on the other lower one before him and searched for his cigarettes in the pockets of his ash stained cheap nylon purple suit.

After lighting up, taking a deep draught of smoke into his lungs and then exhaling, Stannheim stared at Peters.

'The press office is going bananas. We promised them radio silence and now we have got it out in full stereo. And we probably have a jilted journo who is going to go full frontal this weekend about her "relationship" with our killer about whom we know next to nothing. What a start to the week!'

Peters noticed that the dark lines insomnia had mined underneath Stannheim's eyes were blacker and deeper than ever.

'I'm sorry sir. We made a deal with Heike and WAMS but we never guessed "Christopher" would go elsewhere. I'll get the team to check with the rags how they got the story. Presumably he mailed his snuff movies to them.'

He was trying to think of ways of recovery, of suggesting something that might convince Stannheim they were making some semblance of progress. Reluctantly, Peters thought of Riedel and what he had picked up in Blucher's shop.

He cleared his throat as if the idea of Riedel carrying in a breakthrough might make him retch.

'There may be an entry point sir.'

'Go on.'

'It's something Riedel picked up in "Boyz R Us'. Something one of the customers said.'

'Which was?' Stannheim asked as he lit his second cigarette of the day.

'That they were missing someone. Someone who hadn't been in the shop for a while. As I said before there is a link between our two film stars and the shop. Maybe if we could talk to the customers missing their mates.'

'Ok. If they come again get Riedel to ID them and we can pick them up for questioning. Is that all?' Stannheim's question was seared with sarcasm.

'Yes, I think I'll call Heike Numann. Try and keep her on side. I don't want a first-person account of how the killer contacted her and we tried to cover it up.'

'Ex-fucking-actly Martin. That's what we'll be crucified for. Trying to hush the whole thing up. The media don't like being treated like idiots. They'll be out for blood, even your friend. I mean look at this shit. "Bild has learnt that polizei are investigating a possible link between the two murders on camera and the de-capitated corpses found on the Havel shore. Detectives fear this may the start of a major Russian mafia war..." The only thing I fear is crap like that seeping out because we are going to be left to shovel it up.'

More sarcasm, thought Peters, and puzzlement too. After all, how did he remain fiercely loyal to an officer like Stannheim whose mission in life seemed to be to constantly point out the mistakes of his chief subaltern? And then he remembered Angi's observation, blurted out in a rare moment of frankness at a Christmas party, that Mannfred Stannheim only ever criticised one man on his team because he was the only one he ever wanted to succeed him.

When he returned to his desk Angi was holding up his landline, her face as grim as Stannheim's had been a few minutes earlier. She uttered the words Peters was dreading to hear.

'It's Heike on the phone sir.'

Peters took the set from her and answered. What he heard both pleased and astounded him.

'Don't worry Martin I'm not about to bark,' she said, her voice quivering down the line.

'He's been on the handy again. Christopher. He's told me to be at an address in Wedding within the next two hours. I'm going. Care to join me?'

When she disconnected the call after reading out the street Heike was instructed to be in Peters felt as if his body had just been subjected to a short burst of electric shock. It took him about 30 seconds to recover and then he leaned over and whispered to Angi:

'Get the team together. All of them. No sirens. No noise. Just make sure the firearms unit aren't far behind us. Make sure everyone is armed including yourself.'

Seventeen

Berliner Strasse was a single row of pre-war five storey apartments facing onto a small public park in a rundown part of Wedding. The ground floor of the flats was a miserable strip of grimy shops run by Turkish and Maghreb immigrants along with a bakery and a launderette. At the very far right corner stood a seedy 24/7 pub which at this time in the morning had just two customers inside, an old pair of insomniac codgers playing chess at the window, sipping occasionally at their Kindls and Korns.

Peters was relieved that Heike had been 'summoned' at this time of the day, especially the way she was dressed. With her above the knee skirt and shiny black boots and the way she stood nonchalantly dragging on a cigarette she wouldn't have looked out of place filed up alongside the lines of whores who used this pitch late at night. He had recognised the park immediately when he set up the snipers and their spotters in the undergrowth across the road from the apartment block. Just over two years earlier Peters had been sent here one cruelly bright summer morning after local uniform came across one of the girls that had only started working the area; a savagely beaten Natasha whose Russian pimp had taken exception to her open air 'freelancing' outside from the knocking shop he and his cronies ran down in Charlottenberg.

At least Peters had had the satisfaction of putting that particular bastard behind bars in nearby Moabit for life. He would often quite deliberately drive past the prison in the middle of the residential district wondering what kind of lives the men he had put in there were now living. Constantly miserable, he always hoped and prayed. For Martin Peters had no faith in the redemptive power of incarceration.

For Peters man's (it was almost always men) warped sense of their own honour, self-image and machismo drove them to brutalise the women and children they sought to either control or covet. They would not change either inside or out of prison; he was sure of that and the necessity for them to stay there rotting until death.

He then recalled that moment of certainty, that sense that he had finally snared his quarry, that instance of clarity when it was time to arrest and put the charges to them. Surveying the banality of his surroundings Peters knew today, instinctively, this was not yet 'Christopher's' time.

Siberia was back once more and Heike was shivering as the unforgiving wind from the Urals whipped against her while she stood there as a martyr to her fashion sense in the penetrating cold. The only other living things moving along Berliner Strasse was a scavenging mongrel snorting around the bins outside the shops and a balding, ascetic looking postman dragging a yellow coloured trolley from the end door of the complex in the opposite direction of a dog. Peters tried to guess where exactly any of the bored and freezing marksmen crouching in the bushes on the other side of Berliner Strasse had aimed their red-eye gun sites. The cold-flushed exposed bald pate? The little 'Bundespost' bugle sewn into the breast pocket of his overcoat? The flattened crotch that suggested either castration or the tightest trunks in central Europe?

'Whatever you do don't go postal!' Peters whispered down the mobile to the sharp-shooters' team leader. There was a short burst of sniggering down the crackled line, it was the last thing Peters heard for the next two to three minutes.

Berliner Strasse's mid-morning torpor was suddenly shaken by a dull, reverberating thud followed by the ripping squeal of glass exploding and then a discordant symphony of house and car alarms wailing and whining. Temporarily deafened Peters could only feel his heart pounding in his chest, his feet pedalling forward as he dived on top of Heike in a belly-flop long jump over the journalist. When he looked up Peters felt Heike's body beneath him writhing while above the stunned postal worker, frozen in shock, put his right hand behind the back of his head and then brought it back in front of the detective to reveal a medal of blood in the middle of his palm, as if the bald 'Bundespost' employee was offering up stigmata.

Peters glanced up to the right where the second floor flat right above where the seedy pub used to be, papers billowing in the air, a column of acrid smoke seeping out into the unforgiving morning air, the window of the corner bar shattered, the old boys staggering forward, chess pieces strewn across the pavement along with smashed bottles, beer glasses and ashtrays.

When Peters got to his feet the postman had fainted and Heike was golfishing at him, all around them armed men and women in green and mustard coloured uniforms running towards the shops, halting traffic, escorting shopkeepers from their businesses; not in slow motion but rather in a velocity made surreal by the muffled temporary silence of Peters' consciousness. Heike was prodding him in the chest not so much in protest but rather her feeling the re-assurance of human, tangible touch. While above them the charred confetti falling from floor 2 was blending in now with a sudden flurry of pollution flecked grey snowflakes descending through the Berlin sky.

'It looks like Christmas Heike and I can hear bells ringing in my ears,' Peter shouted out when his hearing finally returned. For a few seconds he was back in Taceles amid the ear-drum splitting feedback of Vomitorium, trying to be heard above the seething din.

He felt a short sting on his left cheek as Heike swung at him and screamed:

'Fuck you Martin. Fuck you and your radio silence!'

Uniforms were entering the building out of which poured shaken pensioners and young mothers clutching children in their arms. Peters grappled with Heike and almost struck her back.

'He's playing games with all of us Heike. We're all on the same side here. Don't forget that,' he yelled pushing her back onto the pavement.

In front of him stood a breathless Angi, her eyes wide open boring into Peters'.

'When you two stop rowing I think there's something you need to see Captain inside the building.' Peters guessed the collective shock coursing through his team had prompted Angi's uncharacteristic recalcitrance.

'Show me,' Peters replied sheepishly staring now at Heike who was lighting up, stamping her foot, cursing him barely under her breath. He went closer to her and said almost apologetically: 'If there's anything in there of interest I can withhold I'll keep it for you. That much I promise.'

Heike turned her back on him, still shaking, staring at the gathering crowd staring back towards the scene of the explosion, some holding up mobile phones in the middle of the road to film the mini-chaos engulfing this quiet backwater in Wedding.

'Someone should stay with her,' Angi said as they stepped over the still unconscious postman, Peters signalling to the uniforms to help him out.

'You go back to Wams when she disappears. That's where she's going, to convince her editor she's closest person to 'Christopher' on earth,' he told Angi.

Alone, he entered the apartment block and climbed up the undamaged staircase towards the second floor and the blasted open door of flat 2B. Inside lying prostrate between two uniform cops, one blanched with horror, the other trying to take photographs, was the latest target of 'Christopher's' campaign, a pot-bellied man in his sixties with surprisingly long greasy grey hair tied back in a pony-tail. The dead man was dressed in a Levis suit of quarter length jacket and jeans, a stained T-shirt and fluffy Mickey Mouse slippers. Almost of all his body remained intact apart from the far right side of his face which was peppered with smouldering pin-pricks filled with what looked like metal filings and a single nail embedded deep into one of his eyes out of which streamed a red congealing delta of blood.

'He didn't die that quickly,' Peters muttered out of earshot of the two uniforms. 'He designed it to make him suffer a bit. Broadening the battlefield are you "Christopher"? So be it Tavarich.'

Right beside the victim's head lay a split open black video box which contained a series of melted circuits and wires and a half burnt postcard from Sri Lanka. Peters picked it up, making sure he used a tissue around his fingers and turned over a fire-scarred palm tree and beach scene. There was no stamp but rather a simple scrawled message on it: 'A present from paradise.'

Eighteen

Gustav Husak's last revenge felt like Play Dough but without the smell. Semtex had been one of Czechoslovakia's few export successes in the time of communism. Invented in the year of his birth Peters later saw at first hand its lethal effects. He remembered a rain sodden miserable November two years after the Velvet Revolution when he had been taken to the wreckage of an old police friend's car outside his driveway in a quiet, neatly kept cul-de-sac on the eastern fringes of Belfast. Peters had asked to survey the scene just hours after the explosion that killed one of his closest contacts in Special Branch. The memory of that miserable mini-destruction site drove him and his agents on to counter the threat of Husak's dubious gift to the world.

They eventually devised an odourless substance similar to the explosive that Peters managed to get his informers to replace with the real thing hidden in countless supposedly secret little arsenals across Greater Belfast. Some bombs definitely stopped going off. A few rocket launchers failed to trigger too. So when Angi Domath mentioned 'Semtex' in their briefing later that morning after the Wedding bomb Peters felt his blood chilling and it was Stannheim who was, naturally, the first to detect his fear.

'You look like you've seen a ghost,' Peters' boss whispered as Angi carried out a verbal deconstruction of the device that had killed 'Christopher's' third target.

'Just some nasty blasts from the past,' he replied to Stannheim. 'When I hear that word I'm back in Belfast during the dark days.'

Husak's exports kept turning up all over the world even after he and his henchmen had been miraculously toppled from power just after the Turn in Berlin back in '89. They were still killing Peters' friends almost ten years later. Now for the first time since his last tour of duty in Northern Ireland, in the same year his father finally checked out of 'Terminal One', he was confronted again by this old toxic foe.

When Angi had finished her briefing on how the bomb had been built Peters marched to the top of the murder room in Kottbusser Strasse and took charge.

'Well as Angi has explained it seems our "Christopher" isn't just a competent swordsman with a powerful batting arm. Our man has dabbled in the black arts of bomb making too. Which only confirms what we already knew – here lies a specialist soldier buried somewhere deep in Berlin.'

Bauer had been busy taking notes, trying to appear assiduous and a little less arrogant now that Riedel was busy undercover in 'Boyz R Us.'

'Sir, if I may. Access to that kind of stuff would have been extremely unusual. We are talking about a limited number of specialist units. I have some old contacts in the NVA I could look up. They might pin point who these units are.'

Peters nodded and told Bauer to get going immediately.

'The rest of you start checking the files, find out if anyone has been done with explosives offences over the last 15 years or so. Keep examining lines on homophobic attacks as well. And will someone please come up with an ID job on who our film stars are.'

Stannheim shot up his hand again: 'Captain Peters! Have you put an ID to our friend with the nail in his eye?'

'Yes. We found a passport in the name of Eric Tisch. 64 years old. Single with a lot of entry visa stamps from Thailand on its pages. We're doing a cross reference on him now to see if he appears anywhere. So far we've nothing from the apartment to link him to our two friends but I'm still certain they're connected.'

'As for our media management campaign you and I should have a coffee in "Anna's" later. Maybe you can bring your WAMS' friend along.'

The old man having fired his parting shot for the day skulked back into his glass cubicle, shut the door tight and dropped the blinds. He wouldn't surface again until the pub was opened. The boss knew "Christopher" was running rings around us, Peters thought but dared not speak out loud. Stannheim was clearly taking it personally.

'Angi you do the running check on Tisch and see if anything interesting crops up. I'm going to call Riedel.'

Riedel was barely audible above the mixed din of trance music and the sound of human grunting inside Blucher's shop; even though it wasn't yet lunchtime 'Boyz R Us' sounded busy.

'Go outside, Riedel. I can't hear you in there,' Peters shouted down the line.

'But it's packed in here. What if things go missing?'

Peters was tickled by the idea of Riedel as Blucher's first line of defence against larceny.

'You can frisk them if any come out.'

'Is there anything you wanted, sir?' Rield asked impatiently as Peters heard the heavy door of the sex centre swish open. Once he was sure Riedel was outside Peters continued.

'Look Riedel. Is there any re-appearance of any of those old guys who were chatting the other day in the shop about one of their lot being missing?

'No, why?'

'Because they might know who's who. If any of them return ring me on my handy immediately. I'll come over with the cavalry and take them in for questioning. OK? It's vital you let me know and try to keep them in there.' Peters heard Riedel sniggering.

'That won't be hard they usually spend an hour in those booths watching the films. I should know, I have to wipe them down afterwards.'

The thought of Riedel wearing a pair of marigolds cleaning up the pools of mess left by the clientele of Lothar Blucher brightened up what was otherwise turning out to be another taxing day. Peters then heard a very loud 'fuck' on the line.

'Riedel, what is it? What's going on?'

Again another 'fuck'.

'Riedel, would you kindly tell me what is up?

'The old guys you just mentioned. The ones hanging 'round

those pictures of the boys. I've just seen one on a TV screen across the street. There's an electrical shop just over the road. He was in here a couple of days ago, just after those men appeared on the 'Net.'

Panic was taking hold of Peters now but he tried to sound as firm and commanding as possible.

'Riedel. Listen to me. Keep a look out for anyone else you spotted talking to him. His name is Tisch. Listen out for anyone mentioning Tisch. And Riedel this is an unbreakable order: don't open a single package that arrives with the mail.'

Nineteen

To: heike.numann@wams.de
From: christophswrath@yahoo.com
Subject: Wedding day
What is it they say about terrorism? That it is an act of advertising. The ultimate in the transmission of messages. I have no doubt that by the time you read this what you witnessed in Wedding this morning will be all over the network news. You have lost control of the story Fraulein Numann. For that I am sorry but all the same you have nobody to blame but yourself.

She had thought about pressing 'reply' in the vain hope that he might write back immediately but Heike guessed 'Christopher' was back on the move again, all too aware of how easily mobiles and mails could pin point someone, anywhere on the planet.

He was taunting her now. She had had complete control of the story and she had blown it. 'Christopher' was no longer her property any more. He was being beamed into every living room, the subject of radio chat shows, the fixation of internet paranoia, the raw material (already) of a screen writer hatching a plot to sell to commissioning editors. So why had Heike Numann agreed to lunch with the man who had handed 'Christopher' over to the wider world?

They were sitting facing other, Peters leaning back on the right wall, throwing back a glass of Sale E Tabbachi's house red. For several minutes since she came and sat down they had said nothing. The restaurant as always was full of journalists many of whom were Heike's rivals from other sections of the Springer building around the corner.

A print out of 'Christopher's' latest communiqué lay spread out splattered with wine that had dripped from the bottom of Peters' glass.

'Struggle first and now terrorism. This guy really thinks he's at war. Why is that Martin? What are you holding back from me?'

Judging by Peters' chastised-boy demeanour when she came into Sale Heike sensed she could exploit his need to atone.

'Ok Heike. Here's something you won't read in BZ tomorrow unless of course he walks into their office and personally spills his guts. He was once a soldier. Probably still thinks he is.'

'Hence the bomb', she said smiling and poured herself a glass of the supple, light red from the carafe.

'And the sword.' Peters said.

'The sword?' Heike asked pretending not to be perplexed.

'That was the give-away. It's a specialist present for a Special Forces soldier. He was in the NVA, an elite unit that the SUVs honoured with the presentation of a sword. The guy's got military form from the old days.'

Peters mouthed to her: 'All that's off the record.'

'Don't worry Martin I never expose my sources. Anything else?' she said as the waiter laid down two plates of loose leaf salad which Peters started poking at unenthusiastically.

'Yes but I reckon it'll be out before Sunday. The latest victim is called Eric Tisch and he has form. My boss nearly had a heart attack when I told him what it was.' Peters said.

'Which was?'

'Which was that Eric Tisch, originally from Cologne but living in Berlin since the early 1990s had two convictions for abusing children, specifically young boys. He spent time in jail over in the west before coming to Berlin, probably to escape local media attention in the Rhineland where he was known,' Peters added as he tried to attract the attention of a waiter for another carafe.

'Shit!' Heike said.

Indeed it was shit. A bucket of shit which he was now wading into head first.

'Yep. Comes to Berlin to start a new life of depravity and ends up with a nail embedded into his eye. I'll bet the other gentlemen we were introduced to on film are of the same kidney.'

'So he's killing paedophiles and you have to catch him. That's going to make you really popular Martin,' Heike said, sniggering, visibly enjoying the detective's discomfort.

'Stannheim won't leave "Anna's" since I told him. The poor man can't cope with the fact that we've a caped crusader in our midst. You've got to help out.'

Heike pointed at herself sarcastically.

'Me? You want me to help you out after denying me the greatest scoop of my career? '

'You can have all that stuff about "Christopher" being a soldier, the sword, the lot. And Tisch's background if the opposition doesn't get to it first. But you have got to explain that this guy is out of control and likely to kill anyone that will get in his way. Like this morning in Wedding. There were women and children in that apartment block. He mentions terrorism, well he gets on like a terrorist, someone prepared to kill innocent civilians if they are in the firing line and that is definitely quotable.'

The first course was being taken away, the second carafe of wine delivered to the table with fresh glasses, when Heike finally replied after an unbearably long period of silent contemplation.

'I suppose you would only go to Littbarski anyway and plead your case if I said no.'

'So that's a Yes. There just one more thing...'

Heike rolled her eyes to the ceiling, shook her head and gulped down a glass.

'Just ONE more thing Martin? How much more can you wring out of me?'

'As much as possible. Look I hope one fine day we can be true friends again but I need you do this one thing. I think he's going to call you again, soon. He needs to talk and when he does I want you to tell him about me. Tell him everything about me, all that stuff you know about me before the Turn. And give him my number. Tell him I want to talk. Play up the old soldier in me.'

For the first time since they sat down for their peace conference in the Italian restaurant Heike looked genuinely puzzled.

'What makes you think he'll want to talk to the man charged with hunting him down?'

'Because I think he'll think I might just understand him. He believes he's still a soldier. Maybe he would like to talk to another soldier. Give him my mobile. Insist he take it. And send it via those emails he's sent although I suspect he keeps changing address so there's no history in his outbox.'

They sat in complete silence throughout their second course with Peters occasionally furtively glancing left and right across Sale to survey who was in. Heike meanwhile kept re-reading the printed out email.

'He really does like attention our "Christopher".....'

Peters interrupted Heike's latest thought on her correspondent-killer by holding up his and standing up.

'Hold on. I've just spotted someone across the room. Give me a minute.'

Heike recognised the woman being chivalrously shown to her table by a small, slight man in a grey suit. One of the financial journalists from a Berlin daily she recalled who had worked a couple of years ago on WAMS' business desk when Heike was a cub reporter and was being sent to work across every section of the paper. Peters slid around their table and made his way towards the lunching couple with Heike remaining in her seat.

It was Yanaev. He recognised that nervous twitching gait the second the Russian entered the restaurant.

'Tavarich we should stop meeting like this. People will start talking about us.'

Yanaev turned around, nodded to the attractive slender blonde facing him and replied:

'People are already talking about you.'

'What do you mean Herr Yanaev?'

'You obviously don't read the papers. I only scan the financial pages normally myself but you glance at the headlines sometimes especially when it's a story as big as the serial killer on the loose and the Berlin murder squad haven't a clue who he is,' the Russian said smiling with just a faint trace of sadism across his face.

'Personally I don't read the rags. I only get on with my job. But I'll get my man in the end just like I'll get whoever decapitated those two gentlemen we found in the Havel, Herr Yanaev.'

The blood seemed to drain from Yanev's face, those darting brown eyes the only live feature in a visage that appeared otherwise frozen and lifeless.

'As I said to you before I like a good detective story. So please come back and tell me how you get on because if you don't mind I have to have lunch with this lady to tell her about all the exciting things my company is planning for this wonderful city.'

Peters smiled back at the Russian: 'But of course. I hope to see you very soon Herr Yanaev, possibly in one of our custody suites.' Yanaev shrugged his shoulders casually dismissing Peters' threat.

He then called back to the retreating Peters.

'The next time you talk to me perhaps it should be in the presence of my lawyer. As he will tell you I have nothing to hide and besides, as I said to you before, what makes you think those men were Russian.'

After paying the bill and shaking hands with the Italian waiters, Peters followed Heike outside onto Koch Strasse. It was then he noticed that Heike was firing back invisible daggers at the heavily made up blonde reporter sitting with Avi Yanaev. *They never forgive their enemies or their faces. Hacks are like cops.* Good, it meant they still had a few things in common.

An icy downpour was about to break over Berlin when they stopped outside the Koch Strasse U-Bahn just before they parted.

'Who was the weird guy you went over to?' Heike asked in between lighting up her much awaited post-lunch cigarette.

'Who was the ice cold bitch staring you out beside him?'

'You first Martin.'

Peters took a couple of deep breaths while Heike drew on her fag and shivered against the cold.

'This bit is definitely not for publication...yet. A source of mine, the best source I have ever had, told me that that weird guy is the key to those headless horsemen you wrote about last weekend.'

He bent over and kissed Heike on the cheek and noticed it felt like marble.

'As for the ice cold bitch I don't need to know Heike. You should go home and rest after what happened today.'

She poked the detective playfully in the stomach and then smiled.

'Martin, go fuck yourself, go back to your beloved Angi and Stannheim and leave me to do my job. I promise if he calls I'll offer him a date with you,' she said before racing across the road, avoiding taxis and a long tail of coaches full of tourists anxiously waiting to alight and get to see 'Charlie' and experience the artificial frisson at the old resurrected Cold War frontier.

Twenty

When Peters returned to Kottbusser Strasse Angi Domath was waiting for him with a brief lesson on the nature of blood.

'Serology is the study of blood, which I had to take during my forensic science course,' Angi said in her clipped, robotic delivery while her immediate boss stared down at two blown up photographs of the Havel corpses laid out on morgue slabs.

'In Europe the percentage of Rhesus negatives is higher than in other parts of the world, somewhere between 12 and 16 per cent of the population. But in one part of the continent the proportion of Rhesus negatives can be at least 30 per cent and perhaps up to 42 per cent of European blood. That area is the Basque region of Spain.'

She was standing awkwardly, her hands behind her back, one trainer arched up, the other balancing her entire body which was twitching nervously. All around her others in the squad were quietly working away at their desks, speaking lowly into telephones and handy sets, thock-thock-thocking at keyboards, or poring over notebooks, telephone directories and files stuffed fat with photographs of convicts. Peters looked towards Stannheim's office and noticed that the blinds were up, the lair empty.

'Angi, what is the relevance to our two friends from the Havel?' Peters asked, gently.

'According to serology experts Basques, in terms of their blood grouping, have an exceptionally "European" type of blood. But now we must move on from serology to anthropology. Basques are found to be two to three centimetres taller than the average French or Spaniard. And yet their limbs, despite their muscularity, tend to be quite delicate. These features alongside their blood belong to the men that were found in Lake Havel.'

Angi rocked back and forward on her heels watching Peters attempting to absorb what he had heard.

'So you're saying these men might be from the Basque region of Spain?'

'No. I only started from the hypothesis that they were Russian given the marks tattooed into their skins. But when I checked on their blood types I was curious. Then I had them measured. I remembered a paper I had to do at the university on the importance of serology classifications which mentioned the unique Basque blood. I cannot categorically say that these men are Basque but their blood type is the same and they have some of the characteristics of the larger Basque male. That is all I can say.'

Peters was on the verge of losing his patience with his favourite officer when suddenly he recalled what Yanaev had said to him, not once but twice; the first time at the opening of the Jewish film festival, the second just an hour earlier in Sale.

'What makes you think they were Russian!' now Peters muttered just under his breath, enough so that only Angi could hear him.

Despite his frustration she was one of the few officers in Kottbusser Strasse (the 'basin of scorpions' as Stannheim loved to call it) who he still implicitly trusted.

'Angi. Get the lab to make further checks to confirm all that. And scan the wires if anything came up over the last few months involving Basques doing bad things in and around Berlin.'

He picked up the pictures of the cadavers and brought them almost up to his nose as if he was trying to sniff out a trace of the deathly odour that may have been trapped in these captured frames of horror. Maybe there was a connection between them and the doomed men on film Blucher had led him to. For a start their heads had been severed in what appeared to be one single clean blow. Only a quality swordsman would have been able to do that. Yet there were no other visible signs of torture or abuse on the two Havel corpses.

Their agony had been in no way as prolonged as the ordeal the others had been subjected to in front of the camera. In his bones, Peters knew that he was dealing with two very different assassins.

Bauer, ruddy faced as usual with the flushes of last night's drinking, little pearls of alcohol visibly seeping out of his pores, breathless yet eager as ever to impress, interrupted Peters focus on the photos with news from "Boyz R Us".

'Sir, Riedel's on my line. He's been trying your handy but it's switched off. Insisted I get you immediately.'

The former Vopo who had somehow escaped the purge through the security organs of the East German state after the Wall fell, reeked of stale beer and the sharp, clean laboratory trace of pure Schnapps on his breath.

'Good, good Bauer. I'll speak to him now. Any news from your former friends in the NVA about who our soldier-serial killer is?'

'Not yet sir. I'm seeing some old friends from the old days this evening down in Friedrichshain. Maybe they'll come up with some names.'

Peters ignoring Bauer's desperation to be liked by superiors, moved to the sergeant's desk and picked up the phone.

Riedel was barely audible, whispering down the line on his handy.

'He's here. He's here.'

'Who Rieldel? And for fuck's sake speak up.'

'I can't. He's on his own and there's no one else in the shop. I came into the back to ring you, I tried texting. It's the old perv from the other day who kept wondering what happened to his mate who had disappeared.'

'Shit. Sorry for that Riedel,' Peters was trying to think, he needed to keep this particular customer of Lothar Blucher to stay in the shop.

'Riedel. Keep him talking. Be chatty. Bauer and I will go over now. It'll probably take a while. Text again and send a description. We'll wait outside and pull him in when he leaves the shop. Just keep him interested and smile a lot.'

As he disconnected Peters was certain that Riedel was cursing him under his breath.

'Bauer go round to the car park and get one of the Audis from the pool. I'll meet you at the front. Let's get moving,' Peters said while signalling over to Angi.

'Never mind the headless horsemen for now. Get me three print outs of "Christopher's" victims and take them to the main interview suite, make sure you get the one with the head severed. That'll be our ace card.'

Angi looked bewildered which prompted Peters to add just before he bounded down the wall towards the stairwell: 'All will be clear within the hour.'

Just as Peters was about to push out the swing doors onto Kottbusser Strasse he spotted three satellite trucks and a knot of reporters huddled together in conclave, nursing cups of coffee from an enterprising mobile hot drinks vendor who had pulled up beside the television crews laying out thick, fat cables in the street which engineers were hooking up to monitors and microphones. Peters gave thanks to the heavens that the snow was falling again providing him with a fleeting curtain to hide behind while he jumped into Bauer's Audi whenever he finally managed to negotiate the sleek, shiny-black, souped-up star of the station's car pool out of its tightly packed car park.

Inside the hallway Peters turned on his mobile and noticed five missed messages, one from Riedel, the others from reporters he had either never heard of or he had chosen a long time ago not to work with ever again.

He heard the revving of an engine outside and peered through the glass to see that Bauer had attracted attention, the journalists had dropped their foam cups onto the road and were running over in a pack towards the Audi.

'Oh shit!' Peters cried out bounding through the doors, running down the concrete steps amid a gauntlet of questions.

'Captain Peters. What can you tell us about the latest on "Christopher"?'

'Have you been in communication with the killer?

'Are all three men convicted paedophiles?'

On hearing the last question as he pulled open the passenger door, Peters shouted back:

'You tell me!'

Instantly, inside the bubble of artificial warmth and dark luxury Peters regretted what he had just said. He had just admitted that he knew less than the press. Stannheim would have had a stroke on hearing that one, he thought.

Bauer tore down Kottbusser Strasse, turned left and headed westwards in the direction of Sauvigny Platz. While he drove Peters watched this over-weight grey spiky haired 55-year-old sergeant and wondered why it was Riedel rather than Bauer who was the station's malcontent. He had done well to worm his way into the murder squad as most of the Vopos had been purged from the newly united police force. Bauer however had a fat, bulging contact book full of names of informants and ex-Stasi spooks which Stannheim recognised as a potential asset for the unit. He was elevated from uniform to the murder squad although the chief of Kottbusser Strasse still ensured that the man with the reputation for harassing dissidents and punks while the DDR still existed would never make it beyond the rank of detective sergeant.

'Good man, I didn't need to tell you it was back to the shop. We're here to lift someone. Riedel has done great work there too' Peters said with genuine enthusiasm.

'Of course sir,' Bauer replied keeping his eyes fixed forward, weaving the Audi around the lanes of late afternoon Berlin traffic.

Peters started an interrogation as they made their way towards Blucher's shop.

'Do you ever miss the old days Bauer?'

'What do you mean?' the sergeant asked suspiciously.

'I mean before the Turn, before things fell apart. Don't you think sometimes life was less complicated, more simple and clear cut?'

He noticed that Bauer was watching him, diffidently, out of the side of his eyes.

'Not really. I don't think about the past. Best not to dwell too much there.'

'But do you ever miss it? The clarity of it all. Don't you Ossis not pine for all the security and comfort?'

Bauer ignored Peters barbs and kept his eyes on the road cursing and yelling at the tourist coaches and the cyclists slowing his progress towards Sauvingny Platz.

He must have something he really wants to forget and bury. In silence, they reached the blackened stump of the Kaiser Willhelm memorial marking the beginning of the west end. The English detective reached into his coat pocket and plucked out his mobile. After clicking on 'received calls' Peters found Riedel's handy number and redialled.

'Yes?' Riedel said awkwardly as if he was talking elliptically to an inquisitive wife wondering where he was all evening.

'Riedel, is he still there?'

'Yep, just about,' his undercover officer replied faintly.

'We'll be there soon. Meantime this will keep him rooted to the spot. Tell him the owner of the shop is organising a private trip for clients to Sri Lanka.'

Riedel didn't bother replying.

Just in time, Peters had remembered the half-burnt postcard 'from paradise' lying next to the mutilated head of Eric Tisch and the video box containing the bomb that killed 'Christopher's'' third victim, it was probably the one thing that was going to save another pervert's life.

Twenty One

'6FT 2. LANKY. G'SSES. TARTAN TROUS. BLU. WHITE PUFFD COAT. LVING NOW. R U NR?'

He was midway down the street walking in the direction towards Sauvigny Platz, a plain black plastic bag under his right arm, nervously scanning his surroundings when Peters intercepted him.

Riedel's text message had been brief but accurate. Peters had spotted him the instant he came out the door of 'Boyz R Us.' Bauer thrust the Audi into short jerks slowly in parallel to the pavement only halting when Peters and the man he was following in front reached the junction. The sergeant watched as the Englishman caught up, passed the man and then swivelled around holding his Polizei ID card in front of him.

'If you wouldn't mind sir I'd like you to get into the car,' Peters asked politely.

'I very much do mind!'

Bauer stopped the car engine and bounded out towards the man.

'Get in the fucking car or we'll drag you in,' Bauer shouted in the man's face.

'Am I under arrest?' the bespectacled, awkward looking client of Blucher's shop asked as if already resigned to his fate.

'Just get in!' Bauer kept up his menacing tone.

Bauer sat in the front while Peters kept their 'prisoner' company in the back seat on the return journey to the murder squad station.

'Name?' Bauer demanded while Peters opted to remain silent.

'I want to call my lawyer. Now! I have done nothing illegal.' At that the man fumbled and spilled the contacts of his bag onto Peters' lap.

There were three A5 sized magazines tightly wrapped in plastic film, showing drunken Punks and Gothic boys in various straights of undress at locations ranging from a dockland waterfront to a public park. On the front of one of the magazines whose headlines were written in Dutch there was a Mohican haired punk wearing a kilt performing fellatio on an older pension-age man up against a tree.

'All is perfectly legal and the right age,' the man shot back his confidence growing.

Just you wait chum, just you wait.

From the second he was picked up to the moment they alighted from the Audi at the back of Kottbusser Strasse station and into the labyrinth of halls and office doorways, the man they had gripped continued to demand to see his lawyer. Peters was surprised that he didn't have a mobile phone to call one.

Angi was standing at the entrance to one of the interview suites which was a brightly lit room with a water cooler at one end and a table on top of which sat bottled fizzy water and a jug full of apple juice. She ushered the three of them inside and then slammed the re-enforced door shut.

Once in the room Peters gestured to the water and juice and finally spoke to the man they had picked up:

'Please feel free to have a drink but absolutely no smoking!' he pointed to the No Smoking sign above the desk on the wall beside the clock.

The three police officers stood in strategic positions around the man: Bauer behind him, his fists pumping, his stare glacial; Angi was closer to the door clutching a large envelope tight to her chest and Peters, himself, stood leaning over the table where the man sat. He spoke first.

'To answer your earlier question in the car, no you are not under arrest.'

'Then what the hell am I doing here?'

'Firstly you should tell us your name.'

'Not until I see my lawyer.'

Peters nodded towards Angi and beckoned her over. He took the envelope off her and lifted one of three blown up coloured photo-prints out and dropped it in front of the man. The sight of what he was being shown almost jolted him out of his seat. He blanched in his chair, gripped the table and started retching towards the ground.

'What's a matter sir? I thought someone with a strong stomach like yours would be un-shockable. Aren't you used to the kind of sights the rest of us would regard as revolting?'

The man reached over to the bottled sparking water, wrenched off the top and took a slug, the liquid fizzing out and shooting up his nose. After slamming the bottle back on the table he took several deep breaths and without looking at it again pushed the picture onto the cell floor.

On Peters' instruction, Bauer picked the picture back up and held it up like someone would display a placard at a political protest.

'Look at it. Look at it.' Peters cried. 'Take a good look at it and tell me who the hell he was.'

But their prisoner couldn't look at the image of the severed head captured on camera and copied from screen by the squad's forensic photographer. Instead he kept his eyes fixed on the desk observing the graffiti engraved into the wood by a succession of suspects. His mind appeared to be drifting as he read the carved out messages: 'Jurgen 10-12-98' 'Fuck the cops' 'Turks out' 'Herta Berlin' 'For a good ride ring.....' the last one with the number scrawled over.

'Come on and stop wasting our time. I want your name and then I want his.' Peters said.

'Why should I?'

Peters flopped down in the chair opposite his interviewee and leaned over the table once more.

'Because I think you might be next! Angi shown him our other two friends.'

It was the sight of the second photograph that seemed to conduct a current of terror through his entire frame, which began to shake, his hands trembling so much he dropped the plastic bottle and its contents onto the floor. Peters knew it was that instant of recognition; the faces he knew, the fate that lay for him captured in the terror on the murdered men's visages.

'Right, stop the fucking bravado and tell us your name and theirs – all of them!' Peters stared over his interviewee's head and noticed that Bauer was smiling. Directly beneath him Peters heard the sound of a throat clearing and then heavy breathing.

'My name is Oskar Beer.'

'Well that's a start,' Peters said continuing the pressure.

'And what about this one?' the detective pointed to "Christopher's" first target.

Beer's voice was now trembling in tandem with the rest of his body.

'He is, I mean was, Ulrich Hoeness.'

'And this one?' this time Peters slapped down the picture of the head of number two.

'I think this was Felix Gerster. I'm almost sure it was.'

'And you already know this was Eric Tisch. Tell me, why do think Tisch had so many Thai stamps on his passport? Fourteen to be precise. I counted them all.

'Please I need some air. I can hardly breathe.'

'You're going to stop breathing permanently unless you help us more Herr Beer.'

Angi noted down the names, gathered up the photographs and put them back into the envelope and made towards the door.

'Angi.' Peters stopped her in her tracks. 'Not yet. Just a few minutes more.'

He moved closer to Beer who had his head in his hands.

'Right Herr Beer. Please explain how you got to know this band of brothers. Through the shop I suppose?'

'Yes of course. We used to meet there regularly.'

'What was it you were up to?'

'Up to?'

'Look Beer don't play stupid. I'm going to send my officer out to the computer and check up on each and every one of you. I'll bet you my army and police pension combined that you're all on our records somewhere. Tisch had convictions for sexual offences against young boys. That's what bound you all together. You're not gay at all. That's an insult to the gay community. You were a paedophile club!'

Beer did exactly what Peters had been hoping he would and

rose up to face the detective.

'There is nothing wrong with man-boy-love. It's been going on for centuries. Since the Greeks. There are rights organisations in America fighting for our acceptance.'

Bauer's knuckles were white with fury now. *He's going to hit this fucker in a minute and turn this interrogation into a human rights violation.*

'What I do? How dare you assume you know anything about me.' Beer croaked in protest.

Peters flared at this newly found haughtiness: 'There is one thing for certain I know about you. Do you want to know what that is? No? Well our friend out there who carved up, blew up and battered your chums is coming for you next and WE are the only people who can stop him. So start co-operating more. Besides, if you don't I'll make a phone call to 'Vice and have them turn your home upside down looking for something that is actually illegal.'

'What else do you want to know?' Beer asked, visibly crestfallen.

Staring at Bauer, perhaps for his benefit as much as Beer's, Peter said: 'Me? I'm like the Stasi. My aim is to know everything. So tell me everything.'

Starting with Tisch, Peters' prisoner unravelled the intertwined sexual predilections of this intimate circle who met once a week at 'Boyz R Us' and each fortnight in the back-room of a decaying corner pub in Prenzl'berg. Like Tisch they all shared the same convictions, offences against boys whom Beer protested weakly they had never imagined had either been under age or weren't in any way happy to go along with a bit of fun. Their 'education' as Hoeness used to remark to Beer every so often.

They met under the auspices of a card club gambling in the back lounge of the Kneipe pub playing for a few Euros ever alternating Thursday. No, they did not exchange anything. They simply had found each other out while lurking around that part of Blucher's shop with the images of the cute innocent faces of young boys. Nothing illegal there either, Beer insisted. The group was more like a support network for men who had been inside and suffered the consequences of being the ultimate outcasts in there. They would recall the beatings, the adulterated food, the constant threats, the dark sarcasm of the Screws. They were survivors thrown together who helped each other. That was all.

Peters didn't believe a single word of what he was hearing but what Beer said next suddenly interrupted his fantasy of pistol whipping the old pervert to a pulp.

'All of the group were 'round about the same age. We are all in our sixties. We'd all done time. Except this one guy who joined us towards the end of last year.'

'Tell me about this other guy. What was so different about him?' Peters said noticing that Angi's perceptive powers were also zeroing in on what Beer was now saying.

'Oh apart from his age. Much younger than us. Possibly late forties, early fifties but fit and very good looking. We often wondered at first what he was doing latching onto us. Felix and Ulrich were very fond of him though, but not in a sexual way of course.'

'No I suppose he wasn't their type,' Peters quipped. 'Now tell me Beer what was this man's name? What happened to him?'

Beer made a throttling sound in his throat and added:

'Just after the New Year he told us he was going away. He'd booked a holiday to Sri Lanka. He said he'd been before. He told us it was a nice place to meet gorgeous boys. Cheaper than Thailand. Less commercial. Far more friendly.'

He already knew the answer to the next question but pressed Beer so that Bauer and Angi both heard the answer.

'What did he say he was called?'

'He only gave us his first name. He said he was called Christopher but I haven't' seen him since.'

The trio gathered around Beer were reading each other's thoughts. Angi nodded towards the door and Peters, glaring up at Bauer, accompanied her leaving the room. The former Vopo stayed put in his chair to guard over Beer.

In the hallway Peters kept his volume down to a whisper

'Bring the photo-fit team over pronto and get them to do a make-up of Beer's good friend Christoph. Then find Beer a cell for the night to sleep in.'

'Yes sir?' Angi inquired as she turned on red high heels away from him.

'Oh Angi?'

'Yes'

'Track down Beer's address and when you have it call in Vice for a raid.'

She laughed when she knew she shouldn't have.

'I thought you and him had a deal.'

'Balls to a deal with someone like that. I'm off to bring the old man some good news. I'll let Bauer escort Beer to his hotel room.'

Later on his way to the incident room in search of Stannheim, Peters sent a congratulatory text to Riedel. It had been easier to stomach than a direct call.

'Reidel. Good work. We got our man.'

Twenty Two

To: heike.numann@msn.com
Subject: Manifesto
Fraulein,
Perhaps I have been a bit harsh on you.

To: christophersaint@msn.com
Subject: re Manifesto
Tell me more about you.

To: heike.numann@msn.com
Subject: re re Manifesto
I am not important. What matters is the struggle.

To: christophersaint@msn.com
Subject: re re re Manifesto
You keep saying struggle. What struggle? Why you?

To: heike.numann@msn.com
Subject: re re re re Manifesto
Don't think I'm naive. I know they have your phones bugged and your emails tracked. They would be failing in their duty if they didn't. I would do the same in their shoes.

To: christophersaint@msn.com
Subject: re re re re re Manifesto
There is so much I want to ask you. Is that why you asked to go on MSN messenger, to finally explain what you are doing?

To: heike.numann@msn.com
Subject: re re re re re re re Manifesto
Everything it seems in these times is a commodity to be bought, sold, exchanged and discarded. EVERYTHING! These men simply understood supply and demand. They merely pushed it to the outer extremes. And for such clarity they put themselves in the firing line.

To: christophersaint@msn.com
Subject: re re re re re re re re Manifesto
Your firing line? Is this personal? Has someone hurt you or someone close to you?

To: heike.numann@msn.com
Subject: personal!
This type of pop psychology will get you nowhere. Oh yes, and you can cut that sentence from your 'copy' for Sunday. Permission not granted. I don't wish to cause any embarrassment but please don't try any more of this psycho-babble. The personal is definitely not political. That was a bourgeois concept invented in the west to obscure the true nature of struggle. As I said before these are acts of advertising, the transmission of a message.

To: christophersaint@msn.com
Subject: re personal!
Message? What is the message?

To: heike.numann@msn.com
Subject: re re personal!
We must remain slightly opaque until the time comes and in the right forum.
Just tell your readers and the world this is not some crude self-gratifying crusade. Ask yourself this: what do these men ultimately represent, these beings that think they can prowl around the world with their pockets stuffed with dollars buying up anything that their eyes covet?

To: christophersaint@msn.com
Subject: re re re personal!
You are bugged by the way. I had no choice. The SIO in your case wants to talk to you...

To: heike.numann@msn.com
Subject: re re re re personal!
I'm saying goodbye for now Fraulein. I've been on here quite enough.

It was the third time she had spooled through her MSN messages on the Blackberry that afternoon reading and re-reading the brief exchanges between herself and 'Christopher'. Heike was sitting now right at the back of the hastily convened press conference at the Rathaus, three empty rows of chairs separating her from the rest of the pack hunched together amid a battery of television cameras, lights, microphones and human hands outstretching silver coloured digital recorders. She was enjoying her isolation from the phalanx of reporters as well as the visible discomfort of Martin Peters squirming at the top table in between a silent Mannfred Stannheim and the deputy Federal Interior Minister who had came across from the Bundestag to lend support to the city's embattled police department.

She would make him wait. Once the broadcasters and the daily journalists melted away only then she would approach him and reveal the substance of this weekend's scoop for 'WAMS.'

As her rivals fired questions up towards the police officers and the politician Heike ran over in her mind Christopher's answers. There was a creeping clarity to his rationale. She felt like someone who had wakened with vision temporarily impaired and who was slowly seeing the external world in milky patterns of light.

'Captain Peters! Captain Peters!' she heard the familiar voice of a correspondent from ARD calling out.

'Captain Peters! Can you confirm reports that the explosive

device that killed a man in Wedding this morning contained Semtex?'

Heike watched Peters shuffling nervously in his seat and turning to whisper something to Stannheim who simply nodded. The Englishman raised his head and seemed to blink as he stared back towards the media in front of him.

'I can only confirm that traces of plastic explosive were found in the device but of the type I can't be specific...yet.'

A forest of hands shut up from the rows ahead of Heike.

'Are you saying officially this murder was the work of "Christopher"?'

'Why has he not killed this victim on film?'

'Are you helping paedophiles with their personal security?'

The last question came from one of the mean, lean young hacks out of the 'BZ' stable, the muscular Berlin tabloid whose coverage of the killer and the killings had gone into hyper-drive over the last 72 hours. For the last three days each edition carried an icon of St. Christopher on its masthead with promises below of widespread reportage inside. Further there were 500 psycho-profiles of the killer by one of Germany's leading shrinks. There was even a report that a Hollywood script-writer was flying in this weekend to start researching a movie about Germany's latest real life star. Another, hardly a report more a picture caption, revealed in colour the upper left arm of a middle aged housewife from Dahlem who had just had a tattoo of St. Christopher permanently etched into her skin.

Heike knew that the 'BZ' reporter had scented blood; it was a dubious gift she had also nurtured in herself.

'Once again Mr Peters – are you and the Berlin Polizei actively helping with convicted paedophiles' personal security?'

Mister! She almost admired the way the hack had belittled her ex-lover with formality.

'If you mean that we have informed that section of society we believe may be at risk then yes. But that doesn't mean we send officers out to lock their doors and windows for them,' Peters replied.

There was a smile of sadistic satisfaction on her rival's face. Now she really did feel sorry for Peters.

At the very edge of the journalists, photographers and cameras Heike spotted a very large, overweight woman with straight, lank greasy hair. The woman bulged out of a tight white T-shirt which she was stretched almost to snapping point over a black shirt. There in the middle of it was the Christopher icon.

Just ahead of the woman stood Sigmund Schawboski, or as Peters referred to him 'the laughing Cavalier'. He had been on the crime beat at 'WAMS' at least ten years before Heike but then went over to the other side lured by a larger salary and a pension for life. The rewards of the state sector were visible on his corpulent frame.

Schawboski was frantically trying to catch Peters' attention while moving his ample frame in front of the equally gargantuan woman in the T-shirt. She was not to be silenced or screened off however. The woman stood up and exclaimed:

'Leave him alone! Leave him alone so that he can do God's work!'

The entire press corps turned its attention away from the table to the enormous woman near the wall bellowing out her defence of 'Christopher.' Schawboski made a move to try and calm her but she flailed out at him, screeching now, protesting that she would not be silenced. The press officer was eventually knocked aside by a wave of news crews and snappers elbowing each other to get to the woman who said she was from 'Mothers Against Paedophiles.' As they bunched around her in a huddle listening now to her tale of personal woe, her nightmare upbringing and the years of abuse she endured at the hands of her father and his friends, Heike spotted Peters rising from the table while Stannheim whispered words of re-assurance into the ear of the minister. The only thing audible (which her colleagues appeared en masse to have missed in their rush towards the screeching woman) from the table was the minister's last words to the Kottbusser Strasse murder squad's boss: 'This has been a fucking disaster.'

Heike made a diagonal rush across the room to capture Peters before he disappeared through the back exit.

'Martin, Martin, don't run off.'

Peters looked over his shoulder like quarry checking on where his hunters where.

'Any questions please direct them at Herr Schawboski, Heike. I've had enough of his.'

She sprinted towards him heading Peters off at the door and blocked his path.

'Look, I've something to show you that I don't want to share with the rest of them in here. Something from 'Christopher''.'

He was tempted to tell her the team no longer needed her now that they had a probable ID.

'Martin I'll be in Anna's at about 8. No one goes in there except for you lot.'

Peters said nothing but instead gave her that acquiescent and generous smile which told her they had an arrangement., that she always thought gave him a boyish sensibility.

As he escaped through the exit Heike could still hear the mantra of the woman from Mothers Against Paedophiles blaring out: 'Leave him alone! Leave him to do God's work!' All the while Heike kept repeating the headline for this Sunday's edition over and over in her head: 'This has been a fucking disaster.'

Twenty Three

Even on the U-Bahn it was impossible to escape the all encroaching intrusiveness of television. Many of the underground trains were now fitted with mini-flat screens blaring out news casts every few minutes in between the bombardment of advertising that no longer made travel on public transport such a pleasure for Martin Peters. Today it could have been not just irritating for him but potentially dangerous to use the system. So to avoid the glare of the travelling public who would no doubt see him over and over again as the networks broadcast the first 'Christopher' press conference, he took a taxi across town instead.

Inside the back of the pale white cab, on route once more to the beginning of the west end, Peters looked down at the image of the man conjured up from the memory of Oskar Beer. Staring back at him was the spectral outline of a harshly sculpted, severely handsome face with wing mirror shaped cheekbones, a forehead that jutted out a little too far beyond eye sockets and short, sharply clipped head of spiky dark hair. There was something comic-book about the photo-fit Beer had helped to construct from his imagination; something too perfect; as if the ageing pervert had shaped this picture from the recesses of wet dreamland. *All he needed was a peaked leather cap,* Peters thought to himself as he slipped the photo-copy back into an envelope and glanced up to the front of the cab.

The driver had lowered the window slightly and the wind started to twirl and twist the two decorations dangling down in front of the wheel: a Hertha Berlin mini-pennant and a St. Christopher's' medal suspended on the end of fine blue rope. *Another hanger and flogger, were taxi drivers the same the world over?*

'Did you put up that thing in honour of Christopher?' Peters asked.

His driver was a rotund bald man incongruously dressed in a blue Hawaiian shirt and white body warmer. The driver reached into the glove department and produced a .38 snub nose special wedged awkwardly inside a table tennis racket sleeve.

'Of course! Using this on creeps like that would not be good enough for them. What our friend Christopher is doing is quite right. He should be left alone to do God's work,' the cabbie said on the approach towards Berlin Zoo station.

Peters knew there was no cause for panic, the driver had probably listened to the press conference on the radio, judging by the tiredness etched under his eyes he had probably been working in the cab all day. His anonymity was safe for now at least. Nor had he any wish to engage in an argument about the rights and wrongs of Christopher's crusade.

'Just drop me at the Europa Centre, please,' he called out curtly signalling the premature end of their conversation. After paying the driver and warning him that he shouldn't poke guns at his passengers, even when they were disguised as table tennis rackets, Peters alighted and made his way past the Kaiser Wilhelm memorial to the 20 storey building directly behind it.

It was once the post-war modernist show piece of West Berlin with its gleaming glass frontage and the three pointed star, a show-off symbol to the east, the sky-scraping foil to the television tower constructed on the other of the Wall and an alluring enticement to those trapped inside the DDR.

During the Cold War as well as the various companies' Berlin HQs, the now abandoned ice rink, the first Irish pub in Berlin, the raucous cabaret, it was home to a number of non-descript, semi-anonymous offices that were used by MI6 and their American counterparts who could quite literally keep an eye on the beasty easties eastwards behind the Brandenburg Gate. Peters remembered an awkward afternoon of drinking and eating inside a conference 18 floors up, the verdant splendour of the Tiergarten laid out below, which had been called to absorb and analyse an important snippet of information passed to him during a strange encounter in East Berlin just days earlier. Peters would never forget that meeting nor the man who had originally singled him out in the 'capital of the DDR.'

As he took the lift up to the 17th, Peters only now realised how much he had been stung and humiliated by the indignation and the patronisation of his hosts one floor above back in the first half of 1989. Ascending again inside the centre he recalled that it had been St. Patrick's Day and down below in Moore's Irish pub the all-day party was still in full swing. What would the revellers down there have made of the fact that right above their heads were some of the top Brit spooks gathered anywhere all in one place. They had come to hear Peters' briefing of his supposedly chance meeting with a Soviet army intelligence officer who had delivered a piece of stunning news to his young British military counterpart.

Peters had been in Alexanpderplatz a fortnight earlier posing as a British tourist in town with his family (a woman and child of one year borrowed from a fellow officer based out at Spandau) for a bit of sighting seeing. The 'couple' were shopping in the Zentrum store, East Berlin's premier shopping centre, out for a bargain while Peters picked up a message from a source he had nurtured inside the NVA. He had been instructed to lift up a model of the Soyuz rocket Sigmund Jahn had travelled with his Soviet comrades into space, located on a shelf of the toy department. The specific box would be marked with red line nicked finely onto its right-hand side.

Just as Peters lifted up the one he had meant to buy he felt a hand on his shoulder, male, sweaty, firm and instantly thought that he and his 'wife' would very soon be enjoying the hospitality of the Stasi at Hohenshoenhausen prison. But instead he heard a whisper in Russian, the language he had mastered at Sandhurst along with German: 'I wouldn't advise it Tavarich. The Stasi have been watching your man. Whatever is in that rocket is next to useless because they probably put it there.'

The man whose guiding hand on that late winter afternoon in the year before the Turn had saved Peters from arrest and interrogation was Major Arkady Gavrilov. Sixteen years later the GRU intelligence officer stood facing Peters once more, ushering him into the office he now rented in West Berlin's former inner temple of capitalism.

'Please tell me you have resigned from the force and have come to finally work for me Martin,' Gavrilov bellowed as he shook Peters hand vigorously and gestured for him to sit down on a brown two seater leather sofa at the side of his open plan office.

Not much had changed about Gavrilov's appearance since that first day Peters came across him. But for a few flecks of grey just above each of his ears his hair was still curly, tightly trimmed and jet black, combined always into a neat side parting; he maintained a tightly honed physique despite being a squat and smallish man now surely in his mid-fifties. Instead of the old shiny brown and grey suits Gavrilov sported a pair of perfectly ironed chinos and a salmon pink shirt. The Russian pointed up towards the roof above them.

'They should have erected a memorial up there to commemorate the stupidity of your masters.'

'Well I would exempt the army from that one Arkady. It was a civilian call and they didn't believe a word you told me.'

What should have been Peters' finest hour almost finished him inside military intelligence. For what Arkady Gavrilov relayed to Peters, first while travelling on the S-Bahn out to Ernst Thalmann Park and later still while posing as pilgrims at the Soviet war memorial in Treptower Park, created panic and suspicion amongst MI6 station in Berlin. Even to the extent that Peters was subjected to several days later of gruelling mental interrogation back at Spandau.

Gavrilov had come with a warning that the British should heed. The 'old goats' as Arkady referred to the geriatrics that ran the DDR, were contemplating an armed response to growing dissent and an increasing leakage of people though the Iron Curtain. Later that year, sometime around the DDR's 40th birthday party, Gavrilov warned, there would be a showdown between people and party. The Soviets had done their homework among the flowering dissident groups and realised the thirst for change was unquenchable. The only thing that stood in the people's way was the self-appointed representatives of the people. Which either meant bloodbath or surrender. Arkady did however have one piece of good news which he wanted Peters to pass on directly to his bosses and chiefs in the west. The Red Army itself, never mind Gorbachev, had no wish to prop these old bastards up. They wouldn't lift a single Kalashnikov to help them.

'It's just as well it all worked out the way we hoped it would although that was by sheer luck and accident Martin,' Gavrilov said as he stood up and went to the water cooler to fill up two transparent plastic cartons.

Peters took a sip on Gavrilov's return.

'They were almost laughing at me during that de-briefing. They had brought over some top notch experts from universities in England, you know, people with a spook past who worked in analysis for the security services. These guys with their plummy accents and their flawless Russian and German, who were just playing guessing games. Most of them had never been out of Cambridge or Oxford in their lives and there they were telling me I was talking through my arsehole. That you were playing some kind of double-game of bluff. Well at least we managed to get our man from the NVA out in time before the firing squads got him. I'll always be grateful for that even if our lot weren't buying what you were telling them.'

The Russian reclined in the sofa, put his hands behind his head and surveyed all that was now his around him. Peters noticed that almost the entire workplace was comprised of slender young women in tight trousers and dark T-shirts sashaying around the office carrying files, getting into whispering huddles, studiously poring over computer screens or making phone calls without causing a distracting din. One or two of them on passing smiled at Gavrilov and seemed startled to see Peters sitting beside him. It was then that Peters noticed the bank of television screens at the far end of Gavrilov's domain.

'Well anyway Martin Berlin has been good to both of us. We

each put our craft to good use when it all collapsed.'

'As you predicted it would Arkady.'

'As I predicted it would and no one listened before it was almost too late. I used to catch spies for a living. That's how we came across you and your NVA contact. We even knew about your earlier defecting General the year before the Turn but kept that quiet from our old "friends".'

'I'm relieved you did,' Peters said loudly.

'Martin you see adultery is just like treason and the adulterer is just like the enemy agent. All you need to do is find the trace, uncover the clue, feed your gut suspicion and the hunt begins. Unlike the Cold War this type of hunting is very lucrative.'

Arkady Gavrilov ran one of Berlin's most talked about private detective agencies, which specialised not only in tracking down cheating husbands and even the odd wife but also pilfering employees and industrial spies. The ex-GRU officer, whose English and German was as fluent as Peters' Russian, preyed on and profited from the eternal paranoia of man. 'Dark Corner' received regular glowing praise in both the broadsheet and tabloid press, which was not unconnected to their work for a number of investigative journalists based in Berlin.

'So why are you here? I suppose it's to do with that business about the serial killer everybody has fallen in love with.'

Gavrilov was as good as sensing desperation as he was fear.

'Yes that and I want to open up a second front as well,' Peters said.

'Which one do you want to start with then Martin?'

Peters took out the photo-fit from the album, showed it to Gavrilov, explained 'Christopher's' military history and the targets of his campaign. When he finished Gavrilov didn't appear as daunted as Peters had expected him to be.

'If you want to find someone you will find them. I'll start with the archives, get one of the girls to hit the libraries and the on-line filing systems. There's bound to be a picture of that guy somewhere in one of the old DDR publications.'

'What makes you so sure of that Arkady?'

'Because as you said he must have been some kind of local hero back then. We even gave him a special sword for his efforts. Knowing our old "friends" I would suggest the old goats couldn't resist making a star of this boy. Think about it – handsome, fit, brave, dedicated to the cause of Actual Existing Socialism – an ideal icon. I'll bet he is buried somewhere in "Nueues Deutschland" or "GDR Review" showing off a chest full of medals.'

'Don't you think he probably knows that,' Peters tried to dampen Gavrilov's optimism.

'Of course he has but do you think he cares? In the end most serial killers want to be caught and I'd guess our friend is no different. Anyway, once we have a name you will get your man. The trouble with being a comrade, of being part of the collective is that it's harder to hide.'

What would Gavrilov make of Peters' 'second front'? *When he would be asked to start hunting a fellow countryman?*

'The second thing I want to ask you Arkady is closer to home, for you at least.'

Gavrilov was re-filling his glass, Peters noticed there was none of the usual copious amounts of vodka on tap unlike the old times when they got together again after the Wall came down and they were still both in uniform.

'Go on Martin. Shoot.'

'Avi Yanaev.'

'What about him?' Gavrilov's tone had suddenly darkened.

'I want to know all there is about him. I think he has something to do with two headless corpses turning up on the Havel shore.'

'Shit I read about that,' Gavrilov whistled, 'a nasty business.'

'And a message to someone Arkady.'

'The message translates as "don't fuck with us" Martin. My compatriots, especially those in the import/expert business, don't believe in doing it subtle.'

'I want to find out why. Why go to that extreme.'

It wasn't just Gavrilov's tone that was darkening, his pallor seemed to lose its glow, the smile on his face retreated into a studious scowl.

'He is a weird guy Martin who never leaves a trail. Owns a lot of property....'

'And a six story knocking shop, a different kink on every floor,' Peters interjected repeating Blucher's description of it.

The Russian was shaking his head dismissively: 'No, No, No Martin. You've got it all wrong. The property and the prossies aren't the real source of his wealth. It's something bigger and more dangerous. Well that's what they say back home in Moscow.'

'What's bigger? What's more dangerous?'

'Things that kill you. Guns. Bullets. Bombs. The word up has always been that Tavarich Yanaev makes a lot of money flogging off the surplus arsenal of my old army. But he does it via one or two persons removed.'

Gavrilov reached into his pocket and plucked out a packet of Lucky Strikes and a lighter. After lighting up and taking a long draw on his cigarette, the Russian added: 'I can only do so much Martin before this place would get torched. I'll ask around but believe me this guy keeps his tracks well covered and besides, he has some powerful friends back at home.'

'There is one thing. One thing line I'd want you to pursue Arkady.'

'What's that?'

'Has he had any dealings with Basques? Basque terrorists, Spanish criminals.'

'Okay, Martin I'll ask if Yanaev has ever done business with ETA or been in Euskadi. That's the Basque name for their homeland by the way, I had a girl from San Sebastian working for me one time when we were tracking an errant banker from Dahlem who was banging a mistress over in Bilbao. I promise I'll ask around but be careful.' Peters noted that it was the first time since the Wall fell and the Cold War ended that Major Arkady Gavrilov (retired) had demonstrated any outward sign of fear.

After leaving 'Dark Corners' and reaching the ground floor of the Europa Centre Peters slipped into the Irish bar in the basement which was almost entirely empty except for a group of ruddy faced tourists from Ireland, all male, no doubt in Berlin for a stag weekend, their table groaning with pints and long stacked up towers of shorts. The Englishman chose a quiet corner screened off from the revellers, called over a bored looking waitress and ordered a double Black Bush, his favourite tipple since his tours of duty during the Troubles.

He would decline Heike's offer of a drink and an information exchange over in 'Anna's'. It was too near work and thus too near the gathering gaggle of news crews outside his station. Besides it was his turn to get indignant with Fraulein Numann, he would knock back the whiskey, find a cab and return to Heer Strasse waiting for what 'Christopher' would do next.

Twenty Four

It is spotting the incidentals that can save your life.

Peters recalled this advice while panting and sweating on the pathway he pounded every morning through the Grunewald before work. One of his Special Branch contacts had passed this on during an extremely busy, often precarious tour of duty operating undercover in the Ulster countryside. He remembered the cop retelling a lucky escape when he clocked a gunman just in time coming towards him and his wife while out shopping in Belfast city centre. There had been nothing suspicious about the young man in a business suit walking in their direction except that when the officer looked down he spotted plastic covering over the hands. Transparent surgical gloves that gave away the man's mission. His RUC comrade had pushed his wife into the doorway of a bank and then dived after her before the terrorist drew his gun and fired and then ran off without hitting his target.

Now it was the identical sportswear they were wearing that first alerted Peters that he was being shadowed.

Two exceptionally tall men, in their late twenties he guessed, jogging at a precise distance behind him for the last fifteen minutes, their shadows in the morning winter sun like dark wings gliding across the clearing through the forest where he had chosen to run. Out of the corner of his eye Peters noticed that they were wearing the same dark green tracksuits with dark black trimmings and the Adidas logo on their breasts. This was definitely a team, the Englishman quickly concluded while accelerating his pace.

And it was the lack of a bulge in the skin hugging 'uniforms' they had put on that day that told him he wasn't going to die, at least for now.

Each time he tried to lose them, the pair speeded up to maintain that precise distance between them and him. Peters attempted to break from them three times before reaching the regular spot where he had planned once more to see Blucher. On the fourth attempt he sensed they had doubled their speed and eventually from the corner of his eyes saw that they were running in parallel now. He glanced on either side and noticed that neither of them had even broken into sweat yet.

One of them, to his right, swivelled his body slightly to move closer towards Peters and then he swung his leg, Peters felt a sharp pain in his right shin and a hard pressuring on his shoulder; then the world tumbled. When the detective could tell up from down again, he was on the dirt path crawled up into a ball.

The two runners were standing over him now and Peters could see that they were even wearing identical trainers. Only the tackler who had upended Peters spoke.

'We are just like you English: we do really hate nosey parkers,' he said in guttural English. Peters detected the trace of a Russian accent. The next thing he felt was the dull thud of thick rubber soles hammering into his upper body and legs. He shielded his crotch with his hands, which turned out to be a mistake because the duo then focussed their kicks on his lower arms stamping on them until Peters lashed and exposed his cock and balls. They rammed their feet into his privates sending sickening shock-waves into his groin. When he began to writhe, they switched to fists which fell upon him like pistons. Just before he passed out ,Peters realised they had avoided his face and head and whispered: 'Message read and understood.' There was a blinding flash across his eyes, the high pitch of pain obscuring his consciousness. Over and out.

When he came to Peter saw a magpie pecking the ground beside him as freezing rain sheeted down and the gleam of silver heels propping up long black shiny boots. Beside them were black stubbier, moccasins rubbing out a still lit cigarette. He gazed upwards and saw Lothar Blucher and Anika directly above him; he in his Crombie, she/he in a three quarter length soft leather coat.

'We heard you moaning and yelping and waited until they pushed off,' Blucher said matter-of-factly.

'They didn't take anything from you so I knew it wasn't a mugging. That's why we stayed in the Volkswagen over there. Not safe to get spotted with you Martin.'

Peters' hands had gone back to cover his now aching dick and testicles. He was then helped to us feet by the surprisingly strong Shemale who yanked him off the forest path in one go.

'That was very noble of you Lothar, ' Peters croaked, 'You're a real hero.'

Anika broke in: 'C'mon dahling. I help you to the car. Get you to the hospital.'

He kept on hand around his groin area and used the other to lean on Anika as they inched towards Blucher's battered Orange VW parked close to the old American listening station. When Peters finally slid into the back seat, the pain of sitting was even more unbearable than he suffered on standing up. He lay back and found Anika stroking his forehead and speaking to him as if he was a child. It had a strange soothing effect on the detective as he lapsed in and out of consciousness on the journey towards the Charite hospital.

As they drove eastwards down Heer Strasse towards the Mitte Peters heard snippets of Blucher's monologues from the driver's seat.

'You have to understand neither of us was capable of jumping them. Although you thought those boys were fit, eh Anika.'

This provoked a shriek of laughter from Peters' fellow passenger in the back.

'They gave you some going-over Martin 'Why didn't you fight back?' Blucher asked with clinical indifference.

'You're lucky that Russian doesn't want you dead because we could have been witnesses and then the game would really be up.'

Before Peters closed his eyes for a final time until he woke again on a bed in a private single room, he murmured: 'You fucking cunt Lothar. You'd have let me die out there to protect yourself. You'd have let Anika die too. You'll always fight to the last drop of someone else's blood.' No one was listening.

Awake again and Peters' body was being caressed by another 'mistress' from the east. Mistress Morphine circulating through his blood, soothing away the pain from the blows that had earlier rained across his limbs and torso. As his eyes focussed through misty milky light Peters realised Blucher and Anika were gone. In their place overlooking his bed was a rakishly thin man in a white coat, with steel round-rimmed glasses, sporting a pinched face and a rather small mouth. The doctor standing above him had his arms folded as if he was about to scold someone.

'You are very lucky Captain Peters,' the medic said in a campish Bavarian accent.

'Whoever beat you up avoided your head and face although they have left you with bruising all over the rest of your body.'

The doctor shook his head as if in amazement, or was it disappointment: 'Not a bone broken. I thought we would find cracked ribs or chipped bones. But no, just a lot of bruises. You will be sore for a while. You must take painkillers.'

As Peters was about to say something, the doctor put his hand up to stop him in his tracks.

'One more thing. Do not have any sexual relations for some time. Your penis and your gonads are very badly bruised. It would not to be a good idea to masturbate either for a while.'

Instantly Peters remembered that tomorrow was Miss Thursday. Miriam. At least she wouldn't have to go through her weekly ablutions.

The doctor interrupted his morphine-charged erotic reverie about his Turkish lover, which was just as well because his cock was going hard.

'A nurse will check your blood pressure and heart rate on the hour and make sure you are getting enough Morphine. You took a series of extremely hard blows. What I just can't work out why nothing was broken or damaged beyond repair.'

'Because they were professionals, doctor, real professionals,' Peters giggled.

'Yes indeed. By the way some of your colleagues are waiting outside to see you. Shall I call them in?'

'Yes please....Oh by the way doctor.'

'Yes?'

'What happened the two people that brought me in? The fat man and the far eastern one...'

'What two are you talking about? The nurses found you on your own with your Polizei ID card laid out over your chest in the A&E entrance.'

Bastard Blucher, thought Peters. He was so paranoid about being seen with me he dumped me at the door.

When the doctor had done Peters was surrounded on either side by Angi and Stannheim. The sight of the two them seemed to temporarily jolt Peters out of his morphinous haze.

Stannheim pointed towards him, an unlit cigarette wedged his forefinger and middle one: 'You, mate, are taking some time off.'

'Get lost Manny will you. I'll be out of here by tomorrow. If I have to climb out the window and hand-glide to freedom I will.'

'Did you get a good look at them sir? Descriptions? Age?' Angi had her mini note book out, as officious and dedicated as ever.

'Fit. Tall. Twenties or early thirties. Russian. But you are not going to catch them.'

'What?' Angi looked perplexed.

'Because it was only a message, isn't that right Martin?' Stannheim was reading Peters' thoughts.

'The boss has got it Angi. He knows what this was all about.'

'If you really want to I can have Yanaev hauled in and put under pressure?' Stannheim said half-heartedly in anticipation of the answer that was coming.

'And what good would that do Mannfred? He'd have a cast iron alibi, the best lawyer dirty money can buy and besides the two boys will already be knocking back the Vodka on the Aeroflot flight home to Moscow this evening.'

Stannheim looked deeply uncomfortable. Peters remembered he had spent months in and out of the same former East Berlin hospital, in the last few agonising laps before his wife finally, mercifully passed away.

'I need a smoke Martin. Besides I've got to get back to the fort. We are being encircled by the Indians. Mothers Against Paedophiles as well as the media.'

Peters nodded over giving Stannheim his exit visa and the old man left the private ward leaving Angi and her notebook still over his bed.

'Angi I need you to do me a favour.'

'Ask away sir.'

He pointed behind him to his left where the personal locker was.

'My keys to the apartment are probably in there somewhere. Rummage around and get them for me. Then go over to Heer Strasse. Take a good look around and see if the place has been turned over. I think I left the sliding door to the balcony open. The front room is probably either freezing or soaking or both. Have a search and see if you can find my mobile. If you get it will you bring it over tonight?'

'And your laptop too?' Angi inquired.

'No the mobile will do.'

Angi was now staring at Peters, her glare preparing him for something he wasn't expecting.

'Heike Numann's here. I told her to get lost but she insisted. She rang for you at the station and Bauer blabbed that you were in the Charite.'

'Bring her in. Bring her in.'

'She says she's something to show you. Wouldn't discuss it with me. Too low down the food chain for her.'

'Just get her in here Angi. Don't take it personally. It's a game between her and me, that's all. Information is her power.'

The two women passed each other in the ward doorway without their eyes meeting, a slither of air and light between them as Angi disappeared and Heike got closer towards Peters. On arriving at the bed she was holding up a mobile phone.

'Jesus Heike normal people bring in flowers and grapes for patients. You bring in a handy, thanks a million,' Peters sniggered, his consciousness still gliding on the air stream of morphine.

'Is your head in gear for what I'm going to show you Martin?' she inquired as Peters shot up in the bed wriggling his back on the pillows.

'Now more than ever Heike. Now more than ever.'

She held the LCD screen close to his face and said coldly: 'This was sent this morning. It's dated from a month ago.'

The first thing Peters saw in the video was a close-up of the Berliner Zeitung just as Heike had said from exactly a month ago. Then the phone's tiny camera started to pan around a living room, bringing into focus the interior of a grubby apartment. For a few brief seconds it trained on flickering images on a television screen. Peters could make several naked torsos of flabby middle aged and elderly men and a fleeting shape darting back and forward from the larger bodies to a much smaller flash of flesh. He could have sworn he heard moaning and crying from the faint speakers of the mobile. The shot went wider to incorporate most of a living room panning left away from the TV and then onto a three-seater sofa and a man, probably in his late 60s or 70s, dressed in a cardigan and striped shirt buttoned right up. His head was kinked backwards and it appeared at first that he was asleep. The screen faded to black for an instant and when it came back to there was a tight focus on a small red smoking circle just about an inch above the bridge of the sleeper's nose. Fade to black again and on return a close up of a passport photograph, the phone's recording eye tracking away from it across the page to the name 'Ulrich Vogts.' A final fade and then the return on the tiny monitor of that familiar logo now emblazoned on walls, T-shirts, badges, posters, tabloids, broadsheets and even the upper arms and breasts of some of his more dedicated followers all over Berlin and beyond.

'His latest "target"!' Peters said softly.

'Or perhaps his first. Check the date. And then there were four.'

'You've got to ring Kottbusser Strasse right away and ask for Stannheim. Give him the name.'

Judging by the entry wound 'Christopher' had used a single clean shot. He suddenly imagined the stench inside wherever this had happened in.

'What I keep wondering is how many more has he left in storage somewhere?' Heike mused out loud.

'I mean most of these guys would have no normal friends or

acquaintances let alone to worry for them. They'd be the easiest to "disappear" ', she continued.

Peters was tempted to press the soft pink button on the plastic wire guiding the morphine into his veins but resisted. Instead, he was trying clear a pathway through his brain once more.

'I'll bet anything our Ulrich Vogts has a record too. That's why he was chosen. Take that over to Kottbusser Strasse and give it to Angi if that's not too painful a task.'

He was delighted that the Numann scowl had returned, the petulant pout and the eyes narrowing.

'No pain at all Martin,' she replied curtly. 'It will be a pleasure doing business with our Angi again. By the way if our man hasn't shared this with anyone else can I have Vogts to myself?'

He nodded his assent: 'I'm happy to be renewing our one to one relationship. Speaking of which did "Christopher" call you at any time before or after he sent his latest home- movie?'

'No, nothing at all. Why?'

The pain in his arms and his groin was returning, but Peters knew that once he released the Mistress back into his body he would stop making any sense.

'Because, Heike, when he does I want you to tell him again that I need to speak to him directly. Tell him everything about me, especially the soldiering bits, the things you know, the Cold War stories I used to bore you with. Give him my handy number, my office number, my home number. Tell him I understand that this is a campaign. Tell him that. Tell him I know about the struggle. It's just a feeling I have. We squared up to each other once when that Wall was out there. He might appreciate that.'

Heike's sharp sky blue eyes started widening again as she tried to take in Peters' increasingly manic pleading.

'You need some rest Captain Peters,' she said reaching over to plant a peck on his forehead. On cue he depressed the tiny pink gateway leading him towards temporary pain-free bliss.

It must have been just after dawn when another apparition before him first entered the ward. Judging by his relaxed demeanour in the seat at the end of the bed his visitor must have been in the room for some time, watching the patient in front of him, asleep, vulnerable, alone.

Peters knew the man in front of him was for real when he noticed a film of sweat breaking out between the end of his nose and his lips. For a second or two he was seized by the thought that this could be him, at least that was until the intruder spoke:

'Good morning Captain Peters. I'm sorry to call in on you so early in the day.'

The man was youngish, late twenties possibly early thirties, the arrogance of youth not yet fully flushed from his system. He wore a brown suede three quarter length coat that Peters guessed was Hugo Boss. The orange scarf and fawn coloured polo neck probably were too.

'You're not the doctor,' Peters said in a weak, almost helpless croak.

'No of course not. My name is Gunther Fest and I have a message from your old comrades in the BND, his old Cold War comrades in what used to be West German Federal Intelligence now the 'spooks' for a united nation.'

The BND! Now Peters got it. The spies that once protected the national security of the Federal Republic, who once hunted for Stasi moles placed in the organs of power all over West Germany, now confined to monitoring the squabbling factions of neo-Nazism and the Arab avengers who wanted to hurt people like Irit Weissman. Peters thought about pressing the nurse call bell but Fest continued.

'For some time now we have been monitoring your investigation into the killer known as "Christopher".'

'What do you mean monitoring?' Peters asked.

'I mean exactly that but now our interest is, if you like, deeper.'

'Hold on a minute. The "Christopher" file is a criminal matter, it's a murder inquiry under the control of the Berlin Polizie.'

'Maybe not any more Captain Peters.'

'I don't see how this is in any way a Federal matter,' Peters interjected.

'Oh come now, Captain. You are well familiar with Semtex. I'm sure you came across it on your tours of Northern Ireland. Well our friend has now resorted to the use of the explosive and in our mind that makes it very much a Federal matter.'

The velocity of anger was rising in Peters in parallel with the pain speeding back through his torso, limbs and groin.

'This is still a criminal murder inquiry under the control of the Kottbusser Strasse Murder Squad,' the Englishman insisted.

Fest rocked back a bit in his chair and shot Peters a patronising smirk.

'You must have slept soundly last night and received no interruptions Captain. Last night Semtex was used on a place that you and your team have had under surveillance since this whole thing began.'

'Boyz R Us!' Peters kept thinking. He's blown up Blucher's shop.

'That gay sex shop was destroyed last night in an explosion...'

Peters visibly panicked and thought about Riedel ...or rather this wife and two young children, both of them pre-kindergarten age. Fest instantly picked up the worry etched all over the detective.

'Don't alarm yourself Captain. There was no one in the premises when the bomb exploded. Your man on the inside was probably sound asleep just like you were at three a.m.'

'This is still none of the BND's business. Your job is catching spies and watching terrorists,' Peters protested.

'And you don't think that this was terrorism?' Fest asked slyly.

'You don't imagine for one moment that the BND can ignore bombs going off in German cities. Your man has already killed Mr Erich Tisch with a Semtex triggered device and now he blows up a building. To our mind that is terrorism.'

Fest took a handkerchief out of an inside pocket and started dabbing the sweat-sapped channel across the front of his face.

'You're giving him what he wants Herr Fest. That is exactly what he wants.'

'That's where you come in, you and your journalist friend from WAMS.'

'I'm no longer in intelligence. I work for the Berlin Polizei and may I repeat myself – this is a criminal investigation not a case of terrorism.'

The BND officer stood up, leaned back slightly and then rocked forward towards Peters.

'You will be obliged under Federal law to co-operate if and when we ask you to.

Here's my card if you need to get in touch.'

'I'm far too busy for that.'

'Well let's lighten your load Captain Peters.'

'Oh Herr Fest, there is one thing you could do for me?' Peters asked.

'What is that?'

'Lend me a couple of Euro coins. I might slip out later and ring you.'

'Of course and I won't take it as an advance payment.'

'Please don't' Peters smiled as the spook dropped a cylinder of bright shiny coins into the patient's hands.

The instant Fest left the ward Peters knew it was time to go; he needed to see Stannheim as soon as possible; he needed to stop the BND blundering all over a path that was leading him slowly but inexorably towards 'Christopher' . Peers too had to stop Heike inadvertently aiding Fest in tracking his man down.

He remembered from basic training how to hook up a casualty to a drip and used the knowledge in reverse to disconnect himself from the machine that had been shooting morphine into his body. Peters took the track suit bottoms, T-shirt and a hoodie he had been wearing when he was attacked, the top and trousers crusted with congealed blood, out from his locker and dressed quickly. Glancing up towards the clock on the wall he noticed it was half past six and instantly thought of Miriam. He had less than h§our to catch her before she came off night shift. She could drop him where he needed to go, all he had to do was to get to a public pay phone and ask the 'Blue Angels' cab company for driver 42.

When she finally arrived about 40 minutes later at the Charite's front doors Miriam at first thought Peters looked like one of the down and outs who scoured the city's hospitals at night for a chance to sleep in casualty to ward off the freezing cold. Yet when she got out of her cab, Miriam saw that it was her lover, shaking and shivering and for the first time, vulnerable.

'I'm sorry to have called you at work,' he said apologetically as she helped him into the back of the cab.

'Don't ask what happened. Not now. Just get me to the "Boyz R Us" sex shop.'

Miriam turned around to stare at Peters.

'Don't worry I'm not a secret customer. It's the place that was blown up the night before last.'

'Wouldn't you be better heading to Heer Strasse instead?' Miriam said.

'No. No. I don't want to hold you up. Haven't you got to take Ayse to school in an hour.'

'Martin please don't play the martyr! Do you need anything else?'

'Yes your mobile phone. I have to call someone.'

He summoned Angi to meet him outside Blucher's shop while on-route Miriam stopped at an all-night chemist near the west end where he bought the strongest pain killers on sale behind the counter just as the last dregs of the morphine were wearing off. When the cab reached the cordon thrown around 'Boyz R Us' Miriam pulled up.

'Shall I call tonight Martin? I'd really like to.'

'Me too but I'll be no use to you or indeed any woman. My cock's....'

She held up her hand to stop Peters' in his tracks.

'There's no need. We can have a bath together and you can tell me all about your latest adventure. ' Miriam blew him a kiss as she sped off eastwards towards her husband and daughter over in Kreuzberg.

Before him stood a pile of rubble from where Blucher once ran his porn mini-empire. Amid the debris behind a white strip of tape and four crash barriers were burnt fragments of glossy genitalia, a collage of semi-charcoaled cocks and orifices. In a skip to the left of where the doors used to be were stacks of relatively undamaged magazines, boxes of DVDs and a pyramid of dildos and even a giant glass fist still incredibly intact.

A couple of green coats stood guard, each casually holding

Heckler & Koch machine guns pointed towards the ground. Between them stood Angi, puffing on a cigarette, stamping her feet in protest against Siberia's return, her cheeks aflame with the morning chill. One of the uniforms looked irked at Peters' presence and told him to clear off. Angi went over and whispered into his ear and the cop then saluted. Peters felt a swelling in his loins as he watched Angi's black gloved hand lift the cigarette and slowly take it in and out of her mouth. He told himself that he deserved the shooting pain which started that instant to ignite across his groin.

'Do you have anything to drink Angi?' he whimpered.

'I've a flask of coffee in the car. What the hell are you doing here anyway? I was coming to you later with your mobile to the hospital. Did the doctor say it was 'Ok' to discharge you?'

'Bollocks to that Bavarian ponce. I signed myself out. Just get me the coffee I'm in agony here and need to wash down these pills,' Peters begged.

She crossed the street and pulled open the front door of the uniforms' car. On return to Peters she produced a small steel flask for him. He winked, knocked back the tablets and then gulped down the coffee.

'Thanks Angi. You're a life saver. Now, who would blow up a nice establishment like this?'

'Forensics say it was plastic explosive, probably Semtex.'

'I know. I know,' Peters protested.

'So we can assume it was our friend. Do you know by the way that 'Mothers Against Paedophiles' have pitched a tent outside the station? There's a woman in it threatening to go on hunger strike.'

Peters tried to repress a laugh but failed, the effort of it starting off another spasm of pain, this time all across his torso. He tried to focus hoping that the medication he took really was 'fast acting.'

'Jesus poor old Stannheim must be having a fit every morning. I almost feel sorry for him.'

'Me too sir. There's a couple of other things that are sending his blood pressure through the roof...maybe yours too,' Angi said while rubbing out her fag on the street with her gloriously inappropriate purple stilettos.

'I'm a big boy now Angi, you can give it to me straight.'

'Okay then. The last victim of "Christopher" was a bit different from the others.'

'In what way?' Peters inquired, already fearing the answer.

'For a start he had no association with this place or what's left of it. We checked him out and yes, Ulrich Vogts had a record.'

'Go on.'

'But it was a record different from the others, the friends of Oskar Beer who by the way is still enjoying Kottbusser Strasse's legendary hospitality, in fact he refuses to leave.'

'As I said before Angi– go on,' Peters butted in impatiently.

'Vogts did have convictions for sexual offences against children but his were for little girls. The TV scene Heike showed you on her mobile phone, we had it doctored by the techies. It's a girl having sex with several men. It's very vague but there is no doubt, it was a child.'

Peters suddenly wondered why 'Christopher' had gone to the trouble of blowing up Blucher's place. After all there was no connection between Vogts and the shop, he must have singled him out using newspaper archives and the web, just like all the others. 'Boyz R Us' was just a convenient way to track down and link up with the boy-abusers.

'Sir, there's something else, something Bauer spotted.'

'Bauer?'

'Believe it or not, yes. He traced the roots of all the men targeted so far. They all had one thing in common...besides being a bunch of perverts.'

'Which was?' he said, happy now that he could feel the effects of the painkillers working on him.

'Which was that they all came to Berlin after 1989. And they all came from different parts of what we used to call West Germany.'

His guard was down; he was letting his thoughts slip out.

'Colonisers. He sees them as colonisers. The worst kind of colonisers.' Peters said out loud.

Angi knitted her brows to signal her incomprehension.

'For him it really is war! He's on a crusade Angi. Listen, can you get one of the uniforms to drive me to Heer Strasse?'

'Sure. You need to get some rest at home.'

'Balls to rest Angi. Come and pick me up in two hours and take one of those photo-fits with you. And don't tell Stannheim. Tell him instead I won't see visitors, just in case he turns up with flowers and grapes at the Charite. Try and get a pool car.'

'Why?'

'Because we'll be heading back east once I get cleaned up and changed.'

'Where are we going sir?'

'To see your papa.'

Twenty Five

To: heike.numann@msn.com
I know they are listening. I know they have you tracked. So I will be brief.

To: christopherwrath@msn.com
It's not my choice!

To: heike.numann@msn.com
Of course not. They have been watching over you long before this campaign began.

To: christopherwrath@msn.com
Don't be absurd, this is not the DDR.

To: heike.numann@msn.com
Are you being deliberately naive as well as provocative?
They would not be doing their job if they weren't eavesdropping on people like you Fraulein. But let's not argue. There is little time.

To: christopherwrath@msn.com
I'm outside, in the open air, using my Blackberry.

To: heike.numann@msn.com
Nice try. I really don't think we should meet up....yet.
I'm only calling in to ask for that number you offered, the one belonging to the detective.

To: christopherwrath@msn.com
Why do you want to speak to him?

To: heike.numann@msn.com
Nice try again. Yes, you can mention that in your article this Sunday if you like, that I'm talking to the guy hunting me down.

To: christopherwrath@msn.com
Ok.

To: heike.numann@msn.com
As for the why, well let's say I'm intrigued.

To: christopherwrath@msn.com
I don't quite understand, intrigued?

To: heike.numann@msn.com
Because we were once soldiers, fraulein. As you already know I carry out my research meticulously. I've been reading up on Captain Peters. It seems that he and I were opponents before. There's a neat circle to all this.

To: christopherwrath@msn.com
Elaborate...please.

To: heike.numann@msn.com
Let's just say we were both equally interested in the fate of a traitor, one who your English friend managed to save in time. Just as the swords were approaching. And now the swords are approaching for me. They are getting closer. Just text the number, his handy preferably. Brevity is safety. Good bye.

The instant he logged off Heike's own mobile rang, it was Mannfred Stannheim calling her.

'Heike, why on earth did you pass on Martin's number to that maniac?'

She was angry as Stannheim had no right to tell her what to do.

'Because he asked, that's why,' she snapped back.

'I sincerely hope you don't print that this weekend. If the public learn that our SIO is having mobile chats with a serial killer Martin will have a picket outside his own door.'

Heike Numann felt an invisible, suffocating weight bearing down on her as she sat hunched over the park bench in the Tiergarten trying to keep warm in the later winter morning chill. It wasn't just the pressure from Stannheim tightening around her chest but the clawing demands of her news desk hungry for more copy on the killer 'Christopher" but also her raging internal conflict about Martin Peters, and rhe inexplicable loyalty she still felt she owed her old lover. Numann sensed Stannheim knew this and would use it against her to blunt her determination to get thes scoop!

She composed herself before replying to Stannheim.

'If you put it like that Mannfred I suppose I don't have a choice. I wouldn't want to be ruining your top boy's career now.'

Stannheim's voice mellowed: 'Our murderer is playing a game, Heike. He's going to mash up yours Martin's head too.'

She lit a cigarette and stood up, realizing that her limbs were aching with the cold and the lack of sleep.

'Alright Mannfred but everything else is mine especially his latest target.'

'Target? You are beginning to sound like him. Try the word victim when you're writing up your report.'

'You stick to detective work, Mannfred and I'll stick to the journalism. By the way, isn't wire tapping illegal unless you have a warrant? When am I going to get my privacy back?' she was almost tempted to shout Fuck You but resisted.

'Nothing is illegal in this investigation; you just make sure to let Martin know he's going to get that call. And Heike, there is one more thing...

'What?'

'This is between just me and you and him. No one else in Kottbusser Strasse will know about it.'

'Really now? How about all those techies in the Berlin Polizei and maybe even the BND for good measure.'

Then she found herself repeating what 'Christopher' had accused her of only a few minutes before.

'Are you being deliberately naive or provocative?'

There was no reply back. Stannheim had disconnected.

Peters' pain was subsiding by the time he knocked back his third beer - Lt Colonel Domath (rtd) was at least a generous, if somewhat un-cooperative host.

Angi sat beside her father on a new three seater sofa which was covered by a woollen, moth worn blanket. Peters wondered if the old man had placed it there to accentuate the frugality of the rest of his living room, as a humble cloak to hide this object of excessive consumerism. Angi must have bought it in the vain of hope of brightening up the place. She held up a copy of the photo-fit sketch based on Oskar Beer's description in front of the Colonel's face.

'Does anyone spring to mind?' Peters called out when he put down his bottle on one of the doilies Colonel Domath had placed on all the tables around the room.

'Does our friend resemble anyone you'd have known in the army? Someone who was in Special Forces? Somebody who had close links with the Sovs?

He watched as the Colonel moved his head, first across from left to right, and then up and down, absorbing the image in front of him. Finally, after a long pause, the old soldier lay back on the sofa and put his hands behind his head. Peters thought the Colonel was about to raise them, as if to surrender.

'I'm afraid not. I don't recognise him, whoever he is.'

'Are you certain dad?' Angi asked. 'Do you need a closer look? Maybe we could leave it with you for a couple of days and see if it jogs your memory.'

The old boy shot his eyes up towards the ceiling in frustration. *Or was it in protest?*

'Angi, if I knew who this was I would have spotted him right away. I have always lived by Chairman Mao's dictum....'

'Which one was that Colonel?' Peters interrupted.

'Always forgive your enemies but never forget their faces!'

Peters burst out laughing, which seemed to unnerve Colonel Domath.

'What's so funny?'

'What's funny, Colonel, is that you're not looking at an enemy, are you? He was one of yours although, as you say, you've never seen him before.'

'I met many soldiers in my time in the National People's Army. We had thousands of men under arms in our republic. It' just a pity we didn't put them to good use at the exact time when they were needed.'

By 'good use' of course, Peters knew, the Colonel had meant shooting unarmed citizens during the summer of 1989 when the dissidents finally lost their fear of the regime and thousands turned out on the streets demanding change. He thought about mentioning that but then retreated into his fourth beer which Angi had fetched from the fridge in the cramped little kitchen next door.

'It's medicinal Colonel, I know it's early in the day but I'm in a bit of pain,' Peters said holding up the bottle. The Colonel showed no interest in what had happened to the Englishman, who was now sitting in his house. He stood up and walked to the window overlooking the internal courtyard. This time he spoke as if lost in thought.

'The other night I saw two kids, barely in their teens, down there buying drugs off some character I've never seen before around here. Two kids who live in Pankow who never knew what it was like before. They think that what they lead now in life is normal. That's what's so sad about it all.'

'Why didn't you call the local cops and shop the dealer?' Peters said.

'I'm an old man and I don't want my windows to be put in. I'm just tired of it all,' the Colonel said, his voice deflated.

He walked gingerly back across the room, lifted the photo-fit out of his daughter's hands and held it up to the shaft of wan light penetrating the gloom of his apartment. This time he said nothing but simply stared at the image on the paper before handing it back to Peters.

After Peters finished the beer and Angi placed two kisses on her father's cheeks, the Colonel crossed to the opposite side of the room, to the other window that looked over the street leading to the local S-Bahn station. He pointed towards the sleek black BMW parked adjacent to the communal door of the apartment block.

'Nice car. That was something we could never do. Build machines like that,' Colonel Domath muttered as the two detectives left the flat.

They didn't speak again until Angi had taken the pool car to Potsdamer Platz in the direction of the Marriot Hotel. Outside commuters were descending into and ascending from the new U-Bahn station entrances strategically located in what was once the dead ground between West Berlin and the Wall, in the place where Presidents and Prime Ministers once came to peer into the east and then make some pious speech about the superiority of their system on this side of the divide. Watching the endless belt of people going up and down the entrances to the underground, Peters imagined he was in some futuristic sci-fi set with conveyor belts of troglodyte proles moving to and fro from the earth's innards.

When she halted at the Marriot's entrance, where they were greeted by a nod from a huge African man in a black top hat and purple cape, Peters finally spoke.

'Do you think your father was being entirely honest with us?'

The instant he said it Peters regretted the question. He recalled the warm embrace and the kisses, those little smears of purple that Angi had planted on her father's face.

'Why do you ask that?' she asked.

'Oh nothing, I just thought he was a bit cagey that's all,' Peters replied apologetically.

There was a long pause; the only audible sound was the rumbling of the engine protesting against being halted.

'He simply doesn't trust anyone. Especially not someone with your background.'

He resisted the urge to upbraid her and remind her that he was her senior officer. She shouldn't talk to him like that. Instead he waved out at the increasingly anxious Marriot doorman who was dealing with a line of grumpy drivers backed up behind the Kottbusser Strasse murder squad's BMW.

'I think our friend out there wants us to push off. Look Angi go back to base and leave me here. I've an old chum to look up, besides the beer is wearing off and the pain's coming back. I need some more medicine. Just keep me posted about what's going on at the station. I'm officially off for the rest of the week,' Peters said trying to sound cheerful as he allowed the Marriot's imposing security man to open the car door for him and gently usher him inside, where the detective was safe from the Arctic gales starting to batter the buildings all around Potsdamer Platz.

Looking inside the BMW Angi's face appeared frozen, her indignation still visible even when she reached into the glove department, took out a twenty pack of Marlborough Lights, took out the lighter from the dash board, lit one up and drove off west without saying a word.

'And you're being a bit cagey too madam,' he said out loud while watching her car disappear amid a beige and black blur of traffic and freezing rain, near perfectly vertical, that was teeming down, now, all over central Berlin.

As he entered the hotel once more Peters' mobile bleeped from the top pocket of his leather fur lined jacket. When he pulled the handy out there was a text from Heike on the LCD.

'Our St. Chris will be in touch with you soon. He says he wants to chat.'

Peters was relieved that it had come after he was shot of Angi. No one, he said to himself, no one except Heike needed to know about this. Then he remembered that he had left behind 'Christopher's' photo-fit in the Domath family apartment back over in Pankow.

Twenty Six

For a man whose business had just been blown to pieces Lothar Blucher appeared remarkably relaxed. Bulging out of one of his dark blue suits, Blucher was in his usual spot close to the bar, huddled over a fully armed chess board, a row of mobiles on one side, a tall glass of Stolychnya on the other. He didn't need to look up to sense that Peters was there. Blucher simply motioned to the Englishman to sit facing him.

Peters pointed at Blucher's electric blue tie: 'Shouldn't you be wearing black today?'

His informer shrugged his shoulders and then placed his right index finger on the Black King, rocking the piece back and forward on the board.

'And shouldn't you still be in hospital?'

'Ah, yes Lothar. I wanted to talk you about the hospital. To thank you really for dumping me at the door. That was very considerate of you.' Peters said acidly.

'You're not safe to be seen around anymore. I'm even a bit concerned about us meeting here,' Blucher answered scanning the near empty foyer.

'I suppose you didn't even go to the trouble of taking a snap of those two joggers with your mobile. Of course you must have got a good look at them. Perhaps we could go down the station and take a statement.'

Blucher looked up at Peters and smirked.

'I don't think that is going to happen....and nor do you. I'm your dirty little secret.'

'Speaking of dirty little secrets where is Anika?' Peters inquired.

'Oh probably up in the room powdering his cock,' Blucher replied in between sips of vodka. He called over to a waiter at the bar and ordered Peters a large Pils.

'He might not be around for much longer anyway,' Blucher sighed not so much from loss but more evident boredom. 'I thought it might be interesting to see both sides so to speak but...,well I can't say it was......interesting that is.'

'Poor you Lothar. Poor you. What's going on? Is she about to run away with that Filipino waiter who put his hand up her skirt?'

'They are welcome to each other! HE has just informed me that HE wants to be a full time SHE. Wants the snip and had the cheek to ask me to pay for it.'

'And being the generous soul you are Lothar you are going to dig deep and pick up the tab,' Peters was really enjoying this.

'Certainly not. Did you know by the way that HE is here under false pretences? Applied for political asylum. He claims his life is in danger because he's from a Muslim part of Thailand and that the bearded loonies are after him for being queer.'

Peters watched Blucher lean over the chess board again, his informer surveying it, mapping out his next moves. He then flicked the black Queen off the board and onto the glass table shoring up their drinks.

'Well of course I first met him in a Bangkok bar and he told me he came from some rat hole in the city. Imagine if someone in immigration or border control were to hear that,' Blucher said in a near whisper.

'Imagine that indeed!' Peters was wearying of Blucher's games already.

'Listen Lothar as the sword and shield for the good taxpayers of Stuttgart and Bavaria who stump up for our hospitality isn't there something more useful we should be talking about.'

'Excellent to know that I've joined the rest of Berlin then in living off the hard labour of our friends in the south. And if you mean those two thugs that give you a going over in the Grunewald what more can I do? I certainly won't be making any statement.'

'No one is asking you to be a hero in public.'

'Good. All I can do is ask my chess partner if they were sent down by Yanaev. You must have really pissed him off by the way.'

'Let's say I ruined his lunch date.'

'He might be a remote control murderer but to ruin a man's lunch demonstrates very bad taste. Whatever happened to the English gentleman?'

'He's been dead since about 1945 Lothar, thank fuck. You and your Prussian artisto clap trap you keep reminding us of. Now, when you have your next daily chess challenge with your Russian chum I want you to raise this subject. Ask him if Yanaev deals in arms. I think there's a link between that and the reason why two headless cadavers were washed up on the Havel shore.'

The waiter delivering a second round of vodka and beer to their table interrupted Blucher and Peters' jousting. As he poured Peters' Pils out, the man appeared to recognise the detective.

'Did I see you on television this week, sir?' the waiter asked.

Peters returned an unresponsive, cold stare.

'You might have. Now just put that on Herr Blucher's tab and leave us in peace.'

When the waiter, red faced, scampered back behind the safety of the bar, Blucher's mood changed.

'We are going to have to stop meeting here. Everyone knows you now. You're the cop that can't catch 'St. Christopher'. Isn't that what it says in these,' he pointed to a copy of today's 'Berlin Morgen Post', which had been placed on the table to cover a pile of CDs below. Peters had sped-read the lead story, a speculative piece that suggested the serial killer may have been a Russian. *Ridel, Bauer or someone else from inside Kottbusser Strasse were at their work again*, thought Peters. *Good, let them fire out as many heat flares as possible, the longer 'Christopher' believed the cops were getting nowhere the better.*

Blucher was shaking his head in mock-disgust: 'There you go again. Displaying bad manners even to the hotel staff. The death of the English gentleman. How tragic.'

'Listen Lothar, you just remember why you're here. You could have been in your shop when that bomb exploded. It's only our generosity that keeps you in this place. By the way what's under the paper?' Peters said pointing to the Morgen Post.

'Something very precious to me Martin. Something sentimental.'

'Sentimental! You dont know the meaning of that word Lothar.'

When the paper was lifted Blucher revealed a cylinder of CDs, most unscratched but without any boxes or covers. He picked one of them up and held it towards the light.

'This was what made me my fortune. The moment I heard he had bombed the shop I sent Anika over by taxi. He retrieved as many of them from the skip your officers had kindly parked outside. He does have some uses I suppose.'

'I take it they are totally legal.'

'Well some of them are barely legal,' Blucher snorted.

'They include my one and only masterpiece. 'Man Every Day'. I'm thinking of filming a remake with my castaway taking his friends back to London. Savages on Hampstead Heath. Can you imagine that? They didn't call him Cruiseo for nothing. Do you think Daniel Defoe would approve?'

'Tell me Lothar, why are you so chirpy? A few intact CDs wouldn't exactly cheer me up if my business had been blown sky high.'

'I've the place insured and don't for one-minute think it was an inside job. To be honest, seriously, it was a loss maker even before this lunatic started killing some of my best customers. Besides, I've just bought a bar,' Blucher said smugly.

'Where? In Berlin?'

'No, no, in a land faraway.'

Often when Peters looked directly at Lothar Blucher he instantly thought about nuclear war and the survival of cock-roaches.

'A land faraway might be a very good investment at present Lothar,' Peters added, getting up to leave, holding the beer glass in his hand.

'Make sure you get your Russian pal to start talking about Yanaev's other business. And stick around until all of this is over. I've got to justify your stay in this place.'

Blucher stood up and tinkled his glass against Peters' and winked.

'Watch yourself Captain Peters. I've told you before jogging and fresh air aren't good for you. Stay out of forests too.'

Despite himself, Peters smiled at his oldest source in Berlin, masking a faint regret that Blucher might be leaving the city for good.

'I'll take to press ups in my apartment instead then. Look after yourself Lothar.'

In the back of a cab on the way to Heer Strasse Peters kept staring at the last message on his handy. He was too nervous to use the phone in order to cancel Miss Friday and confirm that Miriam was on for this evening, needing the latter as a balm, needing to avoid the manic demands of the former.

He got the taxi man to pull over at a filing station where he knew there was a public pay phone. Fortunately, Peters kept a Telekom card reserved in his wallet when he needed to use a public phone to reach an informant. The detective spent the next ten minutes offering limp excuses to Karen and later imploring Miriam to join him tonight. There would be no Der Zug this Saturday, nor would he play bus boy for Frau Schuster in her pub.

When he got back into the taxi the driver finally realised who his passenger was.

'Hey boss you were one of the cops I saw on the news the other day talking about "St. Christopher".'

Peters waited in dread for yet another .38 special to be whipped out of the glove department.

'Fame at last!' Peters exclaimed.

'You oughta watch yourself boss. He's a popular boy our "Christopher". My missus loves him. She's gone out on of those bloody vigils.'

'Vigils?'

'Yeah, night time marches. Mothers Against Paedophiles. Personally I think "Christopher" is doing the right thing but still those women, eh. Bloody never shut up, do they?'

It was a relief for Peters that his driver seemed to have as much contempt for 'Christopher's' growing legion of fans than the killer himself. At least he wouldn't be berated all the way back along Heer

Strasse for standing in the way of 'God's work.' When they reached his apartment Peters had a tip and a request ready.

'Do me a favour mate. Don't tell anyone you had me in the back of the cab once.'

The cabbie saluted the ten extra Euros with a kiss and then stuck up one thumb.

'Good luck boss...except when it comes to "Christopher". You can count on me to say nothing but let him get on with the business.'

The flat was still in semi-darkness, the street lights from the main street partially illuminating the living room, when he fumbled towards the telephone stand checking for messages on his answer phone. There were three, one from the Charite wondering where the hell he was, another from Karen telling him to meet her tomorrow night in a bar down in Friedrichshain or else it was over, the final asking if he was interested in buying a time-share in Majorca.

He placed the handy beside the phone and undressed in the bathroom finally getting the chance to survey the damage the Russians had inflicted upon him 48 hours before. He looked down to where his cock was and noticed that it was a drooping leopard patterned series of yellow and black blobs and that it was aching once more. Peters then went off fully naked throughout the flat seeking out what booze there was remaining secreted in cupboards and sideboards.

On returning from the kitchen with a half drunk bottle of Bushmills, Peters checked to see if someone had called on the handy. No calls. No texts. No answer messages. He sat down on a sofa in front of the flat screen television, found the remote control and switched on. He was just in time for a round-table discussion on one of the satellite channels that included two criminologists, a retired cop, a tabloid editor and a Lutheran pastor debating the moral challenge facing Germany over the killer they called 'Christopher'. Just in time he could hear Miriam's car pulling up outside, the familiar wail of Middle Eastern song being cut dead and the door slamming. Peters turned off the television, drained his glass and went to run a bath.

Twenty Seven

In his exhaustion Peters had crashed on the sofa, a thick duvet from the bed next door that had been cast over him by Miriam before she crept out of the house just before dawn, the candles extinguished, the lights off, the TV put to standby, and the shutters closed over the balcony. The only illumination was a slash of lime green screen emitting tiny bursts of fluorescent light on the other side of the room.

At first he was sure he was dreaming when he heard the soft strains of Bach humming in the direction of the faint green glow. Then Peters remembered that he had switched his setting to 'Classical' from 'Office' and shot up from his half slumber and ran towards the handy on the phone table.

A withheld number patiently ringing and ringing; two missed calls. His heart started pounding and he could hear blood throbbing in his ears. He managed to speak first.

'Yes, Captain Martin Peters speaking.'

There was a slight pause and then a clearing of a throat.

'Excuse me for calling at such an early hour, sir. My name is Chet Miles and I represent a major Hollywood production company that is here in Berlin at present. We were wondering if....'

Peters cut the caller off with a question: 'Who the hell did you say you were?'

'Chet Miles, sir and I represent a major....'

He recognised a southern states' drawl: 'Is this some kind of joke?'

'No sir, we understand that you are, let's say, directly involved in the hunt for the serial killer known as "St. Christopher". On behalf of my company I was hoping if we could arrange a meet....'

'Sorry let me stop you there. I'm not even going to bother asking how you got this number but just be to clear – FUCK OFF!'

The worst thing of all was that Peters couldn't dare depressing the on/off button, pulling out the battery and locking the door for the weekend. He could have easily lay in his flat recuperating, doing odd jobs around the place he had neglected for months, writing to his mother back in England, watching Bundesliga on TV and later catching up with West Ham's progress (or lack of it) on Radio Five Live via satellite, he could've even taken a taxi to a quieter corner of Kreuzberg and enjoyed a lunch alone with the English Sunday papers and let Angi and Stannheim and Bauer and Riedel and all the team at Kottbusser Strasse deal with the toxic fallout of "St.Christopher's" wrath. What was even worse though than being a slave to the call was that the walls Peters had erected around his private sphere, in his life beyond the murder squad with its stresses, strains, politics, were all crumbling. He cursed the Laughing Cavalier for persuading him to attend the press conference in the first place. He would pay back whichever rat inside HQ had passed on his name and numbers first to the rags and now to one of the several American film companies flocking to Berlin to be first to put the story of "Christopher" on screen. He vowed to make that smug little bastard from the BND run around in circles before he would hand his quarry over to the spooks. And he promised himself that he and he alone would get his man.

As the morning wore on Peters found himself, unconsciously, pacing up and down the living room, his hands on his forehead, only released to run through his hair, his whole stature resembling a lovelorn teenage boy waiting in vain for the girl who's meant to ring but never does. Absorbed in the anticipation he had forgotten to tear back the blinds, flick on a light switch or dress himself; he even had stopped thinking about the dull pains still latent across his body from the blows he sustained in the Grunewald.

The day crawled along to noon. No one called, not on the land-line, not on the mobile. It was as if the exterior world knew there was only one message he wanted to receive. He was trapped like a fly in amber, a prisoner of 'Christopher's' own whim and timing. Why was he taking so long? Was he busy dismembering, decapitating or quietly dispatching yet another of his 'targets'? Peters caught himself out using that word. Even he now found it hard to deploy the term he was trained, no obliged under law to use – victim. A torrent of questions roared through his brain and yet he knew the call when it came would be brief, exact and loaded with instruction. He knew he could no longer leave this place until the handy rang and the new phase would begin. His universe would alter, its axis would tilt, his perspective would shift and re-colour. It wasn't Heike he had chosen but him. He sensed this deep down. One lesson learnt from spy craft in the claustrophobia of the late Cold War, when your enemy requests to meet there can only be two possibilities: they have either come to you with an offer or they are seeking one for themselves. What was "Christopher" offering? What could he possibly want?

He recalled the general from "Christopher's" army who had, through Blucher's contacts in the east, opened a channel to Peters. Fearing that he would be ordered to in turn command the People's Army to start shooting the citizen's the General had sought Peters out. The general was looking for help from Peters to defect before there was mass bloodshed and he would have the blood of the People on his hands.

Across town in the top floor of the Springer Building, Martin Peters was being unofficially removed from his role as SIO in the "St.Christopher" multiple-murder investigation.

The same man who had appeared to Peters inside his hospital ward was sitting crossed leg, sipping some coffee, in Christian Littbarski's office. Heike Numann noticed how well turned out he was in his Italian cut light grey suit and black silk open necked shirt. His sleekness made her think immediately that here was someone not to be trusted.

Littbarski was behind his desk fidgeting nervously.Her editor looked slightly deflated, put down, more than put out, by the presence of this other younger man purring intrusively in what was meant to be his lair.

Fest stood up, stuck out his right hand and bowed ever so slightly.

'Fraulein Numman. It's nice to put a face to a by-line. I've always been a great admirer of your work.'

Heike nearly stumbled and fell back in her chair. These were among the first words "Christopher" had spoken to her. For an instant she wondered if he had walked off the street to hand 'WAMS' a world exclusive. Her editor instantly shattered the fantasy.

'This gentleman is from a branch of the BND and he's come to speak to you about the "Christopher" investigation,' Littbarski said, his voice quivering under the strain.

She sat back down and opted to say nothing yet. The spook in the expensive suit did the talking.

'We are all grown up adults in there, would you not agree?' he said taking another sip from his cup before continuing.

'We all know that the Berlin Polizei have been listening in to your calls and monitoring your email traffic since this terrible business first began.'

The editor and his crime reporter nodded in unison.

'What you didn't know up until know is that we are also keeping a close eye and ear on your "relationship" with the serial killer known as "Christopher".'

This prompted Heike to butt in, something which surprised even her.

'What do you mean "relationship"? You sound as if I'm fucking him or something. Not that that has anything to do with you.'

The spook carefully laid the cup and saucer on Littbarski's table and smiled back at Heike.

'Fraulein, the only fucking going on is inside your head. He, I mean "Christopher" of course, has been mind-fucking you and half the Kottbusser Strasse murder squad since he started this crusade.'

Heike looked over towards Littbarski who had his head bent over some pages. She spotted that he was doodling with the fountain pen as if he was trying to cover over his obvious embarrassment. She turned and stared at the BND agent.

'Isn't Kottbusser Strasse in charge of this investigation? Since when did a serial killer become an issue of national security?'

The young BND man folded his arms and smiled again.

'You know we have a lot of great stories we could pump your way.'

'So what exactly is it you are looking for, Herr...? Sorry I didn't catch your name.'

'Just call me a "Security Source" for future reference. Isn't that what you call all your friends in the Polizei who don't want to go on the record?'

Across the table Littbarski was shuffling in his seat, Heike sincerely hoped he was suffering from a severe case of piles.

'Well I'll ask you again Herr "Security Source" - what exactly is it you are looking for?'

Mr 'Security Source' smiled over to Littbarski. 'No wonder you say she's good. With a ballsy attitude like that it's no wonder she gets you so many stories. '

He then turned back towards Heike, his expression and tone much graver than before.

'Kottbusser Strasse may be in charge but ever since this man started blowing people and places up we take that as a matter of national security. That's where we come in and that's where you can help.'

'What do you mean by help?'

'Well for a start how about telling us everything that comes between you and "Christopher". Like for example if you and he decided to have a little moonlight meeting that wasn't organised on the mobile or cyberspace. Or for that matter if he sought out anyone else to spill his guts to.'

'How the hell can I help you any more since you're obviously helping yourselves to my mobile calls and emails?' she protested.

'We are not just thinking about you? How about your old boyfriend Captain Martin Peters?'

That was designed to provoke, she realised that and managed to fight off the urge to erupt. She sat smouldering in her chair.

'C'mon, we know that for whatever reason our "Christopher" has taken a keen interest in Peters. For all we know the Englishman could be in danger himself.'

'I hardly think so,' Heike bit back on the verge of losing it, 'He only knocks off paedophiles.'

'True, maybe, but this is his war and in war sometimes innocents get caught in the cross-fire, Fraulein.'

'I should have known "Mr Security Source" that your sole agenda has been protecting Captain Peters from his mad man. Your concern for Martin is deeply touching.'

'You cannot begin to imagine the stories in the future we can lead you towards Fraulein,'

'Captain Peters is still the senior investigating officer in this case and I wish to speak to him only about this,' she said defiantly.

The spook rubbed his thighs along the perfectly ironed, razor sharp creases of his trousers.

'I'm afraid you would be wasting your time. As of today Captain Peters is no longer in charge of that particular investigation. If you don't believe me put a call into Supt. Stannheim. Captain Peters' is on medical leave and when he returns, eventually, his sole focus will be on the unsolved case of the two headless corpses in the Havel. Supt. Stannheim thinks he's been under too much stress dealing with two different inquiries.

Martin must have told the spook to go fuck himself, Heike thought and was proud that he did. Instinctively she knew what she had to say next.

'But of course. You are right. He does need to take some rest so if you forgive me I have a story, a very long story to write,' she got up to go but he gripped her hand.

'Please remember we are not on opposing sides here. We can all help each other. What we don't want is someone going off on a tangent. That's all.'

Heike ignored the spook and nodded towards her editor who was watching the two of them with ever increasing alarm.

'Christian, if you don't mind I'll get started on the new material about our man. How many words?'

'As many as you like, space is no problem, you'll have the lead and write through inside,' her editor stammered, 'Just let it flow Heike.'

She made for the door and ran straight to the elevator outside, her stomach capsizing with fear and disgust. When she reached the ground floor Heike found a quiet corner inside the giant foyer of the Springer empire and sent a text to Peters:

'M I need some tobacco and salt...now. H'

Twenty Eight

The voice was, as Heike said it would be, precise, calm, forceful. The message terse and to the point.

'There is no time to chit chat Captain Peters. Please listen to what I say and make sense of it. The next time I call I will give you a means towards contacting me. I do not trust these things we are using to speak to each other.

So next time open your ears and your eyes. Do you understand?'

The accent was that of a Berliner, the tone and diction of someone who had lived a life of delegation and command. There was no quiver, no hesitation, no uncertainty. The voice was that of a long term planner.

'How do I know you're for real'" Peters summed up the courage to ask.

'If you want proof I can give it to you....but not for now Captain. As I said open your ears and your eyes.'

Peters got bolder: 'If you are Christopher and not some sad crank pretending to be then explain why you're doing this...'

The line went dead. He would cede no ground, surrender not a second, never lessen his grip.

The call came just before Heike's cryptic text which Peters had decoded on a parallel line of his brain while deciphering the subtext of 'Christopher's' words – if this was 'Christopher'. At this moment he needed to be with her; they were like a self-contained support group, marooned together, survivors cut off from the world by this unique bond. Peters texted back 'ok' and dressed quickly in the first clothes he could find scattered all over the spare bedroom.

Within less than an hour he was sitting in Sale e Tabbachi quaffing the first carafe of house-red and waiting for Heike to appear. Peters sat near the door but gazed down the restaurant towards the spot where he had interrupted Avi Yanaev's lunch and paid for it with a hammering in the Grunewald. When Heike finally arrived about 45 minutes and two carafes later Peters pointed down to the table where the Russian sat and slurred: 'One day they'll erect a plaque in the place where the forces of justice confronted the forces of darkness.'

Heike looked disappointed and ordered a large bottle of sparkling mineral water which she later tried in vain to dilute Peters' glass with.

When their starters arrived Peters shrugged his shoulders, pushed away his plate and called out for more wine. The place was filing up with the usual clientele of professionals who worked around the Springer building, the radical daily next door, Taz and the architect and legal offices at the far end of Friedrichstrasse.

'For Jesus sake Martin hold it together will you,' Heike said in a semi-whisper.

'Open your ears and your eyes!' Peters blurted, his outburst turning several heads from tables on either side of them.

'Does he boss you about too Heike? Does he bark out orders and make you jump?' he slugged at the remains of his wine and gestured to one of the Italian waiters for more.

'Wouldn't you be better off with some mineral water Martin? To keep a clear head. What if he calls again and you're comatose?'

'Balls to him Heike. Balls to him. He's played with us and now it's my turn.'

They paused as the waiter nimbly dropped down another carafe between then and swiftly swept away the starters, one plate, Peters', virtually untouched.

'So that's my news. I get a call from a serial killer. It's not every day you can say that...oh by the way that's off the record for now,' he knew he was being obnoxious, perhaps deliberately so.

'So what's your news then?'

Heike ran her forefinger along Martin's hands; her touch electrifying his skin, the sensation seemed to rejuvenate him.

'A real weird guy from the BND came to see me in Littbarksi's office. Told me you'd soon be off the "Christopher" case. Wants me to tell him everything including anything about you.'

Her news seem to stiffen Peters. 'Did he have beautifully coiffured hair, not a fleck of grey and designer clothes, and a very weak handshake?'

'Dunno about the handshake. I was probably too beneath him for that but yeah the description fits,' she lit a cigarette and returned to stroking Peters' hands.

'His name is Fest and he came to see me in the hospital.'

She burst out laughing and shook her head.

'Is this supposed to be funny or are you just taking pity on me?'

'No. It's just his name Martin. I have been offered a Festian pact.'

He slurped more wine and then winked at his former lover, all the while he caressed her hands the way she used to when they first got together.

'I would strongly advise against such temptation Heike.'

'Which means not a word about our man making contact with you?' she said lifting her glass of sparkling water to toast their new alliance.

'Please! Don't ignore Dr Fest. Give him shit information. Tell him I'm taking leave from the case. And let's hope "Christopher" used a brand new handy when he called me and that they haven't traced the call,' there was a newly regained lucidity in Peters' voice.

'Keep all the stuff about the BND's interference in the case out of WAMS for now. You've enough to go on with the latest killing on film. You're going to get a book out of this Heike and get rich, then I'll marry you and we can buy a little villa in Majorca.'

She kicked his shins under the table, playfully, gently, stubbed out her cigarette and took Peters' wine glass out of his hand and drained it.

'I'll drink to that kind of success...except of course that bit about moving to Majorca with you. For your information mister I've already had three publishers on the phone wanting the exclusive on me and "Christopher".'

'Oh that's nothing darling. Just this morning an American movie producer called me in Heer Strasse wanting to talk.'

He refilled his glass, lifted it up in salute of her and said:

'I told the Yank to fuck off!'

Heike's mood then seemed to switch instantly, her tone harsher, less than playful than before, her line of questioning tinged bitter and regretful.

'That's you all over Martin, isn't it? Always running away from new opportunities, always afraid of taking a risk, at least in your personal life.'

He had a sudden flash in his brain of him drenching her with his wine glass but resisted the urge. Instead he sipped at the house red, leaned back and folded his arms.

'And who are you to talk about anybody, much less me?,' his volume was rising. 'I suppose this is about commitment....or the lack of it. You'd know all about that Heike.'

She shot him back a smile, which did more than surprise him, before mouthing silently: 'Fuck you too.'

Peters replied with an upright middle finger and then continued berating her.

'The only commitment you have in your life is to Welt am Sonntag.'

'And the only commitment you have is to Mannfred Stannheim. Tell me – why are so attached to him? What's so great about someone who would knife you in the back?'

He held his hand up to accede the point before going on.

'Stannheim actually happens to be a first class detective but unfortunately is also a lousy human being.'

'Oh come on Martin, he will do what the BND and the high command tell what do even if that means kicking you off the case. So what's so special that he's done that you can forgive him anything?' Heike asked.

'First met him after a few squaddies, a year before the Wall came down, got into serious trouble. Busted bringing in heroin from West Germany on one of the military trains. They were caught down in the west end flogging the gear to Stannheim's undercover team in a strip club. He handed the men over to my unit, I passed them on to the Military Police and they were quietly shipped back over the border and finally across the North Sea pronto. Kept it out of the papers as well. I couldn't thank him enough nor could the British brass up in

Spandau. So we kept in touch too. Became a very useful contact, let's just say.'

Heike sniggered: 'That's what you seem to spend your life doing! Keeping things out of the paper.'

'He was more than that to me Heike,' Peters said tipping the dregs of the carafe into her glass.

'He ran a network of informers all over Berlin, petty crooks, pimps, prossies, people smugglers, the lot. Some of his secret little army had connections on the other side of the Wall which he knew would be useful for someone with a job like mine. He wasn't just a top detective with a superb strike rate. He had more reach across the frontier than most of our agents, military Int. or 6 put together. We came to rely on him quite a lot when things started to fall apart over there.'

Heike was giggling now, shaking slightly at the thought of these two old Cold Warriors now re-united in a Berlin murder squad.

'It wasn't funny at the time Heike. You really had to be there. Stannheim's network didn't just smuggle a few Ossies over to the West. They saved lives. He saved lives,' Peters retorted defensively.

'Relax babe. Now, are you going to tell me how you and Manny Stannheim played your part in the downfall of communism.'

He leaned over the table and delivered the slightest of his kisses on her lips. Heike, embarrassed, turned away, hoping that the gathering throng of lawyers, journalists and their mistresses had not seen their clinch.

'That my darling remains classified.'

She scowled back him while Peters lifted his glass and emptied it in one go.

'Seriously, you should cut back on your boozing, Martin,' she barbed.

Peters slammed his glass down in protest.

'One woman in my life tells me I should go and seek therapy now another wants me to tread the 12 steps to sobriety. What is this – analyse Martin Peters week?'

'It would take more than one week to de-construct you Martin. Who by the way is the "one woman in my life"? Anyone I know?'

Heike asked.

He waved his hand across his face trying in vain to avoid questions, any questions, about his love life. Heike shifted in her seat like a cat tensing up into attack mode.

'That's your answer to everything. Wave your personal life away, then bury it deep with all the rest of your secrets. Do you know that when I used to ask you in the middle of our all night sessions if you loved me you always said the same thing? You'd shrug your shoulders like a little boy lost and say "I don't know" or "I'm conflicted." You thought you'd fob me off with your indecision thinking I would forget about it all in the morning but I remembered every brush off, babe, every petty cowardly evasion.'

She took out a cigarette and, unlit, used it as a prop to point her pent up frustrations in his direction.

'I'll bet you have a specific day and night picked out for your analyst-girlfriend. Isn't that the way you used to "structure" me? I never spent a full weekend with you Martin, one night the usual, two if you were lucky but God forbid if you allowed me to encroach any further into your free time. No doubt you had some other babe on the go in another part of the city to attend to next day.'

Her close to the bone candour made Peters uneasy, so much so that he tried to convince her he was more drunk than he actually was, by swaying gently in his seat, forcing his eyelids to droop, yawning and feigning wind. Ignoring his play acting she kicked him lightly on the shins underneath the table.

'Your trouble, Captain Peters, is that you don't want to be alone yet you won't share your life with anybody either. Me and the rest of your girls, we're the like the agents you used to run, you get what you want from us, we're so dependent on you but you can drop us like a hot snot at any time and steal back into yet other compartment of your boxed out life.'

Heike must have thought he was mocking her when Peters stood up from chair, placed his palms on the table and leaned over to kiss her on the forehead.

When she wriggled away from him, leaning back wearily against the restaurant's wall and said, this time out loud, 'And once again, go fuck yourself.'

Peters woke up prostrate and face down on a tough leather massage table. When he lifted his chin up he was met with the sight on screen of a diminutive Japanese woman being penetrated by a huge African-American in a khaki uniform. He twisted his body around until he was lying on his back and raised himself up. Facing him was Marion, the co-owner of 'Der Zug' and behind her, at the bar area, her husband noisily shoving and re-stocking shelves of beer and mixers, grunting in protest over the presence of their last customer. Marion lifted a glass of brandy from the bar top and handed it to Peters.

'Good morning Martin,' she said gesturing with a flick of her eyes towards the clock behind him above the video screen. It was 4.15 am. He had blacked out while receiving a rub down from the club's in-house masseuse, a thick-set shot-put built woman who learned her trade in the DDR and now earned a living loosening up the muscles of 'Der Zug's' clientele.

'You've been out for hours! Drink up.'

He gulped down the double helping of 'Hennessy' in one go and shook the glass for a top up – a deliberate and instinctive provocation. Marion's husband banged down the bottle before re-filling Peters' glass.

'I'm really sorry Marion,' Peters apologised, 'I had too much to drink in the afternoon. It's been a shit week.'

She responded with one of her incredulous 'now-you-naughty-boy-looks'.

'We weren't going to let you in. Friday night is couples' night but you were very persuasive.....well you are one of our best customers.'

'Again I can only apologise. Hope I wasn't too obnoxious,' he said polishing off the second brandy.

Marion's husband left the bar and gently pushed her aside. He was naked but for a forest of grey pubic-thick hairs all over his torso and a leather thong with three pointed shiny studs.

'We can't make up our minds whether your presence here was, is, a good thing for our business or not.'

For the first time since he regained consciousness Peters realised he was completely naked. He crossed his legs and sat perched on the side of the massage chair.

'I don't know what you're talking about,' Peters confessed.

'What I'm talking about is that half of my clients think you're a celebrity and the other half are freaked out that a cop is in their club. You were signing your name with Marion's lipstick on the first half's tits and cocks; the other half were complaining that you were Polonium,' Marion's partner lit up a cigarette, lifted up the video controls and switched off the 'GI John does Japan' movie on the flat screen above the entrance to the sauna.

'You're our first celebrity Martin,' Marion giggled, 'The cop chasing "Christopher". We don't know whether or not to advertise that on our website.'

Peters dropped down from the table and propped himself on one of the bar stools.

'Listen you two if you want I'll give this place a wide berth for a while.'

The husband appeared unimpressed by Peters' offer of 'sacrifice.'

'Oh that's really noble of you. In you come gate crashing couples-only night, pissed, pissing off and spooking half my Friday night regulars so what do you want, another medal like the ones they gave you in the British Army?' Mr 'Der Zug' had never been this hostile before; in fact in all the times Peters had known him he was quite the opposite, encouraging him regularly to go downstairs with his wife in the look-but-don't-join-in basement part of the club where he liked to watch.

For a moment hostilities were suspended as the owner scanned his eyes over the black and bruises peppered across Peters' torso.

'What happened to you? Did you get beaten up by the St.Christopher fan club?'

Peters almost told the truth about Yanaev's thugs but that would only have heightened the couple's paranoia. The last thing they wanted to hear was that their most infamous client had incurred the Russian mafia's ire.

'Let's just say it was a very complicated arrest operation that turned nasty,' Peters lied.

'Some of our punters were muttering at the bar about reporters tonight. No that there have been any in here. But what if some journalists start to take an interest in your private life and follow you to our door! Those rags will feast on us. And there are plenty of customers who are very publicity shy. You do understand that.'

Marion tried to sound more emollient than her husband who was nervous and twitchy, a sure sign that he wanted to shut up shop.

'Yes of course I understand that. Up until very recently I would have counted myself as being in the publicity shy corner. The thrill of the chance of being caught never appealed to me.'

She poured him out a third and final brandy which Peters knocked back again in one go.

'Ok. I'll not darken your door for a while, at least until this business is brought to a close.'

'How long is that going to take?' Marion asked excitedly, 'Are you close to getting him?'

Peters winked at her, put down the empty glass and made for the mixed sex showers.

'Closer than we've been yet Marion. I'll call when I'm ready to come back,' he shouted back in her direction.

Usually Marion rang a trusted and discrete cab firm to take Peters and the other regulars home but instead he opted to walk along Korner Strasse and around Steglitz, searching for a late-night-early-morning pub or an Imbiss stand, until 6 when the first U-Bahn trains were running. He dragged himself along the street which ran parallel to an S-Bahn track all the way to the local station. The lack of any sound outside, no birdsong, no rumble from the rail lines to his left, no rattle from any car engine, cast a sinister cloak of stillness over this corner of Berlin. As he moved ever closer to the light of what had to be an open all hours corner pub, Peters used anger to distract himself from the fear that threatened to paralyse him. He cursed out loud in protest over the death of his privacy, the decision that he had instantly regretted to stand by Stannheim at the press conference, his out loud 'fuck you Manny' filling the vacuous silence of a city trapped in the dark throat of late winter.

Twenty Nine

'My name is Albert Briegel and I am a paedophile. I was convicted of sexually abusing two young children, a brother and sister, in my apartment in Essen 15 years ago. I was sentenced to six years serving three in prison and the remainder on a rehabilitation programme for offenders in the Ruhr. When it ended in 2003 I moved to Berlin. I still have a taste for little boys and girls and have travelled many times to have sex with them in Asia, first Thailand, latterly Sri Lanka.'

The clanging sound of what seemed to be two pots or pans being knocked together punctuated the message on screen. This time 'Christopher' had turned on the volume, allowed his captive to speak, sparing him - for now at least - the ordeal the others endured had during filming.

Briegel, a gaunt, emaciated spectre of a man with a pasty pockmarked face, was dressed in an orange jump-suit and sat in medium close up in front of the camera. The clanging signalled he was allowed to speak again. It was obvious Briegel was reading from prompt cards directly in front of him.

'I appeal to you the German public to save my life. You have the power to determine if I live or die. I once placed images of myself with my two young victims on the Internet. Now it's my turn. If you decide I must die, then it will posted be all over the 'net.'

He dropped his head and started breathing heavily as if he was on the verge of hyperventilating. The out-of-vision cameraman angrily battered the kitchen utensils together once more. Briegel raised himself back up until he was in line of sight of the lens. It all reminded Peters of those photo-booths where you have to keep adjusting the swivelling chair until your face is captured in a square perfect frame.

'Your reaction through the media will seal whatever is my fate. Please. I beg you. I have served my debt to society. I want to live. Don't let me die,' croaked Briegel. The film faded to black for several seconds and then cut back to the graphic of Christopher and Christ as a child on his shoulder before dissolving into black.

Peters had one hand fiddling on the keyboard, the other holding up his mobile to his left ear. He was rewinding the posted attached message in his in-box while trying to talk to Angi on the other, all the time attempting to forget about the gale force 9 hangover battering his brain and distracted by the thought of what "Christopher" was planning for his current captive and by what means would he dispatch the old wretch in front of the lens from the world. He clicked back to the last few seconds of film and then froze the final frame of Briegel. There were no signs of fear or self-pity anywhere on his face, not even the trace of a tear drop: Briegel already knew what lay ahead.

'Did you see his latest artwork on film sir?' she asked.

He couldn't believe what he was seeing or hearing.

'Has this been sent out on general release?'

'Yes sir, some of the 24 news channels has already broadcast it. It's all over the 'net. CNN and the BBC are currently talking to us about what they are going to do with it. Schawbowski has asked them to hold back...'

On hearing that name Peters broke in: 'That fool will hardly stop them. He'll only piss them off and they'll screen it in revenge. Have you checked on Briegel's form?'

'Riedel has sir. He looked up an old police-contact from his time in the Ruhr who remembered our latest star. Our colleague over there confirmed to Riedel that Briegel had done time for paedophile activity. Not bad work for a Sunday.'

'Bully for Riedel.'

Angi paused for a few second before adding: 'We've been tipped off that Mothers Against Paedophiles are running a vote on their website.'

'Oh fuck!'

'Indeed sir. When it's up and running the tabloids will get hold of it and then our friend is doomed.'

He felt the sudden urge to make light of the latest development, unable to resist broadcasting his thoughts.

'Vote 1 to have Briegel freed, 2 to have him killed by a thousand cuts, 3 to have him knocked off quickly, 4 to have him.......' Peters stopped himself and darkened his tone. 'Seriously, should I come in today Angi?'

'There's no need. Everybody here works flat out. Anyway the boss still thinks you are in hospital recovering. Or at least he is pretending to for the top brass. The team will still know that you are in charge from the sidelines. Riedel says are you are like the Bayern manager who gets sent off into the stands by the referee. You may not be in the dugout but you are still barking out the tactics on the phone.'

Peters was despite himself more than slightly touched that even Riedel was a loyal member of the team.

'Alright Angi but do me a favour.'

'Anything sir.'

'Book me a meeting with our dear leader mid-morning tomorrow. We've a lot to talk about and then get the whole team together later for a pep talk.'

'Sure thing. He's freaking out, complaining that the minister is sitting on his chest. I'll make sure "Anna's" is open for the both of you tomorrow.'

'Oh, Angi?'

'Yes.'

'Have you heard any rumours about me being taken off the "Christopher" case?'

She sounded genuinely stunned: 'Not at all. Who'd be spreading that kind of shit?'

'Cheers Angi. Appreciate that. Now I'm locking the door just in case Mothers Against Paedophiles find out where I'm living.'

'Check out their website just in case they've already posted up your address.'

'Thanks for being such a comfort Angi,' Peters signed off.

His phone had beeped throughout their entire conversation, he guessed correctly who was anxiously trying to get through to him.

'Yes Heike, I've seen it too. Hope it doesn't blow your scoop away.'

There was a backtrack of garbled conservation, glasses being filled and re-filled, jazz, the odd shriek of laughter down the line – Heike had been out celebrating.

'I'm miffed you haven't invited me to your party madam.'

'Screw you Martin. I still meant what I said in Sale. And I only go drinking with men who can hold their own. I had to pour you into the cab. By the way what is "Der Zug"?'

At least she didn't know that, at least he hadn't been stupid enough to let his defence down completely and tell her exactly what it was.

'Just some late night club down in Steglitz where I go to ward off Lady Insomnia but get to the point Heike. What did you see?'

'I watched it on my Blackberry. I caught it on youtube, it'll be viral in a few hours.He really has done it this time our boy.'

'Yep, he never ceases to surprise us. Next thing he'll be doing one of them live on TV....by the way, you OK?'

'Don't worry about me, two of those publishers are here tonight fighting for my attention. Good luck to the broadcasters if they use this latest stuff. Clever of him to use an orange jump suit, just like the Jihadis. By the way yourself - did you by any chance, actually see my article?' there was disappointment loaded into her voice.

'I'm sorry Heike. I haven't left the place all day, never got a chance to check your web edition,' it was then that he remembered he should normally be in the Widow Schusters' pub playing bus boy for her.

'It's fine Martin. I'll send you a copy or you could read it on-line. I'm more worried about you.'

Heike seemed to sense that he was drifting from her.

'Martin, are you listening to me?'

'Yeah, yeah, of course.'

'You really do need to get some rest, or talk to someone, somebody who can help, who can be objective.'

'For Christ's sake don't get back on your therapy crusade again

Heike,' he snapped recalling those dying days of their relationship when she would persistently urge him to seek help.

'That was some other dame who suggested that.....Martin?' she was calm despite his petulance.

'What?'

'I'm saying all this because I care, because I think I still might be in love with you.' She hung up and instantly he imagined her burning with equal anger and embarrassment for what she had just said to him. Seconds later he was ringing a cab to pick him up in Heer Strasse and take him to Westfalisch Strasse when he should gone to Heike's. He knew what was holding him back; what made it easier to rush into the arms of the widow Schuster; that he no longer had the right to be 'normal' in love.

Later, alone at home, as he watched from his balcony, the short belts of light pulsating that went from west to east and east to west along Heer Strasse below, Peters remembered that first tour of the Gulf when he was seconded by the Military Police to investigate rumours about a massacre of Iraqi POWs in the Kuwaiti desert. The reports turned out to be entirely false but in the course of his inquiry Peters' team had come across a video tape belonging to a squadron from a tank regiment first accused of executing prisoners. It had been taken hours after Day 2 of the Ground War when the troops had pushed into Kuwait and discovered a landscape of cratered graveyards filled with Saddam's soldiers. The ragged conscripts had been caught by the full force of a B52 raid and the shock of the explosions had de-capitated dozens of the retreating Iraqis.

The video cut to a row of giggling and smiling squaddies with their arms wrapped around headless Iraqi troops , some of the Brits had even tied football scarves around what was left of several of the cadavers. A number of others had been stripped naked and their private parts shown off to the lens in full close ups. Off camera were distended voices, one asking where the heads where, offering a reward to the first colleague who came back with one. Then the camera panned to a Scottish soldier using a spray can to paint in luminous orange the words 'Dundee United' onto the side of a charred, upturned Armoured Personnel Carrier to the soundtrack of his comrades singing 'Flower of Scotland'. This was Peters' first breakthrough in his mission. Which was to ensure that the footage never made it on to television or into the papers. In the first war on earth to resemble a video game images of destruction from thousands of feet in the air were deemed palatable for viewing; scenes of desecration on the ground were not.

His other job was to track down and quietly destroy the military careers of those directly in charge of the ghoulish revellers. Once he had identified the NCOs and the captain that led the unit and passed them over to the board of inquiry Peters admitted to himself, finally, that he was retreating, inexorably, from the army. It was then that he knew he would be going back to Berlin for good.

Thirty

'Why did you come here? Why did you come here?'

It was the only words she spoke to him all through a long night of tethered captivity at her house.

In the morning stealing along the tree lined street past a row of twitching net curtains. Inside the taxi taking him back to Heer Strasse to freshen up, change and collect some painkillers. On the S-Bahn as far out as Friedrichstrasse Station relieved that none of his fellow half-catatonic passengers had recognised his face. And on the brief journey by cab down to Kottbusser Strasse and through the gauntlet of reporters gathered outside headquarters.

'Why did you come here?' she had kept up in severe repetition, her smoky breath and tangy, slightly-off cologne invading his nostrils as she maintained her interrogation. The words that had echoed through a sleepless night and a dank grey morning now propelled him forward into the day. He had been prepared. He had told Frau Schuster nothing. She had expected and received just this obedient silence, and he was grateful for that.

His confidence restored, Peters was ready then for whatever those now gathered around him on the murder squad's floor were going to throw at him.

Bauer was first to raise his voice at the morning meeting, amid detectives dotted all over the office, some slumped in their chairs, others with their buttocks balanced on the edge of desks.

'Sir it's good to have you back.' The rest of the murder squad started knocking on tables in approval.

'I spent yesterday trawling through firms that rent out lock up garages, warehouses, mini-factories from the Mitte to Marzan and anywhere beyond,' Bauer licked the top of a pencil and scribbled something on a notebook he was holding.

'I've 12 left to check, the remainder, 242, have no records of anyone matching our friend's description renting out one of their properties,' the ex Vopo looked extremely pleased with himself.

Stannheim stood at the entrance to his glass lair, arms folded, staring straight ahead at his officers, his glare trained on all except Peters.

'12 to go. Well done Herr Bauer. Now can we get down to the business of finally tracking down this maniac before he stages his next execution live on the Internet,' Kottbusser Strasse's boss barked sarcastically.

'I cannot believe that we have got nowhere and I mean nowhere with this investigation,' he added and turned and slammed the door.

Peters marched to the top of the room and replaced Stannheim. Sulky bastard was what Peters wanted to say.

'Right it's time to pound the pavements again. That means not calling any of these 12 businesses but physically going down there and checking on each and every one of them in person. It also means getting around parts of the east where the Stasi and the party were once strong, and quietly, discretely showing a chosen few the face of our friend "Christopher". I want all of his victims checked and re-checked. Knock doors around where they lived, ask neighbours if they have seen this man, pick up any detail no matter how trivial it may seem. Get out and sniff about.'

He tapped lightly on Stannheim's door until he could hear the lock turning in the key. The old man was giving up on the case and his fatalism was spreading like contagion through the entire unit. Peters looked at the clock - 'Anna's' would be open in half an hour.

'I've scattered the troops to the four corners, thought it might be a good idea to make them take in some of the famous Berlin luft,' Peters said on entering while trying to sound enthusiastic.

'Let's go to the pub now that the children have gone out to play sir.'

Stannheim jerked a thumb behind him towards the window overlooking Kottbusser Strasse.

'What about those children down there? The last thing Schawbowski will want to see is the two main detectives in the

"Christopher" case sneaking out to a bar.'

'We can go out the back through the car pool. I'll get a couple of umbrellas because, God is good, it's starting to rain. We can hide from the hacks under them,' now it was Peters turn to point to the window and the deluge outside. Stannheim reached for his nicotine-reeking rain coat from the stand and nodded that they should both go.

The lurid lights of 'Anna's' created the feel of being inside a photographic dark room. Red and black décor all around them, chequer board colours that exaggerated the sinister whiteness of each man's eyes and teeth.

'I think I need to see a shrink sir.' Peters said only half-joking.

There was a snort from the corner where Stannheim had collapsed into.

'Jesus Christ not you too Martin.'

Peters knocked back his Korn in one go and slurped the top of his beer. He hadn't been allowed a drink either inside the widow's bar or later in her place, tethered as he had been to one of the pillars in her hallway,

'Why did you come here?'

He tried to shake himself away from the memory of just a few hours ago.

'Not for me sir! For our friend.'

'We've an army of head doctors and profilers on the case Martin.'

'Well, get me the best one.'

'Whatever for?' Stannheim asked, his interest audibly rising.

'Because I want to ask him a question.'

'Which is?'

'Why does he want to talk directly to me?'

The beer glass almost slipped through Stannheim's fingers.

'Are you taking the piss?'

Peters shook his head and lay back on his chair.

'Martin if he speaks to you then you must speak to me.'

'He seems to have moved his affections from Heike onto me and I think for a reason.'

He noticed that Stannheim said nothing in reply.

'I don't know what that is but it might be worth talking to someone about why he enjoys chatting so much.'

Stannheim lit up and then did his pointing act again in Peters' direction.

'Martin, every call, every chat you have I want to hear about it. Do you understand? There can't be any solo runs here.'

'So you will recommend a head fucker then?'

'Of course but you and I will keep a close eye and ear on your conversations?'

Peters finally played his hand.

'I thought someone was already watching over us, someone from the BND maybe?'

'What do you mean by "us"?' Stannheim interjected.

'Heike and I. She got a visit and so did I. And do you know what our spook chum told her?'

The old man shook his head and returned to his beer. Peters detected that the atmospheric pressure inside 'Anna's' had suddenly altered. Now the weight of interrogation was bearing down on Stannheim.

'No answer to that, sir? Not going to enlighten me as to why the BND think I'm off the "Christopher" case?' against his better self, Peters was revelling in the role reversal.

'I wouldn't want to think that my commanding officer would bend the knee to the BND and replace his SIO. Is that what's happening here, sir? Are you suffering from amnesia?'

Across the table Stannheim twisted in his seat, fumbled with a set of keys and supped at his Pils. Peters hoped his boss was like him, rewinding in his mind their greatest hits together. The pimp that bashed a Natasha's brains out. The father who came back from a weekend break on the Baltic coast to inform the Kottbusser team that he had found his wife and child with their throats slit in their apartment and who neither Peters nor Stannheim believed for a minute. The dentist who faked his mistress' suicide in a fume filled car. The nurse who was convinced she was sending her tiny little charges to heaven with a single jag each inside a hospital's paediatric wing. All of them safely locked away from doing anyone else harm. All of them behind bars in large part due to the deep intuition and innate probing qualities of Mannfred Stannheim.

Very well Manny, Peters thought. *Just keep up this silent, wounded act. Two can play at theatrics.*

Out loud Peters hissed: 'Don't let nearly ten years of loyalty at your side count for nothing now.'

With that the Englishman stood up, drained his beer glass and marched out of the pub, Stannheim following desperately in his wake without settling up their bill at the bar.

'Thank God for the rain,' Peters cried out as he shot across the street trying to elude the gaggle of reporters around the front steps of Kottbusser Strasse station.

Once inside HQ, Stannheim grabbed Peters' arm and held his favourite officer, his unofficial successor, his chosen one back in the hallway.

'I'm doing it to protect you, you fucking idiot.'

'Protect me? What is there to protect?'

Stannheim let go off Peters and made a shape with his right hand like he was holding up an invisible object.

'They told me they have a file on you that thick. Do you know what they call you?'

'And I thought the Stasi had been dissolved?' Peters bit back through gritted teeth.

'Whoever they are they call you the "swinging detective". They know about your private life Martin, that club you frequent down in Steglitz, the married woman you knock off when she's supposed to be driving a taxi, the old dear who likes to tie young men up after the pub. Shall I go on?'

It was Peters turn again to feel the compression, he had been a fool and they had found out. He was about to hold one hand up in submission when the idea occurred to him to storm off towards the inquiry room and create a scene.

When he reached the office Peters was relieved that the majority of the murder squad had been slow to act on his orders to get out and trawl through Berlin. Just as he bounded towards his own desk Peters turned on his feels and pointed at Stannheim.

'Perhaps you can explain to our colleagues here why I'm being taken off the "Christopher" case. You give them a reason because you haven't the balls to give me one, a real one anyway.'

He retraced his steps out of the first floor office and back down the stairwell towards the front exit; Stannheim nodded to Angi to follow Peters outside.

Peters forced open the swing doors of the station with a boot and re-entered the freezing wet external world where the dwindling miserable band of journalists stood huddled together. He spotted the one from BZ who had given him, Stannheim and the minister such a rough ride at the first "Christopher" press conference earlier. The tabloid reporter forced his way through a gauntlet of photographers and cameramen towards Peters.

'Captain Peters. Maybe a few words on the progress of the "Christopher" investigation...or lack of it?' the hack asked.

'Why did you come here?' Peters kept saying into himself, the heat rising in the back of his neck, his internal cooling system, even in the stinging icy rain, failing him.

'Why did you come here?'

He glared at his tabloid tormentor: 'No comment, not to you anyway.'

The journalist backed away towards the rest of the pack.

Angi tore through the doors and almost slipped on the steps, those purple stilettos scraping on the slimy surface.

'Martin!' she shouted breaking the conventions of rank and order.

Peters stood rooted to the spot where he had been facing the reporter.

'I may be off the case, Angi but it's still Captain Peters,' he reminded her and then felt instantly guilty for saying so.

'What the hell is going on?' she asked.

Peters pointed over towards the huddle of reporters.

'You see that reptile in the middle there Angi?'

'Sure I do.'

'I want you to ring up BZ this afternoon and ask to speak to this gentleman.'

Angi stared at her boss as if he had lost his mind, Peters' sensed her incredulity.

'Heat flares, Angi, heat flares. Just call him up and let him know I'm off the "Christopher" case. Tell him I'm spending more time on headless horsemen.'

'Why sir?'

'Just do it. Trust me.'

He looked up and saw Stannheim poking his head through the swing doors.

'You better go. If you make the call make sure you do it in a public phone booth, try one of the railway stations. Don't use your mobile and do let him know I've been taken off "Christopher".'

Her expression meant she was none the wiser about what Peters was up to.

'Angi, I'm not sure what I'm doing. Heat flares. Heat flares,' he said peeling away from the pack surrounding the station and into another downpour wholly unprotected from the deluge falling on Berlin.

A couple of flashes lit up the battleship grey sky around Kottbusser Strasse; the photographers had turned their attentions from Peters to the head of the murder squad. Stannheim beckoned Angi back into the station refusing to answer questions to the reporters at the bottom of the steps.

'Never mind him. There's been another development. Come in and link up with Bauer. Those boys out there are going to love this one,'Stannheim said pointing towards the decreasing media circus camped outside his station. When he noted Angi's look of bewilderment, Stannheim adde, 'Just wait to you see what St.Christopher has got up to next!'

Thirty One

'There is only one honourable way out for you.
Now is the time to do the right thing.
You have no other choice.
Your secret life will soon be out.
You are not safe.
You will be tracked down and it will be slower and more excruciating than you can ever imagine.'

The machine beeped again.

'Pick up the phone.
Don't ignore this message.
Your acquaintances are all dead, you have no friends.
You cannot escape the wrath.
The final hours will crawl along in captivity.
And you will be begging for the end.'

Message three!

'Listen or you will follow them.
You are being given a chance to cut short the wrath.
You will not have to endure their fate.
Take the only option left for you.
If you don't you will suffer.'

Message four!

'Remember you and I have met before.
Don't forget your face is familiar to me.

I know all about you and your friends.

I know what you are.'

Oskar Beer was dangling from a make-shift noose inside the kitchen of his surprisingly large and tastefully decorated apartment down in Schoenberg, his tongue three times the normal size sticking out of his mouth, his neck broken, the smell of excreta reeking from his trousers. Angi noticed he was still wearing slippers on his feet. His steel rimmed glasses lay on the floor tiles, un-cracked and intact. She looked back towards where Bauer stood pressing his gloved forefinger onto the 'play' button of Beer's answer machine.

'There are twelve of them in total,' Bauer said, 'Each one in the same tone, he never changes, just keep's going on and on at Beer. I suppose that pervert just cracked in the end. You have to admire his persistence.'

In her mind Angi was shivering at the inevitable tabloid headlines, imagining their reaction to the news that the man who the Kottbusser Strasse murder squad had booted out of their station's cells and back to his home had killed himself less than 24 hours later. It had been Stannheim's decision, or least his order handed down by the press office and ultimately the minister. The force couldn't be seen to be housing a paedophile, not anymore at least... Beer had to go back because sooner or later someone would leak and then Bild and BZ would have a feeding frenzy.

Now they would have one anyway.

She searched around the kitchen and living room seeking out signs of sustenance that might have emboldened Beer to carry out this final act. There was nothing. Beer had simply flipped having been broken by the cold, ruthless, brutal authority of 'Christopher's' voice.

'This was his first virtual killing,' Angi said in near admiration, 'He talked him into this. As Captain Peters keeps saying "He never stops surprising us." Have you checked the number Bauer?' in the absence of Peters she was now, unofficially, in charge of the case.

'No, private number withheld. The techies are trying to trace it but I'm sure if they do it'll be another mobile that's probably in the river or the lake by now,' Bauer replied.

She flicked open her mobile and spooled down to Peters' number.

'Sir?'

Peters' voice crackled on the other side: 'Anything to report?'

He sounded as if he was in a bar somewhere.

'By the way, please don't talk to me about newspapers, Angi. Not on this line.'

Angi inhaled and exhaled slowly, for Peters' benefit.

'It's something bad, isn't it?' he asked.

'Yep but this time you're not to blame. I am standing in Oskar Beer's flat.'

'Where is Beer?'

'Hanging behind the kitchen door.'

'At least it wasn't in one of our cells,' *Peters was looking on the bright side* she thought.

'The boss made him leave. He had to be literally dragged kicking and squealing out of the cell and bundled into a taxi.'

'You said 'hanging'?'

'Yes, he hung himself. There was no sign of any forced entry. In fact, he had just got new locks fitted that day.'

'Well who is going to care that some paedo has topped himself?'

'There's more sir. Twelve messages on Beer's answer machine. All of them from "Christopher". He talked Beer into doing it. I'm certain of that.'

'Angi, I'm almost glad to be semi-detached from all of this. Don't forget the other thing I asked.'

'I'll call later sir. Anything else?'

'Yeah. Tell the boss I was asking after him.'

She wanted to say 'you're enjoying this' but resisted allowing Peters to go back to whatever he was doing, whoever he was with.

The uniforms had pulled Beer's flat apart, the techies had commandeered his computer and boxes of unmarked DVDs, the forensics dabbing the doors and handles. But no sign of breaking and entry; no evidence, after several hours of trawling through his hard drive and his collection of discs, of anything illegal. Beer had hidden his 'hobby" well, Angi ordered the green coats to start tearing up the floor boards.

Sweat was pumping from Bauer's forehead when he returned to the kitchen after climbing upstairs to interview the Turkish family living above. Angi feared he was about to have a heart attack.

'No one heard a thing. Except of course for the constant phone calls. The man of the house said they went on for a couple of hours through the night. He kept whingeing about having to get up and go to work.....as if,' Bauer said with barely veiled contempt. Angi ignored his jibe against the Turks above them.

'Bauer just get him cut down,' she said pointing to the corpse.

'And get him over to the morgue. I'll see you back in the station.'

'How is Captain Peters?' Bauer inquired.

'I wouldn't know,' she would give nothing away to him; 'He does his own thing.'

She had long straight bottled blonde hair, plump with pendular breasts and a belly that hung over and partially obscured a PVC thong. Her age, confidence and the way she smoked using a black shiny cigarette holder streaked with gold leaf gave her an air of seniority over the diffident younger girls, some still in their teens, who were dotted all around the bar of the first floor of 'Haus Ivana.'

When Peters first came into the knocking shop on this wet and windy afternoon she had made her way straight to him, warding off the skinny, fresh faced whores all desperate to bring in business at such a quiet time of the day.

At first Peters assumed she was the madam, at least until she told him her name was Irina and that she cost €80 for one hour although he would have to pay for any drinks they might share. He had been expecting to be ejected immediately on entering the seven storey brothel. The gold teethed, scarred bouncers reminded him of the men he had encountered in the Grunewald as well the crombie coated praetorian guard surrounding Avi Yanaev. Instead he paid the €10 entrance fee and took the lift to floor one clutching the club's glossy guide with descriptions of what was on offer on each storey: floor one was the straight option, suck and fuck with the girl or girls of your choice leading up to tier five and the S&M dungeon all the way to the top and the TS and TV booths which ranged from the cross dressers acting out their fantasies for money to the fully snipped, clipped, re-designed and transformed.

'Irina' put her plump bejewelled hands into his and pulled him towards 'her' room, entering via a multi-coloured series of vertical strips that revealed a mattress covered by black silk sheets, a couple of red fluffy pillows, a video screen above the opposite wall showing a lesbian orgy and to the right of the entrance a self-enclosed shower. A table beside the window overlooking the quiet suburban street in Dahlem contained an array of lubricants, boxes of condoms, vibrators, butt plugs and an ashtray.

Peters stripped down to his waist and reached into his pockets until he found a wad of fifty euro notes which he held up to 'Irina's' face.

'You won't even have to lie on your back to earn all this love,' he told her.

Her eyes lit up but the expression on her face was one of dread.

'If it's pain you are after darling perhaps you need floor five....but that would be a pity.'

He smiled at her: 'Look no offence I don't want to fuck you. I just need your help and I'll make it really worth your while.'

In her broken German she suddenly sounded filled with panic.

'You're a cop aren't you? Trust my fucking luck.'

'No, no, I'm a private investigator. I've been given a job to find a couple of missing persons for their families and I'm willing to pay,' he lied to re-assure her.

She started to massage Peters' exposed torso, this 'Irina' actually fancied her first client of the day. He leaned back his head while she rubbed his shoulders and kissed her deeply. Then releasing himself from the clinch, he laid out his offer: 'Look babe you can have two hundred now and two hundred when we see each other outside.'

Whispering in his ear she gave him the name of a nearby bar the girls often went to after their shifts.

'You sure you don't want to fuck Irina darling?' she said licking the edges of his earlobes.

'I'd love to but not now babe,' he lied again, 'I'll meet you in that place in 20 minutes.'

The pub around the corner from 'Haus Ivana' was run by two withered trannies, one of whom was dressed as Dolly Parton, the other with pig tails and red dog tooth patterned dress was making a last gasp stab at Dorothy from Kansas including a real yappy Toto look-a-like dog lapping up a saucer of water on the bar top. On entering Dolly greeted him with a 'Guten Abend' while Dorothy raised her glass in salute and smiled. The boozer was virtually empty barring two off-duty teenage hookers, smack heads who mercifully ignored his entrance and maintained their bitching about some fellow sex workers operating in the 'Haus' from where they were now barred from working. Peters ordered a Pils and sat down at a table near a window overlooking the street with a view to the door.

Blucher had guided him towards the knocking shop, passing on a hint from his daily chess opponent, that anyone interested in the headless horsemen from the Havel should first talk to 'Irina.' She was the veteran of the second Russian invasion of Berlin, the one launched just months after the Wall came down when the Red Army got ready to ride back east and the mafia started to move into the new reunified metropolis, into Europe's New York. During their brief exchange inside the bar of the Marriot, Blucher had hinted that the de-capitated duo had paid 'Irina' and her co-workers a recent visit.

She arrived shivering despite her fur coat, her huge tits still semi-exposed through her see through red chiffon dress, smoking from her black and gold holder, one hand on her hip. Peters ordered her a brandy, stood up and pulled a chair out of the table beckoning for her to sit down on. *The ersatz English gentlemen.* Blucher would have been appalled! Despite the bo-ho owners the bar's background music was classic, cheesy German volksmusik, all red roses and romance by the Rhein, hardly the Berlin sound of Romi Haag, Bowie, Iggy and the echoes of the 'city's ripped backed sides.'

Peters guessed that 'Irina' was the source of all of Blucher's chess chum's gossip. Her nervous demeanour, her furtive glances towards the doors and windows, confirmed his suspicions.

'There's four hundred Euros in this for you,' Peters said raising his beer glass towards her.

'Are you sure you're not a cop?' Irina inquired lighting up.

'As I keep saying – I'm working for the families of two men who haven't been seen since they came to Berlin a couple of months ago.'

'So what darling?' she shrugged her shoulders and waved towards 'Dorothy' behind the bar who started pouring another large glass of brandy.

'Alright. Here's what I know,' Peters said folding his arms and leaving back in his chair.

'Two Spanish guys came into your place a couple of week ago. Some of the girls remembered them because they were tall, handsome, a bit off-beat. One of them chose one of the older women on duty. Spent a lot of money and time with her,' he said repeating what Blucher had told him.

Peters' words seemed to make her pleased with herself.

'I might be getting on but I can still pull the good looking ones into my booth,' Irina said proudly.

As she sucked on brandy soaked ice cubs like a child slurping a Slush Puppy, Peters probed further.

'I'm sure you pulled the good looking Spanish boy who came to see you.'

She smiled at the mock compliment and then corrected Peters.

'Good looking Spanish boys darling. I had the two of them,' she said shuffling in her chair like a peacock.

'Now why doesn't that surprise me Irina, but tell me did they come alone or with friends.'

'I wouldn't say friends darling. They were Russian boys, mean looking bastards, they had just completed business and as you must know, there are no friends in business. Any business, even mine.

'How do you know that? How do you they had just done business.'

'Because one of the Spanish boys told me.'

He slid the remaining €200 euro across the table towards Irina.

'There's more here if you can remember when and who they worked for.'

She was sucking on her holder now, her mouth stinging from ice to heat, blowing slow draughts of smoke out of her collagen pumped up lips towards the nicotine stained walls, the twee strains of a Volks-crooner blaring from a radio at the bar.

'Oh darling one day just melts into another, it must have been sometime after Christmas because we still had the tree up, but I do know who those Russian boys worked for.'

'Who Irina?' he asked again already knowing what the answer was.

'The Jew. The one living down in Kopenick.'

'You mean the Russian. Avi Yanaev?'

'No the Jew. I mean yes, Yanaev.'

'And these Spanish boys where did they go afterwards? Did they ever come back?'

'Unfortunately no. And they didn't leave their address or email or mobile either darling unlike most of my gentlemen,' she said with un-menacing sarcasm.

'Did they say which part of Spain they came from Irina?'

'What is this a geography lesson?' she was losing patience with him, nodding in the direction of 'Dolly Parton' to send her down another brandy. She was obviously a regular in this particular pit stop.

He dropped an extra €50 onto the table when her drinks arrived and winked at 'Dorothy' who seemed to enjoy playing waitress to him.

'Please accept this apology,' he said nodding down to the note which Irina picked up nimbly placed into the inside pocket of her fur coat.

'But can you remember if they said where they were from?' he continued.

She threw back her head, tossed her hair about and then leaned towards him. It was a simple command, asking him to re-light her a fresh cigarette which she placed in the holder.

'Funny you say 'Spain' though,' Irina said inhaling some smoke.

'When I asked which part of 'Spain' they were from one of the guys lost it. He kept hammering one hand into the other telling me they weren't Spanish. Then the two of them started yammering in this weird language which definitely wasn't Spanish.'

'How would you know that?'

'Because darling I've been selling my pussy for the last ten years in that place around the corner to buy that little dream home on the Costa del Sol. Which I now own. You have to have the native lingo to work. If you ever fancy a weekend down there by the way I can pick you up at Malaga airport no problem....so long as you are paying.'

'Where did your boys go after their session was over?' Peters asked.

'Back to their hotel I assume. One thing I do remember, ' she re-lit the cigarette at the end of the holder, 'One thing I do remember is that they didn't drink. Unlike most of the guys who you meet in there they were completely sober. Nice clean breaths. I remember mentioning that to them after we finished and they were getting dressed.'

'They really made their mark on your Irina. Did you wonder why they stayed off the sauce?'

'I didn't need to; they said they had an early start.'

'Start?'

'Yeah, they had to go to Magdeburg first thing the next day.'

'Magdeburg?'

'Yeah, Magdeburg. Can't think why they'd have to go to a place like that.'

'Me neither, Irina, me neither.'

He was getting closer to Yanaev now that he knew for certain the two Basques' last pleasure on earth was enjoyed courtesy of the Russian's hospitality and Irina's hard work. A shudder of guilt and repulsion shot through his body as he suddenly saw in his imagination Irina lying face down in a pool underneath the crushing Andalusian sun with her throat slashed.

Touching her cheek lightly as he stood up to leave Peters whispered into her ear: 'Whatever you do Irina tell absolutely no one you went for a drink with me.'

Thirty Two

A Lutheran Pastor, a hero of the peaceful revolution of 89, someone who had given shelter and later hope to the dissenters in those first fledgling months of protest, had been transformed into a target for national hatred and ridicule. On the front page of 'BZ' the following morning the priest's public appeal for mercy to 'Christopher' had spectacularly backfired.

'PASTOR PLEAS FOR CAPTIVE PAEDO' the headline screamed back at Peters and it was then that he knew for sure that Albert Briegel was truly doomed, just like all the others. To the side of the main story ran a single column reporting on an overnight telephone poll taken across the capital which indicated that 85 per cent of those questioned opposed his call for clemency for the self-confessed paederast. The Pastor's plea had been mere camouflage to disguise the paper's real feral agenda, to let the mob howl, to hear them cry for blood. The 'splash' ended with news that the clergy-man was already receiving hate-emails and threatening phone calls.

Peters flicked through the first few pages of the tabloid which were dominated by 'Christopher's Wrath,' searching for references to himself. He eventually found one on page five, tucked away in a single column to the bottom left, a nameless snippet of information consisting of just six staccato paragraphs, informing the world that the English detective was no longer on the case. He had hoped, almost prayed, that 'Christopher' was a thorough reader and would spot the story.

In the commercial centre of Friedrichstrasse Station, at an Imbiss stand, Peters sipped at an espresso, scanning 'BZ' and waiting for Irit Wisemann to join him before he took the 9.30am to Magdeburg.

For several hours after he left 'Haus Ivana' the day before Peters had stayed at home banging the phones, using his contact books to track anyone who might be able to help him in the Magdeburg Polizie. Eventually he put a call into a Lieutenant Fischer who was currently investigating a fatal shooting in the centre of the city shortly after Christmas. There had been one victim, a Russian hit by a hail of bullets from a car speeding out a pub car park on the banks of the Elbe. Suspended by Stannheim from 'Christopher', Peters would spend the next day in the capital of Saxony-Anhalt with Fischer.

He thought how dowdy and grey the commuters seemed compared to the tall, slender, Israeli that was emerging from the crowds in the station, her straight sleek hair, her severely cut, figure hugging green tweed business suit that made her stand out amid the monochrome blur. Peters ordered another cup of espresso and gestured for her to come over and join him at the booth.

Wisemann noticed that Peters hadn't shaved for days.

'You look like one of our Zealots Martin. You wouldn't seem out of place in Hebron and it really doesn't suit you,' she said raising her cup and sipping at the steaming coffee shot.

'You been doing some undercover work then? 'she continued.

Irit had sent him a text late the previous evening, simply mentioning 'something urgent to discuss.' He suggested they meet early next day before he took the train west.

In his duffel coat, white polar neck and four-day growth he must have appeared to her like an off duty sailor.

'I'm trying to hide from the general public Irit,' he said feeling a twinge of discomfort that he had actually sounded and felt temporarily like the misanthropic Lothar Blucher. 'Mothers Against Paedophiles could get militant. They don't like the idea of us hunting down their hero.'

She leaned her face against one hand and stared hard at the detective.

'Martin I need to tell you a few things about Avi Yanaev.'

Peters felt his stomach lurch as if he was on a plane pitched about by violent turbulence. He was expecting the worst from Irit, a hands-off warning over 'their' Russian asset.

'Yanaev, through third parties of course, owns a whore house in Dahlem...'

'Seven storeys high, a different kink on every floor,' Peters interrupted her.

'Well Martin, what you don't know is that the place is hiving with bugs,' Peters almost choked on the sticky thick liquid he had just swallowed.

'How do you know this?'

'There was an Arab diplomat based here in Berlin, a senior Arab diplomat. They got him on film having fun on floor seven where the transvestites and transsexuals ply their trade. Which would have been fatal for him if pictures of that started appearing all over the Internet especially in the Middle East.'

Peters decided to ask a stupid question for which he knew there would be no direct, open answer:

'And how I wonder did you know that Irit? Did your friend Avi tell you?'

She rested her head on both her hands, her elbows depressing on the metallic table.

'We got to hear what they tried to extract from the Arab gentleman and it certainly wasn't money'.

'Not money. What else would they be blackmailing him for?'

'Yanev doesn't need money but he does need friends and connections. Next time you get an invite, if you ever do again, to one of his charity functions work out how many local TV celebs and Bundesliga stars have shown up, all of course being aficionados of "Haus Ivana." He seeks out future favours in return for his silence. Turning up for free to one of his gigs is one of them.'

'So they just wanted your Arab to turn up in a tuxedo for a thousand plate euro feast?' Peters said with a taint of sarcasm..

'In his case no. We were able to find out exactly what Yanaev wanted, it was help in business. Diplomatic bags, private jets, boats, free unchecked access to ports in the Middle East. It was a very long list.'

So Yanaev hadn't been working for Irit and her station at all. He was prepared rather to turn to their mortal enemies to smooth along the passage of his lethal commerce.

'Arms routes. No wonder everyone takes such an interest in him. Tell me this Irit why didn't your people breathe down his neck instead of inviting him to a film festival?'

Another stupid question he left for her to field but this time she appeared to read Peters' game.

'There's only so much I can tell you Martin,' she said checking her watch with the giant clock suspended over the escalator leading to the platforms above them.

'You draw your own conclusions.'

'What happened to our Arab friend then?' He asked as she prepared to leave. Irit shook her hair and lifted her handbag off the table.

'I don't have time for any more of this Martin. Just think about it. Yanaev deals in death. He has no compulsion about dealing it out. As for our Arab friend, since you asked, he was suddenly recalled.'

'Why are you in such a hurry too?' he said checking his own watch.

'I'm off to Schoenefeld Airport. My beloved is back,' she said playfully.

Peters tried not to appear too disappointed that her husband had once again returned from wherever in the Middle East he was acting out his ordained part, his proposal for dinner on his return now redundant.

'One more thing Irit? Why didn't your people lean on Yanaev? Get him work for you?'

'That is a trick question .Let's just say Herr Yanaev is better observed from afar,' she parted blowing a kiss in Peter's direction.

On the regional train towards Magdeburg winter had refused to lessen its grip over the North German Plain. Along the journey westward flat, tilled fields and forests of bare trees were sprinkled and gleaming with frost. Early morning commuters at a line of shabby little stations shivered in the cold as snow blessed the platforms they waited along with thick, soot-polluted flakes. Amid the towns and cities of north-eastern Germany that appeared and then disappeared on the rail journey from Berlin to Magdeburg there were no signs, for now at least, even after 15 years of reunification, of Helmut Kohl's promise to transform the former communist east into 'blooming landscapes.' Instead at almost every human settlement, village, town or city, there were brown and red brick, smoke stack factories lying idle, their windows smashed, their desolate locations epitomising not only the collapse of the old planned economy but also the aftermath of the ruthless free market that came and shut them down. The bleakness beyond the glass, both natural and man-made, only compounded Peters' sense of total disconnection. He caught sight of himself in the window, a gaunt spectral apparition with a shadow slashed across the eye sockets, like the Lone Ranger's mask, a visage permanently stencilled over the passing landscape of the Brandenburg Mark.

He had chosen a carriage in the upper deck of the two storey regional express because it was empty. And also because if the mobile trilled Peters would feel safer and more comfortable taking to his quarry if 'Christopher' chose to call in during the journey. But how long would it take for 'Christopher' to react to the news that the English detective was off his case? And why would he bother? For he could move as quickly, ruthlessly away from him just as he had done with Heike. Maybe it was better to forget about 'Christopher' entirely....at least for now.

The trajectory across the flattened, bleak Prussian plain was familiar to him. He had come here first in the year before the DDR's collapse, on the special British military train that was rolled out of its toy box as a show-off trophy to annoy the 'beastie easties' monitoring military traffic on route to west Berlin. Peters recalled a sumptuous lunch in the officer's dining car, thick linen laid tables, gleaming regimental silver, privates-turned-waiters in red jackets and white gloves delivering the five course lunch, thick studded crystal glasses filled with sharp Sauvignon Blanc and robust Burgundy, all raised up in salute at chosen strategic locations in polite defiance towards the East German military along the checkpoints and watchtowers from Magdeburg to Potsdam while, further down the train, boozed up squaddies reserved their own salute for the People's Army by mooning up at their windows for the benefit of the NVA photographers outside the bubble of British mobile opulence and civility, two-finger salutes towards the dank, drab uniformity of the DDR. Somewhere in the scattered archives of the defunct East German army, Peters guessed, maybe even in a private collection of a retired NCO living in Brandenburg, there was a mountain of exposed hairy British arses.

He had once travelled back in the opposite direction, alone, furtive, concealed in civilian dress, posing as a student inter-railer towards his current destination, that first encounter with his general he would eventually send across the Iron Curtain before the Ministry for State Security closed in on him. Peters wondered if his old contact had ever opted to move back to his home city after the Wall came down. Even if the general had returned how to look him up now? They had given him a new identity faraway in Saarland, in a village within walking distance of France, the top half of a house overlooking a series of allotments and a tributary of the Saar in return for files on Soviet military manoeuvres and that warning of a Tiananmen in the middle of Europe that never actually came. Why would the general ever go back to this depressed eastern region of reunified Germany? Yet Peters wished that one day, when all this was over, he would take time off in pursuit of his former charge and when they found each other they would sip wine together and forget about the old times.

Maybe Stannheim kept in touch with the general to remind himself of past glories. The old man's network had been deployed rapidly to smuggle the general out as the Stasi's focus fell upon Peters' source. Stannheim had arranged safe passage for the general through Hungary in the year when Budapest lifted its border controls and the first holes in the Iron Curtain were punched open. To this day the boss of the Kottbusser Strasse murder squad had never spoken about the mechanics of moving the general out of the DDR. All Peters had to do was turn up with a team in a certain hotel on the Pest side of the Danube and wait to shepherd their charge to the airport, a picture-less UK passport at the ready, a flight to Frankfurt Main booked under the name Goodacre and the general spirited to a military intelligence de-briefing centre near

Falingbostel. His greatest triumph in the corps while living on the Cold War front line.

Then it struck Peters: The general, Yanaev, 'Christopher,' even Stannheim. He was hunting down all his history's cast-offs, swimming in its backwash, searching for the remains of the un-dead armies of his war gone by.

Thirty Three

Fischer's self-description had been as modest as it was accurate. He was small for a cop, bald-headed, pot-bellied, a greying goatee, more like an over-fed Federal civil servant than a murder detective – his own words.

He had been waiting for Peters at the entrance to the Magdeburg Hauptbanhof, the front passenger door of a green Audi left open. Peters noticed that the man in the dark green three quarter length coat was stamping the ground to keep warm.

'Welcome to Magdeburg Captain Peters! Let's do lunch,' Fischer said outstretching his hand. He even sounded like a state bureaucrat. Peters was tempted to shoot back: 'Malzeit!'

'Shouldn't we talk about your case first Lieutenant?'

'We are going to the case Captain,' Fishcher said jovially slapping on Peters' left shoulder.

'Please get in and I'll explain on the way.'

They crossed the Elbe and followed the course of the river towards that part of the old city relatively untouched by the RAF air raids during the war or the Stalinist reconstruction of the DDR years. Fischer kept entirely silent through the short drive to an old fashioned inn with a walled garden close to the waterside.

'We'll eat and then talk Captain,' Fischer pointed to the gravelled driveway as they arrived, 'Here be the scene of the crime.'

Inside, the pub was decorated with hunting portraits, the heads of stuffed dear, horns, ancient rusting muskets, shelves with lines of Steins and brass pots. There were several bored looking elderly waitresses in white shirts and black waist coats standing about at each end of a long mahogany coloured bar behind which stood a tall man with a handlebar moustache washing and polishing beer glasses. On seeing Fischer, he bowed over towards the two detectives and then called one of his staff to attend to the only guests inside. They were ushered towards a snug near a roaring fire, two menu cards dropped onto their table and drinks ordered.

After their beers arrived and their glasses tinkled together Fischer did finally explain.

'The shooting took place outside. I thought it would be best to go straight here. Our friend over there saw most of it. We'll get a chat with him once we've eaten.'

'You sure these guys were Russian?' Peters inquired.

Fischer licked the froth which has been twisted into the shape of an ice cream dollop off the top of his glass.

'No, but he's sure.'

'Why?'

'Because Captain Peters they spoke the language they all grew up with over here. It was compulsory to learn Russian...even for future barmen. He was certain they were Russian. Well, all except for two of the party.'

'I know a bit of Russian myself. What do you mean by a party?'

'Yes Captain, a party of them. Three or four Ruskies and two other guys. Now let's eat.'

Once they had polished off their pig and stodge lunch and downed several more Pils, the two detectives went to the bar.

'This is Herr Karsten, Captain. He was here the day the party got out of hand,' Fishcer said introducing the barman with a sweep of his hand.

Karsten poured out three shots of schnapps and knocked back his in an instant.

Peters flicked open a palm sized pad he had taken from the inside of his coat and started to take notes.

'Sir, I wonder could you tell me about the other men? The ones you didn't think were Russian,' Peters asked licking the tip of the pencil and fiddling it around the inside of his mouth.

'They weren't Russian that's for sure. One of them could speak German but the other only talked in this weird language.'

'Spanish?'

'No. I know a little Spanish. We go to Ibiza every year. It was something completely different, nothing I had ever heard before.'

'So then what happened?' Peters went on.

The barman filled up the three shot glasses again before answering.

'Things got a little out of hand; they were arguing and shouting with one another. Then the fists started flying, the "others" were getting the shit kicked out of them but managed to run to the door. The Russians went off after them and the next thing I heard was boom-boom, a car's wheels screeching and I go outside and there's one of the Russkies lying bleeding all over our car park.'

'Did you get any of what the Russians and the "others" were saying to each other? Before things started up,' Peters asked.

Karsten again knocked back his Schnapps and judging from his breath Peters gathered that the barman had been shoring up his day with several early snifters even before he and Fischer arrived.

'What am I a translator?' Karsten complained before slamming down the shot glass.

Fischer face hardened and he leaned across the bar top until he was within an inch of Karsten's.

'Just tell our English friend here what the Russians told their guests and stop wasting our time.'

'What is there to tell? I heard one of them say "the price has gone up....pay that or you don't get the merchandise." Who were these low lives by the way? Drug dealers?'

'Wrong product Karsten,' Peters interrupted, 'Try arms. By the way, you just keep that to yourself Herr Karsten. I mean, if I was you, I wouldn't want to draw any more negative publicity down on this lovely hostelry.'

Peters felt Fischer's elbow colliding with his arm.

'Ok Herr Karsten thanks your co-operation,' Peters smiled weakly as Fischer paid the bill.

Driving back over the Elbe Fischer was more candid behind the wheel this time.

'Would you believe that that guy had the cheek to ask me to put pressure on to keep his pub's name out of the press? A fucking cheek.'

'Why?' Peters said jotting a few more points down in his notebook.

'A cheek because that place attracts a right motley crew. Russian criminals. Fucking neo-Nazis. Bikers. Football thugs. He whined about having no other clientele, what with being on the wrong side of the river. My guess is that he knew the Russians. Regular customers probably on first name terms but he can't afford to piss them off. Would piss himself with fear if we wheeled him and tried to get him to name a few of them.'

'Well why don't you do just that?'

Fischer didn't reply but instead drove northward out of the city centre, out towards the grim suburbs and beyond to the rural hinterland before taking a B-road through a forest until they came to a small lake with a boating house. Peters guessed that Fischer would feel more comfortable talking candidly in this location.

The two detectives got out and sauntered over to the lake edge, Peters lifted a flat stone and sent it skimming across the surface of the water.

'Karsten's an untouchable,' Fischer shouted unprompted, unprovoked.

Peters knew where this was going, but re-started the questioning anyway.

'We didn't drive for nearly 20 minutes just to get some fresh country air Fischer. Why is he an untouchable?'

Fischer nodded his head slowly to assuage Peters' impatience.

'Just after the shooting my boss called me in and introduced me to this young arrogant fucker who starts to tell me that we can't be hassling Karsten. So I says "What's so special about this glass washer and pint puller?" And this asshole in his "Boss" suit tells me it's an issue of national security. Which I assumed meant that Karsten was an earwig for the spooks at the BND. Which is funny because I checked his file and Herr Karsten is "Gauck Positive." He was a Stasi snitch in DDR times. So anything he's got to say, anything really deep, about his Russian punters goes straight to the BND.'

It was only then that Peters detected from his distinctive accent that Fischer was a Saarlander, yet another 'wessie' who had crossed over from the west after the Turn, possibly, no probably, to train up, to de-contaminate his detective unit of all traces of Stasi taint. Peters felt guilty that he had on first meet suspected that Fischer might have been Stasi. And everywhere Peters turned, in each corner of the two cases, there was the security service minding their sources, closing down entry points, watching their rear. He knew all this because it had once been his job, to obscure, to confuse, to conjure up legends, to protect, at all costs his assets.

'We have something in common Lieutenant. My boss likes to refer up too. Seems we're both being stymied. But don't worry, Karsten might be out of bounds because he's working for the snoopers but I have enough to keep me going.'

'You sure about that? I wish I could help more otherwise I've just got another unsolved Russian mafia hit on my books,' Fischer said apologetically.

'At least we both know now that my headless horsemen were knocked off over some arms deal gone wrong. It sorta confirms a few things I've already suspected.'

'I don't need to ask Captain. You wanna go somewhere for another beer?'

'Why not, as long you're buying, I'm not off to Berlin until tea time. Tell me this, if Karsten is working for BND then he must have known all this is connected to arms deals?'

The Magdeburg detective got back into the Audi before replying.

'Maybe he did, maybe he didn't. But he isn't forwarding any names of his regular clients. I suppose he keeps that for his other bosses.'

Which makes one of them yet another source for the spooks, Peters thought but was reluctant to speak out loud.

They drove back towards the Alstadt, all the way Fischer bitching about his bosses and their craven attitude when the BND started calling. Most of all he complained about Karsten and vowed a lifelong mission to find something, anything that would lead to the closure of his business. As they cut across tram lines in the Audi

Peters' mobile bleeped in the top corner of his pocket. There was a message from Heike Numann.

'Hurry back from the weeds. He's back on the job!'

At the station entrance he shook Fischer's hand, promised, or rather lied, that he would pass on anything he picked up from his headless horsemen from the Havel inquiry back in Berlin. On the train on the way back Peters noticed that every table on either deck had been covered with free-sheet coloured newspapers, all of them dedicated to Christopher's Wrath, the headline recording the public vote on the fate of the paedophile Briegel, an overwhelming majority rejecting pleas for mercy.

Thirty Four

To: heike.numann@wams.de
Subject: a parting gift
Triangulation! Isn't that what your 'sources' call it? To trap a killer who likes to talk on the phone or chat in cyberspace you use triangulation. Track the patterns of the calls and emails, use the latest satellite technology, build the links between messages until you pin point where your quarry is moving? They did well down in Kottbusser Strasse to keep my photo-fit out of the papers. Yes, I know that Beer gave them a good description and that your dashing English detective has been circulating it quietly around the city. So the swords are approaching fraulein and it's time for us to say goodbye...although not forever.

To: chriswrath74@yahoo.com
Subject: re: a parting gift
What do you mean by 'not forever?'

To: heike.numann@wams.de
Subject: re: re: a parting gift
There's that lack of patience again! I won't abandon you fraulein. I chose you for a reason. Just keep faith.

To: chriswrath74@yahoo.com
Subject: re: re: re: a parting gift
I didn't know they had your image.

To: heike.numann@wams.de
Subject: re: re: re: re: a parting gift
I'll let you work that one out. I'm probably more likely to be recognised by one of my fan club. Imagine that! Being caught while being mobbed in the street. But I digress. Do you want to know what my

parting gift to you shall be?

To: chriswrath74@yahoo.com
Subject: re: re: re: re: re: a parting gift
I can hardly wait especially after the last few.

To: heike.numann@wams.de
Subject: re: re: re: re: re: re: a parting gift
You shall find it at 22 b St. Moritzer Platz. That's not far from the west end, further up off the Ku'damm. And do bring a friend.

To: chriswrath74@yahoo.com
Subject: PS...
Why the '74'?

To: heike.numann@wams.de
Subject: re: PS....
Why '74'? Don't you know it was our finest year?

Heike not only heard but felt the faint jets of breath from Martin Peters' nostrils as he leaned tightly over her shoulder while still maintaining a slither of air between their two bodies. Without a word between them they knew that the latest communiqué was meant for them both.

Peters tried to resist a desire to wrap his arms around her, a temptation made all the worse by the expression of exhausted doom on her face. He yearned to stroke her skin softly, but Peters knew he could never make it right any more.

'You're not going to stop me going there even though part of me almost wishes you would,' she said coldly without lifting her eyes from the lap top screen.

Her remark forced him backwards on his feet, further away from her, out of touching distance, adrift.

'Heike,' he used her name apologetically. 'Heike. I have to call in the whole team on this one. We can't afford to be walking into another bomb. I know that street and it's tightly packed. We have got to evacuate it.'

She still had her back to him, re-reading those clipped, teasing sentences in front of her.

'As long I tag along I don't care if you call in the entire British Army on the Rhine Martin. How was your trip to sunny Magdeburg by the way?'

'Useful.'

'Useful for what? This case?'

'No, the other one. The headless horsemen from the Havel. Maybe when you get away from him you can go there yourself. I'll come with you.'

'How romantic! You want to whisk me away to Magdeburg. Is it because you are jealous of "him"?'

'No, I'm just jealous that he's stopped talking to me,' he replied pithily.

She swivelled around in her chair to face Peters and smiled.

'Martin, we could sit here all day and discuss our one to one relationships with a multiple murderer but isn't it time you called in the cavalry?'

Peters looked at the digital alarm clock to the side of Heike's computer. 11pm. Not a great time to be emptying a street of its residents and cordoning it off. He would ask Stannheim to give the order for a dawn raid. Whoever was inside the flat would probably already be dead.

'We'll move in at first light Heike. You can come over on your own. No snappers though. Ok?'

Heike nodded and got up to hug Peters, which astounded him although the embrace was loose, semi-formal, weak, a signal he would still sleep alone if he slept at all. Instead he decided to stay up and resist the lassitude tugging at his consciousness. He would find an all-night Kniepe and sit among his fellow insomniacs waiting for that time before the light breaks through the gloom, when the darkness is crumbling and the air gets chillier in a last act of nocturnal defiance against the emerging sun.

He found shelter in a pub near the Landwehr canal close enough to walk back to Kottbusser Strasse and sat for over an hour with a 'Kindl' working out in his head how to worm his way back into the investigation. Officially, Stannheim had taken him off 'Christopher' so he could concentrate solely on Yanaev and the Basques. Yet Peters had found a way back into the 'Wrath', the 'parting gift', so kindly shared with him by Heike Numann. Peters pondered the balance of forces confronting him. Stannheim might have been spooked by the BND but only he and Heike had this channel to 'Christopher' and, perhaps if his latest tease to the reporter was genuine, the path to the terminus of his crusade.

Around half past four he was shaken from his torpor by a row at the bar between some grizzled vagrant and the young Polish barman who refused to serve him any more drink. Peters went over, flashed his ID and escorted the drunk out of the pub smoothing his exit with a ten euro note pressed into a filthy, calloused hand.

When he returned the Pole had placed a fresh beer on Peters' table. As he sat down Peters was suddenly gripped by panic. 'Christopher' knew about the photo-fit, that was why he had gone back to Beer. But neither he, Stannheim, the press office or anyone in the Berlin Polizei had authorised its release to the media. They had even ordered Bauer and his team only to show the photo-fit to the chosen few among the ex-Stasi and party people whom the Kottbusser Squad interviewed down in the deep east. No one was allowed to hand over a copy of the artist's impression. Now Peters started to wonder if Germany's favourite serial killer had someone on the inside.

Before dawn broke he was travelling in a taxi back through the west end passing street sweeping crews, the hard-core hookers who were just about to come off duty taking shelter in the doorways of the sex centres around the Zoo station, the last of the all night revellers staggering down the Ku'damm searching for that final elusive drink to tip them over into unconsciousness and thus avoid the avenging cruel clarity of the morning. Peters checked in the inside pocket of his Duffel to see if his Glock automatic was still there and not in the hands of one of the drunken and the desperate he had been surrounded by in the pub earlier. Bending over pretending to tie a lace, he slipped the weapon out of his coat and cocked it gingerly.

For someone who had been awarded 'flashes' for expert marksmanship, who had slept in barns with only a Heckler and Koch for companionship on stake-outs in damp dank corners of rural Ulster, who had fired point blank into the leather clad body of a pillion passenger of a motorbike murder team returning from a sectarian killing spree in Belfast, Peters had always hated carrying a firearm around Berlin. His success in the city had been through the force of his mind and power of his persuasion rather than the vulgar threat of cold steel. Each time he was instructed to be armed on an operation Peters felt as if he was once again betraying his beloved, adopted home.

He recalled his one and only encounter with death close up and how he had removed from the earth an assassin the British tabloids had branded 'The Angel of Death.' She was the other girl on a motor-cycle, a murderous Marianne Faithful, a visored avenging pin-up wet dream of the loyalist paramilitaries. Peters' undercover unit had been tracking her and her partner that Saturday morning a year before his transfer to Berlin. From the moment they had picked up the bike from a small lock-up garage on a housing estate at the foot of the Cavehill Mountain, to the 'safe house' in another grim housing project at the very bottom of the Shankill Road where she was given the Uzi to be used in a spray job on a bookmakers shop across the peace-line in republican Ardoyne.

To avoid suspicion Peters and the two other men who had tracked the duo while posing as a group of painter and decorators in a white van, drove their vehicle into a side street close to where the Shankill merges into the northern end of the city centre, discarded their overalls and jumped into a Ford Escort, he in the front passenger seat, elected by command back at Army headquarters to terminate the 'Angel's' career.

By the time they had switched vehicles and taken a parallel route up the Crumlin Road past the Victorian jail then bulging with republicans and loyalists, the 'Angel' was already at her work, emptying a full magazine load into the betting shop, sending punters to the floor, splattering blood onto the walls, filing the air with the acrid stench of cordite and hurling a series of shrill insults at the men she was mowing down.

Peters' car met the motorbike half-way down the Crumlin Road, the killers almost back in home territory. The driver, an SAS trained NCO veered the Ford violently to the left to block the bike's path, the machine skidding to a halt and throwing the passenger on the back up into the air.

After hitting the ground, she seemed frozen, paralytic, perhaps already dead. The bike rider was now being surrounded by Peters' two armed colleagues, his pleas that they 'don't shoot' already audible when he moved over towards the woman. The first thing he noticed about her was her slender frame. The leather jacket she had on tapered inwards towards her narrow, child-like waist. She had a small compact, perfectly formed body. Then he spotted her hand twitching, gliding slowly across tarmac and an pool of oozing engine oil, her heightened breathing an indication of some menacing intent, as she reached towards the Uzi lying on the road beside her. He fired three times: once in the throat, twice in her upper body until the twitching and the breathing finally stopped.

He hadn't spoke or thought about that bright autumn Saturday morning in Belfast nearly twenty years before for a very long time. At least not since the Gulf War. Certainly not since he re-settled back in Berlin after the 'Turn.' True, he had received some counselling in the weeks and months after that fatal encounter with Apollonia Winston, the Greek-Cypriot wife of a former police constable blown to smithereens in the first decade of the Troubles by an IRA remote control bomb. But instead of being the subject of media outcry and internal inquiry Peters found himself promoted from lieutenant to Captain and transferred to Berlin for other duties; his one and only 'wet job' had been a pig-in-the-middle propaganda coup, proof the army desk spooks later whispered to compliant journalists that the British Military didn't differentiate between either republican or loyalist terrorists. Until now on his way to whatever horror 'Christopher' had pre-prepared Peters realised he had entirely forgotten her name even though he could never escape from the unalterable fact that he had killed a woman.

Thirty Five

The stench penetrated plastic face masks, hanker-chiefs, hands over faces, clamped tight lips and attacked the vulnerable membranes of nostrils and throats. It set off instant retching and nauseous groans throughout the raiding party that broke down the door of the flat in St. Moritzer Platz. Several of the uniforms who had got there first into the apartment were doubled-over trying in vain to spit out the foul odour that had invaded their mouths. Even hours later back at the station and for some while after at home, its toxic trace remained clinging in the bodies and the clothing of everyone who had come in contact with the festering smell of the corpse rotting inside the flat.

Above the gangrenous cadaver there was a carousel of Blue Bottles which swarmed in wave-like patterns all around the settee where the dead body had been put to rest. Out of eye sockets and broken bruised craters of decaying skin crawled fat maggots engorging themselves on the flesh of 'Christopher's "parting gift." On his forehead there was a raised black and blue bump while around his neck there was a garrotte of video tape tightly bound over the windpipe. Just like Beer this man's fattened, extended tongue stuck out.

In the air there was the audible menacing drone of more colonies of flies swirling around the living room as well as the sizzling fizz of the tuned out television, still on, directly in front of where the body was sitting. 'Christopher' had ensured there would be an arrangement to all this sickening, squalid dissonance, a centre point for his latest message.

Leaning on a Polizei squad car, trying and failing to throw up, Peters listened to the preliminary prognosis of the Kottbusser murder team's chief forensic officer, Dr Maria Scholl who appeared to be the only one unaffected by the stink and the sights of inside.

'The bang on the head – I don't think that's what killed him,' she shouted trying to compete with the loud, staccatoed convulsions emitting from Peters' throwing up on the pavement.

'What then?' he asked while catching his breath noticing that just across the platz huddled underneath a clump of bare trees was Heike Numann.

'It's early days but I think judging by the wounds over his neck he was strangled to death, probably by the video tape wrapped around him,' Dr Scholl replied in her flat, cool professional tone.

'As you can probably guess and smell he's been dead for quite some time.'

'How long doctor?' Peters had tears in his eyes and water streamed from his nose.

'Really hard to say. A week, maybe more Martin. Funny though that no one in the apartment complex noticed the reek from the flat? Wonder why?'

'Because no one cared, that's why,' Peters added, having restored himself into an upright posture, no longer in need of the car for support.

Heike had crossed the street and was about to enter the hallway to the apartment block where she was met by Angi Domath head to toe in a white zipped up suit.

'I wouldn't go up there if I was you Fraulein...unless of course you want to bring up your breakfast,' Angi said smiling at the journalist.

Peters' mind drifted away from whatever details Dr Scholl was furnishing him with and on to the ongoing duel between the two women. He saw Heike ignoring Angi's advice and bounding through the entrance. Forty seconds later he watched her flee from the building and throw up on the road outside. Angi made no attempt to go to her aid.

Dr Scholl broke through: 'One more thing Martin you ought to know...'

'What's that Doctor?'

'There were two wine glasses and an unfinished bottle of Riesling on the table beside our stiff. The last thing he enjoyed was an excellent tipple from the Rheingau, oh, and he wasn't alone.'

Peters immediately thought about Heike and her 'parting gift.' The moment he said it out loud Peters regretted it.

'He wants to be caught. He's already started the countdown.'

Surprisingly Dr Scholl did not react. She looked at Peters coldly and added:

'Is there anything else we need to focus on apart from our chum and the DNA on those glasses? Anything you're specifically interested in?'

'Yes. The video tape around our friend. Can you get it taken away to see what's on it? Can the tcchies do that kind of thing?'

She looked taken back by. Judging from her face it had been a really stupid question.

'But of course Martin. That will not be a problem.'

The doctor put her mask back on and re-joined her team inside, the cue for a green-tinted Heike to cross over and face Peters.

'You should have heeded Angi's warning,' Peters said with unconcealed cruelty.

She ignored his attempts to rile her and focussed instead on the job at hand.

'Apart from the overpowering pong what else did you find in there Martin?'

She had kept her side of the deal, alerted no one else in the media or Fest from the BND. He had been allowed to get to the latest target before anyone else from Kottbusser Strasse and far ahead of Stannheim. He owed her one.

'He was probably strangled to death....with videotape. Don't ask me his name because I don't know it yet, but the good doctor there is certain he was garrotted. Who said variety is the spice of life. Death certainly is for our boy.'

'Will this get out?' she asked.

'Let's keep our pact going. Unless he posts this on the 'Net we can manage to hold that bit until Sunday.'

Peters wasn't completely frank with her. He would keep the discovery of the two glasses to himself and the team.

'You were there first Heike. You saw it. That should be more than enough,' he added just as the first of the satellite trucks and TV crew vans were pulling up across the road from 22b St. Mortizer Platz.

She pulled up the hood of the windcheater she had on until Peters could only see her eyes.

'I'm taking the U-Bahn before some of my dear colleagues over there spot me and ask for an interview. See you later Martin, thanks for all the help.'

He watched her figure merge into the grey gloom of this early spring morning, posing as just another commuter making their way to work bounding towards the U-Bahn station, ghosting past cameraman setting up tripods and groups of TV reporters from rival stations gathered together in an insincere huddle, jousting and probing to see who exactly knew what. To the side of the media standing alone at the opened door of a sleek black BMW was Fest holding a steel cup of something steaming hot in one hand and a mobile in the other pressed to his ear. He appeared to have missed Heike as she passed by but he did spot Peters and nodded towards the English detective with a cocky smile.

Before Fest could approach Peters peeled off back towards the flats in search of some of the residents still living in the run down graffiti covered block. Several were out in their night gowns and pyjamas, a few of the elderly ones choking and spluttering at the putrid smells from above them on floor two.

Peters stopped a woman of pension age, a small dog under one arm and a copy of the morning paper under the other. He guessed she might have been in her early 70s and judging by the way she spoke down to her neighbours especially the Turkish ones she must have lived in this complex for a long time.

'Your name madam?' Peters inquired in his softest voice.

The way she pursed her lips and breathed suggested she was in no mood for either interrogation or co-operation.

'My name? Why is it so important to have "my" name? Don't you want to know whose name that is upstairs,' she said throwing her shrivelled up little head back towards the staircase.

'Alright madam. Then I shall ask you – what is the name of the man we've found up in number 22b?'

Her body gave a sudden, short jerk as if to signify her contempt.

'Elmar Fuller, or so that's what he said he called himself,' she almost spat as she spoke.

'At least we know what he really was,' she went on with a glint of satisfaction on her face.

'Was madam?' Peters asked feigning innocence that failed to impress the sharp faced pensioner shaking with the cold.

'A paedophile!' she said the word slowly as if it was an explosive device she had to take apart bit by bit.

'Did you know that before we found that man or just there now?'

She folded her arms to make herself appear even more bellicose, pursed her lips harder and sharpened her glare on Peters.

'What does it matter? That's another one gone thanks to "Christopher". Good riddance to bad rubbish.' There was a small circle now surrounding this self-appointed block-warden and they started clapping in solidarity.

'If you people did your job right there'd be no need for someone like "Christopher".' a younger man holding an infant in his arms interjected.

'We didn't even know a monster like that lived amongst us. Who cared about us or our children, no one told us!' he protested pointing to the exposed egg shaped dome of the child he was holding.

Only then did Peters notice that a number of the women who had been forced out of their beds and onto the street from the complex were wearing St. Christopher medals around their necks.

'Why are you wasting your time on scum like that?'

'Do us a favour copper and leave our "Christopher" alone?'

'Hope he died slow and painfully.'

The group-think among them was turning nasty, Peters half expected the mob to go back inside, rush upstairs, drag Fuller's corpse down in St. Moritzer Platz and burnt it in front of the rush hour traffic. They were closing in on him, pointing and prodding, he was 'their' Christopher now.

When Peters turned away from them he almost knocked over Fest, later he almost wished he had.

'You're losing them Captain Peters. Not just you but the entire Berlin Polizei. They're all on our friends' side now and that's what so disturbing,' Fest said these last words with fake relish.

'Herr Fest. How unpleasant to see you,' Peters muttered.

Fest fired back a cruel smile at the Englishman.

'So much for the English gentlemen.'

Peters thought immediately of Blucher and that strange similar sense of nostalgic let down.

'As I said to an old friend recently Herr Fest he died shortly after 1945 when we became the masters.'

'We?' Fest looked genuinely puzzled.

'The people. The genuine British people.'

'I thought you had transferred your loyalty to Germany Captain Peters. But at heart it seems you are still a good old English patriot.'

'My loyalty is to the case I'm working on, the one you seem to be treading all over.'

The spy moved closer until Peters could breathe in traces of an expensive after shave that had wafted across the metallic chill of the early morning air. Whatever Fest was splashed with was helping to temporarily counter the odour of putrefaction that had followed him from 2B St. Moritzer Platz.

'I'm just here to remind you that this is still a matter of national security...not that you are, any longer, the senior investigating officer on this case.'

'Me?' Peters pointed to his chest. 'I was just passing and heard the commotion Herr Fest.'

The BND officer retreated slightly to create enough space between himself and Peters as if he was anticipating a punch or a head butt. Or so Peters imagined. Or contemplated.

'Just remember we are keeping a very close eye on our "Christopher's" progress. If you happen to hear from him or if he sends another billet doux to Fraulein Numann please let us know,' Fest said dropping a white business card into the left pocket of Peters' duffel coat. After Fest got back into his car and sped off, Peters fumbled for it and on finding the card noticed that it only had a mobile telephone number scrawled in the middle. There was no name, no address, no email. He wondered if Fest was as near-blank as the card he had just handed over.

Thirty Six

The tape spluttered and whirred, light and images jerking into focus. From darkness into a brittle sunshine that was refracted through trees and evergreen foliage. There was a distended voice of a child somewhere, squealing, panting, running.

Then she came into view, into this place where the camera was fixed, a clearing in woodland. A small girl in a brown puffed up anorak, short skirt and white school socks. She was being pursued and at every corner, towards pathways out of this small patch of open ground, the child recoiled and ran back to the centre. The tiny vulnerable human quarry with Asiatic eyes, high cheek bones, panto-dame rouge cheeks, was scurrying about for an escape route.

The film went blank for a few seconds although the soundtrack had changed to a murmur of voices speaking Russian. Male and malevolent. Then the same child holding her hand up over her eyes to escape the crushing, disorientating glare of a camera light trained on her.

Sobbing became more audible the closer the two men came to her. Their faces cut off by the camera, only the torso's on display. One of them stretched a hand out to her and exposed on his skin, between the thumb and forefinger was a burst of tattooed stars. It was he who picked up and violently flailed her against the brick wall behind her, the light still shining, the sobbing subsiding. The star man placed both hands on her skirt while she lay wriggling on an orange coloured fluffed up carpet. By now the other one had joined him standing over the girl's face, the child still holding her face over her eyes. His glands were exposed, the film tightening on the penis dangling half-drooped over their captive.

'This was a mistake. This was a horrible fucking mistake,' Peters kept repeating into himself.

All around him stood the Kottbusser murder squad, arranged behind him in a D-formation, arms folded, plastic cups crushed in fingers. Tears in Angi's eyes. Smouldering anger on the faces of Riedel and Bauer. Peters noticed that Stannheim simply had his eyes closed.

Just as the star man startled to paw his way over the girl Peters pressed the Off button on the VCR.

'I think we have seen quite enough,' he croaked barely unable to speak to the gathering of detectives around him.

He waited for it and knew instinctively that it would come from Bauer judging by the way he was clenching his fists again until the knuckles went white. He had done that once before in the presence of the late Oskar Beer.

'Maybe, just maybe, we should let "Christopher" get on with it and let him kill all the bastards,' Bauer said breaking the dense uneasy silence inside the station.

It was then that Peters knew he would have to make the speech of his life. And he never felt as alone as now in this place, not even compared to the nights on covert surveillance Ops in Ulster or playing the part of someone else behind the Wall. Not even in the days, weeks and months after Apollonia Winston. His isolation was compounded by the sight of Stannheim beating a retreat to 'Anna's' where he would, no doubt, try at least to blot out those imagined horrors of what was ahead for the child in the puffed up brown anorak in the film found in the flat at St. Moritzer Platz.

Peters knocked on the table which supported the television and video next to Stannheim's office to get their attention. He cleared his throat, rocked back slightly and used his left hand to cling onto furniture as if to keep himself steady.

'What you have just seen will no doubt sicken and appal each and every one of you,' he began.

'Supt. Stannheim has informed me that a police psychologist is on call to talk to you either by phone or in person if you feel the need after this. All of you have been emailed a number if you want someone to listen to you.'

He turned to stare at Bauer.

'I'm actually grateful for Sgt. Bauer's comment because it leads me to what I must say to you all. In the last flat we burst into back in Wedding there were women and children living that block. They could easily have been the victims of our "Christopher's" wrath. They could have been casualties if that parcel bomb had been delivered to the wrong address or if the explosive had been too powerful and taken a couple of apartments out let alone the target's head.'

Target. Target. Target. He was infected by the language of 'Christopher.'

'The point I'm trying to make is that the longer this goes on the chances will increase that someone completely innocent will be harmed or injured. Either that someone is going to get caught in the cross-fire of this maniac's war or else he is going to pick someone by mistake who has no connection to what you have just seen.'

He examined their expressions which were still bearing the mental scars of shock and repulsion.

'The point is that only WE are the law. We are delegated to protect the public and put the criminals, all criminals, away so they can do no more harm. If we allow those lines to blur then it's a free for all. And in a free for all the innocent do often get caught up with the guilty.'

He was thinking about Northern Ireland again, about the stories and pictures of young men crippled for life, in some cases beaten with nail studded bats, holes bored into their bones with electric drills, the victims of instant 'justice' meted out by men whose own crimes eclipsed the venial sins of those they had branded 'anti-social elements. Those savage memories steeled him to go on. He could hear his own voice rising, getting stronger and more confident.

'Colleagues, we must catch this man before this happens. Because it will happen, be sure of that. And remember that when you are going about your work. Bear in mind that your duty is to the law and to the constitution. We cannot be driven by the hysteria of the tabloid media. We are the law.'

He felt utterly exhausted now, in need equally of air but also the suffocating enclosed warm squalor of the pub next door. Peters was so overwhelmed by tiredness that he didn't ever hear his mobile phone ringing on his desk on the other side of the office.

Angi picked up the handy and answered for him before passing it over to Peters. As he nodded, to her and the detectives returned to their desks Peters overheard Riedel whispering to Bauer.

'Who does he think he is?'

Peters ignored the back-bite and spoke into his hand set. It was Lothar Blucher sounding smug and all knowing.

'Your latest stiff my English friend....

'What do you want Lothar,' Peters asked wearily.

'Your latest stiff over in St. Moritzer Platz was Markus Frankel. I know that because he was a client of our Russian friends.'

'What? You don't mean the ones involved in a shoot-out over in Magdeburg?'

Blucher grunted a laugh down the line, a put down for Peters.

'Don't be ridiculous! Why would someone so big as Yanaev want anything to do with a creature like Frankel? No, our pal had a few contacts with the purveyors of very dodgy movies shot back in the motherland.'

'I'd like to meet those purveyors Lothar. Seriously I really would. Just a pity Frankel isn't around to help us track them down.'

'I'd like to help you there but I don't like crossing our Russian comrades, even ones who satisfy the desires of men like Frankel.'

You had to be there to see it; Peters thought but resisted to say out loud.

He instantly saw the terrified child on the partially damaged tape that had been wrapped so tightly around Frankel's windpipe. He also stopped himself from saying that he hoped Frankel's dispatch from the world had been slow and excruciating.

'Listen to me Lothar. I know Yanaev spooks you but I insist you get names of those behind that film. Otherwise we will have to think about whether or not we keep paying your bar bills at the Marriot.'

There was a pause down the line, the rattle of a throat being cleared, the distinctive snort from the man who resented no gain from helping his fellow man.

'Ok Captain Peters. You win this time but if I get names I want some serious cash this time. Enough 'Geld' to get out of Berlin and go somewhere safe and sunny for quite some time.'

'You make sure you do Lothar,' Peters countered and then paused before adding, 'Anything new on Yanaev by the way?'

Blucher ignored the question with one of his own: 'How was your day trip to Magdeburg? Were you going on a sentimental journey?'

Here was a man with many paymasters, Peters concluded. He almost admired the way his oldest asset hedged his bets.

'Never mind where I take myself off to, Lothar. You just get me the names of those who are flogging that filth and you can forget about Yanaev at least for now,' he said as if giving Blucher absolution.

When he snapped his phone shut Peters went over and pinched Angi's arm gently.

'Let's go into the hallway for a little chat,' he whispered to her.

Out in the corridor with its 24/7 strobe lights, thick carpet and framed photos of top brass gone by; Peters looked gravely at his most trusted officer.

'Angi, I've got to talk to the boss about where I stand in all of this shit. So meantime make bloody sure that forensics puts that tape under lock and key. If details of that get out they'll break down the door and trash this place and stop us from doing our job.'

She nodded and let off a mini salute from her temple with two fingers.

'Of course sir, I fully understand.'

'Good because I fucked up. I truly fucked up again. I should never have showed that film to the team.'

He repeated exactly the same words to Stannheim ten minutes later when he sidled into the one of the red lit booths of 'Annas', two beers in hand. The boss of Kottbusser Strasse raised his glass and licked the foam that had been delicately sculpted by the pub's owner on top of the golden coloured liquid below it.

'You thought it was "Christopher's" last communiqué,' Stannheim growled,

'I suspect you even thought he might make an appearance.'

Peters downed half of the glass before replying, the froth shooting up his nose forcing him to sneeze violently.

'I'm not sure what I thought,' Peters replied when he had recovered from his mini convulsion. 'It's knocked the stuffing out of the team. You can see it in their faces. There's no fight left in them.'

The subsequent period of silence seemed to underscore Peters' conclusion. Stannheim agreed, the squad had been thrown off course by what they had been forced to see.

'He's playing more games with you Martin. He wanted you and your unit to watch that child with those men. He even wants to win you over to his side.'

'Maybe I should ring up that on-call shrink sir.' Then he was panic stricken by a new fear.

'Fuck if any details get out about that tape they'll be marching in their thousands down the Ku'damm demanding that we leave "Christopher" to get on with it. Bauer already said so...'

'If it does get out one of us could be lynched,' Stannheim was in no mood to provide any comfort.

His commanding officer suddenly looked lifeless, his yellow taut skin compounding Peters' image of Stannheim as an elasticised waxen manikin, someone hollowed out from the inside.

'Strangely enough I still think we are close to the end. This might have been his spectacular,' Peters mused.

Stannheim was about to say something in reply when Peters' wafer thin mobile emitted a bleep. Peters flicked it open and clicked to messages and then his In-box:

'Meet me @ the Island. A.M. Ur friend Arkady.'

Thirty Seven

Gavrilov had chosen the camouflage of crowds, the foggy throng of tourists marching in phalanxes to and fro over the bridges spanning the Spree, past the Berlin Dom and milling around the steps leading up to the Pergamon museum, for him and Peters to conceal themselves from any prying eyes.

Earlier Peters had taken a serpentine route on the U and S-Bahns, first heading westwards to Spandau, then south through Steglitz and Schoenberg, before leaping into a taxi that left him back in Kreuzberg before finally ending up via the underground all the way to Alexanderplatz and a short hop on the tram towards Hackersher Markt where he popped into one of the bars underneath the railway lines above for a quick beer in order to survey the streets around him.

All the time on the trains there were subtle glances over the shoulder, sideways surveys of fellow passengers to see if any were paying him undue attention, noting without staring at whoever joined his carriage at each stop. Old Cold War tricks for new games. At Alex he bought a key to a baggage locker, placed the mobile inside with the battery taken out and hoped that Arkady Gavrilov would be able spot him emerging from the hordes of visitors around the Museum Island, a tourist guide book he had just bought from the station in his hand, feigning the bewilderment of an out-of-towner lost in Berlin.

On his fourth circuit around the culture trail Peters felt a hand grip his arm and when he turned on his heels he saw Arkady Gavrilov dressed as if he had just stepped out of a spy thriller. Peters wondered if the former GRU man was wearing the hat and flaps down as an in-house joke. Even the weather played its part as insipid shards of melting sleet dropped onto the shoulders of

Gavrilov's three quarter length grey woollen coat.

Peters noticed a rolled up piece of paper peeking out of the inside pocket of the sports jacket Gavrilov wore under his overcoat.

'You looked lost Tavarich. Allow me to guide you on your way, ' the Russian said who then used his eyes to gesture towards the Television Tower one quarter of which was submerged by the low lying steel grey sky.

They said nothing as they crossed the wide lanes of Karl Liebneckt Strasse avoiding the tourist coaches and the darting lines of traffic shooting off in either direction. The two men maintained their silence right up until they were in the lift taking them to the viewing area of the show-piece construct that old Eric and his chums had built in 1969.

When they had reached the 11th floor Peters was first to speak.

'Which side do you want to look out on – east or west? Which one's best?'

The Russian pointed westwards and replied: 'There was only ever one-way Martin and that was over there. How many used to come up here to dream about what it was like on the other side.'

Peters could see the three pointed star atop the Europa Centre peaking still through the gloom.

'Did you ever think you would end up working in that place, Arkady?' Peters said pointing towards the west end and the Russian's office.

'No, I just dreamed about it. Often.'

Gavrilov took out the paper from his inside pocket and flicked it flat along a line of railing parallel to the glass front of the TV tower.

It was a photo-copy of an English language magazine, the words in capital 'GDR Review' tucked away on the top left hand corner and below a headline.

'GDR honours hero who trained Angolan comrades.'

Beneath there was a picture of an elderly African man in a business suit pinning a medal onto the chest of a proud youngish looking man in a peaked officer's camp at a military ceremony, two girls in Young Pioneer uniforms flanking him, with bunches of roses in their hands.

Before he could read the picture caption below Gavrilov interrupted.

'Hans-Joachim Streich,' the Russian said prodding the extract with his forefinger.

'You are looking at one of the heroes of the "National People's Army".'

Peters could feel his heart pounding through his chest, his pulse beating a little faster, sweat beads starting to form on his forehead. He found himself whispering to Gavrilov even though there were only a handful of visitors around them all pretending not to be disappointed that their view of the city's western skyline was obscured.

'What are you trying to tell me Arkady?'

'I'm telling you that he is your man.'

He stared down at the grainy image of a man in his mid to late twenties, just under six foot, short cropped dark hair, a handsome chiselled face and a confident bearing. The pips on his shoulders indicated that he held the rank of Captain back in July 1982 when the photograph was taken. Peters guessed he must now be hitting fifty, about the same age as the Russian beside him.

'"GDR Review" was the foreign propaganda magazine for the old regime,' Gavrilov continued, 'and men like Hans-Joachim Streich were its posters boys.'

'Are you absolutely sure this might be him?' at first Peters didn't want to get carried away.

Gavrilov's confidence unnerved him: 'I've checked the name with some old friends back in the Motherland Martin. Some of the Spetznaz boys remember him from joint training exercises in the eighties. He was a big name among the Special Forces' guys stationed here. Highly decorated for training the MPLA in Angola. Awarded a string of medals for action in Afghanistan. One of the youngest officers to be promoted to the rank of Major before he was 30. Volunteered to go back to Africa to fight

UNITA and the South Africans in '88. Was involved in joint training with the Red Army in the Motherland a year later when it started to fall apart. Missed the 40th anniversary parade in October '89, which is probably just as well as he was about to be promoted to the rank of Colonel and had written a paper for the military arguing for a Tiananmen-style response to the "counter revolutionaries" on the streets. This guy was a true believer right up to the end.'

'And what happened next?' Peters asked.

'Then it's a blank,' Gavrilov shrugged his shoulders.

'He disappears from everyone's radar. It's as if he simply packed up the tent and went away into the sunset with the rest of them. Which is odd.'

'Odd?' Peters was visibly puzzled.

'Odd, because, my British comrade, there was every chance he could have been absorbed into the new united Federal army and gone on to greater things.'

'Maybe he set up a private detective agency like you did Arkady.'

'If he did I would have known about it and I would have bought him out and then re-hired him,' the Russian said only half-joking.

The English detective hoped, in vain, that Gavrilov might still be wrong, that his researchers had excavated someone else from the archives, not 'Christopher' but rather some other Special Forces soldier. Peters took out his wallet which bulged with fat rolls of Euros.

'What do we owe you for this Arkady?'

The Russian stuck one of his hands up: 'Zilch! Again, just promise me that when you get fed up with all the back biting down in Kottbusser Strasse you'll come and work for me.'

'Don't tempt me Arkady, don't tempt me,' Peters said smiling at the Russian, imagining a life beyond the squad, the politics, the pressures, Stannheim's depression, the often absurd orders from high command.

Gavrilov was about to turn on his heels when he stopped,

remembering something else he wanted to say.

'Martin, who do you think is trying to track you? Why all the stealth and cover today?'

'German Int. Don't know why but I don't like the smell around it at all.'

'Are they still as useless as they were back in the old days?' Gavrilov asked.

'I only wish they were. There's one of them who's been on my back for a while. He even threatened to get me taken off the case.'

'Whatever for?'

'National security. A need to know business. All the usual bollocks. Once 'Christopher' started using Semtex it became a "Federal" matter.'

'Semtex? He used Semtex?' Gavrilov seemed taken back.

'On the booby traps Arkady. Seems the spooks think he's a terrorist which is exactly what our "Christopher" wants them to think.'

Peters sensed that the mention of 'Semtex' had shaken Gavrilov slightly.

'So who flogs Semtex in Berlin these days, Arkady?' he went on.

Gavrilov rolled his eyes to the sky as if in protest against the very question.

'Come one Arkady, who can get access to the Czech play dough that easy? '

The Russian blinked nervously looking directly into Peters' face.

'Guess who?'

'Jesus, Arkady, you are joking.'

'I only wish I was. They say back in the Motherland that Yanaev is the only one who knows where the entire explosive is buried around Berlin. If anyone is selling Semtex it has to be his outfit.'

Peters stared out over the city beneath them, the western aspect with its showcase capitalist architecture, its wide boulevards and expansive green spaces. He wondered what Gavrilov had once thought when he gazed across the old frontier, towards the forbidden zone beyond. And then he thought about the man the Russian had brought to him and what was driving him towards his quarry now.

'You think he's running our man Streich?' Peters asked.

'I don't think so,' Gavrilov said shaking his head.

'Yanaev is not a risk taker. He keeps the trade as far away as possible from his front door. I can't see him getting close to someone who would bring so much trouble to those electronic gates down in Kopenick. He's enjoying your discomfort over "Christopher" and probably guesses our man's booby trap toys are set off with his firecrackers but he is no gambler. Yanaev keeps his distance from everyone.'

In that instant Peters realised he trusted Gavrilov more than most of the Kottbusser Strasse murder squad. Arkady's instincts were usually on the money, Peters reminded himself. Yanaev was probably getting some perverse kick out of his Semtex being used by Streich but the chances of them ever meeting were remote.

'You can keep this copy. Happy hunting. It's probably better if we don't see each other for a little while,' Gavrilov said tapping the paper before he disappeared into the lift leaving Peters alone to stare out of the glass bulge of the Tower overlooking the western cityscape beyond.

When the Russian was gone Peters went to the restaurant area of the Tower which turned on a gentle revolution taking the diners inside on a slow east-west journey. He ordered coffee and croissants and laid the photocopy out on the table in front of him, using the condiments to hold down the crumpled paper until it was completely flat.

For some inexplicable reason Peters ran his right forefinger along the outline of the soldier's face in front of him trying to imagine what 23 years had done to these sculpted, harsh but handsome features. He would take it back to Kottbusser Strasse for the techies to play with. Peters had heard that they could 'project' the face of a man in his twenties and come up with an image of the same person n his fifties using the latest computer technology. They would even be able to match this fragment from 'Christopher's' past life to the sketch providcd to the murder squad by the late unlamented Oskar Beer.

What the computers and the techies couldn't answer was what exactly had trip switched inside this man's head. Sure, he had been used to seeing violence in the sweat, the dirt, the humidity and squalor of Africa's civil wars. He had been trained to fight and kill even at close quarters. But Peters still wondered what had driven this one-time hero of a state that no longer existed, one that would never be reborn, to return to the business of death and terror, to hunt and kill as the entire basis of his existence.

What the computers would confirm he already knew. Peters implicitly trusted Gavrilov and the sources he drew upon. The Russian's connections rippled across the eastern half of the continent, all the way to the Urals, down to all those old military general's enjoying their retirement on the Black Sea, to the Berlin veterans now back in Moscow running businesses similar to Gavrilov's, to the Afghansti's who had managed to slip safely back into the Motherland through the Salang Highway after Gorby pulled the plug; this good Russian was at the centre an organism of impeccable contacts and long standing exchanges, of old favours rewarded and new alliances forged.

Hans-Joachim Streich! He hated the certainty of it all almost as much he feared the killer's ever increasing proximity. Carrying around the name in his head felt like he had his thumb compressed on the open pin of a hand-grenade.

After descending from the TV tower Peters walked westwards across to the spot to where the statues of Marx and Engels still stood. A group of his fellow countrymen, obviously in Berlin for a stag week judging by their prematurely inebriated state, were having their photographs taken with the 'old men.' One had wrapped a Leeds United scarf around Marx's neck. Peters avoided them and continued his search for the nearest functioning phone booth.

Thirty Eight

To avoid arousing the suspicions of the Mothers Against Paedophiles' encampment and the media vigil outside Kottbusser Strasse they each slipped out of the station alone to make their way to 'Anna's.' Angi, Bauer, Riedel and finally Stannheim filed their way into the pub towards one of the luridly lit snugs out of sight and earshot of the two early morning drinkers at the bar. On Peters' instruction the owner laid out a tray of Wursts and slices of baguette on the tables.

When they were all in place, each a beer in hand, Peters began by holding up the photo-fit mined from Oskar Beer's memory.

'Hans-Joachim Streich! Meet our chief suspect.'

Stannheim was chewing unenthusiastically on a piece of sausage and spat some of it into the ashtray.

'Why all the cloak and dagger stuff Martin? Don't you trust the rest of our colleagues back in the station?' the Boss asked only for the benefit of the others and not Peters.

'Hans-Joachim Streich!' Peters continued, 'or should I say Major Hans-Joachim Streich retired. A highly decorated soldier in the National People's Army, served with East German Special Forces, trained the Angolan MPLA, worked with the Soviets in Afghanistan and, worst of all, was, no is, a true believer.'

The 'kitchen cabinet' sat frozen in their seats, their beers untouched, their eyes fixed on the razor sharp features sketched out by the Berlin Polizei's best artists. Peters refused to answer Stannheim's question and immediately launched into delegation.

'Bauer! Go east and seek out your old contacts over there. There has to be someone who remembers him, somebody who might even know where he is now residing.'

Bauer tried to say something but Peters ignored him too.

'Herr Riedel. I want you to search for every Hans-Joachim Streich in the phone book. Take the number and the address. And, oh yes, print out a Google Earth map of each and every one of their areas. I want to see what's around the houses in case we have to knock down a few doors. After that get onto the banks, ask if any Hans-Joachim Streich's have been using Visa cards to book on line, buy mobile phones or rent a quiet, little lock up somewhere.'

Again Bauer moved to interrupt and this time Stannheim gestured to allow the former Vopo to speak.

'I have been knocking on the doors of dozens of rental offices, places that lease warehouses, garages, workshops that kind of thing.' Bauer paused for breath; the hiatus allowing Peters to say 'Go on.'

There was sweat again trickling down Bauer's forehead, Peters guessed judging by the way his hands shook, that his Inspector had had another heavy night.

'What I'm trying to say is that I'm down to my last six, all of them in eastern Berlin. Permission to try them first before looking up any old contacts.'

Bauer's intervention set off an alarm in Peters' head. He wanted to keep the name out of the media that was the reason why he had convened their conference in the bar instead of the station. And he was also determined to stop Fest intruding.

'Riedel, make sure that when you talk to the banks about Streich you are investigating a major fraudster. That will make them sit up and take notice. Make no connection to "Christopher." And that goes for everyone else outside this circle you talk to, whether in the bar, on the phone, using email.'

When Riedel and Bauer left, Peters turned to Angi who hadn't drank a drop of the Pils bought for her.

'Take this to the techies and get them to make a comparison with the Beer sketch. Let's see if they can match them up.'

'And after sir?'

'After, how about dinner?' Peters said half as a joke, half in hope mindful that the night was stretching ahead of him in Heer Strasse, alone.

'I'm sorry sir, but I promised my father I would eat with him tonight over in Pankow.'

'That's alright Angi,' Peters said, his cheeks reddening slightly, barely concealing his disappointment.

'Just get me that match so we can be absolutely sure. Then hit the archives, scan for anything about our friend.'

She turned and walked towards the pub's main door, her heels scraping slightly on the hard tiles underneath her feet. Stannheim had downed not his own beer but those of Angi's and Riedel, only Bauer had bothered drinking his, a cure no doubt, thought Peters.

'We seem to have forgotten about Albert Briegel,' Stannheim said suddenly.

'Briegel shoots to national fame like a "Big Brother" contestant, is subject to a public vote and then nothing.'

'He's probably dead sir,' Peters said.

'No, I don't think so,' Stannheim countered. 'He's saving Briegel up for his grand finale. If you're right about him, "Christopher", I mean Streich, then Briegel's the star of his final show. He's keeping him for something special.'

'And your point is?'

'My point is Martin that he's still using a secret place somewhere, still keeping Briegel alive, and so, is still vulnerable. We might just stumble across him yet.'

Peters wondered why his commanding officer was still upbeat about their chances. Stannheim appeared to divine what he was thinking.

'Trust me Martin. He's planning something spectacular for Briegel.'

'Like what?' Peters asked demonstrating impatience.

'Like a live beheading on the Internet, I don't know. Whatever it is he's keeping Briegel holed up somewhere for the big night.'

Stannheim picked up a fully intact Wurst and pointed in the direction of the owner who was helping himself to his third Korn of the morning.

'He's probably bought them from the Imbiss at the S-Bahn

station. Bastard has charged double the money that the stall flogs them for,' he gnawed on the sausage and then added, 'You going back to the station?'

'No sir, I've a contact to look up. The headless horsemen. We can't neglect that case either.'

'No, that's a good idea Martin. Let our friends watching over us think you're only concerned with what happened to our two Basque chums. I'm staying by the way, trying to avoid Herr Schabowski and his press office,' Stannheim raised his glass to dismiss Peters.

Lothar Blucher was carving a slice of Wiener Schnitzel soaked in a rich white wine sauce with his knife, shoving a pile of pork and speared red cabbage into his mouth, pausing only to swill back a mouthful of smoky, brown Franconian beer, pretending to ignore the man that had sat down in front of him.

He had chosen Maximillion's, a Bavarian restaurant on Friedrichstrasse with a 12ft statue of a paunchy Munchen libertine in Liederhosen at the entrance, for their next meeting. Blucher's preference was for pig and stodge over the delicate dishes of the Far East that were becoming increasingly popular in Berlin.

'Don't mind me Lothar,' Peters whispered as he sat down, called one of the waiters over and asked for whatever Blucher was drinking.

'You rang my Lord!' Peters affected the tones of a snooty English butler.

There was the protest snort before the complaint. Blucher was dressed in a dark three-piece pin striped suit and with his copy of the Financial Times affected the pose of a respectable businessman out to lunch.

'You are late and I have already started. Once more we see the death of the English gentleman.'

The waiter came back with a tall glass filled with foamy brown beer and asked if Peters wanted to eat, which he declined.

'You not eating? You'll get sick,' Blucher said with his mouth still full of food, a piece of dumpling flying across the table and hitting Peters' sports jacket.

'If you could see what I see you'd lose your appetite quite rapidly Lothar. Now tell me why I have been summoned.'

Blucher drained his glass, put down his cutlery and leaned forward with his arms folded.

'My chess partner's been over to see me. He says it's for the last time. I'm too toxic according to him.'

'Surely not Lothar,' Peters said sniggering.

'Don't make light of this shit,' Blucher said, his mood darkening, 'And so it seems are you. Toxic. A contaminant. Lethal to be beside. That's why I'm getting out of Berlin for a while.'

'What are you talking about?' Peters inquired.

'What I'm talking about is that they know you were down in that knocking shop recently chatting with one of the older Natasha's.'

Peters suddenly felt nauseous thinking about Irina and her dreams of retirement on the Costa del Sol.

'What I'm talking about is that you were seen in a bar with her asking questions about her fellow countrymen. I hear she's gone back to the Motherland.'

'She just wanted a little place in Spain by the sea,' Peters interrupted gravely. 'Jesus Christ.....I have killed her.'

'Then you are well and truly toxic my dear English boy. Far too dangerous to be seen around with at all. I'm really glad to be getting out of here now that you tell me that.' Lothar Blucher demonstrated only concern for himself.

'This guy Yanaev isn't like those other Mafioski, Tavarich. He doesn't wrap himself in bling or have a show-off trophy wife on his shoulder everywhere he goes.'

'No chance then of him taking over West Ham then, Peters interjected.

'I'm afraid not. Yanaev's only addiction I'm told is art. He collects paintings. Apparently he has a vast collection hanging on his walls down in that mini-fortress he owns in Koepenick,' Blucher said continuing to shovel carefully chopped morsels of pork, dumplings and cabbage into his face.

'Oh yes, art and of course exerting power over people. He likes lording it over people. Awards those who are loyal, turns on those who he thinks betray him. Hence your headless horsemen. Hence your hooker friend who has gone on the missing list.'

'You sound as if you admire him Lothar.'

Peters' informer polished off his beer and licked the froth from his upper lip while Blucher continued.

'What I admire is his sense of self-preservation. People like Avi Yanaev are to be respected for that at least....and feared. Besides why become fixated on Yanaev? Why worry about a couple of terrorists who lost their heads challenging the Ruski mafia?'

'Because I don't like people like Yanaev, people who think they can decide who can live and who can die, people who always imagine they don't have to answer to anyone. People like Yanaev – I like to bring them down from their clouds.'

Blucher was shaking his head and grimacing.

'You follow your own crusade Captain. I've done quite enough as it is.'

'So you're saying you can't help anymore.'

'Don't sound so disappointed. It's not forever. It's never forever for your oldest friend in Berlin.'

Peters thought about Irina's fate and how he had first imagined her with her throat slashed, her blood turning her pool in Andalusia crimson. Instead now she would suffer an even worse fate, back in some frozen backward best forgotten corner of Mother Russia. Peters remembered the reports he used read back in Military Intelligence HQ at Spandau, of Russians agents the British had recruited and that the KGB had eventually unmasked, of their sudden disappearance from the east side of the wall, of their handlers' quiet desperation as the lines to them went dead, of their inevitable fate, of the single bullet to the back of the head, a release after the torturous hours of sleep deprivation and rough interrogation. At least in the end they had been granted a final instant exit from their torment - no such 'luxury' surely awaited poor Irina.

'Stop sulking Martin,' Blucher said interrupting Peters' imagined horrors who instantly retaliated.

'Where's Anika by the way?'

'Gone!' Blucher answered with genuine indifference.

'Gone? You don't seem so heartbroken Lothar.'

Blucher held up two fingers and gestured to the waiter for another round of beers.

'Anika got these ideas beneath his station. Started to DEMAND I pay for the op. What use is he without the equipment down there? If I ever see that Filipino waiter again I shall shake him by the hand with mine stuffed full of Euros. Anika's living with him now and good luck to them both.'

'You're such a sentimentalist Lothar. And by the way you'll have no Euros in your hands unless you start being useful to the Berlin Polizei.'

Blucher took out small, ringed notebook, flipped it open and started writing on the pad. He tore off single piece of paper and handed it over to Peters.

'29(A) Immanuelkirche Strasse,' Peters read out loud.

'Who exactly is at home here Lothar?'

'Some Russians. Film distributors to be precise.'

Peters folded the note and popped it into his breast pocket.

'Thanks for that Lothar. I mean that. For once in your life you did the right thing without expectation of payment. The world will never be the same.,' Peters said patting the top of his jacket, standing up and putting on his overcoat. The informer sent back another snort maybe as much in embarassment as contempt.

Peters ambled south towards "Charlie", checking his mobile for calls and texts, concealed under the hood of his Duffel, buffeted in the gales that had started to batter Berlin. At Koch Strasse U-Bahn he crossed over to the corner newsagents, his attention captured by the BZ headline. It was a speculative picture led splash with pictures both of 'Christopher's' targets alongside several blank, grey boxes. He counted 12 frames, some full, others empty beneath the headline: 'The Dirty Dozen – Dead.'

On finding one near Bebel Platz, he rang the Kottbusser Strasse general station number and asked to speak to Angelika Domath. It took several euro coins before she came to answer.

'Angi, listen to me and say nothing,' Peters said with firm, cold authority.

'Convene a meeting of the "kitchen cabinet" for the next hour. You know who I mean by the "kitchen cabinet"?'

She hesitated for a few seconds: 'Yes, sir as you've called them before.'

'Good. Have them meet me in the Boss' hideaway and speak to them only in Braille. See you before lunch, ok?'

'Okay sir, see you in there.'

Peters dropped the receiver down gingerly, left the booth and retraced his steps eastwards to retrieve his mobile from the left luggage in Alexanderplatz.

Thirty Nine

The bouncer doing the day shift on the door of 'Haus Ivana' looked like he had been built by Lego. His body was a series of connected blocks, sharp-angled shoulders, flat pack torso and a square head. He didn't bulge so much as branch out of the CSKA Moscow tracksuit he was wearing and kept slapping one fist into his palm.

As Peters tried to enter the doorman blocked his way almost shoulder-charging the detective onto the ground.

'You are barred from these premises,' the security man said with one hand on Peters' chest.

'I'm not a customer you dumb fuck, ' Peters retorted pulling out his ID card. 'Get me your manager or preferably your owner.'

'The manager is not here,' the goon replied in broken German.

Peters pulled out his mobile and pointed it towards the Russian sentinel.

'If you don't call your manager, and I know fine rightly she's in there, I'm calling in Vice to raid this fucking place which will piss off your boss, your real boss Tavarich. So, your choice chum – let me speak to the manager or I call for assistance.'

Lego-man grunted, moved his head sidewards and stood aside to let Peters through. He was led towards to a ground floor office passing a couple of exhausted looking whores in nightgowns who had just come off shift. Inside was an elegant woman in her early 40s, blonde, wafer thin steel glasses, a pin striped business suit, sitting behind a desk.

She stood up and greeted Peters with a weak handshake and gestured for him to sit down in front of her.

'How can I help you officer?'

'That's a good guess, miss?'

'Miss Pfeiffer actually. I'm the manager of "Haus Ivana" and I can assure you everything about our business is above board. Apologies for the misunderstanding on the door by the way.'

'Don't worry, I'm not here to inspect your books. All I want to know is what's happened to one of your employees.'

'Which one? We have lots of girls working here and of course some boys who like to be girls sometimes.'

'Her name was Irina. An older Russian woman. I spoke to her a couple of days ago in here. It seems she's disappeared since then. Know anything about that?' Peters asked, taking a note book out of his jacket and fiddling with a pencil, his actions seemed to unnerve Miss Pfeiffer.

'I'm sorry we don't keep tabs on the girls once they walk out on us. We have a big turnover of staff. Girls come and go. They make some money, go home, get a new life, no questions asked.'

That sounded too much like a programmed answer, Peters said into himself. He decided to get straight to the real point of his return to the knocking shop.

'Miss Pfeiffer I want you to convey a message from me to someone. I want you to tell your boss Avi Yanaev that I'm coming to get him. I want you to tell him I know he's had Irina killed. And I want you to tell him that a hammering in the Grunewald won't stop me either.'

She had turned scarlet from the neck up by the time Peters had finished trying to compose herself by clearing her throat.

'You are mistaken sir. I don't know anyone called Avi Yanaev. Whoever he is he has absolutely no connection to our business, which is perfectly legal and once again, above board. And speaking of legal can I suggest that the next time you want to speak to me or anyone connected to this business you do so in the presence of our lawyers.'

Peters dropped one of his business cards onto her table before leaving.

'Make sure you pass that on to your real boss, Miss Pfeiffer. Tell him I'm still coming for him.'

He felt the foul beery breath of the bouncer on his neck, the light darkening around Peters thanks to the Lego-man's looming presence. Peters turned around to face him.

'Don't give me an excuse to arrest you Tavarich!' Peters said. The doorman had returned to slamming one fist into his other palm.

When he got back outside a relieved Peters noticed that his mobile was ringing, Angi's number appearing on the LCD.

'Sir? Where are you?'

'Down at a whore house in Schoneberg Angi..'

There was a pause on the line as Angi tried to make up her mind if her commanding officer was joking or not. Then she decided to continue.

'We got a result from the address you gave us, sir.'

'Go on Angi.'

'It was a kind of clearing house. We arrested two men and found hundreds of DVDs. There were lots of jiffy bags, books of stamps, address books too. They had a network of clients they connected to all over Europe.'

'What about these men?'

'Two Russians. They've started coughing up once they were in the station. Protesting that they didn't know what was on the DVDs. Gave us names of the group producing the films back in Russia. Riedel is already on to Interpol with a list of them. The old man is out celebrating. We might have just cracked a ring of these perverts.'

Peters closed his eyes and for the first time in a very long time he inwardly thanked Lothar Blucher. He was finally paying for his time in the Marriott.

'Brilliant Angi. Well done to the entire team. Make sure that chancer Schabowski sings your praises in the press over this.'

'Sir?'

'What Angi?'

'There's one more thing. Bauer wasn't on the raid in Immanuel Kirche Strasse. He's been busying himself down in Friedrichshain. He called in and asked to speak to you, only to you. Sounded important.'

'Tell him to go back to where we were earlier and wait for me. And call in and see the old man. Make sure he's there too. Now say no more on this line.'

He suddenly recalled those grey blank spaces on the BZ headline, took out the mobile phone and immediately called Angi back.

'Angi, listen to me. That list of names in the address books, check out the ones living in Berlin. Look them up in case some of them have gone on the missing list too. I'll see Bauer and the boss in about an hour.'

Peters switched off and pulled out the battery reminding himself to drop off the phone at one of the main stations before returning to Kreuzberg. He was about to walk off in the direction of the closest U-Bahn when he spotted one of the younger hookers from the night he had shared a drink with Irina going back into the same bar. After about a minute staring at the pub's front door, just as an icy shower began to sheet down Peters crossed the road and followed her inside.

Spread over the bar top, 'Dorothy' had transformed herself into ersatz femme fatal, a skin hugging red dress, black stockings, red high heel shoes, dyed black bob, red lips, black nails, she reminded Peters of a piece on a draughts board. 'She' flashed elongated false eyelashes at Peters when he entered and ordered a coffee.

'What's she drinking down the back darling?' he said jerking a thumb towards the emaciated girl sitting on her own.

'Brandy. They always have brandy darling after their shift. Brings them back to life inside,' the tranny barmaid replied cattily.

He asked for a double Courvoisier with one cube of ice and carried it down to the bottom of the bar.

'I'm not working. If you're looking for a suck and fuck the day shift have just started,' the girl muttered without raising her eyes off the table where Peters had just slammed down the brandy.

He took a seat facing her and noticed how wasted and washed out she appeared. She also reeked of too much of super-imposed testosterone. From her smell Peters guessed it must have been a busy night.

'I'm not looking for business love. I'm just trying to find an old friend. Someone I was in here with a couple of days ago.'

She seemed too jaded with exhaustion and whatever she had taken to get through last night's 'shift' left her either able to register or remember.

'How's the brandy?' Peters asked as he watched her gulp the brown liquor.

'What the fuck do you want?'

'I'll get to the point. Do you recall Irina who used to work across the road?'

The girl shrugged her shoulders.

'Did you know that she's gone?... Sorry, I didn't catch your name.'

He took out a fold of twenty euro notes and laid it carefully on the table next her glass. She put one of her hands on the money and stroked the paper as if she was caressing something she loved, something she undoubtedly did love. Above the wrist where her skin was revealed beyond the cuffs of a battered leather jacket Peters observed the tracks of a heroin user.

'Who are you, Irina's pimp?' she asked sulkily.

'No, just someone she owed money to. A business deal down on the Costa del Sol that she has run away from.'

'Truth be told she was a big mouth. Liked to boast about how she could still pull in all the good looking clients.'

'Like Spanish boys for instance?' Peters enquired.

'Yeah. She was bragging about those two who came in with those Russian pigs. They were hard to forget, all the girls were 'round them like flies 'round shit. But Irina was queen bee on our floor and had to have them both. The rest of us were left with the Russians. Which was as bad as working with the Joes on the streets.'

He fluttered a couple of fingers in the air in the direction of the barmaid for more brandy. When the tranny arrived with another double the girl continued.

'She was even boasting about you.'

'Me?' Peters said taken back.

'Yes, you, she told us you asked her for a drink over here.'

'So what? What the hell is there to boast about?'

'That she was out with someone so famous. You must think I'm completely brain dead but I know you're the cop who's hunting "St. Christopher". We've all seen you on the TV. She couldn't wait to tell us all. So all that shit about her owing you money was just crap. I don't care who you are as long as you're paying.'

So he hadn't been followed by Yanaev's goons at all, Irina had simply spoken to the wrong person inside 'Haus Ivana'.

The girl raised her glass and faked a smile: 'Here's to Irina. Well done for getting out. She's probably sunning her fanny down on the Costa del Sol as we speak. Lucky bitch.'

On the U-Bahn north Peters stared down at the discarded copy of BZ on the seat in front of him and those frames, the faces and the grey spaces, looking up from the pages. No one would miss or care for Irina. Not even her co-workers like the young smack addict who had just taken sixty Euros off him simply to confirm what he feared, what in truth he already knew. Irina's face would never grace the pages of the Berlin papers. She had been swallowed up by the cloying vastness of her homeland, absorbed into its anonymity, and then dissolved from its memory.

When he ascended from the innards of Berlin at Kottbusser Tor station Peters once again hid under his hood, concealed all the way to 'Anna's', protected from the gaze of the Mothers Against Paedophiles encampment and the media vigil. Before reaching the pub door he stopped to search for his handy and the battery and clipped them together. He had meant to drop it off on route at one of the larger stations with a left luggage section. For some reason he couldn't explain Peters had kept it with him. When he turned the mobile on there was one single text message, sent from an unfamiliar number which Peters at first tried to call back. There was no reply on the other end, no answer message but simply a two-line instruction in capitals: 'GO HOME.'

Forty

Mannfred Stannheim's favourite snug had been transformed into a geography classroom. There were several maps sprawled over the two tables on the nook where the old man went to escape from the world. Berlin was laid out in a light brown mosaic of districts interconnected with red, black and blue lines denoting U-Bahn, S-Bahn and tram routes, the harsh colouring broken up by webs of white depicting the wide boulevards and main streets running from east to west. On top of them lay a couple of A4 pages with spidery, unintelligible scribbles and diagrams, arrows shooting off in different directions, a number of addresses underlined in double lines of green ink.

Peters remembered Bauer telling him that in his pre-89 life he used to like collecting 'Thomas Cook' European time tables, the bible of the inter-railer from the 1970s onwards. Bauer used to get the annual red covered travelling tome every Christmas from a distant relative in West Berlin. Unable to travel west Bauer said he dreamed of long overnight train journeys across the DDR's forbidden zone, of hurtling along the rails through the Black Forest at night, of wakening up in the rejuvenating light of Florence or Rome. Now he understood Bauer better than before. He once had a life laid out in neat rectangular patterns which abruptly ended like the last tourist street guide of East Berlin, published in September '89, the one that Peters kept as a souvenir, into white nothingness. Behind the Wall, on the map there were the white spaces of West Berlin; in his DDR life Bauer had simply filled in the blanks of this Terra Incognita by emigrating in his head every night.

On one of the maps Bauer had used yellow highlighter to mark out a section of 'Friedrichshain' close to the Ostkeuz station. Stannheim was tapping one of his long bony fingers on it.

'Sergeant Bauer has been extremely busy,' the old man said looking up towards Peters who was standing over the both of them.

Bauer looked pleased with himself, enough to almost finish his beer in one go, eyes shut, again sweating profusely.

Peters sat down beside them and tried to make sense of the paperwork scattered all around them.

'Well, Sergeant, please enlighten me,' he said while at the same time putting one finger in the air to order a Pils from 'Anna's' owner.

The ex-Vopo in the cheap shiny suit licked his lips in triumph and began to explain.

'First I got on to the Techies. I asked them if there were any patterns to his calls or emails.'

'His? You mean "Christopher" don't you?'

'Yes of course,' Bauer said taking a breath and then launching straight back into his lecture.

'They spotted something very interesting. Clusters of calls from certain areas, mainly in the south east of the city, a lot of them from booths close to the Spree. He does move about a bit. There were calls from S-Bahn stations in the west, a few were made from the West End. But mainly, mainly they are from areas he would be more familiar with.'

'Alright Bauer. So he prefers the east to the west, big deal. That's still a lot of ground to cover.'

Stannheim interrupted to defend Bauer. 'Let him continue Martin.'

'Maybe it's a big area sir but the patterns suggest he works mainly in the south east and that's where the footwork kicks in. Yesterday I asked Lt. Domath for permission to pound the pavements. I checked every warehouse and lock up within a mile radius of Ostkreuz and eventually, I got lucky.'

Peters' expression of bewilderment only encouraged Bauer further.

'I rang up every storage business in the area, in some cases I even went to their doors and asked them if they had rented anywhere from this man,' Bauer had pulled out a photocopy of the "Christopher" photo fit and placed it above the map with the highlighted segment.'

'You did what?' Peters exploded, banging the table with his palm.

'Martin, give Bauer a chance, listen to him,' Stannheim said.

'Thank you Sir. Captain Peters sir, I never made any reference to "Christopher". I said we were looking for a "fence" who might be using a warehouse or garage to store some stolen computers. I made him more co-operative when I said this guy was probably a foreigner.'

'Him? Who's him Bauer?'

'The warehouse owner. Barely out of his teens the little shit. Makes a fortune out of renting these places out down by the Spree. Mainly for techno-parties, photo shoots, performance art, all that kind of Boho crap.'

'So did he buy your legend?' Peters asked in spook-speak, which Bauer seemed to understand instinctively.

'Sure. He panicked and offered to help immediately. Claimed he met the guy about a year ago and that he paid in advance. In cash. Told him he wanted the place for about six months.'

'Where is he now, this owner?'

'Across the road in the station, sir,' Bauer replied matter of factly.

'I told him we needed him to make a formal statement, that I couldn't be absolutely sure he wasn't in on the gig too. He keeps blabbering about wanting a lawyer. I thought that once we picked him up this morning it could buy us some time.'

'Good thinking Bauer. Well done. If you'd have told him the truth, he would have went straight to the press and sold his story.'

'Or contacted Streich,' Stannheim butted in, 'He could a member of the fan club for all we know.'

'Any background on this owner?' Peters said.

'Clean, sir. He's just some arrogant young prick who saw an opportunity and got lucky. Owns about ten places down there. He bought them when they started evicting the squatters. He's wearing a Che Guevara shirt by the way but at heart he's a good little capitalist.'

Peters stood up and almost knocked over the piles of paper that Bauer had brought with him to the pub. *Six months!* He only wanted the lock-up for six months. His time was nearly up. His task almost done. "Christopher" was now in the final phase, Peters realised. The kidnapped Briegel would be his grand finale.

He excused himself and went to the toilet, making sure to lock the door behind him. Then he took out his mobile and spooled down to his messages, the last one that implored him to get back to Heer Strasse. The number had been withheld.

On his return to the bar Peters congratulated his Sergeant, paid the beer bill and without speaking summoned his underling and his commanding officer back to Kottbusser Station.

After running the gauntlet of reporters desperately scratching around for news, any news, of the 'Christopher' investigation and the shrill protests of the Mothers Against Paedophiles, Peters got inside and started searching for Angi, Bauer peeled off towards the custody suites and Stannheim retreated to his office where he once again dropped the window blinds to keep out the rest of the world.

When Peters found Angi fiddling on the keyboard of a computer in the murder room he tapped her on the shoulder.

'Where's our latest guest?' he whispered. She pointed to suite number two which had a red light on above the door.

What they found inside was a man in his early twenties, red hair pulled back into a pony tail, a fringe of hair sprouting from his chin, wearing rimmed glasses, the Che T-Shirt, an army jacket and camouflage trousers, a pair of thick soled trainers plonked on top of a table. Bauer stood behind him, those fists clenched white at the knuckles again, old habits the ex Vopo clearly found hard to bury.

Peters sat in the seat directly in front of the young man, stared straight into his eyes for a second and then said, quietly but with force: 'The last man to sit where you are now sitting is dead. Do you know why that is?'

There was a smirk from the other side of the table.

'No, you going to tell me cop?'

'My name is Captain Martin Peters. What's yours?'

'I don't say anything until I speak to my lawyer. Unless you are going to charge me with something I demand to be freed this instant.'

'Ok mystery man, we can keep up the pantomime if you wish but you should know this is serious stuff. The reason the previous occupant of that seat is dead is because he came into contact with the man you did business with down in Ostkreuz.'

Bauer was starting to smile; he could see the neck of their interogee reddening by the second. Peters meanwhile pressed on.

'The man you rented that warehouse to happens to be the most wanted man in Germany. The serial killer called "St. Christopher" - maybe you've read about him. He's been slaughtering his prisoners on your premises and now I'm wondering if he had an accomplice.'

Peters leaned back, folded his arms and waited for the terror to rise like mercury in heat through the man's body.

'He said he was working on an art project, a piece of installation art involving machines and video. I swear to God I knew nothing about him. I didn't even go near him.'

'Which is just as well Herr...?'

'Lichtenberger. My name is Utz Lichtenberger. I swear to God, sir, I hadn't a clue what he was doing in there,' he was on the verge of tears, shaking, his earlier cockiness consumed by this numbing, physically evident fear that had taken hold.

'Herr Lichtenberger I need you to tell me, and this is urgent, the exact address and location of the warehouse,' Peters said.

'Angi get this man some coffee and while we wait Herr Lichtenberger can tell us what he knows.'

Lichtenberger lifted his face from his hands and looked at Peters with a mixture of desperation and protest.

'What can I tell you? What is there to tell? A well-dressed guy turns up one day at my office and offers me six months rent in advance for the use of a warehouse. Cash too. No questions answered. No interference. No hassle. That's all there was to it.'

'Did he give you his name, leave a home address, say what he did for a living?'

'Only his name. He told me he was called Herr Schultz.'

'Anything else?'

'No, except he kept asking me if I had been born in the DDR. I told him I was from Potsdam originally. He seemed to like that.'

'He would. So Herr Lichtenberger where exactly is this place of yours?'

'It's in a car park, to the left of the Water Tower overlooking Ostkreuz station. It's the only lock-up there.'

Bauer had noted down the location and left the room leaving Peters alone with Lichtenberger who was now in tears.

'You're going to have to stay here for a while as our guest Herr Lichtenberger. Contact whatever friends or family you have and tell them you've had to go away for a few days on business. Do you need a mobile?'

'No. I have one.'

Angi returned with the coffee, handed it to Lichtenberger and was ushered outside by Peters. In the hallway, with Peters continuing to check through the glass over Lichtenberger, Angi spoke first.

'I heard him say he has a handy with him. If he rings out he could blow our advantage.'

'I know Angi. I've got Bauer out in the station rounding up the heavy gang. All we need is a fucking convoy of satellite trucks following us down to Ostkreuz. We've got to shut him up for a while. I'm going to do a deal.'

'A deal?' Angi looked perplexed which tickled Peters.

'I've learned a few things in my time out socialising with journalists Angi. I've a brainwave for our young friend in there,' he said. 'I'm going to appeal to the one thing that always got me what I wanted in the bad old days.'

'What's that sir?'

'His greed,' Peters replied pushing open the door back into the interrogation room.

'Herr Lichtenberger, I have a proposal! Have you ever thought of branching out into the movie business?'

Lichtenberger slurped at his coffee and leaned forward across the table to face Peters again.

'What the hell are you talking about Captain?'

'I'm taking about an American film producer whose been calling at my house all times of the day looking for help on a movie he's in town researching about your tenant down in Ostkreuz. If I was to tell him I could get him the actual place where "Christopher" carved and chopped his way through his prisoners our Yank friend would start waving the cheque book.'

'And why would you do that for me?' Lichtenberger asked slyly.

'Because I want you to do something for me. I need radio silence on your lock-up for the next few hours. If you are going to make any calls out I want Angi standing beside you to make sure you don't happen to mention that you've been renting out a place to a serial killer ... not yet anyway.'

Bauer interrupted entering the suite looking twice as heavy as normal. Peters saw that his Sergeant was wearing body armour; the team must be ready to go.

'Well Herr Lichtenberger do we have a deal then?' Peters said.

'Yes, we have a deal.'

'Good man. Angi stick close to Herr Lichtenberger.'

Once back in the nerve centre of Kottbusser Strasse station Peters found himself surrounded by burly uniformed men, all of them nursing Heckler and Kock machine guns, each with mounted sights and lights on them. Stannheim stood at the entrance of his lair, looking graver than ever. Some of his plain clothes squad like Riedel were putting on flak jackets, checking their short arms, one of the uniforms wielded a sledgehammer, another held a chain cutting device down by his side. The room was filled with the sound of weapons clicking and the murmur of men and women suppressing panic with small talk. For Peters it all felt like the eve of the ground war back in the Gulf years before. He needed to gain their attention.

'Colleagues!' Peters cried out above the din. 'Colleagues. First a few ground rules. We are going to Ostkreuz without a siren wailing or even in a cop car. I want unmarked vehicles preferably ones which the general public can't see into. Second, no gung-ho shit. No one opens fire unless on my command. Finally, I will lead the unit into the building. That's all. We move once the cars are ready. Riedel you are in charge of securing the transport.'

When he had finished Peters saw Stannheim returning to his office, the blinds once more dropped, the shuffling of doors being pulled open as the boss searched for whatever medication he was taking at the time. Peters followed him into the room and shut the door.

'You sounded like that Major on the eve of battle,' Stannheim said slyly.

'Thanks for the promotion sir.'

'You are welcome. Speaking of promotion do you think we should elevate Bauer?'

'Why not sir. He has the nose of a bloodhound. To be fair Riedel might as well get one too. They've done well even thought I would never have them them on my Christmas card list.......Anything else?' Peters asked.

'No. I just wanted to wish you luck.'

Forty One

The tower that cast a shadow over Ostkreuz, once held all the water used to power the steam engines that criss-crossed this rail hub of eastern Berlin for more than a century, resembled a hybrid of a First World War Wermacht spiked helmet and the head of Darth Vader.

Peters' team had arrived in almost complete silence, fanning out of their People's Carriers and hiding, crouched down, behind the lines of vehicles in the car park outside the lock-up belonging to Utz Lichtenberger, all of them trained their Heckler and Koch machine guns or their Glock automatic pistols on the chained up door of the single storey warehouse. The only sound around was the decelerating and accelerating whine of the S-Bahns running east and west, halting at the platform and the muffled crackled voice of the station's PA announcing the ultimate destinations of the suburban trains.

Peters was the last to draw his Glock out from the holster strapped between his left breast and arm pit. The sight of so much carbon-coloured weaponry suddenly produced a churning, reeling sensation in his stomach. This was not how he wanted it to end. He immediately tried to block out a mental apparition of Appolonia Winston.

Leading from the front Peters strolled across the gravel towards the black wooden door of the building and was relieved to see that the chain had been padlocked. *So no one at home*, he said to himself.

He looked over his right shoulder in the direction of the Ostkreuz platforms and noticed that a small crowd had gathered to watch him, at least one was holding up a mobile phone. Pretending he hadn't seen this little gathering audience, Peters signalled to two uniforms, one with the manual chain cutter, the other with a battering ram, to join him at the door. He whispered to them to get it done quickly as possible before someone phoned, texted or emailed from the S-Bahn station.

'Break the chain, knock the door down but don't follow me in. You understand?' he said to the two green-jackets. They both nodded back in unison and went about snapping the links in the chain and bashing down the entrance within a matter of seconds.

Peters went from the fading afternoon light into complete blackness, for every window inside had been obscured. He retreated back to the entrance and summoned the firearms unit to follow him, their lights mounted on top of their guns switched on before plunging into the artificial darkness of the warehouse. Little bulls-eyes of illumination bounced off brick work, thick black curtains, a familiar looking chair and two internal doors at the far end of the room. Peters meanwhile fumbled first on the wall to the left of the entrance and then, crab-like, retraced his steps slapping his way along it until he found what felt was a round switch which he compressed downwards. Immediately the room lit up to reveal only Peters' armed back up. They appeared to be entirely alone.

Behind stood a breathless Bauer, red faced and sweating as always, his own Glock clasped in both hands.

'I had to send some of the uniforms to keep those onlookers back but it can't be long before the sat trucks arrive,' Bauer said almost into Peters' ears.

'Never mind them. You take the door on the left, I'll get the one on the right and fucking be careful,' Peters said through gritted teeth, as they paced forward slowly, past the seat where 'Christopher' had battered Ulrich Hoeness to death in his first film. Beside the chair on the right was an open silver flight case with a DVD camera protected in grey foam inside. On the other side was a closed up slim white Apple laptop laid on the ground. Peters suddenly put one of his forefingers over his lips and then wagged it at Bauer.

From behind the right-hand internal door there was a squeak that grew increasingly audible until it reached the pitch of desperation. Peters signalled to Bauer to cover him as he inched forward, one hand holding the Glock, the other stretching towards a rusting iron bar slammed into a latch. He wrenched the bar's flap upwards and then pulled it across the door which creaked open.

They were met with a revolting stench that temporarily blinded them as well polluted their nostrils, Peters imagining as if he was walking into a gas attack. But the sounds from inside indicated that the prisoner in front of them, arms tied tight behind his back with handcuffs, legs bound together with roll upon roll of thick battleship-grey masking tape, the same coloured tape over his mouth, his trousers and pants pulled down at half mast, resting on a foul smelling toilet bowl, was still alive, if only barely.

Placing one hand on the twitching body, Peters put his gun back into the holster and tore off the tape over the captive's face.

'Herr Briegel I presume,' Peters whispered without a flicker either of sympathy or horror, his only disdain being for the overpowering reek of rotten food and misdirected archipelagos of faeces spread all around the W.C.

He could hear Briegel attempting to suck in the toxic air all around them as he laid him down and began to unwind the tape that his legs had been wrapped in. Just as Peters was about to call out to the uniforms for an ambulance he looked sideways towards where Bauer was standing. His sergeant seemed captivated by something he had seen on the upper end of the left side door. Lights from the Hecklers bounced off it and made the object twinkle and gleam. It was a brand new bright, shiny door key. Before Peters had a chance to shout a warning Bauer turned it clockwise and the door blew out on top of him.

The blast knocked Peters off his feet landing him parallel to a prostrate Briegel who was shaking and jerking violently on the floor. There was a seething, hissing noise in Peters' ears and a hot, wet trickling sensation on his face. He touched his cheek and discovered a clump of thick bristles protruding from his skin. Then his legs gave way.

As he writhed on the ground in pain, Peters sensed a parallel force juddering on the opposite side to where Briegel lay dying. The uniforms had tore off the door on top of Bauer to reveal man with a smoking crater where the left side of his face once was filled with tiny pin pricks of hot metal. Close to Bauer's Adams apple there was a nail embedded deep into his skin. A hysterical Riedel was standing over his friend, trying to punch in a number on his mobile while all the time begging Bauer 'to hold on.' In the distance Peters could hear the faint sound of sirens wailing. His hearing had started to return along with the searing pain now shooting across the side of his face.

Peters used the palms of his hands behind his back to force himself onto his feet again. As he staggered forwards Peters saw a medical team surrounding Briegel.

'Treat him later,' he cried out. 'My officer first. Treat my officer fucking first.'

Two of the firearms unit had grappled Peters under his armpits to prevent him from falling again. As they dragged him towards the entrance Peters looked back to see Bauer now obscured by the paramedics around him; there was no sign of movement at all from Briegel's body.

A booby trap, Peters kept repeating to himself outside, a booby trap. Perhaps 'Christopher's' grand finale wasn't Briegel at all but something altogether more spectacular.

The crowd had thickened on the Ostkreuz platforms when Peters was taken outside into the air. The car park was filling up with ambulances and satellite trucks. A throng was surging forward towards a green, arm-locked line of uniforms while a plain-clothes officer he recognised from the station rolled out a line of white tape between two lamp-posts at a half-way point from the cars to the warehouse.

Someone bundled Peers through the side-door of the black Mercedes People Carrier in which the armed back-up had travelled from Kottbusser Strasse. Inside sat Manfred Stannheim wearing body armour over a dark pin stripe suit. For some inexplicable Peters could not resist bursting out laughing.

'You look utterly ridiculous sir,' Peters said.

The old man bent over and lifted up a small green plastic first aid case underneath his feet. Stannheim flipped it open and threw a piece of bandage torn from its plastic wrapping at Peters.

'And you once again look like you're back at war. Put that over the wound.'

Stannheim bent across Peters and slid the door shut. Now that they were inside no one could see them. The Englishman collapsed into his seat, threw his head back and pressed the bandage tight to his cheek. A delta of blood started forming beneath the gauze, some of it cascading out of the bandage and disappearing into the soft dark carpet of the MPV.

'Bauer isn't going to make it,' Stannheim remarked, fiddling at his earpiece, tuning himself into the pandemonium going on just a few yards away inside 'Christopher's' lair.

Peters glanced out and saw a stretcher being carried out of the warehouse, no drip hooked up to a body, just a sheet pulled up over the head, only for a pair of bony bare-feet sticking out that indicated the cadaver was Briegel.

'Briegel's dead,' Peters said and had to break hard and stop before he added 'at least.'

'Multiple lacerations and a severed artery, they're saying. Lost too much blood, heart-rate flat-lining' Stannheim reported with the clinical detachment of a consultant talking to a group of first year medical students.

'Too much blood lost,' Stannheim said conclusively pulling the listening device from his ear, plopping it into a coat pocket and tearing off the flak jacket.

'I have decided to stop looking ridiculous Martin. Now the Mothers Against Paedophiles can tear me apart if they wish,' the old man said motioning the gesture of surrender.

Of all the officers under his charge it had to be Bauer, the one cop in the squad who had more in common, probably even agreed with Streich, Peters thought.

'What a total fucking sick joke! A sick fuck of a joke! And you know why?'

Stannheim simply shook his head at Peters' question.

'Because Bauer was the only one honest enough in the squad to have his doubts about what we were doing. That time in Vogel's place and after when we watched that film with the little girl in it.

Bauer thought maybe we should just let him get on with it. That none of them were worth saving. Look what happens to the poor bastard when he does try to save one of them. And just when we were thinking of promoting him. He even led us to "Christopher" and that booby trap. I should have spotted that, sir. I've seen them before, a long time ago. In Northern Ireland. Crude but effective. Deadly. I should have spotted that.'

The old man was smoking now, probably to steel himself for what he had heard and what he was about to see.

'Of all the people. It had to be Bauer. The only closet fan our "Christopher" had inside Kottbusser Strasse,' Peters repeated

Something bleeped which prompted Stannheim to reach into the back pocket of the driver's seat in front of him. He rummaged around and pulled up a mobile with a message warning winking on the LCD. After reading the text Stannheim moved towards the vehicle door and slid it back.

'Instructions! I'll bring you in to get properly cleaned and patched up and then we have somewhere to go, Martin.'

'Where's that sir?'

'To the turning point!' Stannheim said before planting his feet on the gravel below, retracing his unit's steps back to 'Christopher's' make-shift studio and into the arms of Bauer's inconsolable best friend and ally.

Forty Two

The 'Laughing Cavalier' kept patting Peters' arm which in other circumstances might have provoked him to punch Schawbowski. He couldn't figure out if the repeated gentle slapping was to steel him or a demonstration of Schawbowski's nervousness in the face of the press pack. There was no point in worrying. They appeared defanged and sheepish rather than their normally feral selves.

Peters and Schawbowski sat alone on the top table of the raised stage of the Berlin Polizei's conference room. They both blinked at the constant mini explosions of light pulsating from beneath them. Yet the atmosphere in the room was strangely still, the only noises audible were the whirr of the recording devices and the constant click of digital cameras.

Schawbowki tapped one of the two microphones in front of them and began:

'Ladies and gentleman thank you for coming at such short notice,' he took a breath and then a sip of water before continuing his preamble.

'This afternoon the murder squad of the Kottbusser Strasse station went to a location close to Ostkreuz. They were acting on intelligence that a warehouse near to the S-Bahn station was being used by the serial killer styling himself "St. Christopher." Having entered the building, they located one Albert Briegel, the man kidnapped by "Christopher" whom we have all seen on our television stations and in our newspapers. I can now confirm that Albert Briegel died at the scene having been held chained up in appalling conditions for so long.'

'We can also confirm that there was one more fatality at the scene. Shortly after freeing Herr Briegel one of our officers accidentally trigged a booby trap bomb device. He was Sergeant

Hermann Bauer. Although there was no sign of the man we now seek for questioning over a series of murders in Berlin over recent weeks, we are confident that this location was used by him not only to torture and kill but also to film these killings as well.'

The head of the Berlin Polizei's press division bowed his head and then turned slightly to face Peters.

'Beside me is someone who is now familiar with you. Captain Martin Peters wishes to say a few words about his colleague who fell in the line of duty today, who died in front of his eyes.

'I cannot emphasise enough the enormous stress and pressure on Hermann Bauer's colleagues in Kottbusser Strasse at this time. They are still in deep shock over the loss of their fellow officer. They need time to grieve. They need space. So with that in mind I hope you will understand that there will be no questions following Captain Peters' statement.'

Peters decided to toy with them for bit by creating a short gap of silence between Schabowski's opening remarks and his own. He used this hiatus to scan his eyes around the room, to zero in and out on friends and foe alike.

Behind the front line of television reporters standing to attention beside cameras mounted on tripods he saw the scribblers, among them, Heike who appeared detached and uncomfortable. Further back he could make out Fest doodling on a notebook with a pencil wrapped up in his long woollen coat, trying and failing to look conspicuous from the pack. When it was all over Peters reminded himself to make a lightening exit otherwise someone definitely would get slugged in the face this evening.

He focussed on one of the cameras, directly towards the team from ARD and kept his glare on it like a prime minister or monarch does when about to talk directly to the nation in times of crisis or at Christmas.

'There are two sets of people I want to address,' Peters said carefully without the need of a script or notes.

'First I want to speak to you the people of Berlin, of Germany, even perhaps the world. Some of you out there might think that what the serial murderer who calls himself "Christopher" is doing, somehow, worthwhile. That he is killing people that many of you regard as candidates for the death penalty. But the law is the law. And it is the job of those who uphold the law to catch and convict men like Albert Briegel. No one else. Those who uphold the law such as Sergeant Hermann Bauer. He was a servant of this city who dedicated his life to protecting you. His entire working life was spent first in uniform and later in my detective unit serving the public. Sergeant Bauer is an innocent victim caught in crossfire. I want you to understand that we, his colleagues, are devastated over our loss. I want you to appreciate the sense of shock and grief my team are enduring. And I want you all to remember his wife and grown-up son who have lost a husband and a father. Remember us all too, his grieving colleagues, the next time you rush to cheer-lead a multiple murderer.'

He clasped his hands together as if in prayer before continuing:

'The other person I want to address is the killer himself,' with these words Peters almost could physically feel the tightening focus of the battery of lenses trained on his face.

'You too were once a loyal and faithful servant - just like Hermann Bauer. With this death surely the time has come to give up your crusade. Because you have killed a serving police officer. With this you have crossed the threshold. You know that! Time is up and you must hand yourself in whatever way you can. Bring this insane campaign to an end before there are more casualties caught in the middle, before further uninvolved civilians are killed or injured.'

He paused once more and added, softer in tone and delivery this time: 'You were once a soldier, so was I. You and I both know when it's time to leave the battlefield. That time is surely now.'

Then something happened that Peters had never expected, that Schawbowski had never experienced in all his years first as poacher and later as gamekeeper, the audience of journalists, camera operators, sound recordists, photographers broke into spontaneous and thunderous applause. Peters bent his head to the right during the ovation and noticed that Fest had got up and skulked towards the exit. He had been the only one on the floor down below that hadn't been clapping. Fest and, also, Heike Nummann who was advancing towards the stage.

She was holding up a mobile phone, displaying a line of text on her LCD. Peters nodded in the direction of the door to the right of the stage. He took the short flight of stairs off it and whispered into the ear of the uniform guarding the door. The green coat pushed opened it and ushered first Peters and then Heike through while Schawbowski started a walk-about amid the media throng some of whom were still applauding.

Peters chose a back room which had been turned temporarily into an information centre printing out statements from the press office relating to Bauer and Briegel's deaths. He asked the PR girl guarding over the printer to give them five minutes. When the press officer had disappeared Peters took the handy off Heike and studied the message.

'TELL HIM TO GO HOME!' he said reading it out loud.

'It's you he wants,' Heike said barely unable to conceal her jealousy.

'I see that now. When did it arrive?'

'Just before you started to speak so eloquently.'

'How do you know it's him?' he asked ignoring her barbing sarcasm.

'Because he used the same number this morning. To tell me your team was getting closer.'

'He must have known then that we were on our way to Ostkreuz because he seemed to have left in a hurry. Anything else?' Peters hadn't meant to let this out and had tried to camouflage it with his question.

She shook her head: 'Only up until a few minutes ago nothing. I expect that that's the last time he will use that number ever again. Maybe the last time he'll ever speak to me.'

Peters thought she looked drained and washed out, her hair lank and greasy, no make-up, even her clothes were all dull greys and browns, as if she too was curling up to conceal herself from the external world.

'I need a cigarette,' she complained.

'You can't Heike. We adhere strictly to the smoking ban. Maybe we could go to Anna's instead.'

'Or how about Heer Strasse?' she added acidly, 'Or would I just be coming between you and him?'

'It's not like that Heike,' he felt he was on the edge of losing his temper without even knowing it.

'And you know I'll tell you everything and then some.'

'Ok then, what's his name?' she asked Peters.

'I can't tell you that yet.'

'I'm not publishing until next Sunday for fuck's sake Martin. I'm hardly going to run to "BZ" tonight am I?' Numann protested.

She stopped for a moment and thought: "How about a trade then?'

'What have you got?' he asked sceptically.

'I know the reason why your Russian friend had those two Basques decapitated.'

'Tell me something I don't know,' Peters countered coldly.

'It's not what you think. They were double crossed. I mean the Basques were. And when they lost the rag one of Yanaev's soldiers got killed. For that there had to be payback....and a message as well. I have my sources Martin.'

'And the message was?'

'The message was to ETA. "Don't come to Berlin a second time seeking pay back. That we are serious people".'

So she had found out about Magdeburg and the shooting in the pub car park, the Basques later killed in revenge for the Russian who got clipped. Peters realised she had more and wondered if she had finally succumbed to Fest's temptation.

'In what way were the Basques double-crossed?"

'They had been sold a pup. They had been sent on an arms buying mission and were disappointed with the goods on offer when they arrived here. ETA got in touch with Yanaev and his empire because they heard he and his team could get their hands on anti-aircraft weapons. New Russian hardware that could take down planes.'

Peters never realised how good Heike was or how extensive and deep her contacts were throughout the city. Even Gavrilov hadn't been able to dig that far into Yanaev's network. The thought of her knowledge terrified him especially if the woman that he hated to admit he still loved had really had entered a 'Festian' pact with the devil from the BND.

'Go on,' Peters said with trepidation in his voice.

'My sources tell me ETA was going to use the weapons to spook tourists from all over Europe. They had planned to film a pilot-less aircraft being shot down with one of their new Russian toys. Then ETA would circulate the video to every broadcaster in the EU and beyond along with a statement warning that unless tourists stayed away from Spain they would do the same to a charter jet anywhere flying over Spanish airspace, possibly one on route to the Costas. Without killing a single soul they could then devastate the Spanish tourist industry and bugger up the economy and perhaps bring Madrid back to negotiate with them.'

'When you say "my sources" I suppose there's no chance of telling me who told you all of this.'

'I think I've told you quite enough. So now what about our "Christopher" then?'

Peters own mobile bleeped. It was a message from Stannheim, a summons to join him in Anna's. When he exited from text messages Peters smiled at Heike.

'His name is Hans-Joachim Streich. Formerly of the National People's Army and a hero of the German Democratic Republic. If you have any contacts in what's left of "Neues Deutschland" you'll find him somewhere in their archives marked under "Heroes".'

She did not reply, but visibly appeared to be absorbing what Peters had just told her.

'Maybe that was his major problem after all,' Heike smirked back after a while at the Englishman, 'Perhaps he just missed being a hero and decided to go after some paedos for renewed glory.'

'Wish it was as simple as that Heike. Oh and by the way he is not in the phone book,' he called out as she left the press room and headed for the door leading back into the chaos of the briefing room.

Forty Three

A phalanx of green coats had surrounded an inconsolable Riedel who was hunched over the bar at 'Anna's'. They had screened Bauer's best friend off from the pub entrance so Peters had managed to elude him on his path towards Stannheim's alternative 'office', the snug where he preferred to hold court. After Peters slid between the tables he sat down beside his boss who already had a Kindl and Korn waiting for him.

'Riedel will be carried out of here tonight,' Stannheim observed as Peters knocked back the snaps in one go.

'Sir, I have a request to ask of you,' Peters said ignoring the old man's concern for Bauer's grieving ally.

'Go ahead Martin.'

'I need to go home.'

'Naturally. You are in need of a rest. You have been for some time by the way.'

'It's not for a rest sir. I think if I'm home "Christopher" will contact me.'

Peters explained the texts to Heike and the messages from the killer that he should return to Heer Strasse.

'I believe not only will he contact but he's going to give himself up.'

'Belief? Cases aren't solved on the grounds of faith Martin,' Stannheim retorted.

'Sir, I know that but I just think he will be in touch.'

'Ok. There's no harm in giving you 24 hours R&R but if and when he does contact you call me immediately after.'

Stannheim's expression then became graver seeming to detect what his officer was planning.

'Under no circumstances are you to meet this man alone, Martin.

He's already killed one police officer; I don't want to lose another one. Don't be so sure he is ready to end all of this.'

'I've no intention of going on any solo run, sir,' Peters found Stannheim's eyes and smiled his way though a lie.

'Good! As long we understand each other. Anything else before you slip off?' Stannheim asked in between several draughts of Pils.

'Yes, Heike Numann.'

'What's she done now?'

'Not what she's done more what's she knows. Our Heike has weapons-grade info on what happened to our two headless horsemen.'

The boss leaned closer into Peters to make sure what he was about to hear.

'Our decapitated duo were Basque terrorists seeking to buy surface-to-air missiles that could shoot down planes. Charter jets to be precise. Hardware that could scare off the tourists from the Costas and smash the Spanish economy. Problem was the deal went wrong, a Russian got whacked and then the Ivans went ballistic. Angry enough to chop the heads of the two Basques.'

'And who the hell is leaking all this stuff to her?'

'I can't be sure sir. Possibly our friend from the BND, maybe some other spook. Whoever it is our Heike is way ahead of the game, ahead of us even.'

Stannheim rubbed out the cigarette he was smoking which made a grinding noise in the ashtray before lighting up a second.

'Be very very careful of Fest, Martin.'

'What makes you think it might have been Fest who gave Heike her scoop?'

'I'm not linking Fest to Heike,' Stannheim said a little too defensively for Peters.

'I didn't suggest you were. It's just that everywhere I turn Fest keeps appearing. Do you know why that is? '

'Because he wants to know everything,' Stannheim bit back sharply.

'Well this inquiry is none of his business while I'm the SIO,' Peters responded.

The old man switched the subject back from 'Christopher' and onto the Russians.

'The last thing we need in Berlin now is a shooting match between the Ivan Mafia and ETA. I just hope the Basques understood the message loud and clear. I'll bet you my pension those two heads were sent through the post back to Spain. If this other nightmare ever ends I'm thinking of sending you down there. I'd like to know what our Spanish colleagues know about all of this.'

'Maybe Yanaev was working for Madrid,' Peters suggested.

'Anything is possible in the world you came to us from,' Stannheim agreed before adding.

'So what did you trade for info on Yanaev and the Basques?' he was looking at Peters slyly.

'The name of the man we seek.'

Stannheim looked like he was going to explode but attempted to avoid detonation by bending over and burying his head in his hands, an old tactic Peters was well used to. After a few seconds of deep heavy breaths Stannheim reclined back in his seat, sunk another Korn and said.

'You are taking one hell of a gamble Martin. If our man is still at large by Sunday and she publishes it every nutter in Berlin will be coming forward saying he is Spartacus. And Streich, meantime, might just decide to disappear for good.'

Peters tried to stay firm: 'I don't believe Streich intends to disappear at all. Why would he given all the publicity he obviously enjoys! I repeat - I'm convinced he wants to bring all this to a close. That's why I need to go home. Besides the name's going to leak out. What we got out of Heike was priceless in exchange. It was a good trade, sir.'

'That's your opinion!' Stannheim snapped.

The old man's favourite detective rose from his seat and threw a ten euro bill onto the table. Stannheim in turn rolled the note up and lobbed it back at Peters, which he then dropped back onto the table. As the Englishman left the bar, carefully avoiding a drunken, distraught Riedel, he wondered if this was what marriage was like.

Outside the pub he thanked the heavens for the rain, pulling up the hood of his Duffel and hailing a cab to take him back to Heer Strasse. Passing the station Peters saw that despite his admonitions the Berlin public were still in thrall of 'Christopher's' wrath. The Mothers Against Paedophile camp had swelled to four new tents that were pinned down against the exterior wall of the station. Crudely drawn banners on white canvas which pledged open support for the killer were strung between the tents and the ledges of Kottbuser Strasse window sills. One enormous woman with scrunched up bleached-blonde hair wearing a T-shirt with the 'St. Christopher' icon printed on it defied the freezing Baltic rain to give an interview on the steps of Peters' HQ. He closed his eyes and yearned to be home soon.

On the journey west his attempts to snooze in the back of the taxi were constantly interrupted by the bleep-bleep of messages on his mobile. The first was from the widow Schuster inviting him over to Westfalisch Strasse for a mid-week drink.

'You've been ignoring me u naughty boy!' she added in her second text which Peters decline

d to reply to realising he was already in 'trouble' with her.

Next came a rare text from Karen advising him to shave off the beard otherwise she wouldn't turn up at 'Taceles' on Friday night. Peters didn't recall that he had even made any arrangements to see her this week.

The final one came from Angi who informed Peters that she had gone to see her father and would try to jog his memory and see if he recalled one Hans-Joachim Streich. Peters spooled through his contact list until he found Lothar Blucher's number.

'Hello Lothar. It seems you are not so well informed as you like to make it,' Peters teased down the line.

He could hear the glug-glug, clink clink of his informer still enjoying the Berlin Polizei's largesse. Blucher then blew his familiar snort of contempt before replying.

'I see you found Briegel before our boy made him into a TV and Internet star.'

'I wasn't talking about Briegel or our friend "Christopher", Lothar. I'm talking about our other friends from the east. There was a tiny bit of detail you conveniently happened to leave out about why our headless horsemen washed up on the Havel shore.'

Blucher's straight-forward, determined response both surprised and pleased Peters.

'You are an impossible man to track down at the minute. I sent a message to you via Fraulein Nummann because no one in your station seemed to know where you were.'

So it had been Blucher and not Fest who had found out about ETA and the missile deal that never was. Peters was instantly filled with gratitude that Heike was still on side.

'Then I apologise profusely Lothar. You are, after all, remarkably well informed. It's just a pity you didn't tell me first.'

'Does it matter? I knew she would rush over to tell you. I can't do things like that by myself of course. Discretion's the name of the game. By the way I think she is still in love with you. Poor girl does she know you are a swinger?'

'How's Anika by the way, any news?' Peters retorted.

There was a chuckle down the line.

'If you think that's going to rile me then you are even stupider than you look. We should both celebrate her departure. It's costing me far less now that she's gone, which is good news for the bean counters of the Berlin Polizei as well.'

'Your sense of civic duty is admirable Lothar. Just don't be putting any rent boys on our tab.'

'Anything else or can I return to my aperitivo?' Blucher said impatiently, ignoring Peters' last remark.

'You have one on me Lothar and the good taxpayers of Stuttgart and Munich. I've got to keep this line open,' Peters said before pressing 'red' to end the call.

Before pulling up on the side road adjacent to the Heer Strasse S-Bahn Peters got the cabbie to stop near the traffic island where implausibly stood a small Lebanese owned restaurant. He bought a bottle of Chateau Musar and some falafels and got back into the taxi, Peters then asked to be driven around the streets running behind his apartment block for about 15 minutes until he was sure no one was waiting to pounce on him with a camera or notebook.

Once in the flat he switched off as many lights on as possible to ensure anyone watching from below knew he was still not in. Peters cooked up the mobile with his charger and made a make-shift bed for the night on his couch. He decided to keep the television set off and sat in silence wolfing down the falafels.

Bauer lived alone but had a family from his first wife, Peters recalled. In what way would they be remembering the former Vopoo whom Peters had saw and heard drawing his last breath?Would they be fishing out the few remaining faded colour photographs of Bauer in the old days before the Turn? Or had they already junked the happier memories and momentos whenBauer was a loving husband, a dedicated father as well as a loyal servant of a state gone by? Our would Bauer suffer the same fate as the country he once served and be dissolved in the acid of time and forgetting?

Mid way through his red wine Peters got up and went across to a book shelf on the far wall that contained several thick photo albums. He plucked down two from either end, one a series of childhood and teenage snaps, the other from his first couple of tours of duty with his regiment.

Opening the first at random he came across a faded colour picture of a Christmas long ago, a lanky ten-year-old shivering in the snow down in their garden wearing his first ever West Ham kit, one studded boot balanced on an orange ball, his father behind him wrapped up against the elements in the kind of fur lined jacket bookmakers and 1970s soccer managers used to wear. The picture must have been from the very early part of that same decade when the pop stars and the people inhabited different planets, the rising stars of Glam in their sartorial sci-fi silvers of oranges and blues while the masses were still fading to grey in freezing fog, the 3-day week, strikers huddled around braziers to keep warm as the nation shivered in power cuts, all in the drab dull blur of Britain in decline.

He thought about Hans Joachim-Streich's own early teen years back then. The state that nurtured him and whom he served to the end had entered what was possibly its only optimistic decade, with the Wall now a permanent feature and all the faces penned behind the barrier turned away from it towards their own internal lives, of old Eric's construction programmes piercing the sky, of the 'friends' from Moscow Centre preparing the first German to go beyond it to soar into the cosmos. It suddenly dawned on Peters that had his father not chosen to flee to England when the Wehrmacht marched into the Sudetenland he could have ended up after the war was over in the Soviet controlled zone and he, like his son later, could have lived a life very much like the one that had shaped Hans Joachim-Streich.

His father was even then an old man in Peters' eyes when that photograph had been taken, greying around the temples, the hair-line receding, the steel-wool mane at the back left to drop just below the ears as if in some kind of existential protest.

He had been in his early forties when he fathered Peters to a woman he had been promising and failing to marry for just over a decade. For his father had already lived 'another' life elsewhere and so chose to glide through his second one with an attitude of passive, discrete contempt. British suburban banality never ceased to bore Peters' father even if he was eternally (but only of course ever in private) grateful to England for giving him refuge.

Despite his gratitude to the place of exile he bitterly resented his son's decision eight years after this picture was taken to apply to Sandhurst once his German and Russian A 'Levels were over. For Kurt Peters had dreamed instead of a son with a place at Oxford, a law degree, then a top post with a leading City firm, a country pile and a legion of nanny-nurtured grandchildren to visit.

Why had he defied his old boy and joined the army? His father's very own nature contained the answer to that question. Because Peters senior revelled in being the contrarian whether at work, pub, union meeting or even at Upton Park. He turned on the revered and defended the put down. He recoiled at what he saw as the fake camaraderie of consensus. He rebelled eventually against the rebellion itself.

Peters found what he had been looking for in a series of other photographs ranging from 1978 to 1980. They started with his DIY Punk phase, the ripped up school blazer, the chain-mail arrangement of safety pins down one of the arms, the red armband on the other, the dog collar around the neck, the spiked hair defying gravity with the aid of starch and the home made tartan trousers tucked into DM boots. The next photo towards the end of the following year witnessed a radical make-over. All from the Punk image but for the DM boots had gone. In its place were drainpipe stay-press trousers held up with red braces over a white Fred Perry T-shirt, red bomber jacket with the furry tartan interior liner, a claret and blue striped scarf knotted around the throat where the dog collar once was, hair cropped tightly. Several pictures further on, taken just before his A Level exams, and his image had altered once more, pared down now to a basic uniform of claret and blue shirt, straight blue jeans, chunky heeled trainers and a wedged foppish haircut – now the rebel without a sub-cult. Because he had simply got sick of the poseurs and band-wagon jumpers. Enlisting in the army, shocking his parents and peers alike, was the final act in his revolution against revolution, his private counter-attack on the teenage rampage.

Later, flicking through the second album and the pictures of his Sandhurst class and those first tours of duty Peters started to imagine the flight paths of his own career and that of Streich's far beyond behind the wall shooting off in parallel directions. For they had both risen rapidly through the ranks of their chosen units. Peters in a regiment that specialised in covert surveillance and undercover operations; Streich in Special Forces where contact meant kill or be killed. While Streich had been taught to hunt down and physically dispatch the class enemy, Peters was destined for 'humanint', the eyes and ears first in the secret war against the IRA and its off-shoots, and much later the interpreter, the recruiter, and the link to allies and foes on the other side of the Cold War's most infamous divide. Only once had Peters been asked deliberately to stand in harm's way when he and the unit he commanded ended the life of the Ulster loyalist assassin Appolonia Winston.

Forty Four

'3.45'

The digits on the top right of the tiny screen reminded Peters of his school, of the time when the last bell clanged in the classroom and the day was finally over. Only this was A.M when he should have been lying on the side of his bed fast asleep.

Its noise jolted Peters out his semi-sleep state and off the sofa where he had been lying. He rolled onto the painted wooden floorboards to break the fall and found himself directly beside where the handy had been charging all night.

'Withheld Number'.

He punched the green button and for some inexplicable reason said his last name, a common German trait on the phone that he had always found pointlessly formal. The voice down the other line had the same clipped, commanding tone as before.

'Speak in Braille. Only in Braille. I do not like these things,' Streich said.

Peters rubbed the grit from his eyes as he tried to compose himself.

'I know who you are,' he said and immediately felt ridiculous.

'Go to the window!'

Peters did as he was ordered, wrenching back the slide door leading to the little balcony overlooking the main road below and the S-Bahn station on the other side.

'Now open your ears as well as your eyes,' the killer said as if he was a teacher beating out a rhythmic message to a subservient classroom.

'Ok. I am,' Peters replied realising how craven he was sounding.

'Can you hear it? Can you hear anything?'

Outside the night was still, no clatter yet from the trains, just a distant faint hum of traffic from somewhere way to the back of Heer Strasse, too early for birdsong, too cold for late night revellers to return by foot from the west end. The only noise that was audibly close was a metallic ringing sound coming from the yellow public phone box down below parallel to the bicycle lane and the line of green, yellow and brown recycling bins by the footpath.

'Can you hear it?' Streich asked, Peters detecting irritation in the voice.

'Yes. I hear it.'

'Then go! We will not be needing these things to communicate again,' at that Streich's mobile phone went dead.

Peters searched frantically around the room for these trousers, a woollen cardigan and a pair of trainers which he put on without bothering to find his socks. When dressed he looked about for a piece of paper and a pencil and then dashed out of the door unsure if he had slammed it and by doing so could have probably lock himself out until the concierge on the ground floor woke some time at after 6.

Down in the street the temperature felt as if it had plummeted by several degrees in twenty seconds. He shivered at the entrance of the apartment block and stared at the yellow painted plastic and glass booth. Peters was relieved to hear that it was still ringing.

The black receiver felt heavy and cool when he picked it up and spoke.

'Feeling more comfortable Streich?'

'I thought I told you to speak in Braille. If you can't I can put this phone down and talk to someone else.'

'I don't think you're going to do that.' Peters said.

'Don't push your luck Captain.'

'You've been riding yours for far too long.' Peters had regained some composure.

'We can have this debate some other time. The priority is that we meet, don't you agree?'

Peters scoured around to see if anyone was passing or taking notice of the unusual sight of a man making a phone call about 4 o'clock in the morning. When he was sure he was still alone Peters answered.

'Yes. I agree.'

'Very well. Let's work out then how to do that,' Streich broke off for a few seconds before continuing.

'Now, I want you to think. Do you know how they represent me?'

'As in your name?' Peters replied before being interrupted sharply.

'Don't mention the name, that is not important. But I shall tell you what is.'

'Please do.'

'Do you know how they represent me? What symbol do they use? Don't say it just make me happy that you understand me.'

Peters had formed a mental picture of the symbol that came into view on that first DVD, when the scenes of horror dissolved initially into black and then to the badge representing the bearded man with a child on his shoulders crossing the river.

'Yes, I understand.'

'Good. Now ask yourself this – what is the secular version? And where is it?'

There was a longer gap this time as Peters searched his mind, his brain physically aching not only from insomnia but being caught in the quick fire of Streich's blunt interrogative tone.

'You can't stay in that booth all night Captain. Somebody going to work is going to report something odd to the first cop they see. And, as you can appreciate, I need to be on the move.'

Peters kept mulling over what Streich had told him again and again in his head. 'A secular version'. At first he was perplexed but then as he started to keep focussed on the image itself of St. Christopher holding the baby Christ a picture formed in his mind. He was roaming mentally across the city, imagining himself flying in the air above, scanning the cityscape in slow motion, gliding over the familiar sights beneath him. In this mental flight Peters felt increasingly close to his destination the further east he soared, until he saw it at last, then he cleared his throat and answered.

'I can see it. I know where you mean. A child on top of a man's shoulder. I need to go east.'

'That's quite enough then. Say nothing more. I don't care how you get there but make it around dawn. Then we can really talk.'

'I suppose it's a stupid question but how will I know it's you?'

Streich sounded amused by Peter's question: 'You are the most famous policeman in Germany, Captain. Let me find you. It shouldn't be too difficult. Now get moving.'

He almost responded with a 'yes Sir' but Streich butted in once more: 'One more thing. Definitely come alone and come unarmed. Is that clear?'

'As crystal.'

'Then go.'

The sound went dead again on the other end of the line and Peters was left feeling completely alone in the booth, a ridiculous sight in his sock-less shoes, a more disturbing one for any early morning passer-by who might have seen him. Peters needed to get back and change and be on the move eastwards as soon as possible.

He was relieved when he found the keys to his apartment inside one of his cardigan pockets. Back inside the flat he immediately went to the sock drawer in his bedroom, found his Duffel coat, put it on and was ready to leave. As he went around the living room trying to find his wallet Peters stared down to the floor at the mobile, now fully charged. This time he opted to leave it at home rather than take it with him as far as one of the S-Bahn stations and his chosen luggage section. He switched the television on and surfed the channels until he found BBC News 24. Leaving the set on a low volume Peters switched on a lamp beside his bookcase, making sure that anyone peering into the flat would think someone was at home. With his socks on his feet and trainers in his hands Peters opened his front door and tip toed back down the block of stairs to the ground floor. He even avoided slipping on his shoes inside the complex in case they squeaked against the polished marble flooring beneath.

Hooded and huddled deep into his Duffel Peters darted across an empty Heer Strasse towards the S-Bahn station. He thought that he must have resembled a diffident novice in cloisters rushing to get to matins on time, if there had been anyone outside to see him.

There was no one behind the ticket counter yet so he fed a couple of euro coins into the machine just ahead of the stairs and bought a Day Card for the whole of the city. Down below on the platform there was no sign of life either until the first train of the morning came into view and Peters could make out the driver of the S-Bahn rumbling in from Spandau.

He took the train five stops up to the Zoo, alighted at the platform and descended into the bowels of the station. On the newsstands a familiar face had replaced the 'Christopher' logo on the front pages – the smiling, podgy, vinous visage of Hermann Bauer. Nervously Peters scanned the papers for any sign of himself delivering his speech the evening before. There were none. They were probably tucked away on pages three or five. Relieved, he made his way through the overnight drunks and junkies being harassed by a patrol of Green Coats near the entrance leading on to the west end. He searched among the human debris being swept out into the morning for any sight of Paul Stannheim but couldn't find him.

Peters walked southwards to the Wittenberg Platz U-Bahn station before seeking out a public telephone booth in order to ring Paul Stannheim's father.

'Sir?' he asked down the line when Stannheim finally took the call.

'Martin. Why so early?'

'I could ask you the same thing,' Peters said knowing that the boss rarely slept for more than a few hours a night especially if his son was on the prowl for smack in town and could return any time in search of a bed or, at least anything he could steal from his father's home.

'Bauer's the most famous face in Berlin....at least for today,' he continued.

'But not for long, eh?' Stannheim replied slyly.

'No. I suppose you're right sir.'

'So why are you calling me at quarter to six in the morning, from a public telephone?' the boss asked.

'I'm on my way to meet our man, sir,' Peters said flatly.

There was a brief hiatus of awkward silence between the two of them, Stannheim's breathing audible, Peters hearing his own heart thumping in his chest, instantly regretting that he had opted to call his commanding officer. Peters was surprised by Stannheim's reply.

'Where are you Martin?' The question sounded more like a command.

'Not far from the west end, why do you ask?' Peters replied, suspiciously.

'Where is this meeting?' Stannheim answered with another question.

'Somewhere in the east, sir.'

'Where's somewhere?' Peters detected frustration in Stannheim's voice.

Peters didn't reply which prompted Stannheim to take a different tact.

'What makes you so sure you won't be next in his firing line? Don't be so arrogant to assume you would never end up in one of this films as his prize captive. Remember – in his eyes you are still the enemy. The ultimate enemy.'

'I'm well aware of what he's capable of but I'm certain he wants to bring this to an end,' Peters tried to sound convincing, even to himself.

'You're taking a hell of a chance with your instincts and they can never be certain.' Stannheim interjected; Peters sensed that the old man was deliberately stringing out their conversation and now cursed his decision to ring him in the first place.

'I'm bringing him in sir, just trust me. I'll be in touch,' he said putting down the phone before his boss could reply and made his way towards the U-Bahn entrance.

He had cut the old man off. He didn't want Stannheim and the team from Kottbusser Strasse to follow him out to Treptower Park, all the way to the Soviet war memorial where 'Christopher' had chosen to meet up. And nor did Peters want to admit that deep down he really wasn't certain what was ahead of him, or what Streich had in store for him. For the first time since he had picked up the mobile earlier that morning and first listened to "Christopher's" commands down the line Peters felt an entirely new sense of fear and dread. He had seen at firsthand how "Christopher" had been prepared to put others in his firing line to dispatch his main targets; "others" such as the residents of Berliner Strasse and Sergeant Hermann Bauer. Why should he be any different? Why would Streich spare him if the killer thought for a moment that a former English spy would get in his way?

Trying to shake off these gathering doubts, as well as anyone who might have been trailing him Peters went first on the U1 green U-Bahn line westwards only as far Hallesches Tor, ascended to the street and then hailed a cab which he took all the way eastwards to the Planterwald S-Bahn station, just one stop south of Treptower explaining to the Turkish taxi man on route that he was a landscape gardener on his way to a freelance job.

Then Peters got back onto the S-Bahn line again, boarding a train north this time with a final destination to Karow, making sure there were no familiar faces in the carriages he might have spotted all the way from his serpentine journey via Heer Strasse and the Zoo. Just one stop later he was on the platform of Treptower Park blinking and squinting as his eyes got used again to the neuralgic light of the sharp, cloudless bright morning.

A few of the early bird suited commuters on their way to work at the gleaming glass high-rise 'Allianz' building adjacent to the station gave him furtive, bewildering looks almost expecting this seemingly half-blind and bearded oddity to start yelling at the top of his voice that he was the Son of Man. No one dared take notice of him.

Forty Five

Even Arkady Gavrilov had once confessed to Peters, in between their endless toasts of vodka as the two of them bade farewell to the Cold War, that when he set foot in the memorial park parallel to the Spree, in the south-east of the city, a lump would form in his throat and tears would well up in his eyes.

'You are treading on 5,000 of my predecessors,' Peters remembered Gavrilov mouthing into his ear after their bacchanalian binge to mark the end of the old order, the Russian's breath reeking of 'Stoly', his face flushed, his arm in a vice-like grip around the Englishman's neck.

'Don't forget what they did Tavarich! Don't forget what they did.'

The women of a certain age in eastern Germany had another name for the Soviet Cenotaph. They called it 'The Tomb of the Unknown Rapist' in memory of the Red Army's mass rape rampage on route to the Reichstag in 1945. Those women never forgot what they did either.

Peters paced slowly through the main avenue extending from north to south of the gardens, past the 16 monuments with carved reliefs of Soviet soldiers, through the gap between the two dark red granite portals resembling the old USSR flag. Beyond stood two stone sentinels down on bended knee each of whom Peters shot a respectful glance towards and instantly wondered why he did so. Perhaps it was the thought of his friend Arkady and that moment alone in the hotel bar back on that incredible night in November '89 when he realised the Russian's mourning for the soldiers who fell on the spot where he was now walking on was also for a life of service Gavrilov had lived in vain.

Now ahead of him stood the 12 metre statue of the soldier towering over the park, a sword at rest by his side, a child on his shoulder, a crushed Swastika beneath his feet. The figure was meant to represent Nikolai Masolov, a Battle of Berlin veteran whom Soviet propaganda would have it found a lost girl wandering around the chaos of Potsdamer Platz, rescuing her from danger and taking her to the safety of a nearby orphanage. A caring, sharing poster boy for Proletarian Internationalism, a friend for the new first workers and peasant state on German soil. As Peters walked in a diffident pace towards the monument he imagined Streich in his formative years being taken to pay homage here first in the white shirt and red neck tie uniform of the Young Pioneers and later the dark blue of the FDJ youth movement. For a generation of Streichs born after the war and nurtured by the state this was the closest they would have come to religious ritual.

Peters changed tempo and started to make as much noise as he could while charging up the steps leading towards the altar beneath the sculpture. He could hear the percussion of his rubber soles striking on the stonework echoing all around him as if beating out a message that he was coming for Streich, camouflaging the inner fear Peters that felt building up, suppressing the tremor of terror now raging within.

But at the entrance to the inner portal Peters suddenly stopped himself, stood for a few seconds, took in breath and closed his eyes. When he opened them again he was inside it, noticing the morning sunshine bouncing off individual golden squares of the secular Icon in front of him. He could make out eight figures imprinted on the wall, two of whom in military uniforms were crouched down laying a wreath. There was also a real wreath directly in front of him of red and white ribbon, Cyrillic writing in gold on each side of an arrangement of fresh red roses.

To his right out of the corner of his eye, partially obscured by shadow, leaning away from the laser-shaped shards of light penetrating this inner sanctum, stood a man whom Peters guessed was about six feet two tall, thin but with broad shoulders. In this penumbral refuge, Peters could also make out that he was a wearing a fur lined three quarter length leather coat that was zipped up to his throat, jeans and Doctor Marten shoes. The outline of his hair was short and prickly and cut more severely at the sides.

'Move back. Closer to the entrance,' it was the same tone of near impatient authority as before. Peters stepped back a bit and could feel an icy blast of cold wind howling up the avenue from outside.

Streich moved carefully into view until he was as fully illuminated as the men and women painted on the mosaic behind him. Peters silently saluted Oskar Beer's powers of description. The wing-mirrored cheek bones, the hooded but piercing blue eyes, the chiselled dimple on the chin, the sharp nose and the swarthy skin. And all around his face a bluish hue that suggested he had spent a long time in the early hours in front of the shaving mirror.

Peters looked down to where Streich was holding a Glock pistol and thought that if he open fires in this instant his guts would explode and he would die in an agonisingly slow, internal fire-storm. In that instant he was no longer sure that 'Christopher' had come to surrender.

'You told me to come unarmed, how come you are?' Peters protested nervously.

'This is just a bit of insurance, to buy some time, to explain oneself,' Streich answered apologetically.

'You are under no threat from me Captain Peters. I give you my word. I think you already knew that.'

'Hardly as a Prussian gentleman though, Herr Streich. Pointing that at me is hardly boosting my confidence.'

The killer shook his head and smiled at Peters while continuing to train the pistol at the English detective's stomach region.

'Only an English Imperialist would say something crass like that. But I have to praise you all the same – you did well to work out where to come. I hope you weren't as successful at elusive action in your spy craft days.'

'Successful enough to see the system you fought for collapse and die,' said Peters impatiently. 'So let's get down to business Streich. You know and I know all this has to stop.'

Streich continued to smile: 'That's funny coming from a man who has a gun pointed at him. Your bravado is very transparent

Captain Peters and you assume far too much.'

'There's nothing funny about watching one of your colleagues die in front of you. This has gone beyond you kidnapping and killing paedos Streich. Your booby trap toy killed one of my officers, who himself used to be a loyal and faithful servant of the DDR.' Peter's truculent reply surprised even himself.

The news that Bauer had been a Vopo in the East Berlin police seemed to temporarily shake Streich. Peters sensed he had scored a direct hit.

'I want to make it clear to you that I never had any intention of hurting any of your colleagues.'

Then he added as if standing to attention, as if making a speech from the dock:

'I wish to express my sincere condolences to his family and all of his comrades.'

Peters kept his finger on the pressure point.

'You took wanton risks. Think of the passers-by you could have killed when you blew up that sex shop near Sauvigny Platz,' Peters stopped and noticed that Streich was shaking his head vigorously.

'What bombing at what sex shop? You think I blew up that place where those ageing perverts used to congregate. I had nothing to do with that. I will own up to everything but I can assure you I had no hand in that incident.'

Peters tried to conceal his terror, the realisation that it had probably been Yanaev's 'soldiers' who had destroyed Blucher's business and not this morbid mass killer in front of him.

'All the same, they were all just collateral damage to you Streich. That's all Hermann Bauer was to you.'

'How dare you call down 'Collateral Damage' to condemn me since you would know all about it? How much 'Collateral Damage' did you and your army do when you were bombing bunkers in Baghdad and television stations in Belgrade! You see I've read your CV Captain Peters and you took part in Operation Blood for Oil back in '91 when you and the Yankees thought you could go around policing the world. So don't think you can launch any salvoes from the moral high ground especially when you are in a place like this,' he said the last four words in a whispered reverence.

To mask his growing terror, brought on again by the way Streich's tone had instantly darkened, Peters feigned guile.

'So what's this all about then Streich? Do you see yourself as Nikolai Masolov up there rescuing the kiddies?'

'As I said to your good friend Fraulein Numann, your crude pop psychology won't work on me, Captain. My motivation was purely political.'

'Political? If it was political why not go out and bomb a bank or shoot a leading industrialist.'

Streich looked insulted by Peters' incitement to terrorism.

'That's what student anarchists would do, don't take me for one of them. They tried that in the seventies and it only led to reactionary forces being strengthened. Besides even bankers and business tycoons have families and loved ones too. Eventually even the worst bosses who you would shoot would gain some sympathy from the public. As for those I targeted, well there was and is no quarter, no sympathy.'

'I really don't see how killing a few perverts and posting their deaths on the Internet is going to shake Capitalism's monopolistic foundations,' Peters jibed.

Streich looked frustrated at being unable to convey his logic.

'Because Captain Peters these beings understood the laws of supply and demand. They scoured the world, the so-called free world, with dollars and Euros in their pockets, coveting anybody they saw. In their case the most vulnerable. In your rotten system anything can be bought, anything! They understood that...clearly. And that is why I chose them as my targets.'

'And what is the bloody point of all this then?'

He ignored Peters' question and fired off one of his own.

'Tell me Captain how come your German is near flawless except of course for that Swabian tinge on your tongue.'

'I'm half German,' Peters replied curtly.

'Which half?'

'On my father's side. He was a refugee from Hitler who fled to England in '38.'

'But you are not Jewish?'

'No, he was a Sudeten.'

Streich now seemed puzzled by Peters' personal history and so the Englishman continued, convincing himself that the more he engaged with the killer the better the chances of his eventual surrender.

'He was one of the few who didn't want to be liberated by the Fuhrer and his chums. He was a Social Democrat who knew the choice was either exile or a KZ. Luckily for me he chose England. He worked for the BBC during the war, writing up broadcasts in German encouraging Wehramacht units to give up on a lost cause.' Peters gave a short pause. 'And how about your father?'

There was a grunt of contempt from Streich and then a smirk.

'I see we are back with the pop psychology again. I'm not doing this because my father abused me or disappeared or something of that ilk. I was the son of a railway worker who used to be a Red before the Nazis took power. He survived the war and opted to stay in the DDR and resume his real politics. I had a very happy childhood in our republic and I don't remember any weird uncles with wandering hands around me back then either. As I said before Captain Peters my struggle is purely political.'

Peters noted with alarm the growing impatience in Streich's voice, the ever darkening tone, the hissed hint of menace.

'Is? Shouldn't that be was? Isn't this what our encounter here underneath Nikolai's feet is all about? To bring this all to a close?' Peters felt the frenetic rhythm of his blood hammering in his ears. Was he pushing Streich too far? Was he riding his luck, relying too much on his own confidence? He looked in alarm again at the Glock pointed towards his mid riff.

'There are many phases to this struggle Captain. You served in Northern Ireland. You must have heard the phrase "armed propaganda" before?' Streich asked.

Peters nodded recalling that anaemic euphemism used to mask the blood splattered campaigns and counter-campaigns of sabotage and assassination of the Troubles.

'Then you will realise that this has been nothing more than an advertising campaign. A rather negative one it has to be said. To highlight the rotten core of a system where anything and everybody can be bought and sold. Even children.'

'Nothing more? Is that all Hermann Bauer's life was worth then? An act of advertising?' Peters suddenly heard his angry outburst now echoing around the chamber.

'Calm down Captain Peters. Don't ruin your greatest triumph by losing your temper. I have to be certain I can trust you. If I can't I don't know where we go after that. I repeat that I never meant to hurt anyone beyond my targets. I will apologise before the world for that.'

'Briegel is dead,' Peters said.

'I have to confess I have mixed feelings about that. The world won't miss the likes of Briegel but still his demise wasn't the one I had planned for him.'

'What was Tavarich? Go on, I'm intrigued.'

'If your team has done their work they would have found my sword by now. I had it locked away in my HQ down in Ostkreuz.'

'You were going to behead him, like the second one?'

'With an important difference, Captain. Briegel's execution should have been in real time, live, as it happened. I was looking forward to that one. I would have enjoyed that.'

'Why the delay? After all you were so meticulous,' Peters asked attempting to suppress his repulsion.

'Because other swords were approaching. I was on my way there when I learned you were closing in. I had to make other arrangements quickly, to ensure that whatever was to happen to me, my message would be transmitted. Nothing should stop that Captain. Not even you.'

Streich paused for a few seconds and then twirled the trigger guard of his Glock around, spinning the weapon in a rapid revolution until his palm cupped the gun barrel while the automatic's butt faced Peters.

'It's time to come in from the cold and explain a few things Captain.'

A more generous smile this time broke out over Streich's face as he looked up towards the roof of the chamber.

'I still can't believe how easily we surrendered back in '89,' he sighed.

'If only we had been tougher. That's what I have learned. That's what guided me on my way across the river as Christopher, Captain. The necessity to carry it out through. The clarity needed to transmit the message,' Streich started to laugh.

'And to think that an English Imperialist will help guide me through to the next phase. Still, I'm glad it's you....'

In that instant two jets of blood spurted out of Streich's forehead, from a dead centre point just above where his eyebrows were. His body pitched back against the icon-mural and a lurid delta of runny red matter splattered against the tiles and then slid in a blasphemous trajectory down the image of a Russian mother, her head bowed in honour to the fallen. The squealing ricochet of the bullet when it exited from Streich's skull created a deafening cacophony in the altar room and Peters felt a sharp pain in his ears that felt like the impact of rapidly changing air pressure on a flight's descent.

When he took his hands off his ears there was still a reverberating, hissing noise in them which reminded him of feedback, but, more potently, of the bomb in Ostkreuz.

The floor beneath him appeared to be dissolving as the room began to spin. Peters backed his body into the wall to shore himself up against the impression that the ground was turning spongy and viscous. In his attempt to steady himself and avoid passing out Peters failed to see the other living person now in the memorial. Only when he had regained a grip on his consciousness did Peters realise that he had been joined inside by Fest.

The BND agent also at first seemed to be oblivious to Peters' presence walking past him as if he was invisible. Fest then crouched down beside where Streich lay, his gun shoved back into his long woollen coat out of which he plucked a cigarette box, flicked it open, nimbly took out a gold slender Ronson lighter and a Marlboro Light and lit up, the smoke rising from its tip curling up and joining the smoke from the entry wound on the serial killer's head.

Fest was transfixed on the linear movement of the two smoke

trails intertwining and rising up in a single noxious blue column towards the ceiling which supported the statue outside. Fest rose up from his position and took the gun back out of his coat pocket.

Now another pistol was being pointed at Peters, this time in the direction of his head. It was as if Fest sensed that Peters was thinking about rushing towards him. At first he couldn't make out what the spook was mouthing but then Peters started to hear his own breathing, the feedback receding, the silent commands becoming audible.

'You have just killed my prisoner,' Peters heard himself saying.

'No, you have just murdered my prisoner.'

He searched Fest's face and noticed that nothing had flinched, his slightly slanted eyes still stared blankly at him, not a single nerve muscle rippled, his whole bearing was frozen. Fest's diaphragm didn't even appear to be moving to draw breath.

The agent dropped his cigarette and rubbed it out using one of his heavy brown brogues on the floor before picking up with a gloved hand, taking out a plastic money bag from his coat and placing the fag end inside it.

'Streich was pointing his gun at an officer of the Berlin Polizei and I had to act,' Fest said in a tone of theatrical rehearsal.

'It was an instantaneous decision. I had no choice. We have already lost one esteemed colleague of the Berlin Polizei. I felt that it was my duty to save the life of another,' Fest said for the benefit of any future tribunal and not Peters.

'You have just murdered my prisoner,' Peters repeated provocatively.

Fest refused to rise to the bait and just smiled, all the time his Glock still pointing at Peters' forehead.

'You are under a lot of stress Captain Peters. You have seen two men die in front of your eyes in the last 24 hours. This was not murder. It was an act of defence. Your defence.'

He realised that Fest had indeed been in rehearsals, he had prepared every line after the execution perhaps even have anticipated that Peters might be wearing a wire or using a mobile's recording device.

'This isn't exactly the time or place to be debating over what happened here,' Fest said maintaining his ice cold grip on the situation.

'You need to speak to your superiors later but for now - ' he broke off and turned slightly, his left ear cocked towards the entrance behind him as the wailing sound of sirens started to pierce the still of the morning.

'Oh listen. Here comes the cavalry. Time for me to go.'

He inched back until he was at the steps which was when Peters cried out.

'Fest! This isn't over. You can't get away with executing suspects. You've become exactly like him.'

The face suddenly de-frosted as Fest sniggered and shook his head.

'Who the hell is Fest? The only Fest I know, Captain Peters, is our distinguished historian of the Third Reich. And now I really must be off before the Keystone Cops from Kottbusser Strasse get here. So I'm afraid to say that it is very much over.'

He turned swiftly and charged back down the steps into the memorial garden leaving Peters, his legs now wobbling, his hands shaking, his body choking with an enveloping nausea, standing over the cadaver of the most popular murderer in German history.

Forty Six

When he was sure the BND agent was gone Peters crouched down over Streich's body and began to pat his coat until he found a thick chocolate bar shape bulge inside the serial killer's top pocket. Peters gingerly pulled back the zip and using his thumb and forefinger delicately pulled out the mobile. He noticed that it had been switched off and decided to keep it that way until he was as far away as possible from Treptower Park.

Back outside two black blurs of iron and armour brushed past Peters as he stumbled into the light. When he reached the penultimate step he turned around and called back to the firearms unit now entering the altar: 'Don't waste your breaths. The only thing moving in there is his blood on the wall.'

Facing Peters was an even thinner, slightly crestfallen, sunken Mannfred Stannheim. Peters noticed that the boss had his hands clasped in front of his crotch; he looked like a soccer player defending a free kick protecting his loins. He waited until he was close enough to sniff the familiar stale odour of cigarette smoke around Stannheim.

'Just fancy meeting you here, Mannfred. Did you wait until your master left the scene?'

Stannheim pursed his lips, shrugged his shoulders and attempted to stiffen up.

'By the way where did Fest go? Or whatever he is actually called,' Peters continued. 'Did you know that that wasn't his real name?'

The old man shot Peters a grave look before taking a cigarette box from of his trench coat, flicking it open and pulling one out. He waited until he torched up before finally speaking.

'I assume our friend up there is dead.'

'You assume right sir. Fest executed him but I assume you probably knew that too. When did you make the call by the way? Was it this morning when I called you?'

'There was never going to be a trial, Martin. Never.'

'So Fest, or whoever he is, and his masters opted to kill him. They're just as bad as Streich was. Judge, jury, executioner...' Peters stopped himself, recalling his last tour of duty in Northern Ireland and the fate of Appolonia Winston.

'Listen Martin. These people were never going to give Streich his day in court. He was preparing to put an entire system on trial. So I repeat they were never going to let that happen.'

'And you set me up to draw him out. You made that call,' Peters hissed.

Stannheim shivered slightly and moved back a few paces before putting his hand out until it was touching Peters' chest who immediately flicked his boss' fingers off his body.

'Now get out of my way.'

'Where are you going?' Stannheim asked with panic in his voice.

'Straight over to Heike and the Springer building. I'm going to give her the scoop of her career.'

'No you are not.'

Peters shook his head in disbelief.

'You just try and stop me Mannfred.'

Stannheim keeled forward and gripped Peters by the shoulders.

'They know everything about you Martin. Everything! The swingers club, the old dear who owns the pub up in Hallensee with the mini-dungeon in her house,' Stannheim tried to go but was cut dead.

'As I've told you before I don't give a fuck what they know or what they want to do with it. If they publish it in Bild or BZ, I couldn't care less. It doesn't bother me Mannfred what they say or do, not any more. That's my private life, the life beyond the walls of Kottbusser Strasse and I don't break any laws.' Peters interrupted his boss and stormed off back down the central avenue of the Treptower war memorial. Stannheim turned and ran to head Peters off.

'Listen to me Martin. Listen to me. It's not just about you, not any more. They know everything and that includes not just your Turkish lady friend, the married one, the old kinky dear who owns the pub, and worst of all your girlfriend the ghost.'

Peters froze and felt the blood draining from his upper body.

'What are you taking about Mannfrend?'

'Don't insult my intelligence or yours. You've been knocking off a female Turkish taxi driver for nearly two years behind her husband's back. Fest, or as you so rightly point out, whoever the hell he really is, even knew the number of the cab firm she works for and that her hubby spends most of his spare time doubled-over on the mosque floor. But what 's much more important to me is the reputation of the squad and yes my favourite officer - the one who shot and killed a woman in Ireland. Fest's knows all about your tour of duty over there. I am not the only one who can call in Cold War favours. Fest must have spoken to some of your old chums in MI6.Just imagine the headlines in BZ about your history.' Peters realised that Stannheim had regained his authority, reclaiming his power with this single sordid piece of knowledge, which he held in common with Fest.

'What's the score here, sir? What are you threatening me with?'

Stannheim looked genuinely disappointed at the questions.

'I'm not threatening you at all Martin. This is not about me. Whoever Fest is and whoever he works for is who you should really fear. He could unleash real damage on us all.'

'I've just seen what he's capable of,' Peters tone too had softened slightly.

'Well then, you'll understand that he's prepared to drop you and everyone you know in it including your lovers and more importantly your colleagues.'

'So I just sit and shut up about the fact that a government agent executed my prisoner in front of me?'

'In a word, yes.' Stannheim answered apologetically.

'After all whoever Fest is working for will bite back that you did exactly the same thing all those years ago in Belfast.'

'Oh, I'll think about it Mannfred but not for your sake. Not anymore! Meantime you just think about this. If I go along with this charade you put any idea you might have had of throwing in the towel and buying that little apartment in Majorca or Ibiza out of your mind. You're staying in that glass cell of yours back at HQ. At least there we can keep an eye on each other until they come for the both of us, 'Peters said.

'They?' Stannheim asked.

'You don't seriously think this scandal can be covered up forever Mannfred? I'm just letting you buy time – again for the both of us! Just you wait and see, they'll come for us. Eventually we'll hang together for this one.'

As he prepared to turn on his heels and head out of the memorial garden, Peters suddenly noticed that someone was absent from the units now fanning out on either side of the statue and the lines of white coated forensic officers charging up the steps towards the altar above the giant crushed concrete swastika.

'Where's Angi? I thought she'd be taking the lead on this one,' Peters inquired noticing that it was Riedel in his puffed up Porsche jacket and driving gloves conducting the enclosure of a forensic screen around the steps and the entrance to the Soviet war memorial.

'She's putting the finishing touches to her own latest triumph. Her eagle eyes have once again solved yet another case. She had the guts to rewind that awful tape we found of that little girl being raped and she spotted something every interesting at about 2 am this morning.'

'Which was?

'Another tattoo. Not of battlefields but of a name. "Misha", to be precise. Angi spotted it on one of the hands that was tearing off the child's clothes.'

'And what was the significance of that, sir?'

'It was the same name tattooed in exactly the same place on the hand of one of the Russians we picked up who were distributing this shit from a flat in Prenzl'berg. Turns out they weren't just distributors but the producers and actors too. Dirty bastards.' Stannheim said.

Peters jerked a thumb behind one of his shoulders towards the direction of the statue.

'Maybe it would have been better to have let Streich just get on with it and take them all out.'

'That's what Bauer said and look what happened to him,' Stannheim said shaking his head.

'So we all succumb to blackmail in one way or another, sir.'

'Try not to see it that way Martin,' Stannheim attempted in vain to sound re-assuring.

'Don't worry, sir. I'm changing my plans for the rest of the morning. Heike can wait for another day. Can I borrow your handy? I left mine back in the flat.' Peters asked with mock effusion.

Peters put his hands his pockets and stroked Streich's switched off phone with conspiratorial caresses while Stannheim handed over his own flicked open mobile. On the top left hand corner the digits told Peters that it was only 7.20 am, still time for him to contact Miriam before she ended her night shift when on weekdays she would pick up Ayse for school. He texted her to meet him at the entrance of the Treptower Park S-Bahn station and then, concealed from his boss, instantly erased the sent message.

'Thanks, Mannfred,' he said handing the mobile back.

'Where are you off to now?' Stannheim asked.

'To see yet another equally stupid stubborn old man,' Peters said and turned again on his heels, the sound of the grit and stones grinding underneath his feet. He picked up a pace and ran zig zagging through an approaching arrow of reporters, photographers, camera operators. But the media throng simply ignored him as they appeared to be riding on a hypnotic wave, being drawn towards the statue at the far corner of the park, towards the final end of 'Christopher's Wrath.'

A few curious commuters were standing around the S-Bahn entrance observing in the distance the crowd advancing towards the white tape and the green lines of uniformed officers blocking their progress. Like the newspaper reporters and the network journalists, the workers paid absolutely no attention to Peters.

He only had to wait for about ten minutes because Miriam normally finished her shift in the south-east corners of the city close enough to Kreuzberg where she lived and Friedrichshain, the headquarters of the cab firm she worked for.

Sliding in to the front passenger seat beside her, Peters almost leaned over to kiss her but Miriam shifted slightly to her left and he had to do with her forefinger gliding over the palms of his hands instead.

'Where to Martin? I think we need to get out of here.'

'Take me to Pankow, near the Viner Strasse U-Bahn, drop me there and I'll walk the rest of the way.'

She looked across to him and narrowed her eyes inquisitively.

'What's going on over there?'

'We've got our serial killer at last. The people of Berlin and the world will be in mourning today. Just drive, love.'

He signalled that he didn't want to go on talking about what he had just seen by closing his eyes, throwing his head back against the seat and rubbing his hand up and down the skin tight jeans over Miriam's thighs.

As she pulled up underneath the bridge of the overhead S-Bahn line Peters shook himself out of his torpor and twisted in his seat. He squeezed her hand tightly and stared straight into her eyes.

'Miriam. We have to give each other a wide berth for a while. Once they get over the loss of their greatest story they're going to come after me. They'll be camped out at Heer Strasse for weeks. I don't want you getting caught in the crossfire.'

Then Peters leaned over and planted a lustful, wet kiss onto her lips before backing out of the car.

'Martin, I know why but hopefully not forever,' she called back to him as Peters made off in the direction of the Domath family home. Her words left him with a faint sense of hope.

The Colonel looked perplexed when he yanked open the iron, rusting door to his apartment, the entrance to the Socialist sarcophagus from which Angi's father had locked out the world. Peters followed him up the hallway in the dim orange light deciding this time to keep his shoes on very deliberately against the Colonel's orders.

When Domath returned from the kitchen with two bottles of beer he scowled at Peters.

'Where is my daughter?' he asked as he popped open the bottle tops with his DDR flag opener.

'She's busy putting some really bad men behind bars. But even if she wasn't busy I would still have come alone,' Peters said nursing the beer bottle close to his chest in a defensive position. He spotted that the lower hem of the Colonel's pyjama top peeked out of the moth eaten lamb's wool jumper pulled over his torso. His breath was beery and his eyes watery. Peters wondered if Angi's old man was finally giving up.

Peters waited until the Colonel sat down and placed his beer on one of his doilies by the table at the side.

'Streich is dead.' Peters said.

The Colonel looked up towards Peters but showed no surprise.

'How did he die?' Domath said without any emotion.

'He was shot during an attempted arrest but that is not why I'm here Colonel. I'm here because you tipped him off that we knew his name that we were closing in. Tell me this – did you make the call after Angi came to see you?'

The Colonel seemed to be staring at some point on the opposite wall just beneath a framed portrait of Che Guevara.

'Am I under arrest?' he asked flatly.

'No. We'll not go down that road Colonel. I just want to know how you got in touch with him and why you never bothered mentioning it to either Angi or myself.'

'It's not so complicated Captain Peters. Once Angi told me the name of your suspect I realised who this was.'

'And then?' Peters butted in.

'And then it was a simple case of ringing some old comrades, tapping into the network and coming up with an address. He had a little flat up in Strausberg. I knew the place well, I've been up there a few times for conferences, to meet some old friends.'

'So you just took the S-Bahn north and rapped on his door.'

'No. I left a number in his mail box and urged him to call. Which he did.'

'Why did he not smell a trap?'

'Because he knew who I was and what I had been,' the Colonel said in an angry protesting tone, pointing into his chest.

'He knew that I could be trusted.' Domath added.

'When did he phone?' Peters went on.

'About 48 hours ago.' Peters realised it was about the time just before they raided Streich's lock-up at Ostkreuz and that he might have been there but for the fact that 'Christopher' had rang the Domath's house.

'And so you told him that the game was up, that we knew who he was. Presumably you mentioned that you knew me, that your daughter worked in my unit. He was always going to take someone like you seriously, wasn't he?'

The Colonel put down his bottle and again folded his hands together as if in prayer.

'Are you wearing a wire Captain Peters?'

'Don't be ridiculous Colonel, we're not living in the DDR anymore?'

'Mores the pity,' Angi's father grumbled. 'More's the pity.'

'But let's not get sidetracked here,' Peters continued.

'The issue comes back to you wiring off Streich and preventing us from arresting him at the scene of where he acted out his crimes. Thanks indirectly to you Colonel, Streich in the end gets clipped.'

Peters kept twisting the knife: 'So I hope you realise what you did. That you ruined our element of surprise and as a result things got messy.'

Domath shot up from his chair and leaned forward into Peters' face.

'If you want to arrest me go ahead. I have nothing to fear from the likes of you, never had, never will.'

'There you are being ridiculous again Colonel. Thinking you are fighting the old struggles. Sit down there in that chair before I knock you down or least knock some sense into you,' Peters snapped back, the force of his bellicosity driving the old soldier towards where he had been sitting.

'I'll get you another drink Colonel, you just sit there and relax,' he said parting the long multi coloured strips of tape that marked the boundary between the living room and the poky kitchen.

When hc had retrieved two more bottles, popped open the tops with the East German flag opener and planted one on the table beside Domath, Peters resumed, this time sounding more emollient than before.

'I repeat Colonel, you are not under arrest. Angi is far too important to me.'

Peters walked over and clinked Domath's second bottle still standing on the table.

'I just want you to know why I'm not charging you with obstructing justice. I don't want Angi dragged into any scandal. She's the best I have. She'll go far. I'll make sure she does.'

The Colonel stood up again this time with his head bowed as if once more about to break into prayer. Or perhaps to click his heels.

'Then I want to thank you Captain. You really do care about her don't you?'

'As I said she's the best I have. The most trustworthy. The most reliable.'

Her father extended one of his bony hands out to shake Peters who instantly declined the offer by shaking his head.

'There's a final thing I want you to think about Colonel, as well your stupidity in tipping off Streich. Because he wasn't there when we came calling at his lock up in Ostkreuz a good man died.'

'You mean your sergeant?' Domath asked diffidently.

'Sergeant Hermann Bauer. At one time too a loyal and faithful servant of the German Democratic Republic. If Streich had been at home at least he would have had the manners to tell us where his booby trap toys where. Think about Bauer too when you can't sleep at four a.m and you're pondering over your decision to jump on the S-Bahn up to Strausberg to help out an old comrade.'

After leaving the Colonel's home Peters made his way back to Viner Strasse and took the U-Bahn one stop to the Schonhauser Allee and then two more clicks east on the S-Bahn to Greifwalder Strasse, all the time keeping a picture in his mind of a teenage Angi Domath, rigged out in her deep blue uniform, flowers in her arms, in front of the giant sculpture of the DDR's home grown adopted wartime martyr.

When he finally arrived at the statue Peters sat down and took out the mobile he had stolen from Streich's jacket earlier that morning. Peters pressed down the on-switch, waited until the master screen appeared and then searched for the video gallery. The last item recorded showed the previous day's date, he had found exactly what he had anticipated that Streich might do.

A frozen frame of Streich standing facing a camera, the red flag and the banner of the DDR pinned up on a bare brick wall, inside what Peters guessed had been his private execution chamber in Ostkreuz, suddenly jerked into motion.

'I am Major Hans Joachim Streich or as you probably know me better as St. Christopher. This film has been made to ensure that my reasons for all that I did during this campaign are explained. In the event of my arrest, or death, this may be my last message to you.'

Peters nursed the phone with a claw like grip holding it up in front of his eyes, faking texting movements with the digits of his other hand in case anyone was looking even though there wasn't a single soul around.

'What I did I did as a soldier, in a war. That war was conducted against the worst exploiters, against those who regard even children as products that can be bought and exchanged in this so called free market. In the system that promised freedom and choice and boundless prosperity.

'I merely targeted its rotten core. Its putrid essence. These beings that I executed were selected not only over what they did but for what they represented. The struggle against them was and is the struggle against that entire system.'

The mini screen froze again capturing Streich's truculent stare into a lens, his head bowed slightly. Peters worked the screen until he found the emails and opened up a sent page, attaching the last of the video files to it before flicking on the digits until he found Heike Numann's 'Wams' email address. He was about to make his ex-lover the most famous journalist on the planet.

Once he was sure the message had been sent Peters switched off the power, broke off the battery and dropped it in a bin nearby before walking west to the Prenzlauer Alee S-Bahn. When he made it back to Kreuzberg, at a strategic distance from the Kottbusser Damm and the station, Peters walked to the Landwehr Canal. Hunched over the railing of the waterway close to where the old frontier once stood that cut off Kreuzberg on three fronts from the rest of what was then West Berlin, he poked out the phone's Sim card and with forefinger and thumb snapped it in two. He flicked one half of the card into the water, and walked along to the end of the canal. Peters kept the remaining half inside his wallet reminding himself to ditch it in one of the bins inside Zoo station on route to the refuge where he had already chosen in his mind to hideaway.

Forty Seven

To escape the intrusive persistence of the media camped outside his apartment Peters surrendered into captivity. For the next nine days he hid in Frau Schuster's' house down in Dahlem acting out a 'work routine' the widow had mapped out for him on the first day of his voluntary refuge.

She had agreed to run the bar during the day, letting the Polish girl she had recently hired to take charge of the pub in the evenings. So on her return each afternoon the widow would come through the door, drop off her shopping bags filled with organic vegetables, white fish and the flintiest of wines from the Saar and Mosel in the kitchen in order to carry out her daily 'inspection.'

She would don a pair of white opera gloves, roll up the sleeves of her shirt or jumper and go sailing around across the living room, her fingers gliding along the surface of sideboards, the piano next to one of the bay windows, the drinks cabinet, the coffee table, the top of the television set, over the brown leather arm chairs, the CD player, even the door handles. Each night she completed her scrutiny and then peered disapprovingly over her thick half moon glasses towards Peters, holding up a finger or two polluted with traces and smears of grey-black dust and dirt. It was all part of the game; he was always doomed to fail her test.

In this temporary luxuriously stifling sanctuary he submitted to the ritual, to thc humiliations and subjugations. Failure was followed by an order to strip naked, to tighten the dog collar that was thrown at him and allow himself to be led on a leash towards her DIY dungeon in one of the spare rooms she had transformed a long time before into a museum commemorating her late husband and hers' lifelong devotion to their fetish.

In this purgatorial bolt-hole there was the home-made St.

Andrew's cross her old man had hammered together one Saturday afternoon in winter; there were the padded cuffs he had welded and bolted onto the wooden structure; there was the mini-throne the couple had found to their delight in an antique shop in Schoneberg; there was the opened suitcase containing a variety of canes, whips, paddles and clamps; there was the teak mirrored wardrobe behind the Saltire deliberately left ajar to reveal a tightly packed rack of rubber, PVC and leather costumes and to the side of it a table laid out like an altar, on either end a thick red candle perpetually burning while upright on a sheet of black lace stood a row of vibrators.

There were no more questions this time, no more 'why did you come?' Until she released him the only other thing audible beyond the thwack of short, sharp corrective strikes, the low hum of her toys and his muffled resistance on entry was the widow's smoky breathing, sounding trance-like and ethereal in the tenebrous, artificial twilight.

After each session he was untethered, sent to a hot mineral infused bath, dressed after drying in a furry hooded robe and summoned for dinner an hour later. For eight days the television and radio inside the widow's lair was switched off. Neither would talk about what had happened to him or what was to greet him when he re-entered the world again. After their meal they would swill thick medals of brandy beside the fire, wrapped around each other, she tenderly stroking his hair and face. Then they would retire early under the fresh coolness of new bed linen and make love only in the missionary position just as he had agreed to when he first signed the contract she had waiting for him on the very day that Peters had asked for temporary asylum.

Looking back later, Peters admitted to himself that those Dahlem days had been among the happiest, least complicated of his life lately and was so overcome with gratitude that he had actually promised to go on holiday in the Med with her that summer. Frau Schuster seemed startled that he had finally relented and from her position of strength summoned up the courage to ask the questions she had dared not pose since they first met on that dank, wet autumn evening a year and a half earlier.

As they lay back together under the Egyptian cotton duvet on one of the last evenings of his incarceration, she rolled over on her side to face Peters planting one of her hands on a shoulder.

'There's something I've been meaning to ask you for a long time, to be honest since the first night you stayed over,' she said staring directly into his eyes.

'What's that then?' Peters croaked back wearily, fighting against the tiredness that was tugging at his consciousness.

'It's not what you might think. It's not about the age gap or anything like that. It's just that I often wonder why it's all one-way traffic?'

Peters propped himself up in bed and rubbed his face.

'One-way traffic?' he asked perplexed.

'You take it but you don't give it out darling...unlike my late husband,' she whispered conspiratorially.

'We liked to have it both ways. Don't worry I'm not complaining. In fact, these last few days have been divine, delicious. I'm just curious that for someone who is in such control can roll over so easily.'

'Do you want me to start beating you then?' Peters replied which provoked wicked sniggering from the widow.

'You'd only look ridiculous darling. Anyway, I've been around the scene long enough to know the master-side is not for you. And you know why? Maybe it's because you need that switch over, to reverse your role. That's why a lot of guys I used to know on the scene, usually always the bigger, the harder ones, loved to cross-dress. They had to cross over to their feminine side but you just need to lose control.'

Peters rolled out of his side of the bed, crossed the room to the widow's dressing table and returned to her side with her cigarettes and lighter.

'There you go darling,' she said as he lit her up, 'The will to serve. As always!'

Then she kissed him lightly on his lips and ran her forefinger down his cheek.

'Look, Martin darling, I know you are not in love with me. At my age I'm lucky to get what I've got from you. And what's more important to me is not whether you are sub or dom but why you haven't found some nice girl to settle down with.'

It was Peters turn to snigger: 'Nice girl? I'm not interested in nice girls only the naughty ones.'

'That's too easy darling, far too easy an answer. You see you like to lose control with me once a week because for the other six days you have to be totally in control of everything else.....and everyone else, no?'

'I suppose so, I try not to think about it too much.' Peters answered.

'Now we're getting somewhere. Now we're making progress. You don't try not to think it about; you avoid thinking about it. You know why? Because you're afraid. Don't worry – I'm not trying to judge you darling. I judge no one.'

He was impressed by the feeling in her voice, and her authentic concern for him, enough for him even to open up, slightly.

'It's not fear. It's just that I don't deserve anyone to make that kind of commitment to me. I couldn't give them what they would really want.'

She kissed him again softly, smiled and closed her eyes in a gesture of what seemed to Peters like overwhelming gratitude.

'Deserve darling! What an interesting word to use. That's more progress. Now I begin to understand you a lot better. Whatever it is you are trying to get over you should seek out some help and eventually get away from it Martin. It's weighing you down, sometimes I can even feel it bearing down on top of you, physically. You come over here, put your burden down for a few hours and then pick it up again as you go. It's going to crush you no matter how many lovers in bolt-holes you have dotted all around Berlin. And that's something you don't deserve. I watched my husband play in those clubs with lots of other women while I played with plenty of men. But we always went home together and I had 36 wonderful years with him. I still miss him, terribly, but that loss doesn't make me regret a single day we spent together. You deserve the same! Because I sense that there is still is someone really special for you, she always has been and you won't admit at least not yet.'

He was shaken by her insight and candour which made him in turn feel uneasy and nervous. Blinking as he stared at her close up, Peters pursed his lips and shuddered.

'I'm sorry you feel the weight too. You shouldn't have to,' was all he could say back to her.

She placed the palms of both hands on his face and compressed his cheeks slightly.

'It's not a rock you carry around with you but a pillar. You're a wannabe Sebastian, my darling, tethered to stone and peppered with arrows. I'm going to print out a picture of that saint and put it right over the bed here to remind me of you. Stop punishing yourself!'

St. Sebastian in pursuit of St. Christopher, Peters almost laughed out loud but resisted for fear of souring this moment of unsettling revelation.

On the ninth day, the widow offered to switch on the television or radio for him now sensing that he was ready to reconnect with the outside. Instead, Peters asked for half an hour on her computer so he could search for the one thing he wanted to be certain of.

In one of the spare rooms that she had transformed into an office where Frau Schuster did her accounts, ordered on-line, booked her cruises and linked up via webcam to the world wide S&M community, Peters logged on and searched for the Guardian Unlimited.

In the website's search engine he typed in 'Christopher's last will and testament Berlin' and found 39 direct links. He clicked on the first and it flashed up that frozen image of Streich standing in front of the flags and on the top right corner of the mini screen the words 'Courtesy of Wams.de.' When it played there were English subtitles at the bottom. Eleven hits down the list of searches Peters opened a file containing an interview with the journalist who had received Streich's final message, who had corresponded with him during his reign of terror; one day Heike Numann would thank him for these triumphs.

Although there were 112 missed calls on Peters' mobile when he switched it back on after returning to Heer Strasse he only answered three. His first call out was a reply to Heike who had wondered in one of her messages if he was dead.

'Heike, it's Martin. I'm back from the underworld.'

'My God, where have you been hiding?'

'As I said, the underworld. I just came up for air to congratulate you.'

'You haven't exactly been around to share my good fortune. Did you see "Christopher's" video?'

He paused before answering, resisting the urge to scream down the line about all what he had done for her, or over what he had seen.

'Yes and once again congratulations,' he replied weakly.

'Then for fuck's sake let's go out and party when I get back' she shouted down the line.

'I can't Heike. I'm getting out of this town for a while. Probably go to England for Easter,' Peters said thinking on his feet, forgetting her last four words.

'You lead such an exciting existence Martin and as usual you are not listening.'

Her voice was drowned out by a ping-pong jingle and the rushed nasally voice of a woman calling out various destinations.

'Where are you Heike?'

'In Tegel. I'm on my way to Bilbao.'

'Don't tell me you're walking barefoot all the way to Santiago de Compostella for Holy Week, Heiki,' Peters jibed, reminding her of her Catholic Rhineland roots.

'You're more in need of that than I am,' she served back, 'I'm off to see some people who might have known your headless horsemen from the Havel.'

She was on her way to the Basque country, in all likelihood Peters realised, to track down ETA's political allies, to ask them directly if any of their people had disappeared in Berlin.

'For Christ's sake be careful down there,' he implored as her line started to crackle and break up. All he heard from her was that she was passing through security and would call him when she got there. There was something equally confident and dismissive in the way that she had signed off, Peters felt. He cursed himself for not having the courage to tell her what he really wanted to say to her, to repeat the words she had once let slip to him in a previous call, that he too was still a little in love with her.

Later after he had packed a rucksack full of clothes and toiletries and booked himself via his own laptop on the boat train to Hoek van Holland and the Harwich ferry, Peters reminded himself to return another call.

Peters made several attempts to ring Blucher but each time the weird bleeping tone on the other end of the line sounded like he might as well have been on another planet. Eventually he gave up and called Angi on her mobile; fortunately she wasn't in the station when she answered.

'Angi, I want you to do me another favour?'

'Sure, sir, just say it.'

'Tell Stannheim I've taken more leave. I need a few weeks more away from all this madness.'

'Where have you been hiding? I came around to your place a few times but you were away.'

'I was staying with a very old friend. As you probably noticed there were lots reporters and snappers milling about the place. I have no intention of talking to any of them.'

'Schabowski is doing his nut. He keeps insisting you turn up and give your side of the story.'

'Screw Schabowski. No, on second thoughts don't. I wouldn't wish that even on Riedel. Did you know that there were two rival American film producers pestering me?'

'You could be sitting by a pool in Hollywood next week, sir,' she sniggered down the line.

'Bastards spent most of their calls bad mouthing each other. It sounded a bit like Kottbusser Strasse,' Peters said.

'You got that right. Sir, where are you now?'

'Back in Heer Strasse but don't tell anyone. I'm going to sell up here and move somewhere else.'

'A wise idea as long as you don't put in for a transfer. The boss would throw himself out of the window if you left us,' she said.

'How is the old goat?' despite himself Peters had inquired, kindly, after Stannheim.

'Worse than ever. It's because you're not there to drain all that negative energy out of him. He misses his sparring partner.'

Peters felt equally unnerved and touched over what Angi had just said because he knew it to be true.

'You tell the old bugger I miss him too.'

'I will sir,' Angi hesitated slightly before adding, 'Have you seen her lady-ship? She has been a constant presence on television screens and headlines for the last week and a bit.'

Her 'lady-ship'! How he loved Angi's cattiness sometimes.

'Streich stayed loyal to her to the bitter end. I supposed there was only going to be one person who would receive his pay off to the world. ' Peters lied.

'Still you have an even better story to tell I would imagine,' she said.

'And one day I will sit down with you and tell you all about it. Meantime I'm off for a run in the Grunewald, haven't done that for a long time either,' he paused uncertain what next to say to Angi as he was overwhelmed by a strange sense of gratitude towards her.

'Thanks for everything Angi. Just don't forget to mark me down as leave-of-absence.'

She hesitated for a few seconds before replying, Peters detecting a nervous concern in her breathing.

'Sir, I'm glad you called because there's just one more thing. One thing we didn't know about Streich before now.'

'Nothing would surprise me. Go on with it.'

'I don't know whether to run to the boss with this, or Schabowski, or you...'

'You should always consult your line manager first - that's me Angi.'

'I ran a check out of curiosity on Streich's nearest and dearest. He had been married young, before the Wall came down although it didn't last.'

'Who was she?'

'Petra Scharner. She was a teacher from Rostock. They had

known each other from the time they had met at an FDJ summer camp in the early 70s. I asked around, looked up the "Neues Deutschland" archives, consulted some of old friends from the DDR times,' Angi halted momentarily, coughed slightly and went on.'

'There was a trial. That's why there was so much detail about the couple and their child.'

'Their child?'

'Her name was Greta. When it happened she had just reached her second birthday.'

'What happened?' Peters asked.

'Streich was away, on special duties, the paper never mentioned that, just that he was an NVA officer dedicated to defending "Actual Existing Socialism". They had to fly him back home from wherever he was stationed. There was an accident on the Schoenhauser Allee in Berlin. Their little Trabant didn't stand a chance when the Audi struck it at full force head on.'

'Wife and kid killed?'

'Instantly. It was a big scandal for a while. A West German businessman over the limit, speeding, losing control. Streich was promised swift justice and probably a firing squad for the marauding capitalist speed-freak. His name was prominent in the "Neues" and "Berliner Zeitung", at least for a few weeks but then it suddenly disappeared. Everyone assumed that this Wessi murderer behind the wheel had either been shot or else locked away for good in prison. No one imagined he would ever walk or that the West German authorities would barter his freedom in the hard currency-for-bodies exchange scheme with the west. The skin trade between east and west saved him.'

Jesus, thought Peters with growing dread, *I know where this is going.*

'I only found about the driver's freedom when I searched on the Internet, in the archives of the Rhineland papers.'

'What was his name? Tell me his name,' Peters demanded.

'His name was Wolfgang Schultz although he later changed that by deed poll following the deal that secured his freedom.'

This time it was Peters' turn to pause and try to calm down.

'His name to what, Angi?'

'To Oskar Beer. The only one "Christopher" actually never laid a hand on.'

So Beer had sought refuge twice, once after his release from a DDR jail into a new identity back at home in the west, burying the memory of Wolfgang Schultz, and once again when he had to flee this time to the east when his crimes on the Rhine against children were out in the open. The pervert who ended up swinging from the back of his own kitchen door in Berlin, who had painted a perfect mental portrait of 'St. Christopher' for Peters and his squad, had failed to see in this man a younger self whose life Beer had shattered so long before the Turn. Peters now knew that Streich had been tracking the man who had casually wiped out his family and must have stumbled by chance across Beer's sordid, secret predilection – so this was where 'Christopher's Wrath' first began. Streich had chosen to spread out his own pain, to expand his anguish, to collectivise his grief, to cover an entire world gone-by and lash out at the one he was forced to inhabit in which men like Oskar Beer were free to walk and stalk.

He had led Streich to his end without the completion of the serial killer's mission to explain. He had been bait for Fest and whoever else in the BND had given the order to prevent an entire system from being put on trial. Now he felt weighed down by a debt he felt he owed. Peters decided there and then he would keep 'Christopher's' first cause where Streich had hidden it.

'Was Petra Scharner buried as Petra Scharner, Angi rather than her married name?' he enquired softly.

'Yes, sir, how did you know that?'

'Intuition. So was the child I assume. Why don't we leave the two of them to rest in that name! And while we are at it why don't we keep Wolfgang Schultz apart from Oskar Beer! That by the way is an order not a question. Do you understand why I am saying this Angi? ' Peters said this time with force.

'Yes, of course. Now I understand. Goodbye sir.'

Peters wondered if at this moment she was daddy's girl protecting Streich's secret for her father's sake as much as due to loyalty to her commanding officer.

He was about say 'Goodbye Angi. Take care' when something struck him, something that was missing from her brief account of the accident and Schulze's trial.

'Angi, one more thing before you go. Were there any witnesses to the crash? Did anyone give evidence in court.'

'I'm sorry sir I never mentioned it before. There was just one, it was early in the morning. Petra Sharner and her child were on their way to take a holiday in the north.'

'What was the witness' name?'

'General Thomas Weber. He was driving to the Ministry of State Security when he came across the crash scene. He was the only one to give evidence in court.'

Peters almost dropped the phone after she spoke, the second surge of shock felt as if he had been cattle prodded. Bad enough that Beer, as Schulzt, had killed 'Christopher's' family, worse still that the only one to have seen it had been the general he and Stannheim's network eventually later smuggled out to safety in the west.

'Sir, sir? Are you alright?' Angi kept asking as Peters stood frozen, his eyes fixed on the floor.

When he recovered sufficiently to reply Peters dismissed her with a curt 'good bye.'

Later back at Heer Strasse as he showered and then changed into his running uniform of hooded sweatshirt, track bottoms and trainers, Peters tried to think only about the journey ahead of him blotting out any thoughts about Streich and his quest to track down Wolfgang Schulz. Or the NVA general he had saved from a Stasi firing squad.

Instead he tried to look forward to the idea of travelling as a free agent on a Monday morning when the rest of his world around him was trudging in surly silence back to work. He would once again trace the path in reverse he took on that first tour of duty to Berlin at the end of the 80s. Peters made a promise in his head that he would call in on his mother at her retirement home in Basildon, that he would look up old comrades from the regiment who were still in London, that he would visit the graveyard in the east end, that he would sit in the same stand where he had been taken as a boy, that he would wear the same claret and blue colours of the team that his father had adopted long ago as his own.

But Peters still had the weekend alone to annihilate in Berlin. On Sunday he would map out a plan to sell the flat while starting the search for another somewhere deeper and far more anonymous in the east. Yet it was Saturday and he still had the option of a farewell drink in 'Der Zug' with Marion. One last trip there would surely not risk exposure, he calculated. He desperately wanted to say goodbye to her too because he knew he had to give up being a regular at the club. Otherwise someone would eventually ring the tabloids and the private life of 'Christopher's' hunter would be out in the open.

Before setting off for his run, Peters tried Blucher's number again but found that there was still no answer. Instead he spooled through his text messages this time in the vain search of anything from Miriam. As he was leaving the mobile finally bleeped and he ran over and picked up it excitedly. It was a farewell message from Karen: 'No show, no calls, no way mister. Screw U.' At least she had helped him make up his mind. He would definitely spend his last ever night inside his favourite swingers' club.

Peters then took a stool from the living room into his bedroom placed it beside the wardrobe, balancing on it while he fumbled about the top until he felt a small iron locked strong box. He searched through the drawers at either side of his bed until he found a rusting key and placed into the box's lock. After a couple of vigorous turns it yanked open. Inside was another souvenir from the Gulf, a 'Tokarev' pistol handed over to him as a token of thanks by the Iraqi Republican Guard captain who had defected with his entire company to the British just hours after the air war began. Peters took the weapon out of the box and cocked it to see if the firing mechanism still worked hoping and praying he would never have to use it for real.

Through lunchtime and into the early afternoon Peters darted through narrow tracks between the oak and ash trees of the Grunewald. Rays of harsh, brittle sunshine illuminated his way as he criss crossed through the forest, avoiding the main routes used by fellow joggers, unconsciously at first staying clear of the path he had taken a few weeks before when he came across his Russian assailants.

Winter's grip was relenting in the woodland, the air felt fresher, here and there Peters could make out in clearings little beds of daffodil buds, their shapes resembling tiny pale Pentecostal flames; even the magpies no longer had the forest to themselves as the trees transmitted the twittering and yammering codes of returning migrant birds. Light filtered through vegetation and leaves all around him. Peters was filled with a sense of renewed, elated evasion as he thrust deeper and deeper into the Grunewald.

After doubling back, this time at twice the pace as on entry, Peters halted outside the Heer Strasse S-Bahn to catch his breath, clear snot from his nasal passages and find somewhere to lean against so he could do his stretches to cool down.

At the side of the station Peters noticed that a shiny silver six seat VW people carrier was parked across the path leading up from the forest to the main road. Half bent over with a stitch in his side he walked past the vehicle and immediately experienced a sensation of danger all around it. With his back to the van now he heard the action of the side door sliding open and the word 'Tavarich' being called out from inside. Peters froze waiting for that familiar, terrifying clack-click of an automatic weapon being cocked.

But there was nothing more audible though except that word again repeated by a familiar weak voice: 'Tavarich!'

Peters paced backwards towards the open door and saw Yanaev strapped tightly into a single back passenger, looking absurdly childlike. Two bald sober looking men sat behind him who Peters had never seen before. They both wore black crombie coats and dark suits and ties. Peters thought Yanaev's travelling companions wouldn't have looked out of place working in a funeral parlour or in a bad production of a Beckett play.

Yanaev seemed to strain in his seat as he began to talk.

'How fortuitous running into you over here, Captain Peters. It gives me the chance to issue my formal congratulations.'

For a minute Peters said nothing back and simply stared at this diminutive, spectral figure in a grey suit, noting once again that the only sign of life were those darting, chocolate drop eyes.

'There's nothing to congratulate me for, Yanaev. My work is never done.'

The Russian flashed back his wan smile as Peters gulped for air.

'Well it is re-assuring to know that the finest of the Berlin Polizei never sleeps. Especially after bringing to an end "Christopher's Wrath." By the way I understand that that is the name of the first book out later in the summer. I have connections in the publishing industry who tell me this. You should hurry up and get yours done.'

Peters took several deep breaths and kept his hands on his hips before nodding in the direction of Yanaev's fellow passengers.

'Those goons in there aren't your hit squad are they Yanaev? They wouldn't look out of place walking behind a coffin but I doubt they'd put you in one.'

'Actually these gentlemen are my legal representatives and will gladly speak to you at any time to help you with your enquiries. We are on our way to Tegel. I have an appointment in London tomorrow which as you know is such a fantastic city.'

'What are you going there for, an illegal arms convention?'

The two lawyers grunted simultaneously and signalled with their eyes to Yanaev who held his hands up to them in a gesture of reassurance.

'Don't worry gentlemen. Captain Peters has a sense of humour, that's all. Which is a quality I have always liked in the English. That's why I enjoy doing business there. I'm actually off to seal a property deal near your Olympic village. Maybe while I'm there I could buy a football team too.'

'You waste your money how you see fit Yanaev just don't bother buying West Ham United,' Peters answered.

'I only play to win Captain!' the Russian said before using a finger to flick back a shirt sleeve and reveal a diamond encrusted gold watch.

'I'm afraid we have to be at the airport soon. Such a pity we couldn't chat further but just remember that next time we do our two friends here will be in the company.'

Peters leaned into the vehicle and tried to appear as menacing as possible.

'Just remember Yanaev I don't give up on any of my investigations. I have a long memory and infinite patience. By the way I wonder how much you knew about our friend Streich. After all you control the sale of Eastern Bloc explosives in this town. You must have known a former Warsaw Pact comrade was seeking to purchase some lethal Czech play dough from one of your dealers. After all your soldiers aren't afraid to use it to blow things up that might annoy you. Or places either - like a gay sex shop.'

Yanaev seemed completely unaffected by Peters' warning or his revelation about 'Boyz R Us'. Instead the Russian parried with a warning and a revelation of his own.

'My love of England extends to your literature. One of my favourite books is the "Wind in the Willows". And best of all I adore Mr Toad. What a character, always getting into scrapes and mishaps. Just like your slimy friend, the fat one that you like to hold court with in the Marriot Hotel.'

Peter's heart started pounding and panic spread through him as Yanaev pointed to one of his attorneys to slam shut the door. As Peters watched the MPV do a three-point turn and shoot off eastwards down Heer Strasse dark thoughts and images of Blucher, broken, beaten and blood-soaked, entered his head.

He tore through the traffic ignoring the lights and the protesting klaxons running towards his apartment across the road and the mobile inside which was still receiving invitations to sell his story or to consult on film scripts.

There was still no answer from Lothar's number and at first Peters contemplated calling Kottbusser Strasse to spark a missing person's investigation. Later when he calmed himself during more warm-down exercises Peters tried to de-code what Yanaev had told him, guessing that it was a warning rather than a hint that Blucher had been disappeared like poor Irina. Instead of setting off a manhunt Peters left a message on Lothar's mobile imploring him to ring his at any time day or night. Then he rang the Marriott who informed him that Herr Blucher had in fact checked out three days ago but hadn't left a forwarding address even though his bar bill remained unpaid.

After a long bath and a 20-minute nap Peters dressed, called a cab to take him to Steglitz and spent the first half of the night sipping beer alone in the cafe of the Korner Strasse S-Bahn station. He waited until eleven o'clock before marching forcefully down the street running parallel to the rail line until he was at the gates of the club. On pressing the bell whoever was in charge inside kept him waiting for several minutes before eventually buzzing him in.

He was relieved that it was Marion who greeted him at the door, took his entry fee and ushered him towards the changing rooms and the lockers. Peters stripped alone down to his black boxers slipping on a pair of flip flops and entered the bar area.

The train was already in motion as the regulars, each 'car' comprised of a male-female couple, were sliding and shoving themselves around the main room to the strains of the Kylie Minogue version of 'The Locomotion.' No one seemed to have noticed him come in. Peters headed straight for the bar and ordered brandy noting that Marion was on her own tonight.

'Where's hubby?' Peters asked as 'Der Zug's' co-owner swayed her hips to the sound of the club's anthem.

'He's in Hamburg with a few of his football buddies. Hertha are up there this weekend. Do you not read the sport pages?' she said trying to make herself heard above the music, the grunts and groans of the human locomotion, and the moans and squeals of the Japanese women on the TV screen above having sex with black American GI Joes.

'I try not to read any papers Marion, least of all the ones that write about me,' Peters said lifting his brandy glass in salute to the proprietress.

Marion clicked her fingers and grimaced before calling Peters behind the bar.

'You wanna do it over the pumps, Marion? That's not very hygienic for the punters,' he teased.

She put her forefinger over Peters' lips and stroked them gently.

'Shussh. I have a present for you. Come inside,' she beckoned him into the tiny office to the left of where the spirits were lined up.

Peters took his brandy with him into the cubbyhole sized room which was filled with boxes of porn DVDs, condoms and lubricants.

From a table, balanced on top of a row of boxes she took down a rectangular parcel in buff coloured wrapped paper, a thin white thine bound tautly across it in the shape of a St. Andrews Cross. On the front someone had scrawled in spidery writing: 'Martin Peters. C/O Der Zug, Korner Strasse, Steglitz, Berlin.' Peters looked closer at the parcel and spotted that it had a franked post mark stating that it had been posted from Berlin Schoenefeld Airport.

Marion gently slapped Peter's ass, raised herself up slightly on her heels and whispered into his ear: 'You unwrap that gift by yourself and then you can have me down in the basement afterwards.'

When she left the tiny room Peters broke off the rope and tore through the wrapping until it revealed a 10 X 4 framed painting.

It was a copy of 'The Meeting of Wellington and Blucher', the work of Irish artist Daniel Maclise painted to commemorate the British-Prussian victory at Waterloo. Peters had seen the real one once on a visit to the Royal Gallery shortly after he had returned from the Gulf War. He remembered at the time being struck by the impression that the painter had portrayed a mood of grimness and tragedy, that Maclise had been mindful of the reality of war rather than seeking in any way to glorify it.

The two old war horses meeting at the inn known as the Belle Alliance were depicted surrounded by death and loss, of cadavers strewn across cannons, of men dying in their comrades' arms, of a young officer being given the last rites by a priest. Amid Maclise's images of carnage combined with triumph Peters divined a message from Lothar Blucher: his informer was alive and well.

In his impatience to rip open the parcel Peters at first failed to notice a post card placed inside the package. He bent down to the floor, picked it up and held it to the light. It showed the naked torso of a young man in a peak leather cap pouring a bottle of mineral water over a perfect six pack. Above the sun tanned Adonis there was a palm tree and the word 'Florida.' Peters turned the card over and read the single-line message in the same familiar spidery scrawl: 'Wish you were him! Lothar.'

Forty Eight

The single cling-clong chime of the church bell on the French side of the river Saar was the only noise to disturb the deep sleep of Hanweiler in mid morning. He detected that same smug soporific stillness to the border village from the moment he stepped off the little train that had taken him all the way from Saarbrucken's main station to the very edge of western Germany and the pen-ultimate rail stop before it crossed the frontier for its final destination in the Lorraine town of Saargumines. As he ambled down the main street through the centre towards where the old customs post used to stand Peters remembered again that long overnight journey from Hanover in '88, the two of them silent and furtive in the car, he going south-westwards with his charge into safety towards a new life under a completely new identity.

Their only conversation had been as they reached the Saarland when Peters asked why his agent had chosen the region to re-settle after being spirited out of the east.

'Those around old Eric will get the joke!' the general had responded, groggily, attempting to resist nodding off in the passenger seat.

'This was where Hoenecker grew up and where my father came from. At least we still share that in common,' the defector added irritated by Peters' questioning.

This morning, on the right hand side of the street just past an off-license which only sold the local Saar brew, Karlsberg beer, with its door flung open and its elderly owner reclining in a chair beside a gas heater, a languid moulting Alsatian dog at her feet, Peters reached that familiar building once more.

It was a two-storey chalet shaped house with two residences, the extended family of Lebanese exiles were still living on the ground floor, a widower above them, the name of 'Stock' written inside a laminated strip beneath a buzzer.

He pressed it several times but there was no reply from the intercom and was about to do the same to the one below when he heard a cracked voice behind him.

'Herr Stock is not in. He takes a stroll in the forest and then goes over to France for lunch. Every day. There's a dyed blonde French tart that serves him over there who he's always raving about,' there was a jealous cackle in her throat.

Peters turned around and saw that the old dear had left her dog to his slumber next door. He bowed and smiled back at her.

'Do you know when he might come back? I have some papers for him to sign.'

'Oh Herr Stock! You can set your watch by him. Always returns between 2.15 and 2.30. And he goes to bed afterwards,' Peters guessed from her tone that the crone secretly harboured some faint passion for the old boy.

'Then I shall come back for him. This is his lucky day!'

The old girl grinned with excitement imagining that her handsome, reserved but often distant neighbour might have just come into a windfall.

He looked towards the junction where the border used to be and noticed that the bar at the end of Germany with its white net curtains and that omnipresent tangy reek of friend onions was still there. Peters bowed once more and almost clicked his heels in theatrical deference towards 'Stock's' secret admirer.

A few minutes later he was downing his first beer of the day and wondering if anyone had recognised him through the new disguise he took on 24 hours earlier just before he left Berlin. Peters had chosen a salon near Theodor Hauss Strasse and opted to have his hair bleached and clipped severely. From a nearby apothecary he bought a pair of glasses with the weakest of lenses that tinted when the sun struck the glass. Now in the reflection of the window of the little pub where Germany stopped and France started, Peters thought he somehow looked ridiculously camp, like a gay Mod in a light blue Italian cut suit and matching raincoat.

He spent a couple of hours reading the local papers, downing a few more beers and picking unenthusiastically at an insipid dish of Spaghetti Carbonara. Then shortly after two o'clock he reached into his inside coat pocket and felt the pistol's smooth surface wrapped up in a napkin.

'Just in case, General, just in case,' he muttered barely under his breath.

Just as he was about to pay the bill Peters saw a familiar figure passing by, bent over slightly, his hand clutching the top buttons of a fawn raincoat as the rain began to hammer down, as if this gesture would somehow shield the sole pedestrian in the street from this sudden deluge.

Peters rushed to the counter, slapped a 20 euro note down on the bar top and went outside to follow the crouched over figure walking ahead back into the Germany village.

As 'Stock' struggled to force the lock of his building's door open with his key Peters called out behind him in English: 'Don't make a move comrade General. Go inside, go up the stairs and let yourself in. I'll be close by.'

'Stock' stood static for a few seconds and then glanced over his shoulder to see a younger well-dressed man getting soaking wet and pointing a gun at him.

'Very well. Come in,' he grumbled.

Once up inside his apartment 'Stock' took off his mack and flung it over a brown leather arm chair by the wall of the living room, and then lumbered toward double glass doors that looked onto a series of allotments leading down to the river and slid them open.

He wants witnesses, Peters realised. *Very well General. Very well.*

The General leaned over a wooden balcony directly above a mini car park below, his back still to Peters, searching for signs of human life.

'Why are you pointing that thing at me Captain Peters?'

Instantly Peters remembered what Streich had told him in Treptower Park.

'Insurance, dear General. Insurance. To ensure you give me an audience.'

'It's as well I recognised your voice. If you hadn't spoke and I had turned around I would have thought you were one of the old network who'd come to track me down and finally exact their revenge.'

'Don't be stupid General. No one's bothered about you over in the east any more - except me of course. I'm the only one likely to put a bullet in your back for your sins.'

'Stock' turned around to face Peters narrowing his eyes to get used to the Englishman's unfamiliar appearance.

'I suppose the most famous and hated detective in Germany has to go about these days in a disguise.'

'Now we're talking General. Why don't you come in sit down, pour me something strong and we can chat about how all this began? Because I assume that it all started with you.'

Peters settled into a single chair to the side of the living room door all the time training his black Tokarev' pistol on the man he had once saved from a firing squad. Despite all the years of exile and self-concealment, of having to adopt a new persona and stick with it even long after the Wall came down, General Thomas Weber retained his handsome looks, that slicked back mane of now silvered hair, those drilling blue eyes, the slightly pursed lips and a face almost entirely free of wrinkle and line. Peters watched as Weber went over to a tasteful teak sideboard, opened a drawer and pulled out a bottle of 12-year-old Bushmills which he filled neat into two heavy crystal glasses. As the General brought over Peters' drink the Englishman raised his hand in polite protest.

'I'll permit you to go into the kitchen General and get us a little water. The distillers in Bushmills once told me that you need some H20 to make the whiskey expand and release the flavour. If you make a run for it out the door I'll do what your old comrades never got a chance to do and empty this magazine into your back,' Peters warned him waving the 'Tokarev' about in the General's direction.

Weber returned a few seconds later with a small plastic jar and poured a couple of drops of water into Peters' glass.

'A 12-year-old! I'm impressed!' Peters said sipping the whiskey.

'If you remember I got a taste for it in your officers' mess in Spandau during those early debriefings. You've to remember Captain Peters that where I came from a 12-year-old Scotch malt was nectar from the Gods.'

'Where you came from! That is why I'm confused General. Totally and utterly confused,' Peters interrupted deliberately failing to correct Weber's geographical mistake.

The General said nothing in reply and sat sprawled over the leather three seater sipping at his neat Bushmills.

Peters went on: 'You gave us everything we wanted and more. You betrayed your comrades, your army, your state. You fled knowing that if they ever caught up with you they'd most certainly take revenge. And yet it was you General, it was you who guided Streich to his targets. Streich who would have thought nothing of putting one in behind your ear if given the order. I once asked myself what was it that clicked in Streich's head. Now I have to ask you exactly the same question.'

Weber threw back the whiskey in one blasphemous gulp, slammed the glass down and sighed wearily.

'It builds up in you. Constantly. The betrayals. The dislocation. The sense of uselessness. Once the whole thing fell apart, especially after that. Strange, isn't it but when it was all over only then did I start to get nostalgic for the old place. The sights, the sounds, even that weird smell that used to hang in your nostrils in east Berlin. I missed my old friends. Or rather I was curious about what had become of their lives. Of course it was strictly 'verboten' for me to contact any of them, even if they wanted to speak to me again, even if they would rather see me dead. But in the years after the Turn, when I watched the evening news, read "Der Spiegel" or "Die Zeit", listened to the radio about their daily humiliations, about the way their lives had been turned upside down I felt, and I know this sounds absurd, well, guilt. As if I had something to do with it. The way their entire lives had all been exposed as a sham.'

Peters scanned the room and noted that the years of exile had been good to General Thomas Weber: the framed photographs of him and some friends on a fishing boat proudly holding up their catch somewhere out in the Med'; the paintings of the red brick roofs and whitewashed walls of Andalusia hung on the wall; the flat screen television and DVD player; the African spear and shield above the TV; the expensive red and black throw around the sofa he was reclining on which judging by its intricate mosaic patterns had been bought somewhere in the Islamic world. He compared it all to the grim frugality of that other old ex NVA soldier who had also colluded with Streich back in his Pankow mausoleum grimly waiting for nothing more now than death.

And at least Angi's father had expected some kind of sanction for helping Streich, Peters recalled. Weber had the arrogant bearing of a man who knew he was beyond that.

'So why Streich? Why go to a man who would kill you on the spot if he was sitting here right now?' Peters demanded.

'It wasn't an instant decision Captain Peters. It built up inside me over a couple of years.'

'Exactly when?' Peters inquired impatiently.

'It started during a trip to Cologne one Easter a few years ago. I was in the city to visit some old acquaintances, contacts from the BND who helped me re-settle in the west after you Brits had done with me. I happened to be in a bar waiting for one of them down in the Alstadt. I had time to kill and started to read the local paper. And there staring out at me from the front page was a face I recognised immediately.'

'Oskar Beer?'

'No! He was still then Wolfgang Schulz. The man I had identified to a DDR court back in '85 as the driver who crashed into Petra Sharner's car. Schulze had just been sentenced for the sexual molestation of a young boy whose parents were friends of his. The man whom my own government freed within a year as part of that revolting "skin trade" with the west. The paper's report emphasized how Schulz had betrayed his neighbours and breached their trust. I was furious that this shit was getting away with it again. He received an 18-month sentence and then probation. There was an outcry in Bonn where it happened.'

'Schulz was getting away with it for a second time. That first time in the DDR. That is what finally broke my will to stay. An old comrade with connections high up in the party whispered to me that the man I had helped put away had slipped out of the state and home to the west for the price of a few million D-marks. Now I find out he's running east this time, eluding justice, real justice in the west.'

'And then he decided to run away again and become Oskar Beer?'

'You've got to remember that I was a bit of a secret celebrity among the western spooks Captain. I had many old friends in the service, plenty of them who had contacts all over the place. It wasn't difficult finding out what had happened to Schulz after he was freed. Or that he had changed his name by deed poll to Oskar Beer. I kept an unhealthy interest in our friend right up until he moved back to the scene of his original crime and thought he could dissolve into the new united melting pot. In a way that was the tipping point. His guile in going back to Berlin really got to me. I suppose it was this arrogance that killed him in the end.'

'So how did you get to Streich?'

The General ran his hand through the weight of his grey mane and threw his head back in a haughty gesture.

'I was taking a risk, yes but I knew about the network, the old comrades association. I got a few of their numbers, left contacts and waited. I waited for five months before they relayed my message to Streich.'

Peters was conscious that his hold on the 'Tokarev' was lessening, his fingers and palms were now sapping with sweat. He gripped the butt plates and pointed the weapon directly at the General signalling for him to continue.

'I knew Streich and I knew what he was capable of. Although the messages I sent were anonymous I also knew that the second he would see me Streich would recognise the traitor, the face once quietly distributed across the organs of the old state when my absence was first spotted in the year before the Turn. So I couldn't take any chances. I arranged for him to meet in a public place, somewhere I would be confident he wouldn't try anything in case he still harboured hatred against an enemy of Socialism like me.'

'Where then? A railway station? An airport? Tegel? Schonefeld?'

A reptilian smile broke out over Weber's face, sly, all knowing, semi-covert.

'In the spot where it all began Captain Peters. I arranged to see him in the very place where I followed Schulz almost every single day for a couple of weeks. The "Boyz R Us" sex shop near the Sauvigny Platz. We met just the once. Face to face. Whispering underneath the soundtrack of grunting and groaning from those awful video booths. I told Streich that Schulz would be in there soon. That he was now called Oskar Beer and often frequented this place.'

'And what after that?'

'The rest you know. Beer's secret then unravelled along with the rest of his chums. And Streich's hit list grew from one to many,' Weber shook his shoulders, reached for the Bushmills bottle and filled his glass again.

'What did Streich say to you?'

The General threw back another shot of the golden liquid in one go, smacked his lips and lay back again in the chair.

'He said he understood why I was there. He said that I had finally atoned. It was the last thing he ever said to me. I never saw him again after that. I knew I had done my duty.'

Weber paused before continuing.

'I didn't realise what Streich was up to until I read that Beer was found strung up behind his own kitchen door and that it was all connected to 'Christopher's Wrath.' That was a neat trick of Streich's. He singled out the others first, scared the shit out of Beer so much that that bastard topped himself. Then all was clear. All was clear.'

Suddenly, Weber looked drained as if something inside him had suddenly expired.

'And you never thought of contacting me even while we were chasing our tails all around Berlin after this killer?' Peters replaying in his mind the exact moment when he regained consciousness inside the lock-up at Ostkreuz, Bauer lying beside him gasping for air, his sergeant's life waning away.

'Like seventy millions others I was caught up in it all. We cheered him on. I cheered him on,' Weber's reply was relayed in a whisper.

Peters left the old man to this thoughts, finally taking the pistol away from him and shot up from his chair moving towards the balcony with a view onto the Lorraine town on the opposite river bank. He admitted to himself that he had brought the gun along for more than simple insurance and shuddered at the idea that he had even considered using it on this double-traitor.

Replaying his journey to the village there and then he had chosen a stop back along the rail line he travelled earlier; to the closest point where Germany faced France, at Kleinsbittersdorf with its bridge over into the French Grossbittersdorf. He had no more use for the pistol-souvenir in his hand. He would ditch it in the Saar and finally put that last campaign in the Gulf far behind him because now Peter knew: he longer wanted to be a prisoner of his wars gone by.

When he returned to the living room, Peters realised he hadn't heard Weber putting on the television and the DVD player. As Peters got ready to leave, saying nothing more to his former agent, he noticed that the General was now oblivious to his presence, transfixed instead to the screen in front of him. Weber was using a remote control to unwind a short film of a man being cut to pieces with a sword.

Epilogue

Upton Park, East London, 15th March 2006

Seconds after the Bolton keeper's own goal that gave West Ham the lead the ageing skinhead strained his neck up out from the upturned collar of his blue Harrington jacket to reveal two black crossed hammers tattooed around the skin covering his jugular vein. He punched the air, leapt on top of his plastic claret and blue seat, and tried to conduct the rest of the Bobby Moore Stand to join him in his euphoric celebrations. After dropping down back onto the concrete floor he went over to try to bear hug Peters who took a few diffident steps back to avoid the skin's embrace.

It was the accent that first convinced Peters he might be in danger here on the very spot where his father Kurt used to take him on Saturdays in the early 70s when as a boy he marvelled at the skills of Clyde Best or the in-box poaching opportunism of Alan Taylor. From the moment the skinhead opened his mouth to strike up a conversation Peters instantly recognised the Belfast accent.

When they did lightly hug in celebration over the first goal of the FA Cup Quarter Final Replay, Peters touched both pockets of his neighbour's Harrington feeling for the bulge of a gun or the outline of a blade. But there was nothing there that felt lethal being concealed in his coat to suggest that this over-enthusiastic Irons' fan from across the Irish Sea was here on a mission of revenge.

Just before the search the Skinhead had gently kicked his ox blood Doctor Marten shoes up against Peters' own and said, 'Snap!' As he scanned Peters up and down, the Skin noticed that this man who was around his own age also wore the 'uniform' of their old teenage sub-cult: claret Fred Perry jumper, button-down blue Ben Sherman, the light blue jeans and the red DMs. Even the bottle blonde hair Peters had used to attempt to conceal his identity as Germany's most famous cop had been cropped down with a number 2 razor.

'Rich men with a mid-life crisis grab a Ferrari and a younger blonde, all us plebs get are DMs and Harringtons for ours!,' the skin said in that same unmistakable glass-grinding accent from the city that had changed everything for Peters.

Through the rest of the cup tie Peters did his best to ignore his neighbour firstly by scrolling through the text messages both from Stannheim in Berlin and Heike now in San Sebastian.

'Hey mystery man. Where are you? I'm here sending you big kisses on one of the loveliest beaches in the world. Meeting some friends of those lads who were found in the Havel a while ago. Wish you were?. Lol! xxxHeike.'

Stannheim's text almost give him as much hope as Heike's had done.

'Enjoy London and hope your Hammers win tonight. Paul sends his regards and is listening in to game on radio. At home ahead of Rehab. He cannot thank you enough and nor can I. Your commander always…M'

Throughout the rest of the second half and into extra time Peters remembered his father sitting with him in their usual seats close to the touchline and in particular that one afternoon when Leeds United came calling. Kurt Peters had cursed and seethed every time the monkey noises rose up from the away end when Best got onto the ball before turning to his son and whispering to Martin, 'That bastard Hitler was going to make Leeds his new capital if he had won the Battle of Britain. Now I know why!'

Kurt never missed an opportunity to have a go at the Fuhrer for driving him into exile…even while at Upton Park, Peters thought just as Marlon Harewood put the Hammers back in the lead on the 96th minute prompting his Belfast 'neighbour' this time to shoot out of his chair and stating pogoing in celebration.

When the Bobby Moore Stand eventually settled down again Peters noticed that the Skinhead had a holdall with the club's crest on it wedged in between his feet. Perhaps he had not been security conscious enough by thinking that a quick stealthy frisk of the man's Harrington would do the job. He had been too quick to dismiss this Belfast West Ham supporter as nothing more than an excited fan from afar on his one and only trip in a season to their beloved East End home.

He wondered what was in the bag as his paranoia began to return. Was there a weapon in there? Would the skin follow him out of the ground, pressing himself close enough to Peters to blade him or stick a syringe full of poison into his limbs or arse? He had read about how the UVF had tried to kill one of its members held inside Crumlin Road jail who had turned Supergrass by lacing custard served up to the traitor in the prison canteen that had been laced with a toxin stolen from an aircraft factory. The informer-inmate only survived because the toxic substance turned the custard into a green slime like sludge which he immediately sent back to the kitchen. That was the mid 80s, Peters thought, surely in this new century any terrorist group out for a silent assassination would have access to far better concealed lethal poisons! He decided he would stay put until the stand emptied as the jubilant crowds of Irons filed out, until his 'friend' in the next seat left.

After the final whistle blew and the stadium erupted in joy, above the strains of 'I'm Forever Blowing Bubbles', Peters' fellow supporter stretched an outreached hand.

'I'm Kyle, amigo. From Stratford via East Belfast.'

'My name's Doug, nice to meet you Kyle,' Peters replied staring into the man's face to search for any flicker of menace of which there appeared to be none.

'I've not seen you this season. Do you live away?' Kyle asked.

'No, just work and that. I do shifts sometimes on Saturdays usually when the Hammers are at home. Trust my luck. What about you? Are you over regular?'

'Over? I live here now,' Kyle said pulling something out from the tartan interior of his blue Harrington.

He then proudly held up a plastic card that looked like it could be shoved into an ATM for cash.

'I'm a season ticket holder. Have been these last four years chum.

Funny enough that seat you're sitting on is always up for grabs. You meet different people sitting on it all the time. The other week there was a fellah from southern Ireland beside me. Really lovely guy. He even invited me over to their West Ham supporters club annual piss up in Dublin in April,' Kyle said smiling at Peters.

By now Peters had already read the name printed on the claret coloured card: 'Kyle Williamson'.

'Here, Doug mate fancy a pint in the Boleyn Tavern after the match. There are a few top boys from around here that I know. You're old enough to remember the Inter City Firm. They've got some tales to tell,' Kyle said evidently trying to impress Peters with tales from his old hooligan chums reminiscing forever over their exploits in the 80s.

He stood up and shook Kyle's hand in secret relief that this over-friendly, over-eager exile from Belfast was just that and not an avenger sent over to hunt down, stalk and slay an undercover assassin who had killed a woman nearly two decades before.

Peters was truthful for the first time this evening with Kyle, 'I'm sorry mate but I'd like to sit here for a wee while on my own. This used to be where my dad sat. He was a Hammer for all his life in England. Saw Moore, Hurst and Peters play in the 60s. Just want to think about him here in what was his favourite place in the world.'

The skinhead with flecks of grey stubble on each side of his temple and green jagged teeth smiled back generously at Peters.

'No bother Doug. I understand. My 'oul boy passed away over a year ago and I wasn't even allowed back for his funeral. Bastard UVF said if I returned to Belfast they would shoot me dead.'

'I'm so sorry about that Kyle,' Peters responded almost in a whisper as faint cries of 'We all follow the West Ham' from the last of the stragglers echoed around Upton Park.

He did sit in silence and think about his father once the Belfast exile had left for a pint with the ICF veterans in the Boleyn. He did recall how Kurt used to huddle up in winter in his sheep skin jacket; how his father would grimace and moan when the team started playing defensively, barking out in his Sudeten German accent, 'The ball goes forward, that is not the Vest Ham vay!' His father's protests often provoked a couple of 'shat up Kraut' mutterings from behind but most of the faithful knew old Kurt and respected him for his record in the war.

His other 'father' over in Berlin came to mind too, the one whom he had got his 'real' son back from the vortex of addiction. All Peters had done was talk to Paul a few times when he was lucid and persuade him to go back to Stannheim's house, and seek out rehab. Paul had simply needed to hear that from someone else instead of his father. His mother's death and his father's 'marriage' to his other family in the Kottbusser Strasse station alongside bad company must have been factors in propelling Paul into the dark place, Peters imagined. Now they were reunited once more and at least that was something for Peters to hold onto. Because Stannheim and him would soon face an inquisition over what happened to Hans Joachim Streich on the steps of the Treptower Soviet war memorial when Peters returned to Berlin. At least the old man had Paul by his side, maybe even throughout the ordeal to come, Peters dared to hope.

Outside the stadium Peters also thought about his new found friend Kyle whom he had mistaken for his executioner. Kyle had crossed the same paramilitary group Peters' life had become entangled with long ago. Kyle had been banished across the sea forever, not even allowed back to bury his father. Peters meantime would always have to look over his shoulder despite ceasefires and peace process back in Ireland.

As his feet crunched over half drunk beer tins and squelched down yellow styrofoam containers with half eaten burgers and unconsumed piles of curried chips, Peters found a quiet spot before the Upton Park station to spool back through his text messages that evening, all the way back to those intriguing words of Heike Nummann sent from her mobile on the beach at San Sebastian. He worried about her on this assignment where she would be mixing with other dangerous men, using their thirst for vengeance over their decapitated ETA comrades that Peters' team had fished out of the Havel, to get closer to the truth about Yanaev.

Peters was about to compose a reply to Heike but just as he

started to depress the buttons to send her his love, Peters remembered that it was one stop west to Plaistow station, that he would be going underground once more and that down in the earth that that other woman who would appear to him again. Even on the train as it descended into the darkness, when he closed his eyes he would still see her sitting in front of him. A leather motor cycle jacket decorated with studs and the faintest outline of an Anarchy symbol on it. Her helmet at her side on the Tube's red leather upholstery, one side of her revealing soft olive skin, oval shaped brown eyes and a heart shaped face, the other a mess of gore, blood and bone.